A KILLER'S HEART

A POLITICAL THRILLER

SUSAN WILKINS

For Sue Kenyon, who makes it all possible.

PROLOGUE

'No, David! No. This is mad.' She stands in the doorway, towel clutched around her nakedness, hair slicked back, rivulets of water running down her legs and puddling on the wooden floor.

He glances up at her, his boyish face taut with rage. He's sitting on the sofa, pulling on the biker boots, tugging and zipping and snapping down the velcro straps.

The apartment is small and boxy, on the ninth floor, a London eyrie with an expensive view of the Thames surging by in full winter flood.

She steps forward, leaving a damp footprint. 'Listen to me, will you? Don't do this. You don't have to do this.'

'No listen. No more listen.' The growl in his voice and the heavy accent make him sound older than his years. As he gets up, the leather trousers creak. He hoists a motorcycle jacket off the back of a chair, pulls it on.

'Just wait. That's all I ask.' She dabs her face. 'Think this through. You need to be sensible. Be sensible, David. Please.'

He rakes his fingers through his dark curls and the scowl dissolves. 'Sensible. You so bloody English.'

Tilting her head, she smiles. *If he only knew.* 'I thought that's what you liked.'

Even though she's tall, he towers over her. They face each other across the marble coffee table and last night's wine glasses ruby-stained with the dregs of the bottle they'd shared. Stalemate.

But she knows her power. Hair sleek as an otter, those penetrating blue eyes, the bare shoulders, her beauty is her weapon. It stopped him dead in his tracks the first time they met. She can feel his desire, knows how to manipulate it.

Edging round the table towards him, she runs her fingertips along the sleeve of his jacket and sighs. His face softens, and for an instant, his anger recedes.

Sensing the advantage, she says, 'I know you're angry. I get it. It's not gone to plan. But we'll find another way. We will. I promise.'

He shakes his head and skirting round her, he picks up the red crash helmet and disappears down the narrow hallway. He doesn't look back. The front door slams behind him.

Her irritation erupts. She pulls off the towel and pummels her wet hair. Dumping the towel on the floor, she stomps over to the wide balcony window. As she slides open the door, an icy blast hits naked flesh. Somewhere down below, the river rolls by, black and turgid. On the opposite bank, the famous towers and tall canyons of the City rise up, bright gashes of light, red pin-pricks on the cranes, slicing into the wintry darkness.

She stands there exposed and cross, but it's freezing. Stupid bastard. He could ruin everything. Retreating from the chill, she closes the door; her eyes scan the room and stop at the phone. It's on the kitchen worktop next to a bunch of keys. She hesitates, but only for a second, then crosses the room to grab it.

. . .

Metal shutters clatter as they rise to allow a silver Harley Davison to emerge from the apartment block's underground carpark. The motorcycle roars up the ramp and brakes. The deserted lane is carefully cobbled, offering the street's affluent residents a sense of old Bankside with none of the muck or inconvenience. Falling sleet melts and dissolves as it hits the roadway, leaving puddles of slippery slush.

He turns his head, checking both ways and, pulling down the visor on the helmet, he sets off. She thinks he's reckless, particularly on the bike. But not tonight. He can't afford to be.

Now he's out of there, he can think. She gets inside his head, burrowing away. But she doesn't understand. He knows what he's doing. It only looks crazy. This is how he's survived. Anger is a fuel that must be contained and used. Like petrol injected into the combustion chamber, a controlled explosion releases energy, drives the pistons. It gives you power. Why can't she see that?

On Southwark Street he joins a column of traffic; it's late, after midnight, but the streets are still busy: taxis picking up, a night bus, pedestrians warm with booze scampering across the road.

Astride the machine, he feels calmer. Riding has that effect. *Think this through. Be sensible.* She's right, of course. But what difference does that make? This is about what he wants. He'd taken her by surprise. That had been his plan. They'd drunk the wine, had sex. He'd waited until she was in the shower, then, hovering in the doorway, he told her.

He knew she'd argue. She always argues because she assumes she's smarter than him. And that winds him up. Of course he wants her, can't help it, but it doesn't make her his boss.

Passing Tower Bridge he knows the route, he does it most days. Stay south of the river, easier traffic-wise, through Rotherhithe and Deptford. Then he uses the Blackwall Tunnel to cross over and head north.

As he cruises down Jamaica Road, the traffic thins and that's when he notices it creeping closer in his side mirror. The BMW X5 is black, tinted windows, Xenon headlights, a driver and front seat passenger, both male. They seem to be tailing him, he's not sure where he picked them up. He accelerates to open up a gap, but the 4x4 responds. Yes, it's definitely stalking him. A buzz of adrenaline ripples through him at the prospect of a chase. He likes danger, he misses it.

Melded to the bike, his nerve endings charged, he's ready. He wonders what their intention is. To follow? Surely they're being too obvious for that. To frighten him? To run him off the road? Through Greenwich, round the one way system, he monitors them, biding his time.

The sleet has turned to rain and lashes his visor. Hunkered down over the handlebars, he opens up the Harley. It tears down the slip-road to the Blackwall Tunnel. If anyone is actually watching the banks of CCTV monitors, they might decide to alert the traffic cops. But they'll never catch him either.

Burning down the outside lane, he's confident the power of the bike will soon outstrip the much heavier vehicle and as they descend into the maw of the Victorian tunnel, he begins to pull ahead. Even at this late hour, the nearside lane is occupied by a slow-moving convoy, a few cars, the odd truck, but spread out with plenty of gaps for him to weave in and out. He can see in his mirror that the X5 is losing ground. It's way behind. The carriageway is narrow, and his pursuers are in danger of getting smacked by lumbering lorries straying over the central line.

Blood pumping, he smiles to himself. He's won. No way they'll get him now. By the time they exit the tunnel, he'll be long gone. He eases down on the throttle and slows to take the first bend. The tunnel is old, its serpentine twists and dips built for the horse-drawn age. But he knows it well, he can relax. Soon he'll be up and away.

With only a few hundred metres to go, he comes alongside a Luton van, trundling up the final incline, back bumper flapping; it looks as if it might snap off at any moment. He glances across at the driver and as the man smiles back, a jolt of recognition hits him. Tony? How? Hot panic floods his veins. The X5 was the decoy. He's been set up! They know his route, of course they do. How could he be so stupid?

His reactions are swift. Twisting the throttle, the Harley surges as the van swerves straight at him. A hundredth of a second faster and he'd have been clear. Its front wing clips his back wheel.

The motorcycle skids and bucks, flinging him over the handlebars in a perfect arc. He flies through the air, precise and elegant as a gymnast. He feels calm suspended in the moment. Then he falls, bouncing along the tarmac like a rubber doll, until the red helmet smashes into the brick wall.

1

———

DAY 1. 5.05am

In the chilly darkness, Adam Hardy's fingers inch along the wall until he finds the light switch. The hallway is flooded in the eerie glow of the energy saving bulb. His hand remains on the wall as he tries to slow his ragged breathing.

The child's sobs are more muted now. Perhaps Zoe's right, leave him, he'll settle eventually. She's a far stricter parent than Adam. And in the last year she's had to be. He's watched her grow thinner and more stressed, snapping at the kids for trivial misdemeanours. And it all adds to his guilt. The house - this sturdy old Devon farmhouse they both worked so hard to restore - was once full of loud games of rough and tumble, jokes and japes. Now it's quiet and awash with whispers. Everyone knows to be careful around Adam. Illness cocoons him.

He takes several minutes to reach the bedroom door. Ryan is standing up, holding tight to the bars of the cot with his pudgy fists. The warm glow of the toadstool lamp in the corner fills the room and, at the sight of his father, the little boy opens his mouth and wails.

'Hey hey, hey! Sssh! What's all this racket about?' Speaking even a sentence or two makes him breathless. The words seem to stab the inside of his rib cage. Feeling light-headed, he leans on the baby blue chest of drawers for support as he sucks down more air.

With huge effort, he moves across the room to the cot. But the slowness of his progress seems to aggravate the child and make him howl more. The toddler waves his arms impatiently. Adam reaches down, puts his hands round his son's tiny torso and tries to lift. But it's impossible.

Staggering to the stool he collapses. He gasps for breath and after a moment manages to say, 'Sorry, mate. Can't be done.'

He can feel his heart thudding in his chest and he wonders, not for the first time, how much longer the damaged and diseased muscle will hold out.

At the age of thirty-two, he was a tough, six-foot dairy farmer; snowboarding in the winter, sailing in the summer. He had energy to burn. Then he contracted a rare virus which attacked his heart. If he hadn't been so fit, it would've killed him outright, that's what the doctors told him. Myocarditis causes sudden death in twenty percent of younger adults. He remembers the cardiologist parroting the statistics as she continued to stare at her laptop.

Now, a year later, he asks himself if sudden wouldn't have been better. A quick and clean ending. Better for him. Better for Zoe and little Ryan and five-year-old Lily. By now, they'd have recovered and could be getting on with their lives. Instead, they are all trapped in limbo, waiting for the call that will probably never come.

Donor hearts are rare, and most people die before they

reach the top of the transplant list. They made this clear to him. But Zoe keeps a bag packed, she's bought a second phone and carries two with her in case one runs out of charge. Her hatchback always has a full tank of petrol, blankets in the back and a flask of water. She's ready to go at a moment's notice, the route from Devon to the Queen Elizabeth Hospital Birmingham programmed into the satnav.

Adam feels his head swimming. He closes his eyes. He knows that if he sits still, it will pass. When he opens them, she's standing there in the doorway scanning him.

He smiles, speaks slowly, the words punctuated by shallow breaths. 'He's been...down that gym again... Turning into...a right little bruiser...Can't lift him.'

'You know you shouldn't even try.' Her tone is unemotional, but there's a tension in her face, in her body, a contained fury.

'If I can't...be a dad-'

Stepping into the room, she scoops the toddler out of his cot none too gently. Sensing his mother's irritation, Ryan opens his mouth and bawls.

She jiggles the child on her hip. 'Don't be stupid, you are a dad. Of course you're a dad. I didn't realise you were up. Can't you sleep?'

He shakes his head. 'Didn't want...to disturb—'

'Adam,' her lips pucker into what looks like a scowl, but could be an attempt to suppress the tears. 'We've talked about this. If you were to collapse or...you know what I'm saying. I need to know where you are.'

'Mummy!' The voice is small and plaintive and comes from the next room.

'Now she's awake too.'

He dips his head. More guilt. 'I'm sorry, Zo.'

'I don't want you to be sorry, I—'

'I know,' he says.

Downstairs, somewhere deep in the bowels of the house, there's a faint ringing.

Zoe shoots her husband a startled look. 'It's the landline!'

'Is it?' Her hearing's more acute than his.

'Yep.' Dumping her son on the floor at Adam's feet, she bolts out of the room. He can hear her running down the stairs. Something clatters in the kitchen. Then the ringing stops.

Adam strains to listen.

'Yes yes! This is Zoe Hardy.'

2

DAY 1. 6.25am

'How? How is it on social media? Is this someone at the lab?'

Professor Dame Felicity Oldroyd drums her nails on the granite island at the centre of the spacious kitchen. In her other hand she holds the phone. She wears soft cotton pyjamas under a towelling robe. It's an hour and a half before dawn and through the tall plate-glass windows the dark garden is silvery with hoar frost.

The title professor she's earned through years of pioneering research in public health, but the dame-hood is a piece of arcane nonsense that comes with the job: Chief Medical Officer for England, the government's medical adviser.

'Well, I'm briefing the Minister at ten,' she says, 'and I want to be absolutely sure of the fact. Yes, I appreciate that. But these test results need to be double checked. Yes, all of them!'

As she ends the call, her husband Gerry wanders into

the kitchen and gives her a sleepy smile. She returns it. Thirty-eight years of marriage and he's still a handsome devil. They met at medical school. She was the anxious grammar schoolgirl, he was the lazy public schoolboy oozing confidence. But he adores her and has proved the perfect match for a clever and ambitious woman. She stuck to her principles and became a GP and health campaigner; he went into the pharmaceutical industry and charmed his way to the top. Retired now, he has a clutch of City director-ships to keep him out of mischief.

He tops up the reservoir on the chrome coffee maker, switches it on and says, 'What's up?'

She sighs. Days like this, she wonders why she continues to do the job. But she says 'Oh, the usual nonsense. The whole department's turned into a leaky bucket. Every tiny thing and some junior nitwit, who wants to be a hero on Twitter, is thumbing it into their phone before we've even had a chance to draw breath let alone come up with an analysis.'

'Not more hashtag "NHS-in-crisis?" Patients dying in corridors?'

'Worse.'

He raises his eyebrows. 'Worse?'

'A suspicious spike in the influenza figures,' she says.

'Well, it is January.' He places an espresso cup under the nozzle and presses the button. 'Didn't you say the other day you thought the incidence would be up?'

The machine gurgles. A rivulet of coffee trickles into the cup, filling the kitchen with its rich aroma.

Folding her arms, she says, 'It's a bit more complicated than that. The number of confirmed deaths in ICUs are up two weeks running. That's predictable. What is surprising is the strain of the virus.'

'Isn't it Aussie flu this year?'

'Yeah, H3N2. That's what we were expecting. What we've also got is H7N9. That's the nasty surprise. It's a new avian flu strain, only emerged in China in 2013 but by last year they were on their fifth epidemic.'

'Well, if people will go on holiday to exotic places and wander round the local livestock markets, they're likely to come home with exotic diseases.'

'World Health Organisation's worried about H7N9 because a couple of cases could be human-to-human transmission.'

Gerry hands her a cup of coffee and says, 'How reliable is the data? WHO is always in a flap about something. What's your nitwit tweeting? We're all about to die of bird flu.'

She raises the cup to her lips. 'Basically, yes.'

'Are you worried?'

'I'm always worried. That's my job.'

3

DAY 1. 7.58am

A hint of dawn is leeching into the eastern sky as Jason Hardy drives up the narrow rutted track to his brother's farm. Having grown up as townies in the coastal resort of Torquay, it was a surprise to him when big brother Adam returned to Devon from his foreign wanderings, married Zoe, a former classmate of Jason's and took over her family's dairy farm.

With barely two years' difference in age between them, they'd grown up friends as much as brothers and their common bond was sport. Both boys loved it, but it was always Adam who excelled. Jason's natural diffidence made him the follower, but he'd never minded because Adam had always treated him as an equal. Their dad had got them started in dinghies and at nineteen, but, much to their parents' annoyance, Adam had dropped out of university to crew in a transatlantic yacht race. He spent the next five years sailing and seeing the world.

The lights are all ablaze in the old stone farmhouse and, as Jason parks, a heavy sense of foreboding seeps into his stomach. This is all his fault. He can't seem to get beyond that. No one's saying it, but everyone thinks it, except perhaps Adam.

It was Jason's thirtieth birthday, the big three O. Adam had a new baby and a shedload of responsibilities, but he'd been persuaded to accompany his little brother on one more adventure. A trek to the Everest Base Camp was on both their bucket lists. To say Zoe was pissed off about it was an understatement. She made her opinion crystal clear. But the trip had been brilliant, a once-in-a-lifetime experience; crossing the high passes of Cho La and Renzo, seeing the Khumbu Icefall, the breathtaking ice seracs. It was on the long flight back from Nepal that Adam first seemed ill.

He returned home with what appeared to be a feverish cold, which he couldn't shake off. But he had lots of catching up to do on the farm and a resentful wife to placate. No one realised how sick he was until he collapsed in the milking parlour, was rushed to hospital and diagnosed with a heart attack. In a fit man of thirty-two, it seemed absurd.

Zoe's father opens the front door. Phil Rowett gives him a curt nod and says, 'Thanks for coming. How're the roads?'

'Icey. But the gritters are out.'

'I'd drive them myself, but Zoe's insistent we stay with the children.'

'I'm happy to do it.'

Jason is well aware that Rowett doesn't have that high an opinion of either him or his brother. He has a wealthy man's disdain for anyone who doesn't have his entrepreneurial outlook or ambition. Jason follows him through into the kitchen.

The room is large with a flagstone floor. But the Aga is

belting out heat, making it warm and cosy. Adam is dressed and sitting at the heavy pine table, cradling Lily on his lap.

He gives his brother a weak smile. 'Apparently my number's come up.'

'About bloody time, you've been waiting long enough.'

'Year on the transplant list. About average.' His breathing is shallow and laboured and worse than a week ago when he last visited, Jason thinks.

Zoe appears with a thick sweater and a scarf, balancing Ryan on her hip; she gives her brother-in-law a tight and hostile glance. 'You need to put this on, Adam. Make sure you keep warm.'

Jason reminds himself that Zoe's been brilliant. She's stepped up to the plate. His brother couldn't have wished for a better wife in these trying circumstances.

Zoe's mother, Ruth, lifts her granddaughter up. 'Come on, sweetheart. Daddy needs to put his jumper on.'

'Nooo!' The little girl hangs on to his shirt sleeve.

Adam frowns at her. 'Hey sweet pea, be...good for grandma.'

'I want to come. Pleeease! I'll be good.'

Zoe intervenes. 'Mummy's explained. Daddy has to go to hospital again.'

'No more hospital. Hate hospital.'

'Don't be difficult, Lily.' Zoe's tone doesn't brook any argument. She loops the sweater over her husband's head and helps him with the arms. It's a slow process.

Jason watches. Ruth distracts the kids with the bribe of biscuits. Rowett fidgets, picks up a coffee mug from the counter and drains the dregs. This is not the life he'd imagined for his only daughter.

It takes the best part of ten minutes to get Adam installed in the front seat of Jason's Range Rover. He bought it second hand with a good few miles on the clock, but it's sturdy and reliable and much more suitable for the journey than Zoe's little hatchback. Jason can tell from his sister-in-law's expression that she wouldn't agree.

She tucks a blanket round her husband's knees, kisses her parents and children and then climbs in the back. Adam tilts his head and smiles at his in-laws standing in the porch; his gaze rests on Lily, who looks sullen, and little Ryan. Adam gives them all a wave.

Jason starts the engine and says, 'Okay then.' He scans his brother. It's impossible to tell what Adam's thinking. Probably wondering, like everyone else, if he's ever coming back.

But Adam gives him a roguish grin, a momentary flash of his old self. 'Got any decent music in this rust bucket?'

Twitter Feed

DAY 1.

True Health News @truehealthnews
MAJOR ALERT! New strain of bird flu from China. H7N9 is here. Over three hundred cases confirmed by reliable NHS source.
253 Retweets 602 Likes

Jenny Brown @jenandjim76
Replying to @truehealthnews WTF! What does this mean? Should I keep my kids off
school? #Scarystuff

True Health News @truehealthnews
Replying to @jenandjim76
Government is keeping schtum. Well, don't they always. Bottom line is this – has it mutated? If it has, then this could be THE BIG ONE.
437 Retweets 853 Likes

Ravi Singh @rpsingh99
I'm really worried. My dad is 75. I'm his carer. He gets the flu jab but is that enough?

True Health News @truehealthnews
Replying to @rpsingh99
Short answer – probably not. This is a new strain over here so there'll be no vaccine. H7N9 has high mortality rate. Go to our website for more info: truehealthnews.com
674 Retweets 1.5k Likes

4

DAY 1. 12.41pm

Felicity Oldroyd's PA brings her a wholegrain salad box for lunch. On her screen she has the weekly figures from the UK Severe Influenza Surveillance System (USISS), which confirms the number of influenza cases admitted to Intensive Care Units and High Dependency Units at hospitals across England and the number of deaths that have resulted.

She peers glumly at the rising graph, then clicks across to the results from the Respiratory Virus Unit at Public Health England's laboratory in Colindale. The tests have been repeated and double checked to confirm it is H7N9, a relatively new strain of the avian flu virus. But why, suddenly, from nowhere, has it popped up in all these different locations? Is it a mutation? It makes no sense. But then what do we really know about how these viruses mutate? Felicity stares at the screen and sighs.

Tearing open the sachet of oil and balsamic vinegar dressing, she drizzles it on her salad. But she has little appetite.

The morning has been a manic scramble of phone calls and meetings, starting with her encounter with the Rt Hon Hugh Ryder MP, the current Secretary of State for Health. During her tenure as Chief Medical Officer Felicity has seen three Ministers pass through the department on what they hope is the fast track to a safer billet. The myriad complications of funding and running a National Health Service is, in the Professor's opinion, incomprehensible to most politicians and Ryder is no exception.

Under forty, telegenic and rabidly ambitious, he's out to make his mark. On the advice of a bevy of PR consultants, he has decided to make cancer his thing. Money for cutting edge research, albeit raised from charitable donations, initiatives for early diagnosis, photo-ops with patients, he's been diligent for the cause, Felicity will give him that. Although she has heard from her husband the rumours that Ryder is more than willing to be wooed by big Pharma, especially the Americans, who are always after a lucrative slice of the cancer budget for their latest wonder drug. This is especially true now that we're out of European Union and is likely to be a plank of any trade deal with the US.

The morning meeting had found him in a peevish mood. As she walked into his office Ryder continued checking the messages on his phone, a habit which annoyed her, but which she concluded was intended as a reminder that although she was a doctor and a professor, he was the boss.

Eventually he looked up, motioned her to take a seat and said, 'Well, is there going to be a pandemic or isn't there?'

'It's impossible to say, Minister.'

'That's what's all over Twitter. Tell me it's fake news.'

'If I could, I would. But given the severe stress on the system already, I think we need to consider cancelling routine operations.'

Ryder chuckled and said, 'Oh, very slick, Felicity. I get it. Influenza figures are up a bit. You get one of your lab rats to plant a scare story–'

'I hope you don't think, Minister—'

'But I do think. You know my views. I've made a personal pledge to the voters that the NHS will cope this winter. Now you're trying to railroad me by creating public panic with some tale about a dangerous new strain of bird flu. What's actually going on here?'

What is going on here? That question has been bothering her all morning.

The professor took a deep breath; it wasn't the first time she'd had her integrity impugned by him for something she hadn't done. He lied and connived all the time and assumed everyone else did.

'Routine surveillance of weekly data from ICUs and HDUs has thrown up an unexpected result,' she said. 'We appear to have a number of deaths associated with the H7N9 strain of the influenza A virus.'

'What does that mean? Something's mutated? Now people are infecting each other? That's what they're saying on Twitter.'

They? Who are they? 'I don't know. We're looking into it.'

'We've had all this scary stuff about bird flu before. 1914 all over again, millions will die.'

'1918.'

'Whatever.' He glared at her. 'BBC wants me on the lunchtime news. What am I supposed to say?'

He'd given her a surly look, as if this was all her fault,

some problem she'd dreamt up to make his life more diffi-cult. Did he believe she would do that? Probably.

She replied with a neutral smile. 'Say we're looking into it.'

They stared at one another across the desk.

Not for the first time, she'd had the queasy feeling that behind his tetchiness was a complete indifference to other people. Politicians could be self-interested, but Ryder was in a league of his own. Put a camera in his face and he could emote with the best. On the floor of the House of Commons, he could erupt with moral outrage but sitting behind his office desk, he seemed vacant and a little bored. A stupid man under the cover of an expensive education, that was her husband's opinion; he'd been to school with chaps like Ryder.

Folding his hands, the Minister changed tack and said, 'What does Dougie reckon?'

Douglas Lacey was the Chief Executive of Public Health England, the body tasked with co-ordinating the response to major incidents and safeguarding the nation's health. He was also Ryder's man; they always sang from the same hymn sheet.

Felicity had spoken to him on the phone as soon as she got confirmation of the test results.

Wily as a coyote, he was an ex-hospital manager who'd survived several major scandals, including the disappear-ance of dead babies' organs and wholesale theft of NHS drugs, to navigate his way to the top.

He'd told her that PHE's medical director was skiing in Banff (*at the height of the flu season, why?*), the deputy had gone on maternity leave and Dougie, clueless in the absence of their advice, felt that the priority was to investigate further and not to overreact. For once, she agreed with him.

She'd met Ryder's gaze with a penetrating stare and said, 'Obviously my team and PHE are liaising closely. Our shared concern is the wide geographical spread of these results. Shall I explain, Minister?'

With a curt nod, he replied, 'I wish you would.'

'Well, various strains of avian flu affect humans, and some can be deadly. But, so far, all reliable reports tell us that the victims contract the virus through direct contact with infected birds, usually poultry. Now we have fourteen deaths, spread randomly across the country, mostly elderly people and people with compromised immune systems.'

She paused to check she had his attention. At least he'd put his phone down.

She continued, 'How were these people infected? Have they all recently been on holiday to parts of south-east Asia, where they may have contracted the virus?'

Ryder sniggered and said, 'Bloody baby boomers are always off on holiday somewhere, so it wouldn't surprise me.'

'The oldest victim is in her nineties, but perhaps she is an intrepid traveller. We're trying to find out. Has any of the wild bird population that visits the UK become infected with H7N9? Again, we're trying to find out. Or has someone, who contracted the virus while on holiday, infected all these people? What's known as a super spreader.'

The Minister was getting fidgety. He nodded. 'That's possible, isn't it? If it's mutated.'

'Human-to-human transmission may be a factor here. But here's the puzzle: could one or even several people from the same family, who had travelled abroad, come home and infect another dozen people at random locations spread round the entire country in a tight time frame?'

Ryder nodded sagely. 'You don't think they could?'

'It's the geographical spread that's the puzzle. It doesn't fit a natural pattern of contagion. What we'd expect is a cluster.'

He nodded, then the penny seemed to drop, and a look of shock had spread across his features. 'What are you saying? This could've been spread deliberately.'

'That's one explanation that could fit the facts.'

'How?'

'I don't know, Minister.'

'So what are we talking about? Some sort of bio-terrorist attack? How would they even do that?'

'I don't know. It's a possibility. Which is why it would be sensible to cancel routine operations and put emergency measures in place. Although, until we know more, I don't suggest we declare a major alert. That would create panic. Dougie agrees.'

The lethargy had disappeared from the Rt Hon Hugh Ryder's features. His face was grave, but Felicity thought she saw a glint of excitement in his eyes as he said, 'Well, it's serious, that's for sure. Could be the bloody Russians at it again, or some brand of jihadist. I need to make some calls.'

Felicity left him to it.

Forking through her salad, the Professor wonders if she's taken the right approach with Ryder. Dougie's view had been to keep him out of the loop for as long as possible. His argument was that they needed space to find out what they were dealing with before the media shitstorm hit.

Virologists were looking at the figures. PHE had created a number of projections of potential spread from a single vector or multiple vectors. Someone was trying to talk to the

Chinese. But it was all speculation. Was this the jump, the random mutation that had long been feared? Human-to-human airborne transmission of a deadly avian virus exploding into a global pandemic? Or was it the handiwork of some psychotic human agent with the deluded belief they were an instrument of God's will? And then there were the Russians.

Felicity lets her gaze drift towards the window. The sky above the rooftops is an icy-white blankness. The chill of it, or is it fear, soaks through her. She shivers and wishes she'd opted for soup instead of salad.

It feels to her that, at some point, when she wasn't paying attention, the world has turned. It spins on a different axis. The values she'd grown up with have become irrelevant, nonsensical even, and not only to so-called terrorists, but to the people around her. Many in her team, the younger ones, regard her as a bit of a smug old bat and, behind their politeness, she gets a whiff of their disdain. She's always hoped that at the end of her career she would have the affection of her colleagues, that her honest approach would command respect and set an example. That would be her legacy. *Perhaps she is a smug old bat?* But nothing has turned out as she expected. *Does it ever?* People will die, they have already. The real uncertainty is how many.

A brisk tap on the door and her PA opens it with an anxious look. 'Erm, sorry Professor, you've got—'

She has no chance to say more. A short, stout woman barrels into the room. Her hair is pinned in a neat bun, her saggy jowls make her look older than she probably is. A comic figure, that's Felicity's immediate impression. A jolly fat lady from a cartoon or a seaside postcard. She crosses the room with a rolling gait, holds out a chubby be-ringed hand, beams and says, 'Pat Babcock. Detective Chief Superintendent. Counter Terrorism.'

5

DAY 1. 2.20pm

Adam Hardy waits listlessly on a bed in a side room in the transplant suite. He wears a hospital gown, but as yet they've taken no other steps to prepare him for theatre. It feels as if he's been lying there for hours. It probably is hours. He was hungry, but that's worn off now. Nil by mouth is the instruction.

The procedure requires that the transplant team wait to hear from the retrieval team. The donor heart being offered is theoretically a match for Adam, but until the retrieval surgeons examine it, its suitability cannot be confirmed. The transplant co-ordinator – a pleasant enough woman, *call me Linda* – has explained this several times. On closer inspection the donor heart may prove to be diseased or to have deteriorated to an extent that it would be detrimental to Adam to go ahead with the operation.

Timing is crucial. Once the heart is removed from the

donor, there is a window of around four hours to transport and transplant it.

Jason has fetched coffee for himself and Zoe. No coffee for Adam, obviously. Having waited almost a year, the possibility that it could all fall apart at the last moment is a level of torture none of them had expected. Jason squats on the floor, back against the wall, leaving the armchair for Zoe. But she can't rest, she paces.

Linda appears with a sheepish look on her face and Adam braces himself for the news that his operation is off.

Her smile is awkward. 'I'm really sorry about the continuing delay but some issues have arisen at the other hospital.'

'What sort of issues?' Zoe says, arms folded about her, probably to help her resist the temptation to seize the hapless Linda and shake her.

The transplant co-ordinator frowns. 'The circumstances are somewhat unusual–'

'Either the heart is suitable for my husband, or it isn't. Surely that's the only issue.'

'We haven't actually been able to...well, to ascertain that yet.'

'Why not? Is this some kind of bureaucratic cock-up? My understanding is the retrieval team would've been dispatched hours ago. Where are they getting this heart from? Timbuktu?'

Adam smiles. He catches his brother's eye. There is some minor relief in watching his wife go into bat for him.

Zoe reins herself in and says, 'I don't mean to be rude. But this is my husband's life.'

'Of course. I do understand. And–'

'Don't tell me you're doing everything you can. What are these unusual circumstances?'

Linda has the look of a woman splashing around frantically in search of the life raft. 'Perhaps, Mrs. Hardy, you should talk to Mr. Farlow.'

'Perhaps I should,' Zoe replies. 'Who the hell is he?'

'One of the hospital's assistant managers. He has responsibility for the transplant unit.'

'Okay. Lead on.' She shoots a glance at Adam as she follows Linda out of the door.

Adam turns his head slowly sideways and gives his brother a ghostly smile. 'You could almost...feel sorry for Farlow.'

Jason grins and says, 'Nah, I wouldn't bother.'

Adam lets his mind drift. Illness has taught him to weather delays and to expect disappointment. He's not sure he's become more patient, but he has learnt to zone out and wait. Zoe, in contrast, has become less tolerant and more angry.

She's smart and has never been a pushover. It's one reason he married her. Not, as many supposed, because her father is possibly the richest man in the county. The Rowetts had been Devon farmers for several generations, but it was Phil who turned it all into a serious agribusiness. Zoe was in Jason's class at school and had the reputation for being a complete princess.

A brief memory slips into Adam's mind: the first time he saw her. She was fifteen and walked into the yacht club with all the self-centred superiority of a young lady used to getting her own way. Like most teenage girls, she had no interest in the boys of her own age and homed in on Jason Hardy's hot older brother. Her attempts at chatting him up had amused him. But he was about to go to uni and wasn't interested in a fifteen-year-old.

Seven years later, when he came home from his travels

and got a job in a local boatyard, the boot was on the other foot.

Jason gets up from the floor, eases his aching back, and settles in the armchair. 'How you feeling?' he says.

Adam shrugs but says nothing.

Jason tweaks his arm in solidarity.

A mischievous smile spreads over Adam's features. 'If I croak in...here, that'll be embarrassing...for them.'

His brother smiles. 'Think she's already told them that, mate.'

Jason sits down on the floor beside the armchair and for a while they share a companionable silence. There are comings and goings in the corridor, snatches of conversation. Zoe seems to have disappeared.

Ten minutes pass and there's a small commotion, the sound of half a dozen pairs of feet approaching. The door swings open and a neat man in blue theatre scrubs appears.

Stepping forward, he says, 'Mr. Hardy,' and beams with confidence, 'I'm James Chang, consultant cardiothoracic surgeon. I'll be leading the team. May I?' Without waiting for a reply, he reaches down and picks up Adam's wrist to check the pulse.

He's flanked by medical staff, also in scrubs, Zoe, the hospital manager, Farlow, and Linda, looking harassed. Everyone waits in silence as Chang studies Adam.

Adam feels the strong fingers. There's a delicacy, a precision in the surgeon's touch.

Chang nods to himself, gazes down at his patient and says, 'I'm sorry we have subjected you to all this uncertainty, Mr. Hardy. I'm going to hand you over to our anaesthetist, Dr. Gupta, and he'll take care of you, get you ready for theatre. Anything you'd like to ask me?'

'Umm, no...' Adam's surprised, or is he? Zoe's a force of

nature. His thoughts drift. Each breath is an effort. What-ever the outcome, he wants to be done with all this. He catches his wife's eye. She smiles.

Jason gets up and says, 'What was the problem? Was there some doubt that the donor was a match?'

Chang inhales. 'No, not once we got access.' He shoots a reproachful glance at the balding manager. 'And the retrieval team has reported that the organ is in excellent condition. So, we're back on schedule and it will be here.' He smiles at Adam. 'Your wife tells me you're a sailor, Mr. Hardy.'

'Not lately.'

'We'll soon have you back on the water. Scudding over the waves. Don't think about the operation. Think about that.'

'I will. And thanks.'

Chang turns and the cavalcade follows him out. Zoe kneels beside the chair and kisses the back of Adam's hand.

'What happened?' he asks.

'A load of nonsense. Nothing you need to worry about.'

6

DAY 1. 4.25pm

Zoe and Jason have been walking in circles, round the hospital site, round the car park, but the cold and the encroaching darkness drives them inside. They head for the coffee shop.

Jason fishes a handful of coins from his pocket and says, 'What can I get you?'

She shakes her head.

'You should have something to eat.'

'Get lost, Jason! You think I can eat?'

He raises his palms. 'Sorry.'

They wander over to a corner table and sit.

She takes a deep breath, exhales and says, 'I don't mean to be such a total bitch.'

He grins. 'Small bitch, maybe. In the circumstances.'

She sighs. 'If you're hungry, get something. Don't let me stop you.'

'I don't think I could eat either. How about a cup of tea?'

'Okay. I should call home, check on the kids.'

He stands up. 'You talked to your dad about an hour ago.'

'I hate this! I bloody hate it!' Shaking her head, she places a hand over her mouth.

'He will pull through. I believe that. I know my brother; I know how tough he is. He's been fighting for the last year and he'll continue to fight. And nowadays they do loads of transplants. It will work.'

Zoe looks up at him, tears welling. Jason realises this is the first time since Adam got ill that he's actually seen her cry.

He reaches out, puts a hand on her shoulder and says 'Hey...'

She shrugs him off. 'Get the tea. I'm fine.' Pulling out a tissue, she blows her nose.

As Jason walks over to the counter, he notices the large television screen set above it on a wall bracket. A small gaggle of hospital workers are gathered under it. Some are watching it, others are scrolling on their phones. It's tuned to one of the news channels. The sound is muted, but there's a rolling subtext.

A nurse calls to one of the catering assistants. 'Can't you turn it up!'

Jason orders two teas, pays, and waits. He glances across the room at Zoe, who's talking on her phone.

The nurse folds her arms and turns to one of her companions; it's her irate tone that attracts Jason's attention.

'What the hell do they expect us to do in A&E?' she says. 'just carry on? The vaccination we've had won't protect us if it's some deadly new strain.'

Jason looks up at the screen. The sound comes on.

The newsreader speaks directly to camera. '...assurances

from the Department of Health and Public Health England that everything necessary is being done to contain the situation.'

The camera cuts to a middle-aged official in a smart suit and a racy pink tie. The text at the bottom of the screen flashes up: Douglas Lacey, CEO of Public Health England, as the man smiles and says in a soft Yorkshire burr, 'There's absolutely no need for alarm. This is the flu season and what we're seeing is what we would expect at this time of year. This is nothing out of the ordinary and, I'd like to say, that the scaremongering we've seen on social media is totally irresponsible.'

A voice off camera asks, 'But is it true that this is H7N9, a strain of avian flu that we've not experienced in the UK before?'

Shaking his head like a patient headteacher, Lacey replies, 'This is nothing new. We have robust systems in place, plenty of vaccine available for those who need it. I can assure you that no one need worry.'

The nurse turns to her friend and says, 'It's bullshit. Online, they're saying thirty confirmed deaths in a few days.'

Picking up his tray, Jason carries the little metal pots of tea and the cups back to the table.

Zoe is on the phone: 'Mum, I'm fine, don't worry. Yeah yeah, of course. Jason's brought me a cup of tea. Yeah, I will. Love you too.' She hangs up and gives her brother-in-law a baleful look.

He sets the tray down and pours. 'I think I may have found out why there's been all this bother. They're saying on the box something about a serious flu outbreak.'

'That was Farlow's excuse. But what's it got to do with us? Flu is flu. It's another pack of lies to cover for a system that's on its knees.'

'Sounds quite serious.'

'Really? More serious than heart failure?'

He hands her the tea. She picks up the cup, cradles it in her palms, then returns it to the saucer. Hunched forward over the table, her whole body shakes with silent sobs.

Twitter Feed

DAY 2.

True Health News @truehealthnews
Seriously! Do they think we're idiots?
Quoting:**Public Health England** @PHE_uk
There is no cause for alarm. This is the flu season. We
expect a spike in the figures. We are well prepared. Plenty of
vaccine is available. #staywell
1.2k Retweets 1.5k Likes

Keandra Smith @keandraS24
Replying to @truehealthnews
I'm a nurse in A&E. We've had 45 cases through the door
already. Really ill people. Chaos here. It's the big one #pandemic #governmentlies
1.3k Retweets 2k Likes

Pete Harris @pharris510
Replying to @truehealthnews
My elderly neighbour got sick yesterday. The ambulance
came but wouldn't take him. He died in the night. A black
van took his body away. #scarystuff #governmentlies

Sheila Thompson @slthompson2
Replying to @truehealthnews
I'm a widow and I live alone. My son is in Australia. I worry
what will happen to me if I get sick. I've had the flujab but
will it work? Feels to me like the politicians don't care.
#tellusthetruth

True Health News @truehealthnews

Replying to @slthompson2

You've put your finger on it Sheila! THEY DON'T CARE!!!

7

DAY 2. 7.32am

Adam is drifting, a calm sea, a soft breeze rippling the surface. The life jacket buoys him up, he floats on his back, face warmed by the sun. But down below, the current starts to pull, or maybe it's seaweed snaring his legs, dragging him down. He goes under. The undertow is sucking him downwards. Into the dark. Impossible to resist. Water fills his nose and mouth, he splutters, gasps for breath. Fear engulfs him. He's drowning.

It's stuck in his throat, right down his gullet, rough and rasping. It's choking him. If only he could cough it up? He sinks again; this time it's pitch black and freezing.

Shivering, his eyelids flutter and he's assaulted by searing white light. *Rough. Rasping. Choking to death.* He sinks. Darkness is better.

A voice comes from faraway and says, 'Adam? Can you hear me, Adam?'

The light hurts his eyes; he wants to shield them, but he can't move.

A face looms over him, a smell, clean, like shampoo? A vinyl glove on his cheek. 'Adam, we've taken you off the ventilator.'

The pain is everywhere. His chest, his throat, his whole body hurts. His mind is screaming: *darkness is better!*

The air fills his nostrils, sharp and abrasive. His throat is sore. He swallows. More pain. The air is painful.

A warm wave floods through his veins and now he's floating. Another voice says, 'That should help.' Blue scrubs. 'Can you hear me, Adam? Do you remember where you are?'

'Sailing.' He speaks the word in his head, but his mouth won't make the sound.

Wet on his lips. Cool and refreshing. His tongue is sticky, but he licks. And opens his eyes a fraction. Tubes and wires surround him, a monitor bleeps.

'Hospital. You're in hospital.' A voice says. 'You're in ITU, intensive care. You've had an operation. A heart transplant. Remember?'

'Yes.' He hears his own voice. He sounds like an old man. It seems better to agree; he's confused.

'We've adjusted the pain relief and that's going to help.'

The light is too bright, blinding him. He has to close his eyes. Suddenly he's moving fast. Hurtling forwards. Down into a hole, or maybe it's a tunnel. Yes, it's a tunnel. The walls have an eerie gleam, it stinks of diesel. Rushing air strafes his face. The speed is dizzying, exhilarating. He's flying through the air, then tumbling out of control.

A roaring, howling gale sucks him down into a spinning vortex, drags him into a black chasm, devouring the light. *Darkness is better.*

Then, a pinprick at first, rolling ahead of him, inches from his face, there's a ball. At least it looks like a ball. Bounces like a ball. And it's red and shiny.

8

———

DAY 2. 8.45am

Jason Hardy wakes with a start, glances at his phone and curses. He's overslept. It takes him a moment to remember that he's not in his own bed. He's in a Travelodge in Birmingham.

He was awake for much of the night. He'd stayed with Zoe at the hospital until they completed the operation. It was after eight o'clock by the time the surgeon came to speak to them.

Mr. Chang described the procedure as textbook. Adam was in the recovery suite. They could gaze at him briefly through the plate-glass window. Jason wanted to ask what they'd done with his brother's own heart. That seemed an indelicate question in his sister-in-law's presence, but he wants to know. Do they throw it away? That doesn't feel right. How would you keep it? What would you do with it? Pickle it in a jar?

The hospital had provided accommodation for Zoe, but

Jason had to find something for himself. He'd driven around
in a daze for about half an hour. Then he came across the
Travelodge on the edge of an industrial park. It had a pub
right next door, which sealed the deal.

Since his teens Jason had been a drinker, he'd boozed
his way through uni, but in the last year, since Adam had
become ill, he'd adopted a healthier lifestyle. He worked in
an office at a computer all week, went to the gym and
pumped iron at the weekend. There had always been a
friendly rivalry between him and Adam as to who was fitter.
Since Adam had taken up farming, his big brother had
insisted it was him. He could carry a newborn calf on his
shoulders wrapped round the back of his neck. Remembering this boast now reminded Jason how suddenly the life
he'd taken for granted, that they'd all taken for granted, had
spiralled into the abyss.

In the pub, Jason had ordered a pint plus a pie and
chips. He ate his meal on autopilot as he watched the ten
o'clock television news.

Speculation around the seriousness of the flu outbreak
was the top story, with experts repeating the mantra: this
was nothing out of the ordinary. It ended with an interview
in which a self-satisfied academic talked about fake news
and the dangers of social media.

There was a desultory amount of interest from the smat-
tering of customers in the bar.

'Nothing out of the ordinary? They must think we're all
morons,' said a portly bloke. He looked like a sales rep
who'd been on the road too long. Nursing his pint and a
whiskey chaser, he belched. 'Buggered is what we are.'

No one seemed inclined to take up the debate.

Could you catch it from eating chicken? Jason considered
the succulent chunks of chicken in his half-eaten pie, aban-

doned it, bought a couple of cans and retreated to his room. He got out his laptop and spent half the night online trawling the net for information. It filled the time and gave him something to focus on, apart from Adam.

He found an avalanche of theories. Forty of the Queen's swans had died on the River Thames. This had been hushed up said one website, but was definitely the source. Jason had once had a nasty encounter with a swan; it'd reared up to protect its young. He wondered how you'd even get close enough to a swan to be infected.

There were lengthy pseudo-scientific discussions about the evolution of the different strains of avian flu. Sad sepia photos of the 1918 pandemic with row upon row of hospital beds. Opinion seemed divided on whether the virus had mutated naturally or been bio-engineered. Anyone and everyone were blamed from poultry farmers to the Chinese.

Jason knew his way round the net and social media, but in the end he found it impossible to separate fact from fantasy. Whatever was going on, it seemed likely that this had nearly put pay to Adam's transplant. The death toll so far was either twenty or two hundred, depending on whose statistics you believed.

Clips of the Secretary of State for Health were all over YouTube and the news outlets. He seemed calm and confident, reassuring everyone that plenty of vaccine was available for anyone who might've been exposed to the virus. But how would you know if you'd been exposed? With a politician's deft change of tack, he'd avoided answering that question.

After a long hot shower, Jason is awake and ready to cope with whatever the day brings. He hopes for the best but, in his mind, has been planning for the worst. Adam had arranged their dad's funeral. That was bad enough. Jason suspects that if his brother doesn't make it, Phil Rowett will take over. But it won't come to that. Adam will get through this. He doesn't believe in prayer, although at this moment part of him wishes he did.

Snatching a takeaway coffee, he phones Zoe for news but the call goes straight to voicemail. It gives him an unsettled feeling and doubts creep up on him again. He's done loads of research, and knows all about the chances of rejection. He also knows that much depends on how quickly the donor heart was harvested and transplanted. Delays leading to a deterioration in the organ will affect his brother's prognosis. He phones Zoe again, no reply. He checks the time. The phone must be switched off because she's in ITU.

Driving on to the hospital site, everything looks normal enough. Jason walks past the entrance to A&E. There are a few people about. Then he notices a police officer sheltering from the cold inside the doorway. He's cradling a submachine gun and shifting from foot to foot to keep warm. Jason gives him a comradely nod.

For the last three years, Jason has worked as a civilian analyst for the Met. With a background in IT, he covers a range of cases from online scams to possible paedophile rings. He likes the work and feels he's doing something worthwhile; it's more interesting than his previous job on the phone all day selling business apps for a tech start-up.

When he finally arrives at ITU, he's asked to put on a gown and mask to reduce the chances of infection. He finds Zoe seated beside her husband's bed, and Adam has his eyes open. His face is gaunt, and he looks about fifty. It reminds Jason of their father when he was dying of prostate cancer.

Jason paints on a smile, points at the heart monitor and says, 'Works then, the new ticker.'

'Yeah.' The voice is a croak. But there appears to be a serenity about Adam; it's probably the painkillers.

Smiling at his sister-in-law, Jason feels awkward. Even at the best of times, theirs is a spiky relationship. 'Well, onward and upward, eh,' he says. It sounds stupid.

Zoe looks exhausted, her eyes darkly underscored. Now the urgency and the arguing are over, she seems to have lost all momentum. She turns her head slowly. 'Could you do me a favour, Jace?'

'Of course.'

'I've got loads of missed calls from my dad. Can't use the phone in here. Can you phone them?'

'Yeah, no problem. Any particular message?'

She sighs, gives him a bewildered look.

He waits a moment, then says, 'Don't worry. I'll update them. Tell them he's awake and...well, whatever.'

She nods. 'Thanks.'

Jason glances at his brother. His gaze has drifted off. He looks frail, tethered to the bed by a tangle of tubes and wires.

'See you in a bit, buddy.'

Adam's pupils are dark and dilated; he's off somewhere else. Drugged up or dreaming perhaps of the life he once had? He doesn't answer.

Jason feels his own heart thumping. *It'll be okay. Adam will pull through. Please!* As he walks away, he repeats the words over and over. Is that praying he wonders? Maybe that's how you do it.

TWO WEEKS LATER

Twitter Feed

DAY 16.

True Health News @truehealthnews
Today's casualty count: 2561 confirmed deaths. May their
souls rest in peace.
Replying to @PHE_uk
STOP LYING!!! Tell people THE TRUTH #pandemic #the-
BigOne #governmentlies
5.2k Retweets 8.9k Likes

Mark Carter @MCB666
Replying to @truehealthnews
Soldiers digging burial pit in Surrey. See for yourself
bit.ly/5FlKtQa
3.02k Retweets 6.4k Likes

Beth Smythe @basmythe45
Replying to @truehealthnews
We're keeping our kids off school but I've read we could get
fined! How can they do this? They don't care.
453 Retweets 781 Likes

True Health News @truehealthnews
Replying to @basmythe45
This is the problem Beth, it's been over two weeks but
keeping up a pretence matters more to them than our kids
health and safety. You think it's outrageous cause it is!
5.3k Retweets 9.5k Likes

9

DAY 16. 8.52am

Felicity Oldroyd walks down Victoria Street. She's brooding. The last couple of weeks have been the most testing of her career, presenting problems for which she has no solution. As a human being, she finds it shocking and abhorrent that anyone would use a deadly virus to attack us. And yet, in her view, it seems to be the most likely explanation for what's happening. But, as she keeps being told, her training is as an ordinary doctor. What does she know?

A bevy of experts has been drafted in: from the security services, both domestic and foreign, to bio-terrorism specialists, epidemiologists and virologists, and foreign policy analysts with insights into the nasty regimes who might not wish us well.

COBRA, an acronym for Cabinet Office Briefing Room A, where it meets, has been convened daily, but no one can agree. Cases of H7N9 have appeared in over a dozen locations round the country, but the mortality rate is low, hardly two per cent. Most people recover without treatment.

And they still have no clue as to the source. Is the spread of the disease natural or has it been bio-engineered? Is the UK in the vanguard of the fight against an emerging, global pandemic caused by a mutation of H7N9 or the victim of another bio-terrorist attack, designed to show how weak we are? The experts are bitterly divided.

Urgent work is being done on the structure of the virus to compare it with the strain of H7N9 that has occurred in China. The Chinese are being surprisingly helpful. The Americans have already been trialing an experimental vaccine on this particular strain; the results so far have been mixed, but it's being rushed into production.

Ryder has changed his position in favour of a naturally occurring epidemic, because that keeps him and his department firmly in the driving seat. He gets to chair the COBRA meetings and Dougie is backing him, ensuring that the resources of Public Health England are being deployed in that direction.

On top of this, there is an ongoing argument over presentation. What should the public be told? COBRA'S priority is to present a united front and to reassure the public that the government knows what it's doing and has a steady hand on the tiller, even if it doesn't.

Felicity finds it a relief to be out in the chilly morning air, finding some respite from the cacophony of conflicting arguments and opinions.

London is a city that's been her home and workplace for her entire adult life. She came as a medical student and has never wanted to live anywhere else. But over the years, the allure she felt as a young woman has faded. The dark underbelly was always there, but it seems to have grown more sinister: drugs, gangs, knife crime, the forlorn army of the homeless camped out in doorways. On her many journeys around the city, she always tries to walk, resorting to buses and taxis only when pressed for time. She hates the underground, crowded and sweaty, it's always her last resort. Through her regular rambles, she's become as familiar with the pockets of misery as with the glittering shops and historic buildings and as a doctor she feels guilty. How did it come to this, she asks herself? Why don't we seem to care that much about each other anymore?

This morning it's bitterly cold and a leaden sky threatens rain. As she approaches Westminster, she reflects that on an ordinary January day there would be some tourists about plus civil servants like her and other office workers coming and going to their jobs in the area. But the normally bustling streets are quiet. People are passing each other with suspicious glances, most of them wearing face masks of some description or muffled in scarves.

Her husband, Gerry, not a man easily unnerved, has been badgering her to use the private chauffeured car he's rented for every journey, however short. But she's resisted. It's yet to be proven either way, but her gut feeling is that person-to-person transmission is not what's happening. And even if the virus can spread through infected airborne droplets, a mask is adequate protection. Hers, borrowed from her cyclist son, fits snugly to the face with velcro straps and has a filter.

But most of her fellow Londoners are not taking any chances. The net is rife with rumour, anecdote and uncorroborated tales of victims dying grisly deaths. Businesses are reporting rates of staff absenteeism close to thirty per cent. Anyone who can is working from home. Many who can't are prepared to risk being fired. The economic impact is likely to prove as problematic as the virus itself.

Felicity's view is that if they were looking at a pandemic, the death toll after two weeks would be much higher. But the computer models, like the experts, all show different results, depending on the biases of those running them.

The tide is high and the river choppy. As Felicity passes the statue of Boadicea and her daughters on their chariot, she reflects that their defiance in the face of superior Roman might is a better reflection of Britain's place in the world now than it was in the Victorian era, when the monument was erected.

She feels frustrated and daunted in a way she never has before. And weary. The world around her, the city she thought she knew, feels off-kilter, a sea of alien eyes and masked faces. Maybe she's not up to the task, that's her worry. Perhaps she should retire and let someone younger and tougher take over. But wouldn't that be a terrible admission of defeat? Wouldn't she be letting people down? It's her duty to soldier on.

As she approaches New Scotland Yard, these are the thoughts swirling round in her head. Fortunately, in Pat Babcock, she's found an ally, whose robust, no-nonsense attitude seems to help. And it's Pat's job to assume that terrorism could be involved.

Detective Inspector Mehta comes down to the reception area and escorts her up to the offices of Counter Terrorism Command. He's a polite young man on the surface, but Felicity gets a hint of sharp elbows when necessary and a probing intellect. She can see why the Detective Chief Superintendent has him as her sidekick.

The place is crowded and buzzing. They have drafted additional staff in to help process and analyse the ocean of data that's flowing in. Information is being collated from numerous sources.

She follows Mehta through to the Chief Super's office.

Pat beams at her. 'Come on in and take a pew.'

They've been meeting privately each morning for the last two weeks to compare notes and theories. This is over and above all the official brainstorming. For Felicity, this is a moment of sanity in her day, when she can sort the facts from the noise. Their working assumption is that every cluster of cases could have a specific and separate source.

Babcock gives her that piercing look: the canny copper checking her out. At first it unnerved her, now she welcomes it. She's had little to do with the police in the past, but Pat Babcock exudes an aura of calm, like an unruffled primary school teacher in a class of marauding seven-year-olds.

'Coffee?' Pat asks. 'Or is this a green tea day?'

Felicity sighs. 'Oh, better make it green tea.'

The Detective Chief Super inclines her head. 'Sami, get the Professor a nice big mug of coffee. And can you also find that box of tricks they've sent from Porton Down?'

He heads for the door. 'No problem.'

Pat chuckles. 'Young men, such an improvement on the generation we were lumbered with, don't you find?'

The professor smiles. She knows nothing of her colleague's private life and feels it would be rude to inquire. Lifting the laptop out of her briefcase, she opens it up. 'I'm sure you've seen the overnight figures,' she says. 'We've got two more potential clusters.'

'Yeah, I saw. Cirencester and Grimsby. That's pretty far apart.'

'I make that thirteen separate locations now.'

'Hmm, a baker's dozen.'

Babcock rescues a stray strand of hair and re-pins it in her neat bun. She's a fastidious woman, everything she does seems precise and controlled, which appeals to the scientist in Felicity.

Scanning the CMO, she continues, 'But if we change our definition of a cluster, it could be more. Don't get me wrong, I'm not questioning your judgement. I need to be sure we're correctly identifying all the likely locations where the virus could've been released.'

'I have been worrying about that,' Felicity replies. 'Kept me awake most of the night. I got them to run a range of possibilities. PHE has got so many computer models they can't see the wood for the trees.'

'They won't notice one more then,' says Pat.

'If we reduce the cluster to between three and five fatalities, we get another four locations. That makes fifteen.'

'I've asked for some more data analysts to help break this down, so we can be a bit more specific about our ANPR and CCTV trawl.'

'Is this going to work?' Felicity asks.

The Chief Superintendent frowns. 'More locations will help because it's patterns of behaviour we're looking for. Vehicles that crop up at the relevant times in more than one of our target locations. Drill that down eventually to individuals on CCTV. It's an enormous task, takes time. But you let us worry about that.'

'Sorry, Pat, I'm not–'

'No need to apologise.' Babcock gives Felicity a reassuring smile. 'I have to say, you look done in. Perhaps you need to take a break, even for a few hours.'

'I've got a meeting with the Minister at ten thirty. He's gone off on a jag about anti-viral drugs.'

'I thought his money was on the American vaccine?'

'Even the Americans are admitting it needs more work.'

'Is Ryder trying to pin the lack of preparedness on you?'

The Professor nods and says, 'It's going to be down to me or Public Health England. But Dougie Lacey's special skill is media management, so I don't rate my chances.'

'Don't be so pessimistic. You're a doctor and you come over as if you actually care. The public don't trust the suits, Downing Street knows that. They need your credibility.'

The professor leans back in her chair and says, 'How do you stay so calm through all this? Nothing fazes you.'

Babcock shrugs. 'Practice. Sadly, I've been involved in enough of these sorts of investigations to know that it's not the actual thing, it's the fallout that's hardest to manage. Terrorism is not about killing people; it's about creating a climate of fear. Fear is the thing that changes people's behaviour.'

'Yeah, well, walking down Victoria Street this morning I'd say they've succeeded.'

Mehta taps on the door and enters carrying a box and a mug of coffee.

Babcock claps her hands. 'Right, well, the boffins at Porton Down have been trying some experiments to see if they can work out what sort of delivery system is being used to spread the virus. They've sent us some samples of what it could look like.'

Opening the box, she lifts out an aerosol can and hands it to Felicity.

The professor examines it. 'God! Looks like a can of hairspray. Someone's going round the country with a bloody spray can?'

'Just a theory,' Pat says. 'But it gives us somewhere to start.'

10

DAY 16. 10.15am

Adam Hardy sits on the side of his hospital bed. He wears tracksuit bottoms and is bare chested, clutching his favourite old rugby shirt Zoe brought in for him. The haggard look has gone; his face looks fuller, pinker and softer.

Chang faces him, hands on hips. He leans forward, peers through his heavy-rimmed glasses at the long red scar that runs down his patient's sternum.

He smiles and says, 'Yep, I'm pretty pleased with that. How's it feel?'

Adam shrugs. 'Not so bad.'

'Don't be tough about this, Adam. Infection is the biggest danger. Don't ignore any serious pain.'

'I know. I won't.' He pulls the top back on. Moving and breathing with ease, speaking a complete sentence without gasping, is a novelty.

Chang watches. 'You've got plenty of mobility back in

your arms and shoulders. Another two to three weeks, the sternum should be healed.'

'And I can drive?'

'We'll discuss that when you come back for a check-up.'

Adam nods and smiles. 'Yeah, I know, one day at a time. I feel like a recovering alcoholic.'

'You were an otherwise fit man, you're young, there's no reason you shouldn't get your life back provided you follow the rules and take the medication.'

'I'm sure you realise how grateful I am. But thank you.. From the bottom of my new heart.'

Chang grins. 'I have heard that one before. But I like it.'

Adam holds out his hand. Chang shakes it. Then he gives Adam a quizzical look and says, 'Any more weird dreams?'

'The white tiles spinning round. That's the thing that keeps recurring.' He doesn't divulge the feeling of abject terror that comes with it. The panic and the urgency.

Chang nods. 'Well, the anti-rejection drugs affect people differently. Hospitals, white tiles, it makes sense. It'll disappear over time. Try not to worry about it. Anything else?'

Adam is on the cusp of mentioning the helmet; he keeps dreaming about a red crash helmet. At first he thought it was a ball, a shiny red kids' football. Then he realised it was too heavy for that. In his dreams he keeps taking it off, putting it on, a red crash helmet with a visor. He's not sure why he's reluctant to talk about it. He has an odd feeling.

All he wants is to get out of there and go home. Once he's home, everything will be all right. Returning to normal, the farm, his family, his children, has seemed a distant fantasy. But he's almost free, he can breathe, he can get up and walk out of that door. It's all he cares about.

Chang's right, these drug fuelled nightmares will fade.

He needs to get home and sleep in his own bed. He's never owned a motorcycle; they've never interested him that much. For him, hurtling down a snowy mountain slope or skimming over the waves is the ultimate rush.

Aware that the doctor is scanning him, he paints on a smile. Then he sees Zoe walking through the ward towards them and the smile becomes real. If he's honest with himself, he never thought this moment would come. For so much of the last year he's felt under sentence of death, now he's got his reprieve.

As Zoe shakes Chang's hand, he finds he can't take his eyes off her. He's suffused with joy and a light-headedness that is not because of any drug. He realises how much he loves this woman, his gorgeous wife, who nearly became a widow. She can be a secretive soul and they've had some ups and downs over the years, but looking at her now, he knows one thing for sure: he's the luckiest man alive.

11

'I thought Jason was coming to get me.' Adam says, glancing across at his wife as they stop at the exit barrier of the car park. Zoe winds down the window and slots her ticket into the machine. The barrier lifts.

'He's had loads of time off work. I told him it wasn't necessary.' Her waspish tone doesn't escape Adam.

'He only wants to help.'

'Why don't you say you hate my driving and you'd rather be driven by your brother.' The tone's jokey, but Adam can sense she's close to snapping.

He says, 'I don't hate your driving. Your driving's fine.'

'Oh, what!' Zoe slams on the brakes as a van pulls out in front of her. The seatbelt locks across Adam's chest and he winces with pain.

She slaps the steering wheel. 'That was not my fault!'

'Good anticipation. Could've been nasty.'

'Now you're taking the piss.' Her expression softens. 'I'm sorry. Are you all right?'

'I'm fine.' He doesn't want to admit to her that since they stepped out of the hospital doors, he's been feeling as shaky as one of their newborn calves.

'I'll be more careful,' she says 'I promise.'

She edges the little hatchback out of the junction and they join the busy main road.

Adam turns his head to look at her. It's the first time for ages they've been alone, no kids, no medical staff, no worried watchers. The wave of emotion he felt in the hospital hits him again. 'I love you, y'know' he says. 'Probably haven't told you that enough lately.'

Zoe is concentrating hard, but she gives him a sardonic glance. 'First time you ever got in a car with me driving, remember what you said?'

'Something rude and sexist, I'm sure.'

'Yeah. Can't fool me, buster. I know what you really think.' That prickly defensiveness is typical of Zoe, and it makes him smile. He reaches out and pats her knee.

Her eyes dart between the road, the satnav on the dash and the huge signs on the gantries above. They negotiate several roundabouts and head for the M5.

Adam lets his gaze coast along with what seems a helter-skelter of passing trucks and cars, garish shopfronts and massive hoardings. Everything seems to rush by him and he realises he's on hospital time. Life on the ward is slow and governed by routines designed to create a calm enclave for recovery. Now he's lost that protection, he'll need time to adapt.

He watches his wife, the crease between her brows, the tension in her knuckles as she turns the wheel.

'Have you ever ridden a motorcycle, Zo?' he asks.

'No. You know I haven't.'

'I couldn't remember.'

'I had a go on Clare Harri'' scooter at school. Thought I might fancy one. Dad freaked and promised me as soon as I was seventeen I could have a car.'

Adam smiles. 'Well, he would.'

She shoots him a quizzical look. 'Why are you thinking about motorcycles?'

'I'm not particularly.'

'Adam, this is not a time in your life to start riding a motorcycle.'

'Early mid-life crisis? Well, I've already had the heart attack, so why not?' He wants to make her laugh again. Their previous life, as he remembers it, was full of teasing.

But she doesn't even crack a smile. 'You're not serious?' she says.

'No. I'm joking. Don't worry.'

They lapse into silence. He enjoys sitting there, riding along beside her, cocooned and also free. But she seems edgy. 'You want some music, or the radio?' she asks.

He shakes his head. 'Not unless you do.

She's still anxious. He finds it hard to ignore. And exhausting. He's got through the operation, his body is recovering. But now there's yet another hurdle to contend with and he finds it pisses him off. Over the long months of his illness, the space between them has become a chasm.

'I wouldn't have got through this without you, I know that,' he says. 'I'd be dead if it wasn't for you.' The words tumble out, he's feeling odd and jittery. *The drugs?*

She exhales. Then she says, 'The kids are excited you're coming home. They'll be so pleased to see you. Lily's made a banner. And your mum's made a cake.'

Adam frowns. 'What sort of cake?'

'Some recipe she found online for extremely healthy carrot cake.'

Adam hesitates. Since his father's premature death, Gill Hardy's state of mind has been a tricky topic.

'How is she?' he asks.

'Oh, y'know. Jason says she's been quite depressed again. I told him to get her medication changed. But I don't think he did.'

'He's not that good at dealing with her.'

'Well, that's stating the bloody obvious. He's not that good at dealing with anything, Adam. But he needs to learn. Because you can't do it.'

'I know.'

'Do you?'

Finally, he thinks. *Here it comes.* All the unspoken resentments of the last year, all the arguments they never had because he was too ill, bubbling to the surface.

'Look,' he says, 'I know how hard all this has been–'

'Don't do this, Adam. Not now. I'm trying to concentrate on driving the bloody car and getting us home. I'm not ready.' Her eyes are on the road ahead.

'Sorry.'

'What I want is for you to recover and for us to get back to something approaching normal life again.'

'Believe me, I want that too' he says.

'Then stop trying to apologise.'

He nods. They fall silent again. It starts to rain. She turns the windscreen wipers on. They clack clack, back and forth. One of them needs a new blade.

Adam watches them and his head spins. Carsick? He's never been carsick in his life, but sweat is gathering under his shirt. *These stupid drugs.* He takes several deep breaths, fixes his gaze on the carriageway ahead to steady himself.

She glances at him. 'You okay?'

'I'm fine. And I'm not trying to apologise. But...I don't want you to be so stressed all the time. And angry.'

'I'm not angry. But this whole bloody thing is stressful. I'm trying to juggle everything and, okay, that makes me irritable. And I'm sorry for that.'

'Now you're apologising' he says.

'You got ill. It's not your fault.'

'It's not Jason's fault either.'

'That's not fair, Adam. I've never blamed him.'

'Maybe if we hadn't done the trip.' He wipes sweat away from his upper lip. The dizziness is petering out, leaving a weird floaty feeling.

'The trip's irrelevant now. We need to move forward.'

He nods in agreement. Then it hits him. Abruptly, from nowhere, he's seized by a torrent of anger. And he can't stop it.

'You didn't want me to go' he says. 'You made that very clear.' *What's he talking about?* He sounds like a petulant teen.

'We had a new baby and a farm to run,' she says, 'but you couldn't say no to your little brother.'

'Don't fucking argue with me, Zoe!' The words explode from deep inside him, fuelled by a murderous rage.

His wife gives him a sidelong glance of disbelief and says, 'Okay. Don't get so upset. Why are we even talking about this?'

He swallows hard. The fury fizzles out. His head spins. He feels bewildered and close to panic. 'I don't know' he says 'I'm sorry. I didn't mean it. I think it's these drugs. I'm really sorry.'

12

DAY 16. 3.52pm

Phil Rowett is keeping watch from the kitchen window, where he's been stationed for the last half hour. The afternoon is fading into a chilly twilight and he's feeling anxious. How many times has he tried to persuade his daughter to get rid of that beat up old hatchback of hers? He's offered to replace it, he's talked better airbags, he's used the safety of his grandchildren. But when Zoe gets the bit between her teeth, she won't listen to reason. He's bought her cars before, he only has one daughter, what else is he going to spend his money on? Then she goes on about being an independent woman who can stand on her own two feet. He wonders how long that will last.

He glances across the room at his wife, Ruth. The contrariness of women is a fact of life. There's no point in arguing with it.

Ruth and Lily are making sandwiches. Ryan is in his highchair, banging his sippy cup. Adam's mother, Gill, is sitting listlessly in the spindle-legged wooden rocking chair in the corner. It's two years now since she lost her husband and Phil thinks it's time she pulled herself together. That's one thing he and his daughter do agree on.

A wonky pair of headlights track across the front of the house and the hatchback draws up outside.

'They're here!' Phil says. He heads for the front door, but his granddaughter beats him to it.

'Daddy!' She rushes headlong and pulls open the door.

Phil is relieved to see that his son-in-law gets out of the car unaided and withstands a hug from the overenthusiastic Lily. He looks better. The ashen cheeks have returned to a more normal colour, he's breathing without difficulty.

Phil holds out his hand to shake. 'Great to see you, Adam. Welcome home.'

There's a good deal of shilly-shallying on the doorstep as Gill Hardy throws herself into her son's arms and sobs. Phil glances at Ruth, to whom he'd been pretty forthright in his opinion that they shouldn't have invited her. Stupid woman was bound to be silly. Ruth had replied that Adam was Gill's son and so to exclude her from his homecoming would look peculiar and, anyway, Adam would probably like to see his mother. At least Jason, the ineffectual brother, is in London.

Phil's impatience gets the better of him and he intervenes.

'It's freezing out here!' he says. 'C'mon', let the poor man get inside.'

Phil shepherds everyone through the front door. Zoe brings up the rear.

He kisses his daughter on the forehead. 'Good drive, darling?' he asks.

She nods and sighs. 'It was okay. Kids all right?'

Their eyes meet for a brief instant and he feels a lump in

his throat. His precious girl. She looks more haggard than her husband.

He smiles. 'Lily's been busy with your mother. We've got enough sandwiches to sink a battleship.'

Putting a guiding hand on his daughter's shoulder, he steers her through to the kitchen.

Adam is installed in the rocking chair, and Gill, who seems to have miraculously come to life, is hovering over him.

She cradles his hand. 'I can't believe how well you look.'

Adam gives her a warm smile and says. 'The wonders of modern medicine, Mum.'

'So we've got sandwiches and cake. But don't worry, it's a special recipe. Nothing bad in it. I bet you've been missing your tea. Hospital tea is awful. I'm going to make you a nice strong mug of builder's brew.'

Adam inclines his head. 'Actually, I wouldn't mind a coffee.'

His mother frowns. 'You hate coffee.'

Turning towards Zoe, Adam smiles and says, 'What happened to that espresso machine?'

'In the cupboard I think.'

Phil steps forward. 'Want me to root it out?'

Adam nods. 'Yeah, thank you. I know it sounds bonkers, but the thing I've been dreaming about in hospital is a double espresso.'

13

DAY 17. 11.45am

Samir Mehta checks his watch. He walks in long loping strides, his height and spare frame carrying him forward at a breakneck speed as he cuts through the side streets from the Embankment to the Strand. His destination is a small coffee shop on the edge of Covent Garden, and the appointment is for midday. It's always midday. He's made the trip every morning for the last twenty-two days in the fading hope that his CHIS will turn up.

The existence of this Covert Human Intelligence Source is something that his boss, Pat Babcock, wants kept under wraps. The fact that the police were contacted more than a week before the first avian flu fatality was reported and given prior warning of the outbreak is a political bombshell. Only two other people know about it: the head of SO15 and the Assistant Commissioner in charge of Specialist Operations.

But since the first casualties became public knowledge,

the source has gone to ground. Tracking him down is proving a problem. So Mehta keeps coming back to the rendezvous. He orders an Americano, scans the room – tourists sheltering from the January chill, a student with a laptop, a salesman on the phone – collects his coffee and takes a table at the back.

It was through a Lebanese contact of Mehta's in the human trafficking business that the informant first made contact and the tale, relayed through this third party in a phone call, was vague: a possible bio-terrorist attack somewhere in the UK; he had no further details. Counter Terrorism Command was used to receiving information that was vague. But they'd learnt from bitter experience that these things all had to be taken seriously. The Source Handling Unit dealt with such approaches in the first instance and assessed their credibility.

But the informant had somehow got hold of Mehta's name. The fact he was a DI also seemed to be important. He wasn't prepared to talk to anyone, said the Lebanese go-between. It had to be someone of rank. He wanted Mehta. So Sami had agreed to make the initial contact, accompanied by a regular handler from the unit. Their first encounter with the CHIS took place in the street outside the coffee shop.

He was young, only mid twenties with a paranoid wariness. But this didn't seem to proceed from mental instability and Mehta concluded he was an individual who'd lived a precarious existence, probably since his teens.

He'd circled, ultra vigilant, hood up, scoping out the two cops, checking for surveillance. It was a test; he insisted Mehta return at the same time the next day and that he come alone if he wanted to learn more. The few words he spoke were in a heavily accented English. Mehta reckoned he was Syrian and had entered the country illegally, which would explain his connections with a trafficking gang.

The handler was dismissive, in his opinion they were being played. Offering information on potential terrorist attacks was becoming a common trick used by foreign criminals, who couldn't otherwise hope to legitimise their status in the UK. The plots were outlandish and always fictitious. Nail bombs in shopping malls was a current favourite. But Mehta wasn't convinced. He had a gut feeling about this guy and it wouldn't go away.

When he got back to the office, he talked to a mate at the National Crime Agency. Something about the young Syrian struck Mehta; it was one of those judgement calls that couldn't be explained. The NCA were experimenting with a new facial recognition software and Mehta persuaded his friend that this might be a good opportunity to put it through its paces.

They created a facial composite from Mehta's detailed description and they named him 'George', because, in the artist's opinion, he bore a striking resemblance to a young George Michael—the sculpted beard, the brown eyes and sleek quiff.

Returning the next day, Mehta found him tucked away at a table in the back of the coffee shop. The clothes he wore seemed deliberately anonymous: a grey hoodie, denim jeans. But peeping out from under the cuff of the hoodie was a Rolex Submariner with the familiar solid link Oyster bracelet. Despite his youth, George was a man of means and couldn't help showing off.

Mehta took a seat opposite him. George stirred sugar into his espresso, gave the cop a sardonic smile and said, 'You believe me, then? You wanna know more.'

Mehta shrugged. He was well aware that his colleague,

the handler, might be right. This could well be another villain trying to fool them.

'We take all information seriously,' he said. 'But I'm curious why you've decided to do this.'

'You think I'm a weirdo? Make up crazy stories?'

'No.'

'Some illegal scumbag who don't give a shit? Come to this wonderful country of yours to thieve and rape. I got papers.'

Mehta smiled. 'Do I look like an immigrant hater?'

'Colour of your skin? Don't mean nothing. Look at you, man.' He flicked a finger under the tip of his nose. 'All the we-so-cool arrogance of the English. Like the world owes you, like we all owe you.'

The anger flared off him. He found it hard to contain and this, Mehta concluded, was an interesting weakness. He'd dealt with enough belligerent teenage gangsters to know the form. Attack first, get right in your face; it was a pride thing.

The DI had adopted a nonchalant tone. 'But you came here. To this country you despise. And now you even want to save us. I'd like to know why.'

George glared, but the cop sensed his uncertainty. He was conflicted, but he was also driven. Doing this, giving this warning, served some deep-seated need.

Mehta went on, 'And y'know, I get it. I understand.'

The source frowned, the abrupt switch to a sympathetic tone confused him. He wasn't as confident as he appeared, and for an instant the dark eyes wavered before he said 'Nah, you got no idea.'

Mehta steepled his fingers. 'Haven't I? My parents came here in 1972 from Uganda. They had two hastily packed suitcases. Idi Amin, you've probably never heard of him, expelled all Ugandan Asians and stole their property and businesses. My grandparents and parents had worked their whole lives in Africa and they lost everything. My dad saw this country as a refuge, but the only job he could get was as a pot-washer. They lived in one room. The experience killed my grandfather.'

George tilted his head and grinned. Once you took away the scowl, he was a good-looking boy. 'So this why the bosses send you to handle me?' he said. 'See I know the jargon.'

'You asked for me,' the cop replied.

George nodded. No arguing with that.

'You born here?' he said.

'Yes. But I know the contradiction of being an outsider: the desire to be accepted but the resentment of the power they have. I've seen it in my father.'

'What he do with it then?'

'He owns the restaurant that first employed him plus a chain of others.'

George smiled. 'Good for him.' He was relaxing, the ploy was working. It was time to take a punt.

'Was it bad in Syria?' Mehta asked. 'You must've been quite young when the civil war started.'

The dark eyes flashed with hostility. 'I'm not Syrian.'

'Okay.' *So he was Syrian.*

'You think you can read me?' They were back to the fractious teenager.

'No.'

'Listen, Inspector, no more stupid bloody questions.'

'Okay.' Mehta raised his palms. George had a volatile temper. But having got the measure of him, he decided to play it straight.

'Let's talk about why we're here,' Mehta said. 'The information you think we should know.'

George seemed to hesitate, as if a dangerous line was about to be crossed. He threw back his coffee in one gulp. Mehta noticed that although the espresso cup had a handle, he didn't use it. He held the little cup with delicacy between thumb and index finger. Habit? He was used to cups without handles. For a moment, he seemed far away, then the hard stare zoned in on the DI.

'Bird flu' he said. 'New strain, deadly. There's gonna be an epidemic.'

'Started deliberately? How?'

George shook his head. 'I dunno.' *Was he lying?*

'When will this happen?'

'Is already started.'

'Where?'

'Everywhere.'

'Who's behind it?'

Shrugging, the source broke eye contact. 'I dunno.' *Definitely lying.*

'How do you know any of this?' Mehta asked.

'I hear things. People talking.'

'What people?'

'People I meet sometimes.'

'How do you know it isn't gossip?'

'They serious people.'

'Jihadists?'

George gave a sour laugh.

Mehta lent forward across the table. 'Jihadists like to boast. Claim responsibility for all sorts, you know that. I'm going to need some names.'

'No names.' The informant shook his head.

'Then what can I do? How do I stop this?'

George seemed irritated. 'I don't fucking know. You the police.'

'What about locations we can look at.'

'It's gonna be everywhere.'

'Everywhere in the whole country? You know the expression a needle in a haystack?'

George had a sulky look. 'No.'

Mehta changed tack. 'This is certainly serious. Many people could die.' He fixed the source with a penetrating look. 'I think you're a good man and you want to stop that.'

The young Syrian swallowed hard; that got through the carapace, he wanted to be acknowledged. The motive wasn't money, he clearly didn't need it, or even a passport. This was something personal.

George raised his chin and said, 'That's why I tell you.'

'Yeah, you want to do the right thing.'

'I stick my neck out.' His manner was bullish.

'I can see that.' Mehta said 'But you also know, that to stop this, I need names. Or ways I can find out who they are.'

George leapt to his feet. 'I already tell you, man, I got no names! I come to you, to warn you, don't play me!'

'Straight up, I'm not...'

'Oh, my dad came here! He's like you. You think I don't see the tricks? Little story you tell to reel me in. Stinking cops.'

'It's not a story,' Mehta said. 'It's who I am. I'm not trying to trick you.'

'I'm not a bloody idiot!' George's eyes roved round the coffee shop, he'd become aware that his outburst was attracting attention. He pulled up his hood, hunched his shoulders and muttered. 'We done.'

Mehta got up. 'Hang on, please...'

'Tomorrow. Maybe.'

'I believe you. I know you're trying to do the right thing. So let's work together.'

The informant shot him a pugnacious look. He seemed about to reply but turned on his heel and headed for the door.

The DI reached into his backpack and drew out an evidence bag and a pen. He poked the end of the pen through the handle, lifted the espresso cup, and plopped it in the bag.

Detective Inspector Mehta leans back in his chair. He's sat at this table and drunk a lot of coffee in the last three weeks, waiting for George to show up again. In the meantime, the informant's fingerprints and DNA have been fed into the system and checked against all the databases in Europe.

After a week and a half, they got a match from the Italian police. In 2012, they'd arrested a juvenile in Brindisi but released him in return for information on a smuggling gang. A mugshot was provided, and it was George. The Italians named him as Feras Khalid. He claimed to be from Homs, so Mehta had guessed correctly, he was Syrian. He'd played the role of informant to get out of trouble with the authorities before. Was he doing the same again? But what kind of trouble was he in? If it was a gang related squabble, he would be naming names?

Something in his manner and approach continued to niggle Mehta. It felt like George had a different agenda. But what?

Then the first cases of the new strain of avian flu were reported. That changed everything. Mehta went to Babcock. Finding George became an absolute priority.

14

Adam gazes out of the kitchen window at a darkening sky over bare fields as he waits for the machine to stop gurgling and deliver him a double shot espresso. Since his return home, he hasn't ventured outside. The weather has been too cold, with intermittent showers of freezing drizzle. But he's been getting reacquainted with his home, wandering from room to room, remembering the state of the place when they first moved in.

His father-in-law had given them the farm as a wedding present; it's a fraction of the vast acreage he owns. The old farmhouse had been unoccupied for years, and Adam and Zoe lived in a caravan in the yard while they worked to make it habitable. Their shared enthusiasm for the place had turned it from a wreck into a beautiful home, a subtle melding of old and new that wouldn't have looked out of place in a design magazine.

It was Zoe's idea that they would become organic dairy

farmers. Her motivation, as with most things in her life, was to do the exact opposite of what her father advised. Phil Rowett adores his daughter, they're cut from the same cloth, though neither of them can see it. He bullied her into a degree in business studies so she could join him in his highly mechanised agribusiness. She responded by becoming a small farmer, bottling their own milk and distributing it locally. Adam was happy to go along with her plans. He was ready to settle, preferred working outdoors and prided himself on the fact that in a few short years he'd become a pretty good dairyman.

Raising his steaming espresso to his lips, Adam takes a small sip. It's his third cup this morning, and he finds it soothes him like nothing else. Through the window, he sees Zoe striding across the yard from the milking parlour. Her boots splash in the puddles and even at this distance, he can see she's annoyed.

The back door opens with a rush of cold air, then slams. She's pulling off her boots. He can't see her yet, but he hears her. Sipping his coffee, he waits. Such moments are restful, the quiet space between anticipating what will happen and it materialising. She appears in the kitchen doorway, Barbour dripping, hanks of auburn hair plastered to her face.

She gives him a puzzled look and says, 'You okay?' *Why does she keep asking this?* He wishes she'd let go of all this anxiety.

'Yeah. Having a coffee. Can I make you something?'

She shakes her head and pulls her jacket off. 'Every time you drink that stuff, you get a weird look on your face.'

'What sort of weird look?' *Here we go again.*

'Jesus, Adam! I don't know. A strange look.'

'I think maybe it helps.'

'How can that much caffeine help? And two spoons of sugar, really? It can't be good for you. What if it gives you palpitations?'

He shrugs. 'Hasn't so far. What's Ollie got to say for himself?' Ollie is one of Phil's farm managers, who they drafted in to help out when Adam became ill.

'Take a guess,' she says.

'Acting on instructions from on high?'

'Got it in one. Dad has decided, in his wisdom, to cut the milk round in half and use the milk for his new ice cream operation. So he can offer an organic option.'

'He never discussed this with you?'

Zoe shakes her head.

'Perhaps he thought you had enough on your plate?'

'No, Adam. What the cunning old bastard thought is that he could blindside me. Use the fact that I've been backing and forthing to Birmingham to the hospital to muscle in and take control.'

Crossing the kitchen, Adam puts an arm round his wife's shoulder and says 'Well, that's Phil, isn't it?'

She steps away from him. *She keeps doing that.*

'He doesn't care.' she says, 'He doesn't care that we've now got fifty regular customers who we've let down. And you know what the bastard told Ollie to say to them if they complained? That we were having production problems because you were ill.'

Adam laughs. 'Sounds like the sort of devious thing he'd do.'

He doesn't dislike his father-in-law, although he knows Phil had other aspirations for his daughter. He would have preferred her to marry a clone of himself, or maybe not to marry at all. Adam muses on this, the contradictions of fatherhood. He wonders what Lily will be like as she grows up. She has her mother's wilful nature.

'It's not funny' Zoe says. 'None of it's funny.'

'Hey, babe, come here. Don't let it get to you. In the scheme of things—'

'Give him an inch, and he walks all over you. That's what he does. I don't know how Mum stays married to him. Six months ago he was on about simplifying things and reducing overheads by putting all our milk in his bloody ice cream! I said no then. He knows I'm against it.'

Adam tries again, and she lets him draw her into his arms.

'He's like a little terrier that never gives up. But then so are you.' He wipes the wet strands of hair from her forehead. 'Chang says I can go back to work in stages as soon as I feel up to it.'

'He didn't. He said three to six months.'

'Depends how I feel. I'll talk to your dad and tell him we don't want to let our regulars down.'

'I can talk to him myself. I don't need you to do that.'

She steps away from him and folds her arms. Adam watches her. He's always loved her stubbornness. Since the day they met, the battle of wills between father and daughter has been a feature of their lives. Adam knows that of all the problems his illness has caused, having to accept Phil's help to run the farm has been the hardest compromise for his wife.

'I know you don't need me to do it' he says. 'That's not why I'm suggesting it.'

She glances at him, wipes her nose with the back of her hand. 'Why then?'

'I want my life back, too. What better way to get back in the saddle than to sort the old man out?'

She thinks about it for a moment then says, 'If it helps you.'

'Of course it'll help me.'

'Okay. I'll leave it to you.'

He smiles. 'Thank you.'

She moves towards him, lays her forehead on his shoulder. 'Why did this happen to us, Adam? Were we too lucky, or too smug?'

He strokes her hair. 'You're never going to find a reason. There is no reason. I picked up a virus. It was out there, floating around in the air. Now someone's lost their life and I've got mine back. Good luck, bad luck, chance? What does any of it mean? It's random.'

'Do you ever wonder about who your donor might be?' she asks.

'No. I'm just grateful.' A lie, but she doesn't notice.

'Me too,' she says. 'Extremely grateful.'

15

DAY 21. 3.05pm

Parking at the school gate is always a problem. There are signs ordering parents, as politely as possible, not to do it. The crossing patrol lady has been known to shake her lollipop at a delinquent parent in a 4x4. Adam sits in the front passenger seat of his wife's car, watching the daily drama unfold. Ryan is behind him, in his car seat, happily burbling. Zoe's parking technique combines effusive charm and pleading with the lady for special treatment, backed by a private belief that the rules are for other people, not her. It seems to work.

Adam can see his wife nodding sagely; she's at the gate listening to something the head teacher is saying to her and several other parents. She has a fidgety Lily by the hand. Lily waves to Adam, he waves back.

Going out and about is proving problematic for him, although he doesn't want to admit this to his wife. Even walking across the yard to the barn makes him feel anxious.

He has to look around, check who's in the vicinity. The unexpected presence of others worries him, he's not sure why.

When Zoe suggested he come with her to collect Lily from school, he wanted to make an excuse. Sitting in the study, perusing the net on his laptop, has become his principal preoccupation. He's reacquainting himself with the outside world in stages. This is what he tells himself.

Zoe hovered in the doorway. 'Come with me. James says you should get out more.'

Having eavesdropped, he knew his wife has been on the phone, having cosy chats with his doctor. 'Oh, James, eh?' he said. 'Well, if old James says so.' The sarcasm surprised them both.

Zoe gave him a penetrating look. 'Adam, don't be a dick.'

A rush of contrition had flooded through him. He keeps getting irritated with her, he's on a short fuse. *The drugs?* Chang says his body will adapt, but he's plagued by these ridiculous emotional swings. The good thing is, since his outburst in the car on the way home, he's kept a handle on it.

'Sorry,' he said and painted on a smile. 'I've been reading up about this new flu outbreak. Should we be looking into getting the kids vaccinated?'

He made his interest sound casual. But was that true? What he had established was that the areas most affected were cities and larger towns, London, the Midlands, a few places up north. The west country remained largely untouched.

'Yeah,' she replied. 'I was going to ask them at the school what they thought.'

'Good plan.' He met her eye. 'It's the cold, Zoe. That's why I don't like going out. And I worry about picking up some infection. Y'know what schools are like. And if I got this flu—'

'Yeah, of course you're right,' she said. 'Bad idea.'

'No, you're right. I will come,' he said. 'I'll stay in the car.'

Adam unwinds the scarf from his neck; he's sweating. He's growing a beard. Zoe dislikes it. The beard feels scratchy. He's wearing a thick jumper plus a ski jacket, way too much. He watches his wife and daughter heading towards the car. He hates lying to her and, anyway, she always seems to know. She gives him that disappointed look, which is rebuke enough. Before his illness, she would've argued, now she seems distant and resigned.

Opening the back door for Lily to climb in, Zoe helps her daughter buckle up.

The little girl is gleeful. 'Daddy! You came to collect me. When are we going in the beast again?'

The beast is a black Mitsubishi Trojan pickup truck that has been sitting under a tarpaulin in the barn for the past year. It was Zoe's birthday present to Adam after he admitted that his Nissan 370Z, a two-seater sports car, was not a practical vehicle for a farmer. When Lily first started school, Adam did the school run in the beast.

He smiles at his daughter and says, 'When I can drive again we'll take the beast for a spin.'

'When Daddy, when!'

'Soon, sweet pea.'

Zoe gets into the driver's seat and starts the car up. She seems narked. 'The whole thing's a bloody mess. No one knows what's what.'

Adam nods. 'The err—'

'What we were talking about earlier, yes. Some people are getting vaccinations done privately.'

'Okay–'

'Am I going to be vaccinated?'

Adam turns and smiles at his daughter. 'You're a clever little monkey, aren't you? Never miss a trick. You heard the word at school? Know what it means?'

'Will it hurt? Keira says it hurts.'

'Only a bit.'

'Then I won't have it.'

Zoe frowns. 'Where did Keira have it done? At a special doctor?'

Lily says, 'I don't know. Needles hurt.'

Her eyes remain on the road, but Zoe huffs and says, 'I don't understand what's happening. Mum and Dad had a flu jab back in October. But now they're saying it may be the wrong sort, that no one's protected from this new strain. There's a new American vaccine, but it's only available privately.'

Adam feels hot. He pulls down the zipper on his jacket and says, 'Are they going to have it?'

The heat is getting worse. It comes in pulses. He rips at the zipper. He feels dizzy.

Zoe glances across at him. 'You all right? I'm sure you'd feel better if you got rid of that beard.'

She sounds far away. His head spins and he's tumbling down into some kind of crevasse with walls of white tiles. It's so hot.

'Adam?'

'Think I'm going to be sick,' he says.

She pulls over.

Flinging open the door, he leans out and vomits on the grass verge.

She places a hand on his back. 'It's okay, sweetheart. You're going to be okay.' She sounds panicky.

Lily whimpers. 'Daddy.'

The spinning slows. He leans back in his seat and wipes his mouth with the back of his hand. 'I got too hot. Made me dizzy. Sorry.'

'Hey.' Zoe strokes his shoulder. 'My fault. I shouldn't have made you come out. It's too soon. You don't think you've got the flu?'

'No, it's dizziness. It's gone now. I'm fine. But I think we should get you and the kids vaccinated.'

'Nooo!' Lily wails from the backseat.

Zoe's lip trembles. 'Oh, be quiet, Lily!' she says.

16

————

DAY 21. 5.45pm

Jason finds the phone conversation with his sister-in-law disturbing. In his experience, Zoe is level-headed and not prone to panic. He's left work and is heading for the tube.

'Something's not right with him, Jason' she says. He can hear the alarm in her voice.

'Well, have you talked to the hospital?'

'Chang's operating. I couldn't get through to him.'

'He's on a cocktail of drugs, Zoe. That could make him sick. The dosage may need adjusting.'

'It feels like there's something he's not telling me.'

'Like what?' he asks.

'I don't know. He's niggled all the time. Gets upset, then he apologises. Irritation, apology. It's like a bloody emotional rollercoaster.'

'You want me to talk to him.'

'I think he's asleep. As soon as we got back from the

school he went to lie down. He's...I think it's me. I wind him up.'

'Want me to come down tonight?'

'No, it's too far.'

'I'll get the train, it'll be fine.'

'What about work? You've had so much time off.'

'My boss understands the situation.' What Jason fails to mention is that his boss, miserable cow that she is, has also told him it's not her problem. He's used up most of his leave. But a job's only a job. 'Zoe, you tell me what you want.'

'It'll be fine. I suppose I needed to talk to someone. Maybe I'm being paranoid.' Jason can feel her backtracking. She hates looking weak.

'I'm coming' he says. I'll call you from the train.'

'That's stupid.' She sounds relieved.

'No, it's not.' Jason hesitates. 'If he doesn't tell you things, it's because he's trying to protect you.'

She sighs. 'That makes it worse.'

'I'll come down. We'll sort this out.'

'Thanks.'

She sounds grateful and small, not very Zoe.

17

DAY 21. 10.30pm

Adam dozes. He lies on the bed fully clothed; the room is not dark, there's a faint glow from the nightlight in Ryan's room across the hall. He finds it reassuring. If he focuses on its soft aura, it keeps the demons at bay. The abyss is what he fears, the gut-wrenching delirium which sucks him spiralling downwards into a black hole. He struggles to detach, to hold at least a part of his mind in rational mode. The drugs cause these hallucinations, they're not real. He knows this, repeats it to himself. It's not real. This is what he must remember.

It comes in waves; the pain radiating from the centre of his chest. Then the visions begin. They're not proper dreams because he's awake. Definitely awake. And they have a surreal clarity. He's hurtling forward at a dizzying speed into a tunnel. At first there's euphoria and a sense of escape. But it flips when he sees the face. Does he know this man? He has a name: Tony, maybe. Who the hell is Tony? As the face turns towards him, what he recognises is the chilling smile. That's when the dread seizes him.

This is the loop that repeats and repeats, over and over. It's been happening for several days, the episodes getting more frequent. He should tell Chang. Each time it's the dread that paralyses him, returns him to blackness. But now suddenly, from nowhere, comes an acrid taste in his mouth. It's the taint of diesel and exhaust fumes seeping up and under his helmet, and they're belching from the van. Suspended in an interminable instant he observes all the disparate elements: the rust on the van's bumper, the creases in that face, the hard gloating in the man's eye as he smiles, the knuckle-white clenched fist wrenching the wheel across.

The whump of the impact sends him flying over the handlebars. He soars. He glides like an eagle on the wing. Then he drops and smashes, neck cracking in an avalanche of pain.

From nowhere, he feels a hand grasping his and pulling him up from the pit. The relief! Someone is trying to rescue him.

Gasping, Adam opens his eyes. He's sweating from sheer panic. In the gloom he can see a figure looming over him on the bed. He can feel the warm dry palm clasping his.

Does he know this man? Perhaps.

'Adam, it's okay.'

He knows the voice.

'Jason?' he says.

'Hey, buddy. I think you've been having a bad dream.'

'Jason, listen. It was murder.'

'It was a nightmare' his brother replies.

'No, it was murder! I remember what happened.'

'You remember what?'

'It was deliberate. They killed him.'

'Killed who?'

'He killed David. I saw it happen. In the tunnel.'

'Who's David?'

Adam's eyes well up. 'No, David! That's what she said. She tried to warn me.' He begins to cry. 'She tried to warn me.'

Jason cradles his brother's hand. 'Sssh, it's okay now. It's okay.'

Twitter Feed

DAY 21.

True Health News @truehealthnews
Good News! Our sources tell us that a brand new British
biotech start-up has found a cure! In trials a 100% success
rate for their anti-viral drug. Bad news: the government
won't pay for it.
6.6k Retweets 9.4k Likes

Keandra Smith @keandraS24
Replying to @truehealthnews
WTF! We need it now. A&E is like a war zone! Pay attention
@PHE_uk WE CAN'T COPE!!! #pandemic #governmentlies
3.7k Retweets 5.3k Likes

VGS Biotech @VGSbiotech
Replying to @truehealthnews
The neuraminidase inhibitor produced by VGS Biotech
does offer a way forward. Our trials have been peer-
reviewed. Check out the data here: ow.ly/tAHC705zRP

Mark Carter @MCB666
Replying to @truehealthnews
BIG QUESTION. How did H7N9 get here? ILLEGAL IMMI-
GRANTS! We all know that. That's what they won't tell us
#pandemic #governmentlies #safeandsound
397 Retweets 507 Likes

18

DAY 22. 9.35am

DI Mehta sits at his desk twiddling a gel pen, over and over, end to end, between his thumb and fingers. He finds it hard to contain his energy; it seeps out in these repetitive habits. Nevertheless, he regards himself as a patient man; picking through the evidence, having an eye for detail, for small anomalies, has led to an accelerated career as a detective in the Met. He's well aware that certain colleagues he's overtaken on the way regard his rapid promotion to be the result of positive discrimination, not ability. But Mehta couldn't give a toss what people think. Results matter to him and to his bosses. He learnt that in a tough Leicester comp; either you ran with the pack or you kept to yourself, got your head down and played the system to win. Samir Mehta was a natural loner, and he soon discovered that coming out on top suited him.

He's staring at the computer screen and an email that has popped into his inbox from the National Crime Agency.

It's a translation of a document received from a Syrian police official in Homs in response to a request, channeled through the NCA, for information about Feras Khalid. Mehta has been waiting two weeks for this reply, but it tells him little. Feras was born in 1995. This makes him twenty-three which fits. The details about him seem to have been gleaned from the national ID card issued when he was fourteen. They include a faded photo of a frowning youth plus his father's name. The official has typed a cryptic remark at the bottom, which has been translated: father former senior member of medical faculty at Al-Baath University, deceased in 2012.

Mehta continues with his pen twirling as he ponders these fragments of his informant's life. How does the son of a university professor end up in the people smuggling business? By Mehta's calculation, he would've been sixteen when the Siege of Homs began and therein lies the answer. Many academics were part of the opposition to the Assad regime. His father was likely killed in the struggle in 2012, a year after it began, and the same year seventeen-year-old Feras came to the attention of the Italian police. Filling in the blanks remained a matter of speculation. But Feras's story wasn't unusual. There were many refugees like him from Syria's brutal civil war, and he wouldn't have been the first to survive by turning to crime. In many cases, it was the only option.

The mugshot provided by the Italians and the teenager on the ID card are the same person. Mehta pulls up the document of the facial composite made after his first encounter with the informant. The face is more mature, but it's a good likeness and also matches the two photos. At Mehta's request, a couple of analysts at the NCA have run the name Feras Khalid through every UK database at their disposal. The five Feras Khalids they came up with have all been visited and eliminated from the inquiry.

George or Feras must have another identity which he's been using in the UK. But how to track him down? *A needle in a haystack.* Mehta smiles to himself as he recalls the blank look he got from the informant when he used that expression. The watch he was wearing was worth a lot of money, so, best guess, he'd probably obtained a *FOG,* false on genuine passport. They retailed on the black market for between five and six grand and would convince all but the most discerning eye.

Picking up his phone, Mehta calls his friend on the facial recognition team.

'Hey, Sheena' he says. 'How's it going?'

They'd buddied up on a course, got drunk and slept together, then she went home to her husband.

'Sami,' she says, a flirtatious lilt in her voice. 'I got the second photo you sent over.'

'Does it help?'

'Last couple of days we've had the techies in, trying to iron out a glitch in the software.'

'So no progress?'

'Not exactly. I know this is a top priority and so we have been trying a few things. I went on some commercial sites; they're a bit hit and miss. The Italian picture matches him with George Michael.'

Mehta laughs 'Yeah, he looks a bit like that.'

'There was something I came across, though. The DVLA got an application to replace a driver's licence. Applicant sent in a photocopy of a passport. DVLA refused to accept, said they needed the real thing, also questioned why someone in their early twenties didn't have a bio-metric passport. Never heard back. So they flagged it up as dodgy.

The photo pinged on our system as a distant maybe. The picture photocopied from the passport's rubbish. But you've seen him in the flesh, so you might do better than the algorithms.'

'Sounds promising. Send over what you've got. What's the name?'

'David Taylor.'

Mehta writes it on the corner of his pad. 'That's a good one, must be a few zillion of those in the UK. Thanks, Sheena. We should have a coffee sometime.' He doesn't mean it and she knows that.

She laughs and says, 'Yeah, we should.'

Hanging up, Mehta circles the name several times. Then he gets up, crosses the office to one of his DC's. It's a hunch, but, he reflects, it's time their luck changed.

The DC looks up and smiles.

Mehta says, 'Could you cross reference Feras Khalid's prints with the name David Taylor and see if any charges were brought against him in the last, I dunno, two years. Could be drugs, assault maybe.'

Mehta returns to his own desk as a message from Sheena drops into his inbox. He clicks on the image and a starkly lit photo booth snapshot appears on the screen enlarged to the point of distortion.

He gazes at it. The eyes hold him. The face is leaner and gaunt, covered by a fuller beard. But it could be George.

19

———

DAY 22. 9.40am

Jason Hardy sits at the solid pine table cradling his mug of coffee and watching his brother. Adam is feeding cereal to his small son. Ryan is in the high chair, a boisterous, happy child. He accepts a mouthful and his father scraps the residue from his lips with the spoon.

Adam seems absorbed by the task. His face is pale, bearded, his blonde hair sleep rumpled and longer than he usually wears it. Jason notices a slight tremor in his hand as he manoeuvres the spoon.

Zoe has taken Lily to school, so Jason knows this is his window of opportunity. He's observed that his brother has become much more taciturn in her presence. He treats her with the awkward courtesy of people who are bound together but no longer close. But maybe that's understand-able. The last year must have taken its toll on their marriage.

Their relationship had always seemed enviable to Jason.

He'd watched it develop from the beginning. An amazing couple, that's what everyone said. Zoe Rowett had scared him to death at school; all his mates had fancied her. She was popular and pretty—a long crinkly mane of auburn hair and a fiery temperament to match. But, to his mind, she'd always had a spiteful streak. She looked for the weakness in people, and, as teenagers, she'd found it in him. It was only when she got his big brother in her sights she changed her tune and ceased to taunt him.

Taking a sip of coffee, Jason says, 'I could take you to the barbers if you like. Time you smartened yourself up a bit.'

Adam smiles, but his eyes have an abstracted look. 'Is that a polite way of saying I look like shit?'

Neither has mentioned their conversation of the previous night. Jason had sat on the bed and held his brother's hand until he fell asleep.

'How you feeling this morning?' he asks.

'Okay. Bit tired.'

'Any more nightmares?'

'It's the drugs, Jace.'

'Last night, you talked about someone called David. Who's he?'

Adam shoots him a cagey look. 'Take no notice. All this stuff goes round in my head. I'm sorry Zoe got in such a panic and dragged you down here. It's not like her.'

'No, it isn't' Jason replies. 'But, hey, I get to skive off work, which is all to the good.'

'I thought you liked it there.'

'I do. But London's weird at the moment. It's nice to escape.'

'People are freaked out about this flu thing?' his brother says.

'Yeah, walking round in masks.'

'Have you got a mask?'

'Actually, I've been covering my mouth with an old scarf. I look like a bandit.'

Adam laughs. Ryan bangs his tiny fist on the tray of the high chair. His father scoops up another spoonful of cereal and says 'Sorry, mate, are we ignoring you?'

'He's got a good appetite.'

'Zoe says he's a greedy little sod.'

'Takes after you.'

'Oi! Watch it!'

The brotherly banter helps. Adam seems to relax. Jason studies him. Zoe's right, there's something peculiar going on with him. Jason senses a tension, a reserve that he's never experienced with his brother before. The trauma of what he's been through must've had some impact, though; and that seems the most likely explanation.

'Y'know,' Jason says, 'you don't have to put on a brave face all the time. You can talk to me.'

'I do.' His brother feeds the toddler the last scraping of cereal. Ryan scoffs it with gusto. Adam carefully wipes his mouth with the bib.

Jason takes a sip of coffee. 'You know me, saddo that I am, I spend half my time online reading stuff. And I've been reading up about this.'

'This?' It seems as if his brother is avoiding eye contact.

'Heart transplants.' Jason says. 'The drugs. The after effects. All that.'

Adam gives him a side-eyed glance. 'And what have you discovered?'

'Any illness there's going to be things the doctors don't want to tell you. All I'm saying is that whatever you're experiencing, I'm not about to turn round and say you're crazy.'

Adam doesn't reply.

Jason continues, 'The coffee thing too. I get it.'

Adam puts the cereal bowl and spoon in the sink. 'What d'you mean?'

Ryan is burbling and banging his sippy cup.

'I always thought I was the coffee addict in the family, not you. Now you're mainlining on the stuff.'

'Tastes change.'

'And heart transplant patients report developing tastes they never had before. Tastes which seem to come from their donor.'

Adam gives a hollow laugh. 'Well, if it says it on the net, it must be true.'

'All that concerns me is what's true for you.' Jason isn't about to let this go.

Turning on the tap, Adam runs his fingers under the water. Then he picks up a towel, wipes his hands and says, 'Bloody cocktail of drugs swilling round inside me, I feel like some doddery old man.'

'You think it's the drugs causing the hallucinations and nightmares?'

'What else can it be?'

The tone is unexpectedly aggressive. His mood has flipped. Not like Adam, not like him at all. He's the most even tempered bloke Jason knows. This must be what Zoe was talking about.

'You should speak to Chang about this' he says.

Adam doesn't reply. He seems to be struggling to hold on to his temper.

Finally he says 'Sorry, mate. The least thing seems to rattle me nowadays.'

'Understandable. And all the more reason to talk about what's going on inside your head.'

'Even if it doesn't make sense?'

'Especially if it doesn't make sense,' Jason replies. 'Do you remember what you said to me last night?'

'I dunno, some nonsense.'

'You talked about someone being murdered. Someone called David. Who's David?'

Adam folds his arms across his chest, he heaves a sigh, then he says, 'I don't know what's real anymore, Jace.'

'Well, don't try to analyse. Talk me through it.'

'It feels like I'm remembering something that has actually happened to me. Except it hasn't.'

'Like what?'

Adam hesitates, his gaze flickers. He loops the towel over the handle of the Aga, smooths it nervously with his fingers.

He has his back to Jason as he says, 'A motorcycle crash in a tunnel.'

'That's pretty scary. You're watching it?'

'No, it's me riding the motorcycle.'

'Okay.'

'Told you it was crazy.'

'Just tell me. Don't analyse. You're riding the motorcycle.'

'Yeah. And there's this van on the inside of me. I'm trying to overtake it. But I recognise the driver.'

'Someone you know?'

'Yeah.'

Adam turns to face him and there's a dread in his big brother's eyes that Jason has never seen before. 'He looks at me and then turns the wheel towards me.'

'You saying he targets you deliberately?'

'Rams into the side of me, yeah. And I go flying over the handlebars and smash head first into the wall.' Adam swallows hard. 'Then I hear this crack and I realise it's my neck snapping. And the rest of my body goes numb. I can't feel a thing or move.'

Jason exhales. 'Bloody hell! That's horrible.'

Ryan is quiet, eyes darting back and forth, then tuning in to his father's distress he starts to grizzle.

Adam lifts him out of the high chair.

'You sure you should do that?' Jason asks.

'It's fine, don't worry.' Adam leans the toddler against his shoulder and buries his face in his son's back.

Jason watches them comfort each other, Adam's cheek against the soft dinosaur print sleepsuit as he rocks the child.

'So you're him? You're this David.'

'Mental, isn't it?' Adam says, swaying a little.

Jason stands up. 'Here, let me take him. He looks heavy.'

Adam hands Ryan over and sits down. Jason transfers the toddler to his hip, as he's seen Zoe do. Apart from his nephew and niece, he's no experience of small children. It's another country.

Ryan gives him a baleful look. Jason reaches for the stuffed penguin perched beside the high chair and waggles it in his nephew's face.

Adam smiles and says, 'You're getting better at this.'

'I do my best.'

'Make me a promise, Jace. Don't tell Zoe what I've told you.'

'C'mon, mate. You can't shut her out. She knows something's going on with you.'

'Our relationship's messed up enough as it is. I can't put this on her too.'

Jason sighs and says, 'So, let's get this clear, in the dream you're David and David was murdered?'

'It's not a dream.'

'What is it then?'

'I told you, a memory.'

'How can it be a memory?'

'Because I'm not asleep.'

'Okay. But where does this memory come from?'

Adam hesitates, takes a breath. 'David. I think he's my donor.'

'How do you know that's his name? I thought they didn't give you any personal details about the donor.'

'They don't.'

Jason digests this. 'Okay, no one's told you his name, but you think your donor was called David. How do you know that?'

'It's there in my head. I know it. How d'you know anything? It's there.' Frustration fizzes off Adam. He rakes his fingers through his hair.

Jason watches and waits until Adam meets his gaze again.

Then he says, 'Is there other stuff you remember besides this crash?'

'Flashes of things. A woman's voice. She says: *No, David!* I dunno, maybe that's how I know his name.'

'You said that last night, said she tried to warn you. You were pretty upset.'

Adam swallows hard. 'Yeah.' He turns away.

Jason ponders. 'You should talk to Chang about this.'

'I don't think he'll believe me.'

'You don't know, he might've come across something similar.'

'I doubt it.'

Ryan fidgets and bats the penguin to the floor. Jason slots the toddler back in his high chair and hands him the sippy cup.

Adam has his elbows on his knees, face in his palms. He looks forlorn.

Patting his shoulder, Jason says, 'Okay, it's hard to make sense of this, but if you talk to Chang—'

Adam raises his head and fixes his brother with an unwavering stare. 'There's only one way I can make sense of this. Find out if what I'm remembering is true.'

'How the hell will you do that?'

'By finding out who my donor was and how he died. See if it matches in any way. Then I'll know if it's some crazy drug-induced hallucination.'

'Maybe, but—'

'Will you help me, Jace?'

Jason shifts from foot to foot. Yet again, something in Adam's manner has changed abruptly, a hardening of tone he finds disturbing.

Sighing, he says, 'If I can, yeah, of course. But they'll never give you any information about your donor. They have strict rules, you know that.'

'Yeah, I know. But you have access to stuff through your job, don't you? Police National Computer? That's why I need your help. This crash happened in a tunnel somewhere. There'll be a record.'

'It would be on the Met's CAD system. But I can't use that for personal reasons. That's a sacking offence, mate.'

Adam stares at him. There's a blankness in his eye, neither hostile nor friendly, just detached.

Then he sighs again and says, 'Course not. I shouldn't even ask. Sorry.'

20

DAY 22. 12.10pm

Felicity Oldroyd sits in an anteroom staring at the artwork—modern copies of Hogarth's The Rake's Progress. Maybe her Right Honourable boss has a sense of humour after all, or he's employed someone who does. She's already been advised that he's running late. A young woman with a rictus smile, one of his attack dogs, brings her a tepid cup of green tea. She wonders if this is it. Is Ryder preparing to throw her under the bus to save his own skin? She's heard whispers from Whitehall that he's been agitating in Cabinet for it.

In the last three weeks she hasn't slept more than a few hours each night. She's passed through exhaustion and despair and come out the other side.

Despite government reassurances, people are drawing their own conclusions about the seriousness of the situation. Production of the much-touted American vaccine has been halted as its benefit has been called into question. Fresh cases of H7N9 are being reported daily, fatalities remain low and the random geographical distribution around the country has continued. But there is a reluctance, led by COBRA, to admit publicly that some kind of deliberate human agency could be the source of the virus. Behind the scenes, the wrangling continues.

In an interview on Breakfast TV Felicity avoided endorsing the official line, and since then she has become a focus for those in the bio-terrorism camp.

Sensing a chink in the official armour, the media has besieged her home. The family has rallied round and created a human shield to protect her. Her daughter has flown in from the States, taking a leave of absence from her post-doctoral research post. Her son has liaised with the police to get the television crews and the reporters off their drive and corralled across the road from the house. She has uniformed police guarding her front door. It feels like an eternity since she's been anywhere alone; she can't remember when she last had a decent walk. She's submitted to her husband Gerry's insistence that she uses the private chauffeured car he's hired. It has tinted windows and through them she has witnessed her city morph into an alien landscape of suspicion, where scurrying pedestrians in masks avoid one another.

Compared to heart disease and cancer, and the more usual varieties of seasonal flu in the elderly, the actual death toll from the H7N9 virus is low. It hasn't exploded into an epidemic as predicted. No medical staff have died. Which would support Felicity's belief that there's little evidence of easy person-to-person transmission. She feels victims have been exposed in some other way. But, as Pat Babcock has asserted from the outset, this is not about killing people, it's about creating an atmosphere of alarm and disorder. Fear is what's infecting the populace, stoked by hysteria on social media and a barely less frenzied approach from the main-stream press.

A sense of foreboding permeates the streets. London has lost its bustle and buoyancy, and this saddens Felicity as much as anything. She was a small child during the Cuban Missile Crisis and remembered little about it. But she was a medical student in the early 80s when the government came out with their *Protect and Survive* advice about what to do in the event of a nuclear attack. Much lampooned, she recalls the febrile atmosphere that surrounded it. Both she and Gerry went on CND marches, but compared to now it was a carnival. She and her friends were worried, but they were also imbued with the excitement and optimism of youth. When communism collapsed and the Berlin Wall came down in 1989, there was a collective sigh of relief and they all got on with their lives.

Now Felicity finds it hard to separate the toxic mood surrounding her from her own anxieties: is she doing the right things, making the best choices? But these personal doubts must be kept hidden; achieving this, presenting a public persona of competence and confidence, is taking up most of her waning energy.

The attack dog reappears. Her scarlet lipstick and skintight pencil skirt would not have been approved of in a Ministerial office when the CMO began her career as a civil servant.

'Professor Oldroyd' she says, with what Felicity senses is a mocking politeness, 'he's ready for you.'

Yes, thinks Felicity. And I'm ready for him. Or she hopes she is.

As she's escorted into the room, it surprises Felicity to discover that Ryder is not alone. Shirtsleeves rolled up, tie loosened, he's leaning over the oak conference table, peering at the screen of an open laptop. This belongs to a shaggy little man, pigeon-chested, with a t-shirt and an expensive bomber jacket in buttery-soft leather hanging limply on his narrow shoulders. The professor has never been a fan of beards and his is thin and wispy.

Ryder gazes at her over his heavy tortoiseshell spectacles —an affectation to give him a serious air—and says, 'Ah, Felicity. Thank you for joining us. I'm sure you know Dr. Henry Shawcross.'

She doesn't. She's never heard of him, but smiles, anyway. A nervous Shawcross offers her a damp hand to shake. Scruffy academic is her first guess, or researcher rather than medical doctor. Probably the purveyor of some half-baked theory that has caught Ryder's attention. Or maybe a refugee from Silicon Valley? She's seen the familiar uniform at conferences.

Ryder takes off his glasses and nods sagely. 'Yep, I think this offers us a way forward. But of course, Felicity, I need your input.'

Both men stare at her expectantly. She knows Ryder's set her up. This is his ploy to catch her on the back foot. But she can guess the agenda.

Painting on a smile, she says, 'Unfortunately I'm not familiar with Dr. Shawcross's work.' Another freelance buccaneer who claims he can produce a vaccine in five minutes at a fraction of the usual cost.

Ryder flops down in a chair and says 'I'll spare his blushes, but Hal is the UK's leading specialist in viral genome sequencing. But I'll let him speak for himself. Over to you, Hal.'

Hal. Obviously.

Shawcross tugs at the wiry tuft sprouting from under his lower lip and fixes his gaze on the middle distance. 'We've been working on H7N9 for over a year now, with the full co-operation of the Chinese,' he says in an acquired American drawl. 'That's why it's all been a bit under the radar. The neurovirulence of H7N9 is of particular concern, as I'm sure you know.'

What Felicity knows is when she's being patronised; Shawcross exudes the geeky maleness often encountered in research laboratories. You're a mere woman, is what he's saying.

'Encephalitis has been present in some the fatalities' she says. 'Is that what you'd expect? We'd be interested if you've got some data on that.'

He blinks and twitches his beard; he glances at Ryder to see if he's expected to answer.

Ryder is checking his phone.

Shawcross coughs and says, 'We've developed a new neuraminidase inhibitor, which we believe will be a far more successful treatment than any of the anti-virals currently in use.'

'Excellent,' say Felicity. 'The team at PHE is looking at research data on any new anti-virals and indeed a number of existing drugs to see what might be the most effective treatment for H7N9. What we've got at the moment is far from ideal.'

'Ours is the most effective. We've proved it.'

'In clinical trials?'

'In the laboratory,' he says. 'The Chinese gave us samples from lung aspirate collected from a patient with a fatal case. We used it on mice, treated them. They all recovered.' Lucky mice, thinks Felicity.

Shawcross shoves a memory stick across the table at her. He seems petulant, as if having to explain himself is an imposition.

'We'll certainly take a look,' says Felicity. 'And thank you for coming forward. The research community has been offering us tremendous support in what is a difficult and unusual situation.'

It would be more accurate to say that for the last three weeks they'd been trampling over one another to get their particular anti-viral drug considered for the lucrative government contracts likely to be on offer. A deluge of data from bio-tech outfits big and small has poured in from around the globe and a bevy of academic researchers, drafted in from half a dozen universities to bolster the PHE team, is ploughing through the stuff.

She smiles and picks up the stick. Now what?

Shawcross looks at Ryder, who clears his throat and says, 'In a crisis such as this, I think we have to act decisively. I know that doesn't sit easily with you, Felicity. The scientist in you wants proof, clinical trials and all that paraphernalia.'

'I think any responsible doctor wants to know that a new treatment is going to help not harm their patients, Minister. And we are examining all the data as a matter of utmost urgency. I'm sure Dr. Shawcross understands that.'

'Meanwhile, people are dying, which is terrible. And I understand from Dougie that we're not being as open-minded and proactive as we might.'

Has Dougie been briefing against her? Or is Ryder putting his own words into Lacey's mouth? He has a tendency to do this when he wants to reinforce an argument or so he can pass the buck if his idea turns out to be rubbish and he needs to backtrack.

She can't help feeling niggled and says, 'Dougie's in charge of PHE not me. The thirty odd highly skilled researchers we've got reviewing the data work for him. My understanding is that every published paper on every anti-viral is being looked at. So I'm surprised that he doesn't think we're doing enough on this front.'

Challenging Ryder directly is not a smart strategy, but she's beyond caring.

He gives her a sour look and says, 'Your opinion is noted, Professor. But I think it's time to cut through the red tape and try something new like this. I'm telling you now that it has my full backing.'

Afterwards, striding down the corridor from the ministerial office suite, Felicity's weariness has evaporated. Anger at the absurdity of politicians consumes her. She feels both wired and caged and desperate to get out of the building. Returning to her office, she grabs her coat and face mask.

She could phone Douglas Lacey to find out whether Ryder is lying. Instead, she decides to see him in person.

Her walk from Victoria Street to PHE's headquarters in Waterloo Road takes half an hour. The afternoon is raw and overcast, shrouding the city in a freezing smog. The stagnant air is loaded with particulates from belching vehicles and fashionable wood-burning stoves, which Felicity has long argued should be banned in the capital. This, she reflects, is what she should be arguing with Lacey about: how to curb pollution without upsetting the voters. But poor air quality is on no one's agenda today. It feels like a problem from a more innocent time.

The velcro on the face mask chafes her cheeks but as she crosses Westminster Bridge it has the additional benefit of protecting her from the noxious air. It's the first time she's been out in ages and she marches along at a cracking pace, the exercise lifting her mood.

Arriving in Douglas Lacey's office she realises she must look a sight.

Glancing up from his computer he says, 'Felicity! Good God, have you walked here? Setting a fine example, most heroic. I hope the news crews got some footage of you.'

Lacey is a born schemer, but he also has a wry sense of humour, which Felicity appreciates.

Smoothing her unruly hair, she settles in a chair and says 'Sadly Dougie, I think I passed unseen.'

'Oh well. I hear you've upset our master.'

'News travels. Is it true you agree with him? That we should buy vast quantities of a new untested anti-viral drug and treat patients with it immediately even if we have absolutely no clue whether it works or what the side-effects might be?'

He steeples his fingers and says, 'It's a point of view.'

'What's wrong with sticking to the anti-viral drugs we've got; at least we know they have some efficacy.'

'Only with some patients,' says Dougie.

'Yes, but the state of the individual's immune system is always going to be a factor. The success of any treatment will depend on that as much as anything else.'

'You're the doctor, Felicity.'

She smiles. Dougie is a consummate player, and this is the fake deference he indulges in when he knows he's already won.

'Okay,' she says. 'Who the hell is Shawcross? He's been researching H7N9 for a year. But where? In China? What are his credentials?'

Dougie chuckles and says, 'Don't be such a snob, Professor. The company is called VGS Biotech, based in Cambridge, and they have substantial backing.'

'From who?'

'I dunno. Some private equity fund with deep pockets.'

'Mystery billionaires then?'

'Private equity finances a large chunk of cutting-edge medical research.'

'Don't you think, Dougie, we're in danger of mixing up two things here. The political need to be unstuffy and egalitarian and the medical need to have research that's been robustly tested, by competent trained scientists and that can be relied upon.'

'I don't disagree,' he says. 'But Ryder's under a lot of pressure. The PM wants an answer.'

'That depends on asking the right question.'

'There's a lot of fear out there. It's already having a huge economic impact.'

'Jesus wept, Dougie! I know that.'

'We did a poll. Public trust in the government is down to twenty per cent. We need a treatment people believe in.'

'Surely the best way to achieve that is to find something that works.'

'But what if we can't?' he says as he rises from his chair. 'Back in the days when you were a GP, did you never prescribe a placebo? If people believe it works, it works. That's scientifically proven.'

'Well, yes, up to a point, but—'

'What we're planning is a carefully crafted campaign on social media. Information about this amazing new drug will rapidly spread.'

'Disinformation you mean.'

'Personal, individual, emotional stories of survival and recovery. Thanks to a brilliant new drug.' His tone is serious and heartfelt. Felicity can't help smiling.

She shakes her head and says, 'It's pure propaganda. You don't even know if anyone will recover using this drug?'

'I thought the figures were promising. Even most of those hospitalised are pulling through.'

'Well, yes, but they're largely recovering because of the efforts of their own immune system together with standard care. You've had the flu, generally that's how people get better.'

He shrugs and says, 'My dear Felicity, believe it or not, we are on the same page here. But until the bloody security services and Counter Terrorism get their act together, it's our job to get people back to normal.'

Normal is the unofficial PHE mantra under Dougie's stewardship.

'So you do think it's bio-terrorism of some sort?'

Sighing, he says 'Yes, but Downing Street's shitting a brick. The last thing we need is another bloody stand-off with the Russians. There's only so many times you can call someone a liar. They deny it and show your total impotence as they get away with it yet again. We've run out of threats.'

'If we can prove it, then we'll have the moral high ground.'

'The moral high ground?' Tipping back his head, he laughs and says, 'Oh, Felicity, you are such a lovely woman. The moral high ground! Who in this world do you suppose gives a rat's arse about that?'

21

_____

The light is already fading when the taxi arrives to take Jason to the station. Zoe offered to drive him, but when he refused, saying she must be busy, she didn't press the point.

Earlier, he'd followed her out into the yard hoping to have a private word about his brother. Although it was at her request that he'd come down, she has since retrenched into an obstinate silence. She was on her way to check on a cow that was due to calve and seemed to regard his company as an intrusion.

The vaulted barn was a huge steel structure, a recent addition to the farm, financed by Phil and built to provide the burgeoning dairy herd with suitable winter quarters. The fuggy warmth rising from the cattle and the sweet smell of silage filled the vast shed as Jason tagged along behind his sister-in-law. He's never seen the attraction of farming; long hours of labour and the messy nature of animal husbandry doesn't appeal to him, and it had surprised him when Adam had chosen such a life. He prefers offices and computers and high-tech gyms or country walks with a pub at the end.

He'd waited while Zoe had cast her expert eye over the pregnant heifer. The notion of the former Zoe Rowett, spoilt bitch and bane of his teenage years, up to her armpit in the nether regions of a cow, had once amused him. Now their relationship pivoted around their mutual concern for Adam and was far trickier.

Finally he said 'Well, I've talked to him and I think you're right, something's a bit odd.' Mindful of his promise to his brother, he wasn't about to say more.

She was stroking the heifer, soothing the creature, and appeared not to be paying that much attention.

Then she said in a small voice, 'What do we do?'

'I've told him he should see Chang. The immunosuppressants can produce all sorts of side-effects. But I think Chang'll sort it out.'

She nodded, and that had been the end of the conversation.

Adam escorts Jason to the front door and pulls him into a hug. 'Thanks, mate. I appreciate you coming.'

'Remember what I said, you're not on your own in this. I'm at the end of a phone.'

Adam squeezes his shoulder and says, 'I know. I hear you. Dad always said you were the smart one.'

Jason laughs. 'Did he? He never gave me the impression he thought that.'

Adam glances over his shoulder and says, 'I don't know where Zoe's got to. Changing Ryan probably.'

'Don't worry. Tell her goodbye from me.'

Tossing his bag on the back seat, Jason climbs in beside the taxi driver.

The journey to the station through the darkening lanes takes twenty minutes. Jason responds to the driver's attempts at friendly chat with monosyllables. In the end, the man gives up. Feeling awkward, Jason gives him a big tip.

The train comes up from Plymouth and is running ten minutes late. Jason buys himself a large cappuccino and a pack of sandwiches for the journey, although he doesn't have much of an appetite.

I'm thirty-one, he thinks. Will these feelings ever go? But Adam's comment, that their dad said he was the smart one, gnaws at him, churning up all the old adolescent rancour. He's sure Adam made it up to make him feel better. There's no way it was ever true. Jason was the boy his parents never wanted; they'd never said it, of course, but he had no doubt. He knew it in his blood and bones when he was no older than Ryan.

The train glides along the platform, the doors click open, Jason boards and finds a window seat with a table. Getting his laptop out, he plugs it in as a matter of habit but as the train pulls out of the station and for the next ten minutes he stares out of the window.

Lights and buildings give way to ghostly trees and a black hidden landscape. Adam has always been his shield, an emotional bulwark against his parents' indifference. Somehow, his big brother always knew that he needed protection. When their dad derided him as weak or sissy, Adam was the one who encouraged him and taught him how to climb a tree or jump into the pool. Adam kept him safe.

Ever since he can remember, he's loved his brother with a fierce unspoken passion; he's never experienced such an intense connection with anyone else. Sexual desire is by comparison a pale impulse for him, a carnal need which he pursues with detachment. No lover has ever touched him, no relationship has ever lasted. If he could've taken Adam's place and got sick instead of him, he'd have gladly done it.

Turning his laptop on, he pulls up Google and types in a question: how many road tunnels in the UK? He's working on the assumption that his brother's donor heart came from the UK, which seems a reasonable starting point. Wikipedia pops up with a list of tunnels, most of which are rail. But he does a count, coming up with an initial figure of forty-one. More scrolling and questions produce a revised estimate of forty-nine and the fact that road tunnel operators have an association to promote their interests. This is nonsense, he's playing around. He knows if he's serious, he needs to change his approach.

Settling to his task, Jason sips his coffee. Was there ever any doubt that he'd help Adam? No. But there's plenty of open source information out there that he can access without crossing any red lines. Drilling down through an amorphous mass of data to extract nuggets of relevant detail is what he spends his life doing. He prides himself on speed and precision.

The date of his brother's operation gives him a time frame for the crash. He trawls through the various news outlets looking for accident reports, searching a forty-eight-hour window before the operation, and finds there were nine fatal road traffic accidents reported in the UK. Two involved motorcyclists. Another couple of clicks and there it is, a potential match: a motorcyclist killed in the Blackwall Tunnel in London at 12.42am. The northbound tunnel was closed to traffic for several hours.

Flipping on to social media, he wonders if any witnesses

posted a picture. Often they do, the ghoulish appetite to see and to share horrifies him but, in a data search, it can prove useful. All he finds are a couple of blurry phone shots of police tape and a squad car across the mouth of the tunnel. Then, way down in the news feed, he finds a snippet: *dude in a bad way but alive when ambulance took him. Wishing him well.*

Leaning back in his seat, Jason feels the hairs on his neck prickle. If he was alive at the scene but died in hospital later, that makes him a candidate for organ donation. Is it possible he could've found the person whose death saved Adam's life?

His fingers hover over the keys as he ponders his next move. He goes back to the news feed for more details, scrolls through, reads it twice. Sometimes the victim is named. But this happened late at night. The report is brief and he can find no follow up. He checks a couple more London based sites that often carry crash details but the motorcyclist remains anonymous. *Dude.* That's all there is.

Glancing around the carriage, Jason scans his fellow passengers. Across the aisle a woman in her fifties clutches a kindle, but she's nodding off. In the next section down, a young couple; she cradles a new baby while he plays on his phone. When he sat down, Jason staked out his territory—laptop and food on the table, backpack next to him on the seat—and succeeded in discouraging anyone from joining him. He has the surrounding seats to himself. No one will notice what he's up to, which makes it easier.

He reaches into the front pocket of the backpack and extracts his key fob, which provides the security codes for a remote log in to the secure databases he uses for work. Accessing them for private purposes can, as he told Adam, lead to charges ranging from professional misconduct to a criminal offence. But, without even making a conscious decision, his mind has been calculating how to get away with it. And there's an ongoing inquiry he's involved in which could provide the cover he needs.

For the last six months, they've been chipping away at a paedophile ring and a couple of weeks ago, one target disappeared. If he gets caught out, there's a good chance he can use this as an excuse and blag it. He knows of colleagues who step over the line, pursuing some private beef or trying to get the drop on their ex. His boss doesn't like him much, but she's also a lazy cow who rarely bothers to scrutinise the work of her team.

The digital display on the fob provides him with the code for secure access. He waits for the numbers to change, then he has two minutes to type the live code into the VPN client screen on his laptop before they change again. As he keys the numbers in his gut tightens; *this is for Adam.* In seconds he's on the network.

He goes straight to the Met's incident log for the day of the accident; 12.42am, RTA in the Blackwall Tunnel, it's a hundred and fiftieth on the list, not a busy night. From there, he clicks through to the crash report. His palms are sweating.

Scrolling down, he scans the details, and it flies off the screen straight at him: the name of the victim. David Taylor. Victim conscious at the scene. Transferred to the Royal London. DAVID! It takes a moment to sink in. He forces himself back to the report.

They found a donor card on the victim, brain stem death was diagnosed at 13.24 and the transplant team contacted.

Jason stares at the laptop, elation surges through him, followed by panic. His brain is scrambling for a logical explanation. Someone in the transplant team in Birmingham cocked up. Somehow they let the name slip. Adam could have been only partially under the anaesthetic when he heard it mentioned. But would the surgical team even know the donor's name? Or perhaps it's a bizarre coincidence. David is a common enough name. Statistically, what are the chances?

Even as he analyses all the possibilities, Jason feels a wild and chilling unease. This is the man whose heart now beats in his brother's chest, whose death saved Adam's life. And Adam knows his name.

22

Felicity has come home early. Lack of sleep, elevated cortisol levels from the stress on her adrenal glands, she can read the symptoms warning her to stop. But now she doesn't know what to do with herself. She's made a cup of tea and wanders into the sitting room with it.

It's already getting dark, and someone has half-drawn the heavy drapes across the front bay window. Shafts of amber leach through from the sodium street lamp outside. There's a small cabal of reporters shivering on the opposite pavement, but she doesn't feel sorry for them. They've merged into the landscape like the chauffeur driven, bullet-proof Merc belonging to the Azerbaijani businessman down the road, which is habitually parked on the double yellow line.

Putting her cup and saucer on the glass coffee table, she pulls the curtain shut. She likes things to be in order. Gerry teases her about it. As a young doctor, she'd come in after a long shift and hoover the flat; even when she was exhausted, she found it comforting, but he's never understood that.

Her eye travels over the room, checking the familiar details. Someone has left a mug on the mantlepiece and failed to use a coaster. Her husband. He maintains a cavalier attitude towards these things as a point of principle. *Let it go, Flis. Life's too short.* His laid back attitude can be exasperating. The battleground in the early years of their marriage was always about the mess he made and never seemed to notice. Bringing up two children while holding down a job has caused her far less hassle than trying to house train her husband. His idea of compromise was to hire a cleaner. He didn't expect her to pick up after him. That was always his argument. But he worked and earned, he said, in order to avoid doing the menial tasks.

Over the years, she's adapted her attitude to accommodate his obdurate notions. She didn't want to spend her life being annoyed by him. That was futile. But as she walks round the room, turning on lamps and smoothing cushions, she feels her irritation rising. The angry voice in her head natters: in the present circumstances, is it unreasonable to expect him to try? Is it too much to ask? Pick the mug up, carry it to the kitchen, put it in the dishwasher. Is his life of retirement so demanding that he can't fit that into his busy schedule?

She finds that within moments, she's seething. Her diaphragm is rigid with rage. She takes a deep breath. This is ridiculous! Standing in the middle of the room, she places her hands on her hips and forces herself to do a reality check. She scans the room, the elegant Italian sofas, the neat sideboard with her three favourite family photographs carefully placed, the original Eames Lounge Chair Gerry bought from an American collector for her birthday. Nothing is out of place. It's all as it should be.

'Thought I heard you come in' a voice says, and she turns to see her husband framed in the doorway. 'Are you okay?' He pads into the room, bare feet slapping the polished oak boards, another habit that vexes her.

Realising that she's scowling, she shakes her head and says, 'I'm turning into a cantankerous, bad-tempered, angry old woman.'

He laughs. 'Victor Meldrew. Remember him? I don't believe it!'

She sighs. 'I hate it. I don't know what's wrong with me.'

'Stress. And more stress. And—'

'I want to argue with everyone. I had to leave the office. Coming home in the car, I was looking out of the window, and I was thinking what has happened to us, what the...' She bites her tongue. She's never liked coarse language.

'Say it, Flis. What the fuck has happened? It's a reasonable question.'

'Okay, the situation is unprecedented. But the thinking around me, it's mad, Gerry. I don't understand what's happening to people—educated, intelligent people. We've got to get a grip.'

He walks across the room to her, puts his hands on her shoulders and says, 'You can't bear the weight of this, my darling. You can't!'

'Y'know Ryder's latest thing? A new untested anti-viral drug. They're planning some ludicrous fake news campaign so people will be conned into thinking they've got the answer.'

'He's a politician.'

'Lacey's as bad. They're not saying how do we stop

people from dying. They're saying which lies do we tell to persuade the public we have this under control.'

'COBRA will put pressure on Ryder to cover the government's backside.'

'I know we have to reassure the public. But blatantly lying? No proper clinical trials on this drug. Some outfit run from a business park outside Cambridge by one Henry Shawcross. VSG Biotech?'

'Never heard of them.'

'Shawcross left Johns Hopkins under a cloud, as we discovered this afternoon. Came back to the UK a year ago and set up shop to research H7N9 with some kind of private funding and the co-operation of the Chinese.'

'Not a name I've heard, either. But want me to do some digging?'

She sighs. 'You can. All the good it'll do. Ryder's dead set on it. This is going to be his wonder drug. This is where the money's going. Decisive action, that's what he calls it. But the best-case scenario is people strong enough to fight the virus will be fine, the vulnerable will continue to die. No different to now.'

'Even though he's the Secretary of State, he'd be foolish to ignore your advice.'

Leaning forward, she allows her forehead to rest on his shoulder and says, 'I don't think he gives a monkey's.'

'Resign. You've done what you can.'

'I can't give up. Let people down.'

'You can, Flis. You can't take responsibility for his bad decisions. And if you resign, then you can speak out.'

'Oh and you know what'll happen then! They'll close ranks. Forget any terrorists. I'll be the enemy. That's the sort of diversion Ryder would love.'

He strokes her hair and says, 'I worry about you. The strain of this. You're not getting any younger, old girl.'

She gives him a sardonic smile. 'Thanks. Promise me one thing, if that man ever becomes Prime Minister, we'll move to France or Italy. Get a little place in the country and keep chickens.'

They both laugh and he says 'Well, possibly not chickens. How about a little vineyard? Maybe near Toulouse, for the airport. Cotes du Tarn, somewhere like that? I've always thought I might make a good vintner.'

She grins and says 'Yes, my darling, but you need to know a bit more about wine than how to drink it.'

23

DAY 23. 9.40am

Phil Rowett watches his daughter drive into the yard. He's not a man to indulge in negative thinking, but he finds the outlook on this freezing February morning depressing. There's a numbing coldness in the air and a darkening sky suggesting the possibility of snow.

Zoe has just taken Lily to school. Meanwhile his son-in-law is skulking upstairs somewhere. Adam is proving impossible to deal with. He answers questions with a diffident shrug or he doesn't answer at all. Ruth counsels patience, he's been through a lot. But Phil has never seen the value in pussyfooting around. He believes in speaking his mind.

Zoe wanders into the kitchen, dumping her bag on the pine table, pulling off her gloves and rubbing her hands. Her face is pinched, her eyes underscored with heavy pouches. His gorgeous, energetic, laughing daughter has been reduced to this worn shadow and every time he sees it, it's like a kick in the gut. He reaches out, pulls her into a hug, kisses her on the forehead.

She wriggles free. 'What's that for?'

'You look like you need it.'

'Is he ready?' She sounds tetchy.

Adam has an appointment with his consultant in Birmingham. That's why Phil and Ruth are there: child-minding duties.

'Zoe, why don't you stay here with your mother and the children? I'll drive him. Looks a bit like snow.'

She walks away, placing the kitchen island between them. Drumming the counter with her thumb, she radiates anxiety.

'I appreciate the offer, Dad. But I don't think that's going to work.'

'I don't see why not,' Phil says.

'Adam needs support.'

'I can support him.'

This prompts a wry laugh, then she says, 'I know you're trying to help. But the best thing is you stay here, pick up Lily from school and we'll be back late tomorrow.'

'I worry about you, sweetheart.'

'Don't tell me I look awful. I don't need to hear that.'

Phil opens his palms. 'Give me some credit, I know better than to comment on a lady's appearance.' He knows that she finds his old-fashioned brand of gallantry both annoying and reassuring. He has the satisfaction of seeing her smile and meet his gaze.

'You're a silly old bugger,' she says.

'I'm allowed to worry about you,' he replies. 'That's my job.'

Ruth appears in the doorway, cradling a fractious Ryan in her arms.

Zoe frowns. 'Shall I take him?'

'He's fine, full of beans. But I think Adam could do with some help with his packing.'

Her daughter huffs and says, 'All he needs is an overnight bag. How hard can it be?' She scurries out of the door.

Phil draws a sharp breath in through his nostrils and looks at his wife. 'This is getting ridiculous.'

'Sssh! They'll hear you.'

'It can't go on, Ruth. Look at the state of her, she's bloody exhausted.'

'I know that. But keep your voice down.'

She carries Ryan from the kitchen through to the spacious family room, high-ceilinged with a crossbeam roof. It was once a stable for the farm horses. Phil trails after her.

Placing Ryan in his playpen, she extracts a squeaky rabbit and a green plastic Stegosaurus from the toy box and offers them to the toddler. He grabs the rabbit with a gleeful cackle.

She turns to her husband and says, 'You have to stop pushing her, Phil.'

'I'm not pushing her, I'm trying to take care of her.'

'Adam's her husband. She has to do this her way.'

'Oh, so he gets better, and she makes herself ill?'

Ruth shakes her head and says, 'You cannot solve this for them.'

'I'm not trying to. But what's needed here is a bit of plain speaking. When Zoe married him, she didn't sign up for this.'

'I think it comes under the heading of for better or for worse,' his wife says drily.

'All I'm saying is that when circumstances change, then you have to respond and chart an alternative course.'

'This is a marriage, not a business.'

'All transactional relationships are the same, my dear.'

'Oh you do talk nonsense, Phil.'

'Who knows how he's going to be over the next few years and if he'll even survive. Is this what you want for our daughter? Nursing an invalid, bringing up two kids more or less single handed only to end up a widow ten years down the road? The best years of her life, Ruth, are being swallowed up. I feel for the boy, of course I do. It's bad luck. But the truth is she'd be better off if they split up.'

Ruth shakes her head; she's used to her husband's views and ignores them. Reaching into the playpen, she smooths her grandson's hair. 'And would this little one be better off, and Lily?'

'In the long run, yes.'

'You cannot say that, Phil. And whatever you do, don't say it to her.'

'Don't say what to her?' Zoe steps through the archway from the kitchen. Adam follows her. He's wearing a thick sweater and a scarf, his hair uncombed and his beard scruffy.

Phil steps into the breach. 'Oh, I was talking about the ice cream.' He raises his hand. 'But don't worry, darling. I know what you think. In fact, I was wondering if you'd like to take the whole thing over, turn it into a completely organic brand.'

Zoe is staring at him. 'Dad, I don't think I've got the mental space for this at the moment.'

'I know. Don't worry. It was an idle thought. We'll revisit it another time.'

Ruth approaches Adam and pats his arm. 'So, you ready for off?'

Her son-in-law has a faraway look, but he smiles and

says, 'Thanks for looking after the kids again. We appreciate it.'

'Don't be soppy' Ruth replies 'it's lovely for us to have this time with them.'

Phil nods enthusiastically and says, 'Absolutely. Happy to help.'

DAY 23. 5.15pm

Adam sits on a chair in the waiting area, watching his wife pace. On the drive to Birmingham, they've hardly spoken. It was a slog, icy roads and heavy traffic; they listened to a podcast Zoe had found reviewing some of the teams for the America's Cup. As he listened, Adam had wondered if he'd ever do any serious sailing again or whether that life was one more thing lost in the maelstrom of his illness.

Mr. Chang's secretary has arranged a last-minute appointment for him at the end of the consultant's clinic, although he has been advised that he may have to wait.

Mulling over the discussion he had with his brother, Adam has concluded that Jason is right: this is the sensible way forward. Chang is hugely knowledgeable in the field, he's the most likely person to shed light on Adam's disturbing experiences.

Once he'd settled on this course of action, the problem was how to explain it to Zoe. He didn't want to lie.

'Are you in pain?' she said, when he mentioned the appointment. 'Why didn't you tell me?'

'No, but I think there might be some problems with the drugs.' Only a small lie.

'What sort of problems? More nightmares?' He'd watched her anxiety skyrocket, and he wanted to reassure her, to calm her. But he didn't know how.

He said, 'I can go to Birmingham on the train.'

'Why on earth would you do that?'

'Easier for you?'

'You having some discussion with your consultant behind my back? How is that easier for me?'

'It's not like that, Zo.'

He had to admit to himself that she saw straight through him. Cutting her out of the loop is exactly what he wanted to do. He didn't even know why. Was it because of the miasma of unspoken anger that eddied around her most of the time? He knew he'd let her down, he'd let his children down. It was another poisonous thread in the knot of twisted thoughts and tangled feelings inside him.

The door to the consulting room opens and Chang appears. 'Adam!' he says. 'Come on in.'

Zoe is there first, shaking the consultant's hand and being ushered in. Adam follows and suddenly he's nervous. They sit down.

Chang studies him with a practiced eye. 'You're looking well. How are you feeling?'

Although he's rehearsed what he plans to say, Adam is momentarily flummoxed. Sitting in the consulting room with its examination couch, the tray of medical equipment, the antiseptic smell, it all sounds too weird. He's aware of both his wife and his doctor staring at him.

'I feel good physically. But I'm not sleeping that well.

And I've got this stuff in my head.' *Stuff.* This was a stupid idea.

'Bad dreams?'

'Not dreams because I'm not asleep.'

'Sometimes we drift in and out of consciousness. We can be in the dream state without knowing it.'

'Yes, but it feels as if this is different.'

'Different how?' the surgeon asks.

Adam is aware of Zoe fidgeting, wanting to butt in. Chang notices this too.

He turns to her and says, 'You want to add something, Zoe?'

She sighs and says, 'I think Adam's not telling you the whole story. He always tries to tough it out. He won't admit when he's having difficulties.'

Chang glances across at him. 'True, Adam?'

Adam smiles. *Why can't she put a sock in it for once in her life?* 'Probably' he says. 'She knows me too well.'

'I think he's quite fragile,' says Zoe. 'Physically and emotionally. He doesn't even want to go out.'

'That's because it's bloody freezing!'

'Says the man who's sailed the Atlantic in a force nine gale.'

Adam chuckles. It's a front. They're playing the happy couple for Chang; it's happened before. They're colluding to preserve the public face of their marriage, which they both seem eager to retain.

'Patients often feel agoraphobic after major surgery,' says Chang, 'its self protection. Quite natural.'

Still on hospital time, thinks Adam. Chang's words make sense. They also have the effect of shutting Zoe up.

The consultant turns back to his patient and says, 'So, you've been having nightmares? It's not uncommon.

Altering the medication usually does the trick.' He flips open his laptop. 'Let's have a look at the dosage.'

Adam feels a surge of irritation. 'It's not about dosage.'

Chang seems taken aback. 'Okay—'

'Sorry I—'Adam reins himself in. *Spinning in the head again?* He feels hot, the thick prickly jumper, the ridiculous scarf his wife's made him wear tangling in his new beard. He pulls it off.

Chang folds his hands and says, 'It's okay, take your time.'

Adam takes a breath and says, 'This sounds barmy, I know, but I feel as if I'm remembering things, things that happened to me, except they didn't.'

The surgeon nods. 'Can you say more?'

'I remember being in an accident, in a tunnel, on a motorcycle.'

Zoe is staring at him. He can feel her annoyance.

'Do you ride a motorcycle?' asks Chang.

'No, I never have.'

The surgeon runs his finger across the track pad as he ponders.

Then he says, 'Patients do occasionally say to me I remember this thing, but it couldn't have happened to me, it happened to my donor. Is that what you're thinking?'

'Sort of, yes.' Chang knows. Jason was right.

The surgeon nods sagely. 'The question is, is this possible? And the medical answer is no. Definitely not. Cellular memory is given as an explanation for this phenomenon. You can read about it on the net, but I wouldn't bother, because there's absolutely no proof.'

'What explanation can I give you for your experience? Many of my colleagues would say this results from the powerful immunosuppressant drugs we're giving you. And they're certainly a factor. I think there's more to it than that.'

Chang leans back in his chair. 'We're remarkable beings. We make sense of this world, or we try to, no matter what. You've suffered a major trauma, which your brain is attempting to process. It needs a story to help it understand.'

'I think I would know if I was making this up.'

'That's the point, Adam. You wouldn't. To make sense of things, the mind must imagine what the body experiences. Take eyesight as an example. It's not about what is projected onto the retina; perception requires recognition, knowing what you're looking at, that's how the brain constructs an image, based on the story you already have.'

'Why a motorcycle accident in a tunnel then?'

'Your subconscious mind is taking an educated guess. Most donors will probably have died from a catastrophic brain injury. I think it's common knowledge that road traffic accidents provide most organ donors. And a motorcyclist is likely to be young and otherwise fit. You're smart, you know all this.'

Adam smiles and says, 'Now I feel like an idiot.'

'Don't. Making sense of your experience is part of the recovery process, an important part, and everyone has to do it in their own way. I don't have this sort of conversation with many patients, only the more intelligent ones.'

Adam wonders if he's being flattered into submission, but he's also relieved. He wanted a proper explanation, and this is it, from the horse's mouth.

Chang smiles and says, 'The drugs don't help with the confusion you're feeling. Recognising that's what it is and managing it is a learning curve and you will get better at it as time goes on. My job is to help you.'

'You have. And thank you.'

'Can I ask a question?' says Zoe. She's been sitting motionless, shoulders hunched, listening intently.

Chang smiles. 'Of course. Fire away.'

'In this situation, can people's personalities change?'

'You think your husband is different? In what way?'

Adam watches her; she's nervous and avoids his eye.

She hesitates—considering her words, not like Zoe—then says, 'It's his temperament, I suppose. He's so laid-back and breezy normally, copes with anything, it's a family joke. Rarely gets upset. Now he's on a short fuse, quite reactive, and that's not him. It's more me; I'm the stroppy one.'

Adam feels a lump in his throat. Her distress is worse than her anger. He wants to reach out, take her hand, comfort her. But he's too embarrassed in front of Chang. She has tears in her eyes.

It's the surgeon who leans forward and hands her a box of tissues.

'Zoe,' he says, 'this is what serious illness does to people. They get frightened and that can lead to a short fuse as you put it. The mind must heal as well as the body. And that's where Adam is now.'

She dabs her face with the tissue. 'Sorry. I'm being stupid.'

Adam strokes her arm and says, 'You've been brilliant.'

'I haven't' she says. Her contrite glance reminds him of Lily when she's been naughty.

'We should never ignore the stress on you as a carer,' says Chang 'you have to recover from this too.'

She nods and blows her nose.

Adam gets up. He wants to get out of there and out of the hospital. He's had his fill of hospitals. 'I think we've taken up enough of your time' he says 'thank you, again.'

Chang shrugs and smiles. Adam notices how suddenly

care-worn he looks.

They shake hands and Adam says, 'One other thing, can I drive?'

'You feel ready for that?'

'I do now.'

'Then I don't see why not.'

Walking out of his consultant's office, Adam is bouyant. A weight has lifted, the anxiety and confusion are gone, relief suffuses his body. Jason was right all along. Chang would sort this out and he has. He longs to call his brother and thank him.

Without realising what he's doing, he strides off down the corridor. He turns to look for Zoe and discovers she's yards behind him. She has a sullen look.

He stops, waits for her and says, 'Sorry. I wanted to get out of there.'

'I wish you'd talked to me about all this,' she says.

'I didn't want to worry you.'

'Bloody hell, Adam! You think watching you isn't worrying enough? You think I'm stupid?'

'No,' he says. 'Of course not. And I meant what I said in there, you have been brilliant.'

She sighs. 'What does that even mean? Where does it leave us?'

He looks down. The corridor is covered in a speckled-grey vinyl flooring. He traces a line across it with the toe of his trainer.

'Okay,' he says, 'this is it. I'm drawing a line. I'm not ill. That's over and done with. I'm getting better and I'm getting on with my life.' He offers her his hand and smiles, 'Care to step over the line and join me?'

She takes his hand. 'Just like that?'

'Yeah. You heard Chang, it's all in the mind.'

25

DAY 26. 9.50am

As he wanders into the large open-plan office where he works, Jason has his excuse ready: a painful back spasm that put him in bed and necessitated a day off sick. The pain part of it is true, he's been suffering crippling headaches, having spent several sleepless nights in a state of anxiety and indecision. Should he tell Adam about David Taylor? That's only one of the questions tormenting him.

Jason didn't stop when he discovered the name. He dug further into the crash report written by the Traffic Officer attending the scene. It stated that David Taylor was found lying in the carriageway conscious but paralysed, with a suspected broken neck. Traffic was light. Road surface dry. Two witnesses travelling in a black BMW X5 saw the accident and stopped. They stated the motorcyclist passed them at excessive speed, misjudged the bend, and ploughed into the wall. No other vehicle was involved.

The victim was taken to the Royal London, where he lost

consciousness, was placed on a ventilator but was subsequently declared brain dead. By then, they had discovered an organ donor card in his wallet and the decision taken to call in the transplant team. As a result, the crash report had to be expedited for the Coroner. This may have been one reason why no CCTV from the tunnel was checked.

The report ended with an addendum: the victim spoke several words at the scene, but they weren't recorded. The Traffic Officer believed they were in a foreign language, but he couldn't identify it.

Jason had pored over the report, reading and re-reading, most of the way back to London on the train. The witness account didn't tally with Adam's memory, but hitting the wall, the broken neck and the paralysis did. In the time-frame of Adam's transplant, there was no other donor in the UK; so although it wasn't a hundred percent certain it was David Taylor, the chances of another donor arriving from abroad at the same time seemed unlikely.

The most disturbing aspect of Jason's discovery though, was the two witnesses who told the police it was an accident. Jason could tell his brother that he was right about the name, but what should he say about them? Was Adam's version of what happened the correct one or theirs? And if they were lying to the police, why? Were they involved in a conspiracy to cover up a murder?

Since he unearthed all this, Jason has been avoiding Adam's calls. He sent a couple of innocuous texts to give himself space to think and maybe find out more. He kept going back to the files on Taylor to see if he could prize any more information out of them.

Over the weekend, he visited the site of the accident in person. He had used his Met ID to blag his way into the Tunnel control room, where he had spun a tale about CCTV and data analysis. He used enough IT jargon to confuse them and persuade them to leave him alone to rummage through the CCTV. But the search proved futile. The system was archaic and had to be wiped every two weeks to keep it functioning. Transferring to any kind of back-up was time consuming. Jobs had been cut, and no one bothered anymore. A frustrated Jason left empty-handed. If there had been any evidence of David Taylor's so-called accident, it was gone.

As Jason walks to his desk, he notices his boss turn her head to look at him through the glass partition of her office. It seems likely that, before he can even get himself a coffee, she'll summon him for a bollocking. There's a tall Asian or Middle Eastern guy standing beside her. He too glances in Jason's direction.

Putting his backpack down next to his desk, Jason is hooking his jacket over the back of the chair when a colleague scurries over to him and says, 'Sally wants a word.'

He smiles and says, 'Thanks.' The cow is nothing if not predictable.

He considers making her wait, but it's best not to aggravate her. Strolling back across the room, he stops outside the open doorway.

'Come in, Jason' she says. She seems unusually tense.

He has his cover story ready. 'Sorry I'm late this morning but—'

'This is DI Mehta from Counter Terrorism.'

Mehta smiles and holds out his hand. 'Samir Mehta.' His dark gaze is unnervingly direct.

Jason shakes his hand and replies, 'Jason Hardy.'

Mehta looks him up and down. 'I've been explaining to

Sally that we need to talk to you about some of the work you've been doing.'

'On the pedophile ring?' Jason wonders if he should worry.

'Yes' says Mehta. He turns to Sally. 'I'm sure you're busy. I don't want to hold you up.'

Jason inwardly smirks. When in her life was Sally ever busy? Certainly not with work. She spends most of her time gossiping with her mates on social media and redesigning her DIY mood boards on Pinterest.

Sally gives the DI a gushy smile. Could she suck up to him any more? 'Oh, I work closely with Jason' she says, 'and I'm sure I can be helpful on—'

'Unnecessary,' says Mehta. 'But thank you. Jason and I are going to go for a wander and have a chat.'

With an amiable nod, he saunters out of the office. Sally glares at Jason, but before she can speak, he follows.

He catches up with the DI halfway down the corridor. Mehta selects a window overlooking a brick wall and a row of dumpsters. Then, hands slotted in his trouser pockets, he turns to face Jason.

'What's your interest in David Taylor?' he says. ''Cause I'm thinking he's not a pedophile.'

Jason's stomach lurches.

'Erm, well, it seems he may well know someone who—' his brain is scrambling for a plausible excuse and the DI's unremitting stare isn't helping.

Mehta jangles the change in his trouser pocket and sighs. 'This is a serious situation, Jason, and you do not want to get on the wrong side of it. In the last seventy-two hours, you've been repeatedly accessing documents relating to him. Why?'

The DI's cool demeanour hides the stress of long hours, wakeful nights and of an inquiry under severe pressure.

But his hunch that Khalid and Taylor were the same person had been confirmed. On Wednesday afternoon, within an hour of being asked, Mehta's DC had come back to him with the news that he had matched Feras Khalid's prints with the name David Taylor. Taylor was a motorcyclist who'd been arrested after a collision on the M11 and was found to have taken drugs.

The breakthrough had galvanised the team. Mehta had assigned half a dozen other officers and, using the new name, by Thursday morning they'd tracked down his informant only to discover he was dead. It had looked like the end of the road. Then the system had tossed them this bone.

Mehta studies the analyst. Jason Hardy looks nervous. It's clear he knows he's been caught out, but he doesn't come over to the DI as a typical rule breaker. He's too buttoned-up and watchful. This is not habitual behaviour for him.

They've pulled his file, but it revealed little. Since joining the Met, his work record has been exemplary. Several SIOs have noted his speed and proficiency. But if Mehta was expecting a weedy geek, the analyst doesn't fit that profile either. He matches the DI in height, and the well-defined biceps and pecs suggest a serious gym habit.

The DI smiles and says, 'As I'm sure you're aware, at the very least this could be a disciplinary offence.'

Jason nods. Mehta is an unnerving presence. His thoughts skitter. But being found out brings him an odd sense of relief. It was always on the cards he could lose his job with a stunt like this. But he did it for Adam.

Reviewing his options, he realises he has none. He knows the system well enough to be aware that the files he delved into must've been tagged to send an alert. Rumour has it Counter Terrorism does this with persons of interest.

His eyes meet Mehta's. How the hell is he going to explain this? It makes no sense to him. How will anyone else understand? The DI is going to think he's lying or completely mental.

He takes a deep breath and says, 'I wanted to check out how he died because my brother's got his heart.'

26

Boots crunching through frosted tussocks of grass, Adam makes his way across the fields at the back of the house. The afternoon light is fast fading. Max, one of the farm's three border collies, trots at his heels. It's the first walk of any length he's tried, and he feels invigorated, blood pumping, fingertips tingling in his gloves.

He climbs up on to the wooden step of the stile and surveys the scene. He's home and reconnecting with this land he lives on and farms, and with his family.

When he and Zoe left the hospital on Friday afternoon, he'd insisted they call Phil and Ruth to ask them to babysit for another twenty-four hours. Then they'd driven down to Stratford-on-Avon, checked into an old inn overlooking the river, and Adam had ordered a bottle of champagne.

At first, Zoe had been awkward and resistant.

'This feels weird,' she said.

'Weird's okay.'

'Adam, I can't flick a switch and go back to before. All light-hearted and playful. I'm not saying I don't want to but—'

Lifting her hand, he'd put it to his lips, kissed it and said, 'Zo, drink your champagne and chill. I'm not expecting anything.' He laughed. 'Not sure I'm capable of much. I want us to be together and to be at peace. I think we deserve that.'

They'd drunk the champagne, chatting of inconsequential things. He'd kissed her and she'd responded. It wasn't the most energetic sex they'd ever had. They were both tentative at first and then desire took over.

Afterwards, she'd lain in his arms. 'I thought I'd lost you,' she said.

'Takes a lot to kill me,' he'd replied.

'My heart's been breaking too.'

'I know. But it's over now.'

The next morning they'd gone out for breakfast, strolled beside the river and watched the ducks preening and feeding before heading home.

Adam had driven part of the way and teased Zoe about her clunky old car. She'd laughed at his lame jokes and, for the first time in months, she seemed at ease.

Calling to the dog, he jumps down from the stile and walks through the yard, past the barn and round towards the house.

Zoe's old hatchback is parked out the front and beside it a sleek new black Mercedes. Adam smiles to himself. Another new car! His father-in-law is incorrigible. He swaps vehicles like other men change their socks.

As he heads for the side door, it opens and Jason appears.

'Jace!' he says, 'Didn't know you were coming down.'

Jason's face is pale. He has a hunted look. He whispers, 'Listen, mate, we've only got a minute, but I wanted you to know—' His chin quivers.

Adam seizes him by the shoulders and says, 'What's going on? Is it the kids?'

'Kids are fine. I'm so sorry,' he says.

Adam pulls him into a hug. 'Hey, sorry for what?' Then he becomes aware of several figures in the lighted kitchen behind his brother.

He walks through the doorway to find a tall, raven-haired man, sharply suited, leaning on his Aga. Seated at the pine table is a stout middle-aged woman with a neat bun. Zoe is pouring her a mug of tea, and she's eyeing a plate of chocolate digestives.

She looks up, smiles and says, 'Ah, Mr. Hardy. I hope you enjoyed your walk. I must say you're looking well. Your wife is kindly giving us tea. And you're thinking to yourself, who the hell are these strange people and what are they doing in my kitchen?'

Adam shoots Jason a quizzical look and says, 'Feels like, I dunno, we're in trouble?'

The woman sighs; she has an imperious air, Queen Victoria in a Jaeger suit. 'I think you could say the entire country is in a fair amount of trouble, Mr. Hardy,' she says. 'That's why we're here. I'm Detective Chief Superintendent Babcock and I want to talk to you about David.'

Adam perches on the sofa in the sitting room with his face in his hands. Jason is busying himself lighting the wood burner. The kindling flares and catches. Adam looks up, and for a moment, meets his brother's troubled gaze. He feels betrayed. How did this happen? Jason went to some colleagues in the Met and told them Adam was harbouring crazy thoughts about his donor being murdered? Why would his brother do such a thing to him? Just as his life seems to be getting back to normal, some laughing fiend has flipped him on his back again. These people have walked into his house and his life, flashing official looking ID. Counter bloody terrorism? He feels angry and confused.

Babcock settles herself regally in an armchair and focuses on her tea and biscuits. She's leaving it to the man to do the talking. He introduces himself as DI Samir Mehta.

Adam glares at him.

Mehta smiles back.

'Don't blame your brother for this,' he says. 'He was doing an illegal search of our databases, trying to help you, I believe. And it flagged up his interest in David Taylor because of our interest. So blame us for this invasion of your life and your privacy, not him.'

Adam doesn't respond.

'I don't understand how my husband can help you,' says Zoe. She sounds small and nervous, cowered by the forces of law and order or perhaps it's the shock of them turning up out of the blue.

'These are curious times we're living in, Mrs. Hardy,' says Babcock serenely, 'they oblige us to travel down some unexpected roads. When you've eliminated the likely and the probable and the possible, you have to consider the impossible. And that's what we're doing now.'

Mehta sits down beside Adam and says 'We'd like you to tell us about these odd memories of yours.'

Adam bristles. The proximity of the other man feels

threatening. But he senses it's deliberate. He's being interrogated and in his own house. And he's not having it.

'Look, it's all nonsense,' he replies. 'I've talked to my doctor. My subconscious is making this stuff up. Sometimes this happens, I'm told.'

'How do you know your donor was called David?'

'Maybe it's a random guess. Or I overheard something. No one knows. The system isn't perfect.'

'And yet you remember the manner of his death,' says the DI. 'Tell us about that if you can.'

Adam is staring down at his fingernails. He feels the heat rising up, flushing through him. It's making him dizzy.

Taking a deep breath, he says, 'I had this sort of memory of a motorcycle crash in a tunnel. At the time it felt vivid, but I have to take all these immunosuppressive drugs and they can cause nightmares.' *And the dizziness.* He doesn't mention that.

'But you told your brother it wasn't a nightmare, that you were awake,' says Mehta.

Adam shoots a fierce glance at Jason, but this is not his fault. His face softens and he says, 'I'm sorry if I've got you in trouble.'

'You wanted to know if it could be true,' says Jason.

'You telling me it is?'

Jason nods. 'Looks like it.'

'This guy, I've got his heart? Are you sure?' His questioning gaze flicks from his brother to the cop.

Babcock sips her tea and watches the exchange like a large spider keeping a close eye on her prey.

Mehta says 'Obviously we've looked into this too. David Taylor was killed in a motorcycle accident in the Blackwall Tunnel in London. We've checked with the hospitals concerned. He was your donor.'

Adam looks at his wife. Now he understands why they don't tell you. David Taylor. An actual person.

'Whatever happened to patient confidentiality?' Zoe says. 'We were told there were strict rules about that.'

'There are,' says Mehta. 'In normal circumstances.'

Adam closes his eyes. *David? Is that his name?* He feels giddy. Everything is spiralling out of control. The wall is coming straight at him. He forces his eyes open and says, 'Did he wear a red crash helmet?'

'That I can't tell you,' replies the DI.

Zoe perches on the arm of the sofa, takes her husband's hand and holds it tight. Adam feels relieved; he's got Zoe, she's holding on to him. That's good. He looks up at her, but she seems far away. He clutches her hand.

She turns to Mehta and says 'If this is the same person why is Counter Terrorism interested in him?'

The DI glances at his boss to confirm her approval, then says 'We're going to trust you. And you appreciate that this information is confidential. David Taylor was an informant of ours. His disappearance has caused us some problems.'

'What sort of problems?' asks Zoe.

Adam clutches her arm in a panic 'Zo!' He's about to throw up, he dry retches.

'Adam?' she squats in front of him, strokes his forehead. 'Take some deep breaths. You okay?'

He breathes. Nods.

Abruptly, the spinning stops and a cold clarity cascades through his mind; beads of sweat stipple his upper lip and under his chin, but the heat is only an outer carapace. The fear has gone to be replaced by an unexpected detachment.

'I'm fine' he says, 'don't fuss.' *Fuss is stupid.* He pushes her hand away.

Turning from her, he focuses on Mehta. 'I don't know if Jason's told you but I think he was deliberately killed.'

It seems a simple matter-of-fact statement. Suddenly he can't understand why he didn't tell them straight away. Why is he being so wimpy about this? A grown man holding on to his wife's hand like a child.

Mehta nods. 'Tell us about that.'

'My feeling is he knew the tunnel. It was a route he used. He'd nearly got to the end. Up the final incline, he was passing this old Luton van. It swerved deliberately and hit him.'

Adam frowns and closes his eyes, but the dizziness is gone. He feels calm and normal, although he's dripping in sweat. 'I think he recognised the driver,' he says.

Zoe wipes the slather of perspiration from his forehead with her fingers and turns on Babcock 'He's burning up. I don't give a toss who you are! You can't do this to him. Now I'm going to call my father and he's going to call his lawyer—'

'Zoe' says Babcock evenly, 'no one, least of all us, wishes Adam any harm.'

'Then what the hell do you want? He was fine, he was getting better.'

'I am fine, Zo' says Adam. *He's more than fine.*

'No, you're not' says his wife. 'You've gone into this weird space again. Remember what Chang said. You have to recognise it for what it is.'

'What kind of weird space?' says Babcock.

'His personality changes,' says Jason. 'He's not himself.'

'That's ridiculous' says Adam. 'Of course I'm myself. Short-tempered, I'll admit.'

His wife shakes her head. 'I agree with Jason.'

Adam feels his anger rising. But he keeps a handle on it.

'Well, that's a first,' he replies sourly. *Stupid bitch.*

Babcock and Mehta exchange looks.

Then the Chief Superintendent says, 'I don't think any of us understand what we're dealing with here. I think we could do with some expert help. Adam, I'd like you to consider talking to a friend of mine. Jason can bring you to London.'

Zoe jumps up and faces Babcock. 'No way he's going to London. This bloody flu thing! His immunity is shot. He catches it, he'll die.'

Reaching up, Adam clutches his wife's arm and says, 'This is why they're here, Zo, the flu thing. That's why they're in such a panic.'

'Adam—'

'Let it go, Zoe.' His tone is stern, brooking no opposition.

She stares at him as if slapped. He releases her arm. They stare at one another. Her chin is quivering, but he doesn't care. His guilt has evaporated.

For a moment, no one speaks. Jason hovers in the corner of the room. He doesn't know what to do. He's aghast at the chain of events he's put in motion.

Then the DI says 'The flu epidemic? Is that a guess, Adam?'

He shrugs, He's sweating but inside there's a coolness. He stares straight at Mehta. *What a prick?* 'I've no idea' he says, 'it's a feeling. Who's this person you want me to see?'

'She's a doctor,' says Babcock. 'All I'm asking is one conversation.'

'She comes here,' says Zoe.

The Detective Chief Superintendent nods 'Well—'

Adam eyeballs Mehta. 'What about family? Do you know who they are? Did they give permission for the transplant?'

Mehta glances at his boss. She shrugs.

'Yes, I believe—'

'Here are my conditions,' says Adam. 'I'll come to London.'

'No, Adam!' His wife shakes her head vehemently.

'But before I talk to your doctor, I want to meet her.'

Babcock and Mehta look at one another again. The DI frowns and says 'Her? You mean the doctor? Who are we talking about here?'

'No. I mean Mia. That's his girlfriend's name, isn't it?'

The four other people in the room stare at Adam. There's a hollow silence.

He watches them. Zoe and Jason, his wife, his brother, he loves them, of course he does. He knows that. They're on his side. But the two cops. *Fuck them.*

The queasiness and dizziness have passed, and he feels much better. Clear headed. Back to normal.

Wiping his face with the sleeve of his jumper, he stands up and says, 'How do I know about her? I can see that's what you're wondering.' Now he and the prick cop are on the same level. He steps forward to stand inches from the DI's face. 'You want my cooperation? First I meet Mia. Do we have a deal?'

Mehta edges backwards and shoots a glance at his boss. Adam smiles to himself. *Prick cop tried to play me. He was never that smart.*

'Yes' says Babcock. 'If that's what you want, yes.'

Twitter Feed

DAY 26.

True Health News @truehealthnews
We did it! YOU DID IT! #pandemic #powertothepeople
Quoting: **Public Health England**@PHE_uk
The government has acquired a new anti-viral drug to treat
the most serious cases in the current outbreak of avian flu.
Advice for most people remains the same #staywell
8.6k Retweets 9.3k Likes

Pete Harris @pharris510
Replying to @truehealthnews
Shows what we can do when we act together. Visit your
elderly neighbours. Check they're ok. #pandemic #safe-
andsound
3.9k Retweets 5.1k Likes

Mark Carter @MCB666
Replying to @truehealthnews
Great news! Now we need health checks at our borders.
KEEP THE VIRUS OUT TO SAVE LIVES! #Pandemic
#safeandsound
429 Retweets 573 Likes

27

DAY 26. 9.45pm

Professor Dame Felicity Oldroyd is curled up on one of the large Italian sofas next to her daughter, Phoebe, watching *Love Island* on catch up.

'Oh no, seriously?' exclaims the Professor. 'They've got the mentality of squabbling teenagers.'

Her daughter giggles. 'That's why people like it.'

The Professor purses her lips, 'It's soft porn.'

Cuddling up to her, Phoebe says, 'It's romance, Mum! People looking for love, for the fairytale to come true.'

"Emotional hogwash and narcissism,' says Felicity. 'Yeah, I know, I'm a po-faced old biddy.'

Her daughter grins. 'Somewhat.'

Getting up, the Professor stretches 'Fancy a cup of camomile tea?'

'Oooh, please?'

Felicity cuffs her daughter's ear. 'Don't be bad.' She feels a rush of love for her child; everything else may slip through her fingers but that, at least, will never go away.

The door opens and Gerry appears. Felicity wags her finger and says, 'You can make him watch it while I get the tea. He likes young women in bikinis.'

'Actually, we've got a visitor,' he says.

Meeting her husband's eye, Felicity whispers, 'A visitor? It's nearly ten.' She reads his grave expression and follows him into the hall to discover Pat Babcock unwrapping her grey Pashmina.

'Pat!'

'Apologies for the intrusion,' says the Detective Chief Superintendent 'I know it's late. But I need your help. Somewhat urgently.'

'Of course.' Felicity scans her colleague. 'You look worn out.'

'It's been a long and difficult day. But this isn't a conversation we could have on the phone.'

Gerry smiles and says, 'Why don't you ladies go into the study. I've got a pretty decent single malt. I'll fetch it.'

Babcock beams 'Good man!'

Felicity escorts Pat into a spacious room overlooking the garden. It's Gerry's study, but the only concession to his taste is a couple of high-backed leather armchairs and a desk that once belonged to his father. 'Make yourself comfortable,' she says as she turns on a couple of table lamps.

Babcock settles in one armchair, the lamplight throwing her fleshy features into stark relief. The bonhomie she usually practices is absent.

Felicity sits down opposite and waits for her to speak.

The cop rubs her face. 'Well, I don't know where to begin with this. I'm shattered, as you can no doubt see.'

Felicity nods.

'Tired but not crackers' she adds. 'Though you're going to think I am.'

'Okay,' says Felicity.

'You've always thought that this was a bio-terrorist attack.'

'It's the pattern of transmission, it's never suggested to me an emerging pandemic. But, hey, what do I know? I'm not a virologist.'

'What if I told you we received a warning,' says Pat. 'We had an informant, who correctly predicted what would happen.'

'Wow! And you didn't feel you could share that information?'

'What would PHE have done if we had?'

'We might've been prepared. Had some idea of what we were facing. The advice we issued could've been—'

'Felicity, the advice wouldn't have been any different.' The tone is callous to Felicity's ear, suggesting Pat Babcock is far more ruthless than she appears. Or perhaps she's just beyond it.

'How do you know that?' says the Professor.

'I know how government works,' Babcock replies. 'When the shit hits the fan, covering their arses is always the political priority.'

'That's a very cynical view. I'm not sure I share it.'

'We're coming at this from different perspectives.' Weariness has stripped away the facade, revealing a pitiless glint in Babcock's eye which makes Felicity uncomfortable.

'As CMO, my perspective is to put public safety first. To save lives' she says.

'My job is to stop this by catching the perpetrators,' comes the cop's caustic reply.

'Then why haven't you?'

Babcock laughs and says 'Well, good on you, Professor, I've always thought that deep down you were a woman of metal.'

'What do you want, Pat?'

'The informant went to ground before the first cases were reported. We've been looking for him, as you can imagine. Turns out he was killed in a motorcycle accident at the beginning of January. But—'

A soft tap and Gerry enters the room carrying a bottle of Lagavulin 16-year-old, two glasses and a ceramic jug of water on a tray.

Catching the look in his wife's eye, he places it on the desk, says, 'I'll leave you to it' and retreats.

Felicity gets up, pours generous measures into the cut glass tumblers and hands one to Pat. 'Water?'

They each add a splash to their glasses.

Babcock sips and gives an appreciative nod. 'Anyway, here's the thing. He carried a donor card and they transplanted his heart into another man who appears to have, I don't know...' she heaves a sigh, 'memories or visions of things that happened to his donor.'

'Are you serious?'

'Never more so,' says Babcock, taking another mouthful.

Felicity takes a moment to absorb this.

'Are you asking me if this is possible?'

'I'm telling you he appears to know things.'

'Come on, Pat. Have you ever watched a magician? They appear to accomplish the impossible, but it's always a trick. You need to check this man out a bit more thoroughly.'

'We have,' says Babcock. 'But what about theories of cell memory? Isn't all science magic until someone does the experiment that proves something is true?'

'I'm not a neuroscientist. I can't answer any of this.'

'Would you talk to him?' says Babcock.

'To what end?'

'I can't interrogate a heart transplant patient. I might hurt him.'

Felicity stares at her colleague in astonishment. 'So you want me to do it?'

Babcock sighs 'One of my analysts has been doing some digging and thinks we should try hypnosis.'

'Oh for goodness' sake.'

'There seems to be credible academic research it can help release suppressed memories.'

'Your own memories, not someone else's. But even that's controversial.'

'If he could tell us fragments of things—'

'Perhaps he's leading you up the garden path? He could be a fantasist? Time of national crisis, he wants or thinks he can save the world. Wants to be the centre of attention. Talk to a psychiatrist. I'll give you some names. They can tell you about all sorts of mental disorders that could explain this.'

'Actually,' says Babcock, 'he doesn't want to do this. He's a Devon farmer, who got ill, had a heart transplant and wants to get on with his life.'

Babcock knows this isn't strictly true. But explaining her deal with Adam Hardy doesn't seem helpful at this point.

'Then how will you get him to agree to being hypnotised? It won't work if he's resistant.'

'You see, you do know about it. Weren't you involved in a research project once?'

'Have you been checking up on me, Pat?'

'Not in a bad way.'

The two women eyeball one another.

Babcock takes another sip of her drink and says, 'Your husband has excellent taste in whiskey.'

The Professor shakes her head. 'You're seriously asking me to hypnotise this poor man to see if he shares any memories with your dead informant?'

'I know it's a lot to ask,' says Babcock 'but, basically, yes.'

'It's a ridiculous idea.'

'It's also the best lead we've got.'

28

As she crosses the yard, picking her way between the icy puddles, the security lights come on. She hates having to come in on her own so early. It's creepy. But now she's a supervisor, there's no choice. Someone has to open up.

She looks at the van; the beat-up old Luton van is where the stupid tosser left it. It's beyond a joke, beyond annoying. Yet again, they'll have to work around it to load. Three weeks ago, no more than that, getting on for four, she asked him to move it. She said it all politely, explained. She was dead respectful. He gave some lame excuse. Flat battery, he said. Promised he'd sort it. She'd like to flatten his sodding battery for him with a nice big sledgehammer. Except that now he's the boss. Some kind of takeover, she supposes; never a good idea to ask too many questions though.

The morning he dumped the van there, he called her into the office. He's a lairy bastard, everyone thinks that. Even the gang on the estate—they think they're tough little sods—they give him a wide berth. Rumour has it, in the past, he's done stuff for the Albanians. Nasty stuff. Things that if you saw, you'd look away. He's the kind of bloke who probably has a gun or could get one.

But he called her in and promoted her. Out of the blue. And it wasn't the usual case of do more, more responsibility but sorry about the wages. He gave her a pay rise. When she went home that day and told Ma, neither of them believed it.

'Wait and see what happens,' Ma said. 'Bastard like that, you ain't ever gonna know.'

When she got her wage slip at the end of the week, the extra was there, like he'd said.

That night she and Ma and the kids treated themselves to a Chinese. Crispy duck with pancakes and Hoi Sin sauce, her favourite.

You could say cleaning was the family business, that's what she told people, after a couple of pints of lager or when they all went out on a karaoke night. It had a ring to it, a bit of a boast, made it sound like she owned the firm. That was a bloody laugh, and the truth was she wouldn't want to own it. No way. In the ten years she'd worked there, the place had changed hands several times. And at least one boss had come to a sticky end. No one even knew what happened to him.

She'd started doing cleaning jobs as soon as she left school. Ma had always been a cleaner. City offices mainly. It was a decent living back then until the immigrants started taking over. Cleaning firms had been legit, then the gang-masters moved in. An unlimited supply of foreign workers, many illegal, had meant they could pay shit wages, undercut proper contractors and still make a mint.

Personally, she had nothing against foreigners and over

the years she'd worked with quite a few, legal and illegal, and taught them the ropes. Some had even become friends. But everyone sticks to their own lot in the end. That was human nature. She was never the sort to pick a fight, knew how to keep her head down and she'd developed an instinct about who to trust and who was likely to mug you off.

In her time there he's the first bloody Englishman to run the place and he makes a big deal of it, the English thing. She's seen the tats: St George and the Dragon on his right bicep. None the less, she's mistrusted him from the word go. Ma knew a fella who reckoned he was ex-military, and he did hang out in those sorts of pubs, drinking with the football thugs. They all bragged about being in the army and it wasn't ever true. They were hooligans in army surplus.

You could tell real squaddies, they were different. When she was young, she went out with a couple. It never stuck though, which was a pity. Her youngest, Kyle, his dad had been in Iraq. He was such a lovely fella, had a gentle nature, but he went off his nut. They pulled his body out of the river near Barking Creek. It took her a long while to get over that.

She unlocks the deadbolt on the heavy metal door to the offices and keys in the alarm code. The main shift is due to arrive at five thirty. The current staff numbers around thirty, though a couple have done a runner because of the flu thing; they work in teams, minimum of two or three depending on the size of the contract. Until recently, they did private commercial or upmarket residential cleans and never strayed far outside the M25. But the boss before this one had ambition. He got bigger contracts, some with councils and hospital trusts.

And she had to admit it was a smart move. They were better payers, and it was always legal. Some of the staff objected though. Mostly because it involved loads of bog cleaning, always the least popular job.

She's turning on all the lights as a 4x4 pulls up out front. She watches surreptitiously as he gets out. Why's he here this early? He doesn't see her, he's yattering on the phone. He hovers in the outer doorway before coming into the office. A few snatches of the conversation filter through. He's doing this thing she's noticed before. When he talks on the phone he's posher, like that's his natural voice. None of the east end boy patter, which is what he does when he speaks to her and the other workers.

He hangs up, and she grabs the kettle and goes towards the kitchen to fill it as he comes through the glass door into the main office.

He smiles at her and says, 'All right, love. You're bright an' early.'

'Dunno about bright,' she says. 'You want a coffee?'

'Cheers.'

She turns to go into the kitchen but feels his eyes watching her back. It's not a pleasant sensation.

'Hang about, Wendy' he says. 'I came in early 'cause I wanted a quiet word.'

Oh shit! What now? Ma said sooner or later there'd be trouble with him.

She turns to face him, clutching the plastic kettle to her chest, and says, 'Yeah?'

'It's about the van,' he says. Then he grins. His teeth are dead white, like he's had them done. 'You think I don't listen, but I do. Truth is, it's a piece of crap.'

She inclines her head 'Yeah, well, you said it, not me.'

'But I heard from one of the lads that your brother works in a scrap yard in Canning Town.'

'Recycling, that's what they call it nowadays.'

'Yeah, recycling. So I was thinking you could get him to do us all a favour and recycle it.'

'You won't get much,' she says.

'Ain't so bothered about that,' he says, folding his arms. 'In fact, I'll tell you what. You sort it out with him. Get him to come down with a low loader. Take the bloody thing and put it in the crusher. Whatever he gets for it, you and him split it between you. Everyone's happy. Wha'd'you think?'

She sighs and says, 'They have to 'ave the paperwork. No way round that.'

'It's not a problem.' He tilts his head, all teeth and smiles. 'You're a smart woman, Wendy. And I can see you thinking this is somehow dodgy, body in the back, or drugs or something. But it's not like that. Promise you. Look for yourself. Check it over. You know me, I'm a lazy sod. You're a good employee, you keep this place running. I know that. And I thought this is a little perk. A little something for Wendy.'

'I understand that,' she says. 'And thank you.'

'Sweet. So you'll sort it out?'

She nods and heads into the kitchen to fill the kettle. Sweet. Who says that? No one she knows. Sounds like something he heard in a gangster film.

29

DAY 27. 10.25am

Adam and Jason sit side by side in the back of the car; the soft leather upholstery and that *new car* tang appeals to the petrolhead in Adam. It's another sleek Mercedes, also black, and it arrived at six o'clock to collect them.

'This is where all our bloody taxes are going,' said Zoe contemptuously.

It had been late by the time they all went to bed. After the police had left, Adam retreated to the barn, saying he needed to look the cattle over. A concerned Jason went after him.

'You all right?' he said.

What followed was the first serious fight they'd had since Adam was about thirteen and his little brother had tormented him about some girl he was trying to ask out.

He'd shouted at Jason and shoved him into the long metal trough used to feed the cows. Jason had fallen backwards and cut his hand. It was a nasty gash which bled a bit. They'd gone back into the house and Zoe had put a dressing on it. No one had said much to him after that. All he remembers now is the look of abject misery on both their faces. It had made him feel ashamed. He'd retreated to the family room where Lily was watching television. Curling up on the sofa with his daughter, he'd fallen asleep.

When he woke he was alone in the room, the television was off and Lily had disappeared. He'd wandered into the kitchen. His wife and brother sat at the pine table, which was spread with the remains of a loaf of bread, a hunk of cheese and a half drunk bottle of wine. The kitchen clock told him it was ten o'clock.

Turning to look at him, Zoe said, 'Want something to eat?'

He looked back at her, then at Jason, the dressing round the side of his hand; there was a red dot where blood had seeped through. A wave of remorse had hit him. He'd crouched down on his haunches beside the Aga. Zoe came over and knelt beside him. He'd put his head on her shoulder. She stroked his hair and rocked him like a baby.

He glanced up at Jason. 'I don't know what to say. I didn't mean to hurt you.'

His brother shrugged.

'I don't understand what happened,' he added.

'I think I pissed you off,' said Jason.

'What did I say? I can't remember?'

'Doesn't matter, mate.'

Zoe sighed. 'You said you were fed up with him following you around like some limp-wristed queer, asking if you were all right all the time. You told him you hated him, you were ashamed to have him as a brother. You told him to fuck off out of your life and to stay out.'

He got up from the floor and shook his head. 'Christ! That's terrible.'

Zoe looked at him. 'You don't remember any of that?'

'No. I remember being angry and—' his voice petered out. He sat down at the table opposite Jason. 'That's not what I think, Jace. You know that. That's not me.'

'Yeah, I know,' said Jason. 'It's not you. That's not my big brother. Question is, who or what is it?'

'What's happening to me? I don't understand. Feels like I'm going crazy. Do you think I am?'

'Yes,' his wife and brother answered in unison.

They sat in the kitchen until well after midnight, interrogating and analysing the kaleidoscope of alien memories Adam seemed to have in his head. Jason got a notebook from his bag and wrote down much of what his brother said.

What they ended up with was a series of random scenes and snippets. The crash in the tunnel, which Adam had recounted to the police, was the most detailed thing he could describe. But winding back from that, he saw the van driver, the cynical look of amusement and a face he felt he recognised. A name hovered on the periphery of his consciousness. Tom or maybe Tony? But now it all seemed vague.

Jason reminded him of what he'd said on the night he woke up in a sweat, the warning he thought he'd received. *No, David!*

Was this Mia speaking? Adam's sense of her and what she might look like was hazy. Like a wraith, the more he reached out to her in his mind, the less substantial she became.

Jason asked specific questions: hair colour, height, blue eyes or brown? Adam couldn't say. Nor could he recall why he'd felt so determined to meet her. It didn't make much sense anymore. His conversation with the police about her was another fragment which had floated out of his conscious mind, returning to some nether region he couldn't seem to access.

The whole thing left him feeling wretched and confused. James Chang's reassurances and explanations seemed irrelevant. And trying to understand what was going on in his own mind was exhausting.

It was Zoe who said, 'Okay, say it was this Mia who said *No, David!* If she was trying to stop him, she must've had some notion of where he was going. Did she somehow see the danger?'

Adam latched on to this. 'Yes, she wanted to warn him or somehow save him.'

'But the police must've questioned her,' said Jason.

'They can't have found anything out though,' said Zoe, 'or they wouldn't have come here.'

All three of them had taken the decision that he should go to London and meet her. They agreed that whatever James Chang said, something more than a heart, an organ for pumping blood, had been passed from David to Adam. He'd been contaminated, but with what?

A slither of dead man? A kind of memory download? It was mystifying and disturbing, but it was also real and there seemed little point in trying to ignore that.

Jason had promised that he wouldn't let his brother out of his sight.

Adam had been clear in his instructions. 'If I kick off, then grab me, deck me, do whatever you have to.'

Jason grinned and replied, 'Yep, you'll get my best right hook, you'll go out like a light.'

'Try not to break my jaw, little brother.'

Jason pulled him into a fierce hug and said, 'Seriously, you need to stay close and keep telling me how you're feeling. Any freaky stuff, any dizziness.'

'I think feeling sick is a sign,' Adam replied, 'and you'll be the first to know.'

The morning traffic on the M4 is sluggish, but lighter than normal. Those that can are staying at home. Adam gazes out of the window as the suburban fringes of London roll by under a heavy sky threatening rain. Pedestrians on the street wear masks, people in their cars peer out from the safety of their private bubbles.

He turns to his brother and says, 'Weird vibe.'

'It's been like this for weeks,' says Jason.

Jason has put an alarm on his phone—every fifteen minutes they do a check in. Does Adam feel sick or hot or dizzy?

After several hours on the road, it's become tedious. So they've turned it into a game.

The phone chirrups. Jason glances at his brother. Adam pretends to puke into his woolly hat, then laughs. Making a joke of it helps. But the tension between them is palpable.

Adam has had a sleepless night wondering about various forms of mental illness and dementia. Is this what it feels like to get lost inside your own mind? And not even know you're lost. To go mad and forget who you are? To be driven by impulses you can't explain, let alone justify? He has no answers, only a pervasive sense of foreboding.

The Mercedes cruises down the Strand behind two half empty buses. The driver mumbles into his headset and pulls up close to the entrance of the Savoy Hotel.

Samir Mehta stands on the pavement, wearing a loose

cashmere scarf round his face. Passersby scurry round him but he has a cool, unconcerned air. He steps forward and opens the back door of the car.

Adam pulls his woolly hat on, winds the thick muffler round his mouth and gets out.

'Good journey?' says Mehta.

'Yeah,' Adam replies.

"She's agreed to meet you. Her understanding is that you're a friend of David Taylor's.'

Jason joins them. 'Savoy Hotel?' he says. 'Posh. We going in there?'

'No.' Mehta points down the street. 'She works for a PR firm. Their offices are a few doors down.'

'Okay,' says Adam. 'I just walk in and say my name?'

The cop nods. 'How long do you think you'll need?'

'Um, I don't know.' Adam has an overwhelming impulse to bail. He glances at Jason.

'You want me to come too?' his brother asks.

'No,' says Mehta. 'I don't think that's a good idea. Her relationship with David was pretty casual. They met on *Bumble.*'

'A dating app' explains Jason.

'She's shaken by his death, obviously. But she wants to move on with her life.'

'I know the feeling,' says Adam.

30

DAY 27. 11.30am

The entrance to the PR Consultancy is on the Strand, an anonymous wooden door with a discreet brass plaque and an entry-phone.

DI Mehta presses the button, says his name and rank; the door clicks open. Adam and Jason follow him into a mirrored lift, up several floors and through another set of doors into the reception area.

Light floods through from double height windows which cover the back of the building giving a magnificent view of the Thames with the Southbank Centre opposite.

Mehta turns to Adam and says, 'We'll wait for you here.'

Adam is nervous. 'Um, okay.'

The cop stares at him. 'Your call, Adam. You wanted this.'

'Yeah, I do.' Something in the cop's neutral but implacable manner galvanises Adam.

He walks over to the receptionist and says, 'Morning. I'm Adam Hardy. I believe Mia is expecting me.'

'Mia Cunningham?' says the woman with a polite smile.

Adam shoots a look back at Mehta and Jason, who are settling on opposite sofas in the waiting area. No one has mentioned a surname. Adam wonders if Mehta is making this deliberately difficult.

He gives the receptionist a winning smile. 'Only one Mia,' he says.

She nods. 'She'll be right with you.'

Adam hovers. He decides not to sit down. He glances across the room at his brother, who gives him an encouraging smile. To distract himself from the absurdity of the situation, he reads the text painted in large letters on the frosted glass screen behind the receptionist. *Our Values* it says in a curly font. *This is the age of engagement and.*

He doesn't get any further. From nowhere, a small oriental woman has appeared. 'Mr Hardy?' she says in a chilly voice.

Adam stares at her. This is Mia? The woman's gaze is dark and penetrating, a tiny elfin figure. 'Do come this way,' she says. The accent is American.

Walking off down the corridor, she turns to check that Adam is following. 'I'm Mia's assistant. She has a phone call that's run over. She apologises.'

'Oh, no problem,' says Adam. Relief. Confusion. He wonders what the hell he's doing and why as he follows his petite escort. Yet, at the edge of his consciousness, there's a niggle of desire. A want he can't quite pin down and a sense of anticipation. *Mia!*

The office suite is large and open-plan, with long tables in the middle, a high bench of standing desks, sofas and beanbags next to the windows, people dotted around with laptops.

His first view of Mia Cunningham is from behind. Arms folded, she's strolling away from him, wandering in a small circle, as she talks into her headset. It gives him goosebumps. A sense of knowing he can't explain.

'So, yes, okay,' she says, in a cut-glass English accent, then she laughs. 'Don't worry, it's difficult here at the moment. But it's not the bubonic plague. They aren't painting crosses on front doors. Not yet.' She laughs again, light and airy. 'Yeah, we'll speak soon. Bye.' She ends the call and removes the headset. Turning, she sees him and smiles.

The eyes are cornflower blue, the streaky blonde hair is sharply cut in a medium bob grazing her collarbone. Tall enough to be a model, she has a shapely elegance.

Adam realises he's staring. But she's obviously used to that. A flick of the head sends the hair swinging back as she holds out her hand. 'I'm Mia,' she says.

'Adam Hardy.' He shakes her hand; nothing girly about the firm handshake.

'Mind if we go out on to the terrace?' she says.

'Fine,' says Adam. 'Thanks for seeing me.'

The terrace, edged with planters of evergreen shrubs, extends across the back of the building. At the level of the treetops, it overlooks Victoria Embankment. Adam follows her out. It's cold, but although she's wearing a silk blouse over a pencil skirt, she seems unaffected. Adam wonders if he should offer his jacket.

'Aren't you cold?' he says.

She responds with another tinkling laugh. 'I rarely feel the cold. Hot blooded, I suppose.'

This sounds like a line she uses a lot. Even so, the tease works. Mia Cunningham is mesmerising. Adam tries not to gawp. Some women combine physical beauty with a presence, he's seen it before. But not often enough to be immune.

'I gather you were a friend of David's,' she says. 'I have to say I never met many of his friends. But that's London, isn't it? People keep their lives in separate compartments, don't they?'

'I'm from Devon. So I wouldn't know.'

She gives him a quizzical look. 'Devon? What do you do in Devon?'

'I'm a farmer. Dairy farmer.'

'Goodness. That sounds interesting. How did you know David?'

It's on the tip of his tongue to lie. Old school friends? Instead, he opts to prevaricate.

'Well, I haven't always been a farmer. I travelled a lot when I was younger. Did some crewing on luxury yachts. Had a great time, went all over.'

'A seafaring man, okay. Well, that's makes more sense. Given where David was coming from.'

Adam smiles. Where was he coming from? They seem to have reached an impasse. He senses her wariness but knows he has to prod.

'Tell me to mind my own business if this is rude,' he says, 'but how did you and David meet?' He knows the answer, but how else can he get her to open up.

'Oh, you know, one of these silly dating apps. That's how it started. I'm a busy woman with a busy life. I wanted something that was fun. It was a casual thing. That suited us both. I wasn't about to take him home to meet my mother.'

Adam nods. 'It was tragic the way he died.'

She frowns. 'Yes, indeed. He loved his motorcycle, though. Kept trying to get me to go on the back. I did once.

Back in the summer. We drove down to Brighton for the day.'

'Sounds great.'

'Well, I only did it that one time. To be frank, it was a bit of a scary experience. He was quite a reckless driver. A real speed freak. So, when I heard what happened, the accident, I was shocked of course, but not surprised.'

She stares out over the river. Perhaps she's trying not to cry. They're both pensive. It feels awkward to Adam; he's intruding on her grief under false pretences.

He casts around for something comforting to say. 'Didn't he have a red crash helmet? Red for danger, I guess.'

'Yes, that's right.' She smiles wistfully. 'I don't want to speak ill of the dead, Adam. And he was your friend too. But, you know, sometimes you meet people and they're way out there on the edge. They don't follow the normal rules. And I suppose, if I'm honest, that was part of the attraction. Some of my colleagues go in for booze or coke. I had a dangerous liaison. That was my buzz.'

'Was he dangerous?'

'You know his background, surely?'

'Not exactly.'

She tilts her head and gives him a chary look. 'David wasn't his real name.'

'Wasn't it?'

'You didn't know he was Syrian?'

Adam takes a deep breath and says, 'I never met him in person.'

'What? You were a Facebook friend or something?'

'Look, I feel awkward about this.'

'Seriously?' Fixing him with a stony stare, she says, 'I'm not a complete moron, Adam Hardy. The police have been asking me all sorts of questions I can't answer. I've told them what I know. He was a Syrian with a lot of money, a volatile temper, and probably some dubious connections. Now they want me to talk to you. So who the hell are you and what do you want?'

'Did you know he carried a donor card?'

'What's that got to do with anything?'

'I never met him. But I had a heart transplant back in January. David Taylor, or whatever his real name is, he was my donor.'

Mia Cunningham raises her sculpted eyebrows, but the face, with parted lips, remains as perfect and blank and frozen as a Greek statue.

After a moment she exhales and says, 'Well, that's not something I could've ever predicted.'

31

Adam stares out of the window as the Mercedes winds its way round the Aldwych and turns north up Kingsway. Mehta sits in the front with the driver, his brother is in the back beside him.

Jason leans into him and whispers 'How you feeling?'

'Okay,' Adam replies. But what does he feel? Does he even know?

The encounter with Mia Cunningham ended with polite awkwardness on both sides. A complete stranger walks into your office and says: I've got your dead boyfriend's heart. That would be distressing enough for anyone to cope with. In the circumstances she was restrained, although shocked, obviously. But she'd asked for Adam's number and said she needed time to think about what he'd told her.

Throughout the meeting, he'd felt tense, a knot in his stomach, but otherwise fine. No head spinning. No nausea. If it reminded him of anything, it was of his teenage self, out clubbing with his mates, plucking up the courage to chat up the prettiest girl in the room. And it was easy to imagine that Mia Cunningham would be the prettiest girl in any room. Except pretty didn't quite encompass it. Her age, he guessed, was late twenties. She was a beauty. Poised and exceptional, and she knew it.

Mehta cranes round in his seat to look at Adam. 'Did you get what you were looking for?'

'Not sure' Adam replies.

Mehta has the steady, probing look of a cop. But Adam suspects he's always been a watcher. His professional facade is courteous enough, but he has a whiff of cynicism about him. Everyone's guilty until proved innocent.

He nods and says, 'Happy to keep your side of the bargain?'

'Do I have a choice?' says Adam.

'Of course you do,' the DI replies. 'These are strange circumstances, I'm sure we'd all agree. But there's no coercion here. You have agreed to co-operate of your own free will.'

'You want me to sign something? In case I collapse or freak out,' says Adam.

'No,' says Mehta. 'I'm checking you're okay.'

The rest of the journey passes in silence. Adam glances at his brother. Jason gives him a tight smile.

If Jason hadn't stuck his neck out, risked his job, they wouldn't be sitting there. But then, where would they be?

Adam's thoughts are becoming jumbled. The reason he's agreed to this is to protect his brother. He needs to remind himself of that. But he's feeling hot. Outside, the day is raw and freezing but the car's heater is pumping out a fug of warm air. Someone, maybe Mehta, is wearing a sharp cologne. The smell is cloying. Adam loosens his scarf.

'Can you turn the blower off,' he says to the driver.

Jason shoots him a concerned look.

Mehta himself flicks the switch and a draft of cool air wafts across from the vents at the front.

Adam smiles at his brother even though he's wondering: *am I okay?* He focuses his mind on the kids. Lily, when she has a mad half hour, rushing round the house, squealing with glee. Ryan, small but so solid, crawling everywhere at top speed, over grass, stone pathways, nothing daunting him. I'm okay, he tells himself.

The air-con is refreshing. Before he was ill, he never bothered much with scarves and jumpers. Out on the farm in all weathers, he didn't feel the cold. Zoe always insisted on turning the heating up. He walked round the house in a T-shirt and shorts. He was always feeling hot; for him, it was normal. Like Mia Cunningham, hot blooded. What would it be like to sleep with a woman like that? The thought is arousing.

The car pulls up outside a smart double fronted Edwardian house. They're somewhere in north London. Adam isn't familiar with the area, but it's posh. Across the road there are a couple of photographers standing behind a crash barrier, fingerless gloves clutched around steaming coffees.

'Right,' says Mehta 'hat and scarf on. Both of you. Make sure you wrap it round your face.'

'Where are we?' says Jason.

'Straight up the steps and into the house,' says Mehta.

Adam stares through the smoked glass window at the photographers. 'Are they here for us?'

'No,' says Mehta. 'Ignore them.'

32

DAY 27. 12.50pm

The hallway is high-ceilinged and elegant with a polished wooden floor. Adam glances down at his shoes, wonders if he's leaving a messy footprint, traces of Devon mud in this chic London home.

As the police officer on the doorstep admitted them, Adam noticed he had a gun in a holster on his hip. But Mehta was right behind them, hustling them inside.

Adam shoots his brother a covert look as a door opens down the hall and Pat Babcock appears. 'Well,' she says, 'thanks for agreeing to this.'

'I'm not sure what I have agreed to,' says Adam.

Pushing the door wide, Babcock invites them to enter.

Another stylish room, all white walls and expensive furniture. It occurs to Adam that it's the sort of thing his wife would like.

Standing in the middle of the room next to a leather

Eames chair is a woman who looks familiar. A face from the television?

She steps forward, holds out her hand to shake and says 'Hello Mr Hardy, I'm Felicity Oldroyd. And in case you're wondering I'm the Chief Medical Officer.'

'Okay,' says Adam, 'I thought you were supposed to be some sort of hypnotist.'

The woman laughs. But it's Babcock who speaks.

'This is a strange situation for all of us, Adam. It involves issues of national security. But I know you understand that. We're hoping that Professor Oldroyd's extensive medical experience will assist us in this and ensure that your well-being isn't compromised.'

'But you're planning to hypnotise him?' says Jason.

'We're going to try some deep relaxation,' says the Professor. 'It's not brain-washing or anything like that. We can stop at any time—'

'Look,' says Adam, it's hard to keep the desperation out of his voice, 'I know something weird has been happening to me. I've been told it's the drugs. Or some kind of stuff my subconscious is making up. But it feels more like I'm going mad. I do things, say things that aren't me, then I don't remember.'

He swallows hard. *Shit.* He can't cry in front of all these people. That would make him look even more certifiable. But Oldroyd takes his arm. 'You don't mind, do you?' she asks and guides him towards the chair.

She speaks softly. 'It's understandable that you'd feel like this, Adam. You're recovering from major surgery and you're on some pretty strong medication. All these things are factors which will affect you. And you're confused. Anyone would be. Why don't you take off your jacket and make yourself comfortable?'

She helps him remove his jacket and scarf; Jason takes them.

As he settles in the lounge chair and leans back, she pulls up the stool and sits down next to him.

A nod from Babcock and Mehta puts a firm hand on Jason's shoulder and ushers him out of the room. Babcock reaches for the dimmer switch, turns down the wall lights and steps back into an unlit corner.

'Ignore everything else,' says the Professor. 'Look at me.'

Adam can feel the tension in his shoulders, it's making him fidgety. 'I'm sorry,' he says.

'No need to be. There's nothing to worry about.' The calmness in her tone is reassuring. Her face is in shadow, only her rimless glasses are catching and refracting diamonds of light. She takes them off and smiles at him. Her pupils are large and dark. They fix him with an intent stare. It's hard to look away.

'I want to help,' says Adam.

'I know you do.' That gaze doesn't waiver.

'None of this is my brother's fault. I don't want him to lose his job.'

'I'm sure he won't. Just look at me, Adam. Keep looking. And think about your breathing.'

'That's the best thing since the transplant.'

'The best thing?'

'I can breathe again.'

'That is good. So let's breathe together, shall we? And concentrate. Slowly in. Then out again. Does that feel nice?'

He nods as his chest rises and falls. Rising and falling. It's less of an effort to hold her gaze now; the eyes seem to glisten.

'Can you feel the air flowing in? Your lungs filling?'

'Yeah.' He must admit, it feels good. It's certainly calming.

'Now take a bigger breath. Enjoy that air,' she whispers.

He inhales deeply. He does enjoy it.

'And let it go.' He exhales.

'Slowly in. And out again.' The glistening gaze, the silky soft voice.

The weariness of it all sweeps over him. His eyelids tingle and close.

33

DAY 27. 1.05pm

Jason stands in the hallway with Adam's jacket and scarf looped over his arm.

He glares at Mehta and says, 'I promised I'd stay with him.'

The cop folds his arms and glares back. 'They know what they're doing.'

'You don't think that. You think it's all a load of crap.'

'Do I? Well, you're the analyst, aren't you, Jason? So you'd know about these things.'

The tart sarcasm feels like deliberate provocation. But there's something in the way Mehta watches him. Jason's felt this from their first encounter. It's as if the cop is waiting for something. But what?

'I'm surprised that a Detective Inspector in Counter Terrorism runs around like a bagman. Your boss, basically she's got you doing a Sergeant's job, hasn't she?'

Mehta sniggers. 'You think, if you piss me off enough, I'll lose my temper and blurt out something I shouldn't?'

'And what would that be? That you're desperate. And if you mess my brother up in the process of this, not one of you will even care?'

'You think we're that callous?' The cop frowns and for an instant there's a glimpse, the merest hint of something else. Shame? He gazes at Jason, his dark eyes are probing and intrusive.

Jason's steaming and he hits straight back. 'I've worked for the Met long enough to know that's exactly what you lot are. Collateral damage, that's what he'll be in the report. If there even is a report. Cause what are we doing here? In a private house? Off the grid? Is that the idea?'

The DI shakes his head and says, 'Look around you, mate, analyse what you see. Now, in your vast experience of the Metropolitan Police Service, does this gaff look to you like a typical, off the grid, safe house? Christ, have you never heard of the cuts?'

'I'm not stupid. And I'm not your mate. This is her house, your CMO. I got that when we arrived because, apart from anything else, it's featured several times on the news. Talking of which, anything happens to my brother, and I'll blow the lot of you out of the water. On social media, on the telly, I'll be talking to everyone and anyone who'll listen.'

'At least we understand one another. Presumably you'll also be looking for a new job?'

Jason steps forward, right into Mehta's face; the DI is taller but not by much. Jason is heavier, stronger and running on high-octane rage. The desire in him to punch the cop fizzes. He has the satisfaction of feeling Mehta recoil.

'Like I give a fuck!' he hisses.

'Can I get you boys anything?' The voice wafts from the top of the plushly carpeted stairs. Gerry Oldroyd follows it down. 'Got some cold beers in the fridge.'

'We're fine, thank you, sir,' says Mehta.

34

DAY 27. 1.06pm

Adam seems to be sinking, then tumbling downwards, faster and faster into a dark chasm, a black hole.

But up ahead there's a light.

The landscape is bleached and barren, a grey dust eddies in tiny tornadoes between the derelict buildings, and silent, except for the slap of loose cables against a metal pole. This was once a thriving place, but no more. Bombed out, collapsed roofs, crumbling walls; it's hard scrambling over the rubble, even harder to keep his head down as he does it. And carrying the body makes it more difficult. Blood has soaked through the shroud, dry and crusted now, the metallic smell sharp in his nostrils. But he couldn't leave her there, leave her to them.

He glances round to check the boy is behind him. They don't speak. Eight years old, he carries the rifle. Following obediently, the child needs no instruction.

Pausing for breath, he resettles the body on his shoulder; she was never a heavy woman. The grey hair hangs loose. She carried him for nine months, now he's carrying her. He made a promise to take her home, to lay her to rest in a proper grave.

A sudden rat-tat-tat; the automatic rounds whoosh past him, strafing the wall behind, showering him and the boy with exploding slivers of concrete. They dive for cover, he drops her, she rolls.

Grabbing the gun, he checks the magazine and releases the safety catch. It's an old Heckler and Koch G3 semi-automatic with flip-up sights and a wooden stock. It belonged to his father. Resting the barrel on a section of broken wall, he points it in the gunfire's direction. And waits. All he needs is another round, then he'll see the muzzle flash. But nothing. All is quiet. The minutes pass. High above in a cerulean blue sky a buzzard circles.

Then he sees them. His eyesight has always been razor sharp. They're on the move—two, no three of them—putty-coloured fatigues, barely discernible. They're making a run for it. Across open ground. Perfect.

Settling the stock against his shoulder, he takes his time, inhales, takes aim. Hold your breath, squeeze the trigger gently, as his father taught him.

The first body lurches and tumbles; at maybe two hundred metres distant, not a bad shot. Steady, inhale, hold the breath, fire. The second one goes down. Another precise headshot. The third one hits the deck, scrabbling for cover. There is none.

He adjusts his aim. Number three is on his belly, crawling. Track him, wait. Let him think, let him hope. Hope is the best form of torture. He knows that. The hope they had for his father, that he'd be released, until his battered corpse was dumped outside their apartment from the back of a pickup. Those army guys, smoking and laughing as they did it.

Number three struggles to his feet and sprints. Steady aim, inhale, hold the breath, fire. Whomp! He can't hear because it's too far away. But he knows that sound, relishes it every time; another kill, he loves it. Each one is better than the last. In such moments, his spirit soars and he feels alive.

Spinning in a black vortex. Inhale, exhale, *not enough air!* Adam Hardy gulps for breath. A searing, red-hot dagger carves through his chest. The pain erupts from him in a sob. His eyes snap open and he's back in the room, the cool, semi-lit room, not the arid sweep of scorched earth and blazing sun. Heavy, opulent drapes, shadowy pictures on the walls. A smell of wax polish and whiskey.

'Where are you, Adam?' says the silky voice. 'Tell me about it.'

His fingers go to his cheeks, which are wet with tears. 'I'm crying' he whispers to himself, not to her. *Bitch.*

'Yes,' she says. 'Tell me what's upsetting you.'

The faint scent of whiskey. Is it coming from her? She sits in front of him, watching him. No. He looks around. He'd forgotten about the fat cop. She sits in the corner, holding a glass, beady eyes monitoring him. He knows at once that he must run.

Feeling sick, he jumps to his feet.

'It's okay, Adam—'

Not okay. That much he does know.

She gets up too, but there's no way they're stopping him. A couple of strides and he's at the door. He wrenches it open. People in the hall. *Fuck them.* He barges through. Gets the front door open. A hand on his shoulder, he turns and throws a punch. Fist connects with flesh. He feels the crunch. A babble of voices. But he's outside, running down the steps. He's in the street and clear. He runs.

35

DAY 27. 4.45pm

The police put out an alert, but Jason's theory is that he won't have gone far. In the event, that proves correct. The light is fading and an icy drizzle falling when Jason and a uniformed officer find him hidden in heavy shrubbery in a garden at the end of the street. Curled in a foetal ball, he's asleep and damp, not wet, the dense evergreen foliage of the laurel hedge forming a canopy over him.

Jason crawls under the hedge, puts a hand on his shoulder, and eases him awake.

'Adam? It's me.'

Opening his eyes, Adam rubs his face. 'Jason?'

Jason clasps his hand. 'Yeah. I've been looking all over for you.'

Adam peers at him. He seems confused and fearful. 'Oh no, did I hit you again?' he says.

'You hit Mehta. Gave him a bloody nose. But he deserves it. I wouldn't worry. Let's get you out of here.'

'I need to go home, Jace.' The tone is hoarse and desperate.

'I know.'

'Get back to Zoe and the kids, then I'll be all right.'

'I agree.' He pulls off his jacket and wraps it round Adam. 'Stay here for a moment.'

Climbing out of the shrubbery, he says to the police officer, 'Can you go back to the house? I'm bringing him back, but I don't want to crowd him. We'll be there soon. Tell them to wait. Okay?'

The officer nods and trots off.

Jason pulls back a laurel branch. 'Come on, mate. Quick! Let's get out of here.'

As they hurry down the street away from the Oldroyd house, Jason summons a cab. It's already dark when it meets them on the corner of the main road.

The cabbie winds down the window, he wears a tight beanie hat, a surgical mask and vinyl gloves. 'Jason?' The mask muffles the voice.

Jason nods 'Paddington station, yeah?' He pulls on the handle of the rear door, but it doesn't open.

The cabbie is scrutinising Adam. 'Is he all right? Not sick?'

'He's a bit pissed. I promise you.'

The cabbie considers this for a moment, lean pickings for him. People aren't going out. Then he clicks open the door and they get in.

Traffic is light. The silent journey to Paddington takes less than twenty minutes. Adam is drowsy and disorientated. His head dips and rests on his brother's shoulder. Jason lets him doze.

The train is half empty. As they walk through the carriages looking for a suitable seat, people give them hostile glares. This is the new normal; claim your space and create a cocoon around it to protect you from infection. The variety of face masks has proliferated, ranging from the improvised to the high-tech with built-in filters. Some people even wear goggles. They pass a whole family decked out like extras in a sci-fi movie. At the end of the carriage, tucked in a corner seat, an old man sits alone, coughing. There is no one anywhere near him.

When they finally settle, Jason pulls a couple of chocolate bars from his pocket and two bottles of water. This is all he could get at the station; most of the usual kiosks and coffee shops have closed. Lack of staff and supplies have caused many businesses to flounder. Few people linger in public places.

Adam devours his chocolate in three mouthfuls. Jason offers him his own bar.

'Any better?' he asks.

His brother nods.

'What happened in there?'

Adam cracks open his bottle of water and takes a long draft.

He looks at Jason and sighs. 'Don't ask.'

'But I am asking. You freaked out and assaulted a police officer.'

'I'm sorry. I'm so sorry I've got you into all this.'

'I called Zoe. Her Dad's picking us up at the station. But we need a plan.'

His brother frowns and says 'Maybe I shouldn't go home.'

'What do you mean? You said that's what you wanted.'

Adam takes another swig of water. He struggles to hold the bottle steady, the water spills.

Jason reaches across the table, seizes his hand and says, 'You're still my brother. You'll always be my brother.'

'What if I'm dangerous?'

'You mean Mehta? I tell you, I was tempted to give him a smack myself. He's a sarcastic bastard.'

Adam is shaking his head.

'What if I'm a killer?'

'What do you mean?'

'My donor, what if he killed people? Killed lots of people. What if I've got a killer's heart?'

'Is that what you've remembered?'

'It's not a memory. There's something inside me, Jace. I don't know what to call it. A sort of demon that takes over. And I can't control it.'

'We should never have agreed to them hypnotising you.'

'Makes no difference. It's there. Whatever it is, it's in me. And you know what, I wish I'd never had the transplant. I'd rather be dead than this.'

36

DAY 28. 10.15am

Darkness is better. He opens his eyes and looks up. It's not dark. Diffuse morning light is seeping through gaps in the curtains. His gaze roves across the ceiling and stops at the cornice round the edge. There it is! That zigzag crack in the moulding; he's been promising Zoe that he'd get some filler and repair it. Relief floods through him. It's okay. He's home, in his own bed.

Sitting up, Adam glances at the clock and now it all comes back to him. He and Jason took the train from London. His father-in-law was standing on the concourse at Exeter station, arms folded with a belligerent look on his face. He'd started in with a barrage of questions and Jason had said, 'For once in your life, Phil, why don't you shut up?'

Adam smiles. The look on Rowett's face was priceless. Throwing back the duvet, he gets out of bed. He's thirsty. It's after ten. Why have they let him sleep in? He roots out some old trackie bottoms and a t-shirt, pulls them on and heads downstairs.

Making a beeline for the fridge, he takes out the orange juice and drinks in gulps straight from the carton. His wife hates him doing this; it sets a poor example for the kids. But the kids are nowhere to be seen. Jason is alone, sitting at the pine table with a mug of coffee and his laptop.

His brother gives him a wary smile and says, 'Good sleep? How you feeling?'

'Thirsty.' The carton was half full, but Adam empties it.

Jason gets up. 'Want a coffee?'

'I can do it. Where's Zoe?'

'She's out in the barn. Talking to a couple of blokes from DEFRA. They're looking at the herd, reviewing something about Bovine TB, I think.'

Adam frowns. 'From the Ministry?'

'Yeah. Maybe they're planning to gas a few more badgers.'

'Is she pissed off with me?'

'Mate, no one's pissed off with you. We're concerned.' He pauses. 'But don't worry, I didn't tell her what you said last night on the train.'

'Which bit?'

Jason is staring straight at him. Adam notices his right fist is clenched. He taught his little brother this trick back when he was an unhappy teen: you press your fingernails hard into your palm to stop yourself crying. 'That you'd rather be dead' Jason says.

Adam turns away, switches the coffee maker on.

'Look, yesterday, it was all a bit full on. I wasn't exactly thinking straight.'

'Remember where you ended up? Under a hedge?'

'Yeah, I remember. I was trying to keep dry.'

Jason sighs and says, 'However bad you feel you can't do that to them, Adam. You can't.'

'I know.'

'There has to be another way.'

'Like what? I go back to Chang and say give me another transplant. But this time I want a normal heart. No gangsters or murderers or police informants. Minor addictions I can handle: coffee, gin, ice cream. And if you can throw in something positive, like a better taste in music, that would be nice.'

Jason cracks a smile. The ploy works. He relaxes.

Adam smiles back. He could maybe tell his brother about the killing. But the erotic charge he felt with the memory of each hit? The sheer pleasure of it and the itch in his fingers to hold a gun in his hand. How can he make that sound anything other than sick?

'Why don't you make us both a coffee' he says. 'I'm going to pop out to the barn and see if Zoe needs any help. She's got little tolerance for all the official form filling and bullshit we get from the Ministry.'

Jason nods and Adam escapes.

At the back door, he slips on a pair of wellies and heads out.

It's good to feel the raw February air on his body. The sharp cold is cleansing. His thoughts are jumbled. He needs a chance to think, to process. Jason means well but his concern is claustrophobic.

Adam walks across the yard but takes a deliberately circuitous route to the barn. Going to find Zoe was an excuse; she's perfectly capable of dealing with officialdom, better than him in fact.

When they'd arrived back from London it was late. He'd hardly said a word to his wife. He'd gone straight to bed and fallen into a heavy dreamless sleep. That, at least, was a relief. But the events of the previous day remained with him, a kaleidoscope of random impressions. And some searing memories. He had to make sense of all this.

As he turns the corner into the huge vaulting shed, the warm smell of the cattle cheers him. Cows milling about, feeding at the troughs, it reminds him of what matters. He knows all of them individually, and they know him. Reaching out, he rubs the damp nose of an inquisitive young heifer; it tries to lick his fingers.

Zoe and her visitors are standing beside a pen at the far end of the barn. They have their backs to Adam as he approaches them.

The two men wear Barbours and green boots; Adam can hear his wife speaking. She's good at this kind of spiel: the health of the herd, the proper procedures, she always sounds knowledgeable.

As he gets close, Zoe turns and says, 'Ah, here's my husband. Adam, I was explaining how we're...'

But Adam doesn't hear any more. There's a thunderous rushing in his ears as one man turns towards him and smiles.

That smile. The slow turning of the head and the supercilious curl of the lip; it would be impossible to forget it. This face is burnt into his memory. It belongs to the driver of the Luton van. It's David's killer, his donor's killer, and he's here, standing in the barn talking to Zoe.

37

DAY 28. 10.20am

Jason rests his cup under the spout of the coffeemaker. This morning Adam seems okay, but it's impossible to tell. His brother is a proud man, he knows that. As before, after one of these episodes, Adam wants to retreat from his vulnerability. He pretends everything is normal, but what does that even mean anymore? Jason is at a loss.

As the coffee trickles into his cup, he wonders what he should do next. Mehta has left him several curt messages. But the police can't force Adam to help them. Or can they? Phil Rowett has yet again offered the services of his lawyer. Maybe they should take him up on that.

This is what Jason is pondering when the back door flies open and hits the wall with a crash. Adam comes bolting through it.

'Where's your phone!' he screams.

'What?'

'Your phone, Jason. Your phone!'

'Umm, I dunno, the table.'

Adam scans the table. 'Where? Where!'

Jason fumbles in the pocket of his hoodie and finds the phone. 'No, it's here.'

Grabbing it, his brother runs off down the hall towards the front door.

'Adam?' Jason follows. 'What the hell's going on?'

By the time he catches up Adam is outside the front of the house, holding up the phone and videoing a black BMW X5 as it drives out through the farm gate. He runs after it, continuing to video as it turns right into the lane.

Zoe is striding towards him from the direction of the barn. She shouts across the yard 'Adam, what is going on? What the hell was that about?'

The car disappears round a bend. Adam lowers the phone, his breathing ragged from the exertion.

'They're not from DEFRA' he gasps as he collapses on to his knees in the roadway.

Zoe gets to him first. 'What d'you mean? What are you talking about?'

Jason joins them. Adam scrabbles to his feet, clutches his brother's arm and says, 'Listen to me Jace, phone Mehta. Send him the video. They can trace the number plate.'

Zoe is scanning her husband. 'My God, you look awful. What's going on?'

He turns to her, desperation in his eyes. 'I don't know what they told you. They're not from DEFRA. I recognised him. He's the man that drove the van that killed David.'

Zoe stares at him. 'What?'

'I think his name's Tony.' Adam tumbles sideways, Jason catches him.

'I'm going to be sick.'

Jason eases him down until he's sitting in the middle of the lane.

'Just breathe,' says Zoe.

'I'm sorry, I—' his head lolls. His eyes close.

Zoe feels his forehead. 'He's burning up.'

Bending, Jason grasps Adam round the torso and loops one arm round his neck. 'Let's get him inside.'

Jason heaves, Zoe gets the other side and helps. Between them, they half carry and drag a semi-conscious Adam towards the house.

He mumbles, 'I'm so sorry...'

Twitter Feed

DAY 28 .

True Health News @truehealthnews
Quoting: **Keandra Smith** @keandraS24
NHS is rationing supplies of new anti-viral. I'm in A&E
department in Sheffield. Managers say none for us, London
the priority #governmentlies
9k Retweets 14k Likes

Anushka Anand @AA539
Replying to @truehealthnews
In London, Charing X hospital, same here. Anti-viral being
kept for private patients. #governmentlies
10.7k Retweets 11.2k Likes

Keandra Smith @keandraS24
Replying to @AA539
Staff hit too. Nurses have died but they hush it up. You?

Anushka Anand @AA539
Replying to @keandraS24
No one knows. Colleagues disappear.

True Health News @truehealthnews
Time to face the people AND TELL THE TRUTH
@PHE_ukAnd where is CMO? Advising gov to lie? #Pan-
demic #governmentlies #powertothepeople
12.3k Retweets 15k Likes

Mark Carter @MCB666
Replying to @truehealthnews
Dame bloody Felicity leading the cover-up at Yarls Wood.
#Pandemic #safeandsound #callthemtoaccount
873 Retweets 971 Likes

38

DAY 28. 4.20pm

Zoe Hardy paces. Her mind whirls. She can't stop. There are probably a couple of Xanax ligging around in the bottom of her bag. Tempting though it is to take them she resists. She must stay sharp.

Her husband has been airlifted by helicopter to Birmingham. Occasionally, the Rowett millions come in handy and this is one of them. There had been some nonsense from the hospital about whether they'd accept him because of the likelihood he was infected with H7N9. But James Chang was helpful, he felt responsible for Adam, and they provided a special room in the isolation unit set up to treat victims of the epidemic. At present, the unit's half empty but the hospital remains on high alert.

A suite in the private wing has also been set aside for Zoe to use. Since both she and Jason might be infected, they too were asked to remain in isolation until the test results clarify the situation. Chang promised these would be expedited. It probably helped that Zoe was effusive in her gratitude and backed this with mention of a potential donation by her father to one of his research projects.

Zoe can't stop thinking about the Xanax. She pours herself another coffee instead; she must focus. Her mind flits to the children. She worries about the impact of all this on them. Lily is turning into a jumpy, anxious child. The school has expressed concern about her behaviour. Zoe has yet to tell Adam about that.

The little girl clings to him at every opportunity. She knows they might lose him and Zoe is at a loss to find ways to reassure her. Ruth has spent a lot of time with her granddaughter and this has helped.

In terms of the flu virus, when Adam and Jason got back from London, the children were tucked up in bed. There was no contact with their father, so the chances of infection are small. She repeats this to herself like a mantra, although she's not sure whether she believes it. Nothing feels certain anymore.

Phil Rowett had driven the brothers home from the station but insisted he was fine; both he and his wife had been vaccinated with the regular flu shot, which, the government was assuring the public, would protect them. Will it protect them? Zoe can't worry about that, too. There's so much fear and misinformation swilling around, ramping up anxieties. Turn on the television and every news bulletin is in permanent crisis mode. After a month, it's become exhausting. Disaster fatigue has set in.

Her mind skips back to the stopover she and Adam made in Stratford-on-Avon on the way back from their previous trip to Birmingham. For a blissful few hours, it appeared the horrors of the last year had been erased. It was the first time they'd had sex in eighteen months. She'd been nervous at first, fearing that such exertion might do him harm. But it was as if they'd stepped back in time to when they were younger, a new couple, passionately in love but hesitant and getting to know one another.

It had lifted her spirit and given her hope for the future. Then, that hope had been snatched away. The cruelty of it had formed a solid, sour lump in her belly and once again, anger came to her rescue. Over the stressful months since Adam's heart attack, it was the only thing that had provided her with energy to fight back. Like an animal at bay, she'd relied on it to survive.

The room is a pleasing shade of yellow with several comfortable sofas, a small fridge and a kettle. Zoe criss-crosses it diagonally, arms folded; Jason sits.

Being holed up with her brother-in-law is not a situation she would've chosen. He always gives her the impression that they're in competition for Adam's affection. She finds Jason secretive and, at times, resentful. The stupid trip to Nepal was Jason inveigling her husband into yet another private, testosterone-driven adventure from which they excluded her.

She watches him; he's on his laptop, he's always on his laptop. Zoe wonders if he has some network of nerdy friends out there in cyberspace. He has few actual friends, as far as she can see, and has never managed a proper relationship, which is why he continues to leech off his brother.

Jason glances up at her. He seems edgy and nervous, another thing that annoys her. Why can't he grow some balls?

'Well' she says, 'what do you think?'

'DEFRA's website isn't helpful. I've sent them an email

asking if they sent anyone to the farm. I doubt we'll get a reply.'

She sighs. 'Okay, what about Mehta?'

'I don't know if that's such a good idea.'

'Why not? That's what Adam said: tell Mehta.'

Jason exhales and stares down at his keyboard. There's a lethargy about him that never fails to provoke her.

'What's the problem with that?' she says irritably.

'I don't know if we should bring them back in the loop right now.'

'Oh for god's sake, Jason. Adam thinks his donor's killer came to our house and you don't think we should tell the police?'

'How reliable is that? After they hypnotised him, he was in such a state. I don't even think he knows what's real any more.'

'Excellent. And what if he is right and some criminal or terrorist came to check us out?'

'Well, what did these guys say? It could be a co-incidence. Was there anything suspicious or threatening about them?'

'No! I've told you. They said they were reviewing the bovine TB campaign. Asked me what we thought about it. I did most of the talking.'

Jason gives her that look, silent and condescending; you're a woman, he seems to say, you would do that.

She turns away. She must hold on to her temper. Losing it with him plays into his hands. Then he looks all sulky and forlorn, as if it's her fault they don't get on.

'Okay,' she says, 'think about this. There's all this panic going on about the flu pandemic.'

'It's not clear it is a pandemic.'

'All right, but, whatever it is, does it seem likely that DEFRA would think about bovine TB right now?'

'Probably not.'

She gives a satisfied nod. 'Exactly. It doesn't add up.'

Jason stares at her. She finds him difficult to read at the best of times. But she has a strong sense that there's something he's not telling her. He covers for Adam and Adam covers for him. They've been doing it since they were kids. Getting either to speak revealingly about the other has always been impossible.

Zoe decided she was going to marry Adam Hardy when she was fifteen. He was tall and strong-limbed and beautiful. His attitude to life was laid back, but he had a roguish humour too. He always did what he wanted, which is what had made him such an attractive quarry.

Her university years were boozy. She managed enough work for a decent degree, but the boys she dated and dumped never quite erased her teenage crush on Adam. And she was level-headed enough to know it was a crush. When they met up again years later, she expected to be disappointed. She wasn't.

Lean and tough, he looked like the star of a surfer movie, a romantic nomad who'd never settle. It took Zoe Rowett less than a year to walk him down the aisle and turn him into a dairy farmer. All the guests who came to the spectacular wedding marvelled at how she'd done it. They were the image of the perfect couple.

But getting what you want can come with a downside. That was the lesson she'd gradually learned. Happy-go-lucky became slippery; there was something about her gorgeous husband that couldn't be grasped. On the surface, he gave her what she wanted, including two equally gorgeous children, except when he didn't want to. Then, like a will-o'-the-wisp, he eluded her. He wouldn't even row. He shrugged and became evasive. Whereas she'd expected it would always be the two of them. Having adventures together, he liked to divide his life into neat compartments. Her compartment, once lover, was now the wife and family, but there were other spheres where she was neither included nor welcome. She'd discussed this with her mother, who'd said dryly that this was how many marriages worked.

Shortly before the Nepal trip, when he became sick, she'd started a casual affair with a Polish contractor who ran a potato picking gang. The sex wasn't that good, but because it was clandestine and risky, at least it gave her a buzz and the illusion she was back in control. The contractor broke it off when he heard Adam had suffered a heart attack, said it made him feel awkward.

Turning to Jason she says, 'Why do this the hard way? If they were legitimate officials from DEFRA, then the police will find that out in no time. Then we'll know what we're dealing with.'

Jason has no chance to reply. There's a tap on the door and James Chang enters. He's come in person, and what flashes through her mind is: this is not good.

But he beams and says 'Good news on the test result. Adam is showing no trace of the avian flu virus. And we're bringing the fever under control.'

'What is it then?' says Zoe. The knot in her gut loosens.

'I think a more common-or-garden bacterial infection. As I've said to you before, he is vulnerable to such infections. Particularly if he's been under stress.'

The surgeon gives her a quizzical look, but the question hangs in the air. Zoe decides not to enlighten him. Adam wouldn't want that.

'Can we see him?' she says.

'Of course,' says Chang, 'but maybe one at a time. Let's not crowd him out.'

'Not a problem,' says Zoe, and without a backward glance at her brother-in-law, she follows the surgeon out of the door.

39

DAY 28. 4.25pm

Being back in the hospital is the last thing Adam wants. On his back again, staring up at the ceiling. He's looked at too many ceilings. Irritation bubbles up.

He remembers being in a helicopter—the whump whump of the rotor blades—where does that memory come from? Some war zone? Were they dropping barrel bombs? Sweeping in low over the apartment blocks like vengeful Valkyries? Is that what he remembers? He feels confused. But he's learned a new trick. If he lets his mind coast, it's easier. Don't question everything. Accepting he might not have an answer drains some of the anxiety out of the situation. It makes it more bearable. He waits for the ripples to settle. If he focuses on the immediate and the concrete, his choppy thoughts will calm. The annoyance will abate.

There's an intravenous drip in his arm—he flexes his wrist—a clip on his finger and wires connecting him to several monitors. But he feels better. Floaty, but no pain or nausea. They watch him through the glass, the medical staff. At one point, he thinks he sees Chang. Is it Chang? The nurses who come in to tend him are gowned and masked. Does he have the flu? Is this what's happening to him? He's survived a heart transplant to die of the flu?

The blinds are tilted, but the light is fading. It must be late afternoon.

The door opens and two people come in. They wear the full protective rig. Only when one of them leans over him and he sees her eyes, does he recognise his wife.

'Zoe?' he says.

'You gave us a bit of a fright,' she says and he can hear the relief in her voice.

He has to ask, 'Sounds crazy I know, but was there a helicopter?'

'Yes. You know Dad donates to the air ambulance. He made some calls. They were happy to help. They airlifted you here to Birmingham.'

'I might've guessed. Have I got the flu?'

'No,' says the other person. It's Chang. 'You have an infection, but it's responding well to treatment. You should be back on your feet in a few days.'

'A few days?' How long has he even been here?

The surgeon nods. 'But you have to listen to me, Adam. I've told Zoe, and I'm sure she understands. You need to as well. You simply cannot afford another episode like this. You must rest and give your body a proper chance to recover. A good diet, gentle exercise and plenty of tranquility. No upsets, no conflict, no cortisol. You're a sailor, as I recall. Maybe get out on the water once the weather improves.'

Adam smiles. 'I'd like that.' He thinks about sailing again. It's not a lie. He would like it. Ocean racing. Escape. Possibly not what the doctor has in mind.

'Then do it. And if you're tempted to get involved in something you shouldn't, that you know is stressful, ask yourself: does it matter more than my health?'

'I will' says Adam.

Chang nods. Adam wonders what he knows. Was he consulted before the police hauled Adam off to London? Probably not. That was stressful, certainly. Perhaps Chang seems knowing because he's a doctor and part of the bedside manner routine is to appear wise and confident. Nevertheless, he has put his finger on the nub of the problem. What does matter most to Adam? *They came to his house. The killer came to his house.*

'Is my brother here?' says Adam.

'Yeah, we both came with you,' says Zoe.

'Has he got that video on his phone?'

Behind the mask, Zoe huffs. 'You need to forget about that. Let us handle it. You heard what James said. No stress.'

'Did he speak to Mehta?'

'I don't know. I'll have to ask him.'

'Ask him now.'

'Adam–'

Chang and Zoe exchange looks, and the doctor says, 'I think we'll give you something to help you relax and rest.'

A chemical cosh. *Don't you dare!* He wants to lash out, defend himself, but he can't. He's too weak. He has to bide his time. Why can't they understand what's happening? Don't they see the danger? He's become a target. Wasn't he always a target, though? They know about him. *They always knew.* Now they know about his family.

His family? He looks up at Zoe. It's been tough, but she's stood by him. Does that make her a good woman? He wants her to be a good woman, but he's feeling a little giddy again. He remembers carrying a dead woman—his mother?—she was a good woman. But his mother is alive. The thoughts meld. It's impossible to separate them.

It's only the drugs. Chang has stepped away from the bedside to be replaced by another masked figure, who's injecting into the cannula. It takes only seconds for Adam to feel the full hit. He keeps his gaze fixed on Zoe. Zoe is his wife. He has such a rush of love for her.

Except the eyes have changed. They don't belong to Zoe. It isn't his wife. This woman is far more beautiful. Far more arousing. And this woman loves him back. She's the one who can help him, who can save him. That's what he must remember.

40

DAY 28. 6.05pm

It's already dark and Wendy is at her desk checking tomorrow's schedule when the headlights sweep into the yard and come to rest glaring straight at her through the office window. She knows at once it's not one of their vans, wrong colour lights; these have the icy, bluish tinge of a high end German manufacturer. Mercedes is her guess and when the driver extinguishes them, she's proved right.

In her gut she has a sinking feeling, but decides to sit and wait to see what happens next. Since the business with the Luton van, she's been expecting a visit, though not quite in this form.

She did as he'd asked—hard not to—called her brother and got him to come over with a low loader. The paperwork was in order; it went to the crusher. She told her brother to keep the twenty-five quid. In her experience, if you could lie to the old Bill from some sort of moral high ground, it came out better, and they were more likely to believe you.

The driver gets out and opens the back door, never a good sign. Then from the backseat a fat calf emerges, followed by a stout body and a neatly coiled bun. The overhead lights in the yard throw the short figure into stark relief as she marches towards the door. Wendy has a terrible sense of foreboding; whatever is coming her way, it's not good.

Getting up from her desk, she walks through to the reception area to meet the visitor. The other girl in the office has gone home. There are some lads in the warehouse, but apart from that, the place is empty. She feels exposed.

The door swings open and the woman enters. Short but formidable, with the same solid shelf of a bosom that most of Wendy's battle-axe old aunties have. Expensive coat. Long fancy scarf, one of those Indian things that are really soft. What should she do? Definitely not a casual: how can I help you, love?

Wendy waits.

The woman smiles and says, 'Is Tony about?'

'Haven't seen him all day,' says Wendy. 'Well, several days, come to think of it.'

'I've got the right place?'

Wendy hates coppers like this. They treat you as if you're stupid. Why can't she do it properly and with a bit of respect? Pull out the warrant card and ask politely.

It's annoying enough for Wendy to say, 'Is this official, then?'

This seems to amuse the snotty cow. But still no ID and no respect.

'No,' she says, 'not at all. We're old friends, Tony and I. But I haven't seen him for a while.'

Wendy nods. This is a side of him she hadn't imagined:

police informant? A snitch; Ma wouldn't be surprised. She's said all along he was bad news.

'I just work here,' says Wendy.

'What's your name?' says the woman. The tone is peremptory. She assumes she has the right to know.

'Annie' says Wendy. Ma's an Annie, and strictly speaking, she is too. But no one has ever called her Anne. Calling a kid after its parent has always seemed a daft idea and bound to lead to confusion. Wendy gave her kids deliberately different and modern names: Jade, Callum and Kylie.

'Well, Annie,' says the woman, 'I need you to do me a favour. I want you to send him a text.'

'Tony? A text?'

'Get your phone and I'll dictate.'

'I'm not sure I've got his number.'

'I'm pretty sure you do.'

As the woman smiles, her face wrinkles. She seems jolly except for the eyes, which are diamond hard.

Wendy sighs. She doesn't owe him anything. The only question is who she should fear more.

She pulls a smartphone out of her cardigan pocket, finds his number and nods.

The woman leans on the reception counter and laces her fingers; they're covered in expensive rings. The chauffeur-driven car, the rings. She's a boss, no question. This is the correct choice.

'Okay,' the woman says, 'write this: Pat came round this afternoon. She wants to talk. Urgently. Said this is not a request. Get in touch now.'

Wendy thumbs the words in, looks up 'Want me to read it back?'

'No. Send it.'

Wendy presses send.

The woman smiles and says, 'Well done, Wendy.'

She knew all along. Bitch.

The boss cop turns on her heel and strolls out.

41

DAY 28. 10.30pm

Felicity Oldroyd sits at her long kitchen table; her neck and shoulders ache, a tension headache hovers behind her eyes. She pours a ginger and ginseng herbal infusion into a bone china cup as she scrolls back and forth through the reports on her laptop. She sips and scrolls; she's been at it for hours, searching for discrepancies, trying to tease out more information from the data.

But the latest figures confirm yet again what she's been saying all along: the H7N9 virus has not mutated. Random outbreaks are traceable to separate geographical locations, which suggest different sources. A pandemic has been avoided although you'd never think that from the media brouhaha. There have been no new fatalities for three days. But the public is not reassured. In the last survey, fifty-two percent thought officials were lying. The stream of vitriol directed at Public Health England has become relentless, especially on social media. Even Dougie Lacey, its embattled

CEO and a consummate media manager, has been unable to avoid the flak.

Having spent the afternoon at a lengthy COBRA meeting, chaired by a tetchy Hugh Ryder, she feels bone weary. A leading PR consultancy has been brought in to promote the Secretary of State's new anti-viral wonder drug and to calm the situation. Felicity's contention that they should simply tell the public the truth and back it with the statistics has been treated with disdain by these so-called experts.

'What perhaps Professor Oldroyd fails to understand,' said the supercilious young woman, 'is that if people don't trust you, then being right is not an advantage. You come over as elitist and uncaring.'

Elitist and uncaring!

Ryder and several others round the table had greeted these remarks with sage nods. Felicity found some comfort in the fact that Dougie was as irritated by all this as her. He's effectively been cut out of the loop.

Felicity had scrutinised the young PR consultant. At first sight, she seemed a surprising choice for such a weighty task. But her poise and self assurance were impressive. She couldn't have been thirty and yet being summoned to the Cabinet Office didn't faze her at all. It probably helped that all the men in the room, and they were in the majority, couldn't take their eyes off her. She had an arresting beauty, and she knew how to take full advantage of it. Her attitude appeared to be that she was their equal or even their superior, and Felicity found herself envying such absolute confidence.

As the young woman laid out her plan of action, Felicity tried to listen and hold her temper. She managed the latter, but not the former. The gist of the argument appeared to be that perception was all that mattered, a viewpoint the Chief Medical Officer rejected from the marrow of her bones.

After the meeting, as she walked down Whitehall with Dougie Lacey, he shook his head and said 'My dad was a gunner in the RAF during the war. Reminds me of his favourite expression. FUBAR. Ever hear that one?'

'Fucked Up Beyond All Reason?' said Felicity.

Dougie grinned. 'Well, I've never heard you use that sort of language before, Professor.'

'I'm doing a lot of things I've never done before,' she replied.

She didn't mention her ridiculous attempt to hypnotise Adam Hardy. No one in the department knew about that, and for good reason. There had already been several newspaper articles questioning her approach and personal competence in the job. She remains annoyed with herself that she'd ever allowed Pat Babcock to browbeat her into it.

The kitchen door opens and her daughter wanders in. Looking up from the screen, Felicity smiles, takes off her glasses and rubs her eyes. Amidst all the public furore, at least she has the emotional bulwark of her family. But whereas her husband and son protect her in their masculine ways, Phoebe is her real solace.

Her daughter walks over to the table and says 'C'mon, Mum. Isn't it time you stopped?'

'Probably. I keep going over the figures. This is what we should rely on, facts and figures. The evidence. What's the use of science if we don't believe it.'

Phoebe nods and seems to hesitate.

'What?' says Felicity, catching her daughter's eye.

'Have you talked to your cop friend today?'

'Pat? No.'

'Are you still annoyed with her?'

Her mother sighs. 'The whole thing was mad. I cannot believe what we did to that poor man. It's my fault though, I should never have agreed.'

'Did the police find him?'

'Apparently, his brother took him home.'

'That's something. Y'know, I've been thinking. Maybe you need to change your approach to all this. Because it's not only about people getting the flu.'

'Darling, my job is to—'

'Hear me out, Mum. Please.'

Felicity takes her daughter's hand. 'Okay, I'm sorry. I am listening.'

'The news channel I told you about, True Health News—'

'How the hell do they know what's true? This is what's true, the official verifiable figures. Anything else is bogus.'

'Bogus they may be, but a lot of people believe that these sites tell them what's going on. True Health News has got over five million followers now.'

'We've got PR people who are supposed to be dealing with all that. Although they don't seem too keen on telling people the truth, either.'

'I told you that True Health News is pushing the theory that the avian flu was brought here by immigrants.'

'It's all such nonsense, Phoebe. Immigrants get blamed for all sorts. They always have. I think you should ignore it.'

'They're saying that this strain of avian flu is being spread by illegal migrants who escaped from the Immigration Removal Centre at Yarl's Wood.'

'Well, that is rubbish, clearly.'

'I know, but people believe this stuff.'

'Not if they've got half a brain.'

Phoebe perches on the end of the table. 'Mum, they're

saying that you're in charge of the cover-up. That you need to be held to account.'

'Well, I can't be held to account for something I haven't done.'

'I think Counter Terrorism should be looking into who's actually behind True Health News. Who backs them? Where do they get their money from? You should speak to Pat.'

'I think the police have got enough on their plate, don't you? Sticks and stones. The Daily Mail or is it the Sun are saying I should resign because I'm incompetent. You have to ignore it.'

'It's toxic this stuff. It's turning into an orchestrated attack on you personally. We're worried about you. Dad's talking about hiring a bodyguard.'

Felicity sighs. 'Oh for goodness sake! We've already got a policeman on the doorstep. There is no pandemic and eventually the police will find out who's disseminating the virus. It'll all blow over. These awful people'll on the internet will find someone else to pick on.'

'I don't think it's that simple. It's about saying the experts are incompetent. The government is incompetent and you can't trust them. But you're the one caught in the crossfire. Talk to Pat, please.'

'Okay.'

'You promise?'

'Yes. Darling, I don't want you worrying about me.'

'Mum, I don't want to have a reason to worry.'

42

DAY 29. 7.54am

DI Samir Mehta walks into the office as the night shift is preparing to go home. He looks around, an exhausted team, flagging morale. Everyone, including him, is near the end of their tether.

He goes over to one of the junior DS's and says, 'That vehicle trace I asked for, can you check who was given the action?'

As he waits for her to access the action management system, he tries to remember her name; she's new and mousy, drafted in from the Boroughs. 'Doesn't appear to be on the system.' She gives him an apologetic look.

He nods. But it's probably his fault. They're all on overload. Procedures have become ragged.

Late the previous afternoon, he'd received a phone call from Zoe Hardy. She gave him a garbled tale of some incident at the farm. She was phoning from Birmingham where her husband had been readmitted to hospital, which in the DI's opinion was probably the best place for him.

On Babcock's instruction, Samir had taken the day off. He had a split lip, badly swollen, and some bruising to his upper jaw, courtesy of Adam Hardy. Hardy had run at him like a mad bull. It hadn't been his intention to get in the way, but he'd tried to grab Hardy's arm and been punched in the mouth for his pains. He was lucky not to have lost a tooth.

After the phone call, the wife forwarded him a video clip but it came from Jason Hardy's number. This annoyed Mehta all the more since he'd been trying to get that slippery sod on the phone ever since he and his brother did a runner. Jason's phone had been tracked, obviously. So the police knew where they'd gone. But that wasn't good enough for Babcock. She insisted she wanted the Hardys back onside.

The irritation that he feels at the thought of Jason Hardy rises to the surface once again. Why does the analyst piss him off so much? There appears to be no reason why this particular individual should get under his skin. He reminds himself it's unnecessary and unprofessional. But there's something in the way Hardy looks at him that's weirdly knowing and he hates it.

In view of this, he's decided to focus his attention on Zoe Hardy. They don't need Jason. She can be their conduit to Adam.

Approaching his desk, he notices that the Detective Chief Superintendent is already in her office. She might've even been there all night. He assumes Babcock has a life. She wears a wedding ring. Does she have a family? She never talks about them. But the present situation means she's getting relentless pressure from the top.

He strolls over, taps on the door, enters and says 'Morning, guv.'

Babcock is cradling an outsized mug of coffee. She glances up at him. Her face is etched with weariness, but she smiles. 'Quite a smack he gave you. Sure you're all right?'

Mehta shrugs. 'I've had worse. Possible lead came in late yesterday though. I talked to Zoe Hardy. She reckons they had a visit at the farm from two blokes claiming to be DEFRA officials. When Adam saw them, he had a complete freak out and insisted one of them was David Taylor's killer. She sent us a short video clip of their vehicle. I'm trying to trace the plates.'

Babcock rubs her face slowly. 'Did you give that to Pramiti to follow up before you went home yesterday?'

'Gave it to someone. Might've been her. I was a bit out of it.' He fingers his lip.

'Yeah, understandable.' Pat Babcock's flinty gaze comes to rest on his face, but the tone is offhand. 'Pramiti did come and ask me about it. Doesn't look like a goer, though. Vehicle is registered to DEFRA. So Adam Hardy is probably off his trolley. He collapsed with a fever and he's back in hospital. I told Pramiti not to waste any more time on it.'

A shiver runs through Mehta as he meets his boss's eye. He's used to her unnerving stare. But he senses something else; it's tiny, a bat's squeak of tension, of evasion, rippling between them, but it's there. A lie? That makes no sense. Why would Pat Babcock be lying to him?

'Okay,' he says. 'But I thought you were anxious to get the Hardys back onside?'

She lounges back in her chair and sighs. 'Sami, I'm loath to admit it, but I think you were right all along. Some heart transplant patient who's got his donor's memories? It's a load of bollocks. You told me, Felicity Oldroyd told me. We were clutching at straws. Time I listened to sense, don't you think?'

'So we're not interested in David Taylor anymore or the notion he was deliberately killed?'

'It's all speculation. Where does it get us? There's no real evidence.'

Mehta nods and smiles. 'Whatever you say.'

43

DAY 31. 11.15am

Adam holds open the swing door for an elderly couple and gives them a smile. The influx of Saturday morning visitors into the hospital is part of the routine. Worried relatives looking lost, peering at the signs, asking directions. He's familiar with the rhythms of the place. He woke at five and has been wandering the corridors, chatting to a few people, for several hours. The coffee shop opened at nine. He got a double shot espresso.

Zoe has rung, apologetic. She's stuck in traffic. But that doesn't bother him. Walking the corridors, stepping up the pace, reassures him that he's fit and ready to go home. Four days in hospital is enough. Chang's registrar came in at seven, checked him over and discharged him. He has more antibiotics and strict instructions to finish the course. But he feels fine. More importantly, he's got plans.

He stops beside a hand sanitiser attached to the wall, squirts a shot of antibacterial gel into his palm and rubs it over his hands. Taking precautions, protecting himself from infection, he's learnt his lesson.

After the days of fever and confusion, his mind is clear. He's made a decision. Doing nothing is not an option. He must grasp the nettle. He must protect his family. That impulse is strong, but he's no longer in any doubt about where it comes from. *It comes from him.* It's what he's always done. *Family first.*

He knows what Zoe will ask him. *She'll badger him. Women do.* Is he himself? What can he tell her? Thoughts scoot around his brain. He bats them away.

In the middle of the night, he got up and went to the bathroom. As he flicked the light on, they'd almost blinded him: the white tiles. Since then his dreams are full of white tiles. Except, is it a dream? In his sub-conscious, deep down, they were already there, more like a memory—a cold, clinical whiteness, laced with a cloying, sickly smell. But the meaning eludes him. It hovers out of reach. *Wait. Stay focused. It will come.*

He loiters near the main entrance. Each time the automatic doors slide open, a blast of icy February air rushes his way. But he welcomes it. It's fresh and cleansing. The sharp cold of an English winter is pure. Uncontaminated by viruses and infections.

People are scurrying to and fro, faces swathed in scarfs, some wearing more elaborate masks. The sadness of it all hits him for a moment. It raises a lump in his throat. This flu epidemic bothers him. *Surely it bothers everyone.* But David knew about this. The police have said as much. It's yet another thread that he must grasp.

He sees Zoe before she sees him. His lovely wife is making a dash from the car park. The doors glide open to admit her. She looks tense and hassled, eyes frantically scanning until they come to rest on him.

She hurries over and says, 'Oh God, have you been waiting long? The traffic was manic. Some pile-up on the–'

Taking her hand, he cradles it. 'Hey, not a problem. Your hands are freezing.'

'Left my gloves in the car.'

He rubs her fingertips. 'I'll drive home. You can relax now.'

'You sure you're well enough?'

'I'm completely fine.'

He picks up the carrier at his feet. 'Look what they gave me.' He pulls out a plastic pump bottle of antimicrobial gel. 'Industrial strength. I may end up completely OCD from endless hand washing, but I'm never getting another infection.' He laughs.

Her smile is anxious. 'And you've got all your meds?'

'Locked and loaded.' He clenches his fist against his chest in a military salute.

She gives him a puzzled look. 'You sure you feel all right? Properly yourself. You know what I'm saying?'

He smiles. She's nothing if not predictable. *Women.*

'Of course I'm myself' he says. 'Can't you tell? It was a bacterial infection. Now I'm better.'

'Okay.'

He grins. 'Shall we go?'

The doors slide open and they walk through.

Adam turns to her and says. 'Oh, I hope it's okay, but I've invited some people to Sunday lunch tomorrow.'

This stops Zoe in her tracks. 'Jesus, Adam. Tomorrow! What people?'

'We could do a standard roast. Yorkshire pudding,

maybe. Something typically English. We've got lamb in the freezer, haven't we?'

'Are you crazy? You've just got out of hospital. And by the time we get back—'

'C'mon, Zo. Be a sport. You can rustle something up. The kids'll love it.'

Adam starts to walk towards the car park. Zoe has to trot to catch up.

'Wait a minute,' she says. 'What's going on? What about the men who came to the farm? I did phone Mehta and tell him.'

He turns to face her, but he smiles. 'That's all right then. I'm sure the police'll sort it out.'

'You're not worried anymore?'

'No. What I am is fed up with hospitals. I want to go home, get back to normal and do normal things with my family.'

'Who on earth have you invited?'

'Mia. Remember I went to meet her in London. David's girlfriend.'

'Yeah, well, I'm hardly likely to forget your trip to London, given what we've been through.'

'But that's over,' he says. 'I thought this would be a good way to celebrate.'

Zoe scans him. She seems at a loss.

'When did you ask her?'

'This morning. Talked to her on the phone.'

'And she's free tomorrow? It's a bit short notice.'

'Normal people do spontaneous things, Zoe. She understands that, said it was a great idea. She's looking forward to seeing the farm.'

'Adam, we need to think about this.'

'I have thought about it. I'll help with the cooking. Promise. But hey, here's the best bit. Guess who she's bringing with her?'

'I can't imagine.'

'His brother. David has a younger brother.'

'A brother?'

'Nizar. A younger brother. Like me.'

Adam smiles serenely. The moment Mia had spoken the name, Nizar, Adam had felt a rush of joy. There was no way to explain any of this to his wife.

Zoe gives her head a shake and says, 'What the hell is going on? This whole thing is getting more crazy. You're definitely not yourself.'

'No, it's getting less crazy. You need to stop worrying. I know what I'm doing.'

'What about the men who came to the house? Have you talked to Jason?'

Taking her hand, he brushes it with his lips but the tone is imperious. 'I don't need to. I've told you. I know what I'm doing. Now shall we go home?' He holds out his hand. 'Keys?'

44

DAY 32. 8.30am

Samir Mehta often takes his bike out on a Sunday morning. It's a Cervelo road bike, an indulgence he has to admit, but he loves to ride. Sometimes he cycles to Liverpool Street, takes the train to Saffron Walden and does a circuit of the Essex lanes. He doesn't belong to any club—they're all full of middle-aged men—he prefers to ride alone. It gives him time to think.

He lives in Shoreditch, shares a flat with his sister, who's two years older and works for a City law firm. Their father purchased it when they both became university students in London. His argument was it would save him money in the long run. Ten years later, it's done considerably more than that. The block has a roof terrace with a picture postcard view of the City, plus a basement gym, pool and sauna. Samir makes a point of never discussing where he lives with colleagues. If pushed, he'll mention he flat shares, which sounds more acceptable. He never takes anyone back.

His relationship with his sister is amicable, not close. They live separate lives but conspire to prevent their parents from discovering anything that would upset them.

The earlier encounter with Pat Babcock has disturbed Samir. He's had some tough jobs in the Met and he's not naïve, but the idea that the Chief Superintendent may be doing something untoward has shocked him, leaving a gnawing doubt that won't go away. Why would the boss lie to him?

As soon as he left her office, he went in search of Pramiti. The DC is one of the unit's stalwarts, an experienced officer with no desire for promotion but always meticulous.

'You weren't around' said Pramiti, peering over her half-moon specs at Mehta. 'I ran the BMW's plate. Turns out it was cloned. Registered to a garage in Stirling. Phoned them, they seemed kosher, said the vehicle was a write-off six months ago.'

'Definitely dodgy plates, then.'

'Yep.'

'And you told the boss this?' said Samir.

'Obviously. But she said it was a piece of nonsense.'

'A piece of nonsense?'

'Her exact words. Said we didn't have time for stuff like this. We had to prioritise. Told me to delete the file and the video. Take it off the system.'

Samir smiled at the DC. 'Well, she's probably right. You ditched the video?'

'Yeah.'

'Talked to DEFRA at all?'

'No. Sorry.'

'Not a problem.' He smiled to conceal his unease.

Since then, his brain's gone into overdrive. He can understand Babcock's frustration with the Hardys and her desire to move to more useful lines of inquiry. But why this elaborate lie?

He has no reason to doubt what Pramiti told him. She's done her job. And she'd been specifically instructed to get rid of the video. What the hell was Babcock up to? Why had she shut this down so firmly? It smacked of a reactiveness that didn't fit the boss at all.

Scrolling back through the messages on his own phone, Samir found he'd deleted the whole stream from Jason Hardy, probably out of sheer irritation. But was he making a mountain out of a molehill here? He'd been sceptical of Adam Hardy's so-called memories from the outset. He tried calling Zoe Hardy. She didn't pick up. Nor did Jason.

As he puts on his cycling gear, travels down in the lift to the basement car park and gets his bike out of their secure lock-up, his brain niggles around the question. Babcock told him the vehicle did belong to DEFRA, but that was an outright lie. Is she trying to conceal something? But what? And why?

He needs to get out of London. That's his intention. Maybe Kent? He rides down to Tower Bridge, crosses the river. But part of him already knows where he's going.

The traffic on the Old Kent Road is light. People aren't going out. The return to normality that the government is desperate to engineer doesn't seem to be working.

He scoots off through the side turnings. He worked in Lewisham for a while in a special unit targeting gang violence. He knows the turf. He also knows Jason Hardy's address. He's looked at it on Google, a large three storey Victorian mansion that needs a coat of paint and is divided into flats. Jason has a one bed on the top floor. The road is nose to tail with parked cars. Samir has to get off his bike to squeeze between them. The pavement outside the property is freshly strewn with rubbish; it looks like a fox has been at the bins.

Now he's arrived, Samir feels oddly nervous. He tells himself not to be so stupid. Holding the bike in one hand, he uses the other to press the doorbell. No response. After a few polite bursts, he starts to get impatient. Jason's at home, he got an update from the phone tracker. But it is Sunday morning. He leans on the bell.

Finally, the entry phone crackles to life. 'Yeah?'

'DI Mehta. Can we have a word?'

'You are kidding?'

'Open the door, Jason.'

A couple of seconds pass and the lock mechanism clicks. Samir pushes the door open, hoists the bike on to his shoulder and scales the stairs two at a time.

When he gets to the top flat door, it's ajar. He props the bike against the banister. But as he steps into the tiny hall, he sees that Jason is not alone. He's in the narrow galley kitchen, with only a towel round his waist, pressing twenty-pound notes into the hand of a young man.

Man may be an exaggeration. The boy who edges past Samir in the hall with a nervous grin can hardly be twenty. He has almond eyes and a sparse downy beard. He scurries off down the stairs.

Jason Hardy gives Mehta a challenging glare and says, 'Coffee?'

The DI nods. 'Bit early. Sorry. I need to talk to you about that video you sent us.'

Jason folds his arms over his bare chest, smiles and says, 'Oh dear, Detective Inspector, have I embarrassed you?'

'Sod off, mate. Put the kettle on.'

Samir wanders into the small sitting room. It's compact but neat. Sofa, television and a wall of books. The cop suppresses his discomfort by scanning the shelves: an eclectic mix of fiction and non-fiction, plus some serious tomes on maths and computer science.

Jason comes in with a cafetière of coffee and two mugs. He's put on a t-shirt and shorts.

'Hope you take it black' he says. 'So have you been in touch with DEFRA?'

'Slight technical hitch. It's mayhem in our office at the moment, as you can imagine. Seems someone mislaid the clip. I wonder if you can let us have another copy. I did try phoning but you've been ignoring my calls.'

Jason gives him a quizzical look, then sitting down, he pours the coffee. 'It was Zoe's idea to send it to you. Her argument is why would DEFRA be worried about bovine TB with all this other stuff going on.'

'She's got a point. Sounds like you were reluctant to do it, though.'

Jason huffs and shakes his head. 'Adam landed up back in hospital with a serious infection. He could've died thanks to you lot.'

'But he's okay now?'

'Do you care?'

'Yes, of course we do.'

Jason stares at the cop and says, 'Why are you even here?'

'I told you, we mislaid the clip.'

'Really?'

'Yeah, really.'

'Okay,' says Jason with a sigh. 'I didn't want to send it because I think Adam could be imagining things.'

'Why do you think that?' says Mehta.

'It's hard to explain.'

'Try.'

'I don't think he understands what's happening to him. I don't think any of us do. It's making him paranoid. He mixes all sorts of things up. And that stunt with the Professor, well, that tipped him over the edge.'

'Wasn't my idea.'

'Also, let's not forget, it turned out he had a bacteriological infection. He could've been hallucinating.'

'Have you talked to his doctors about this?'

'No. I haven't had the chance. Zoe's... well, protective.'

Mehta picks up his coffee. He paces. He's all too aware of Jason watching him from the sofa.

He sighs. 'Let's play devil's advocate for a moment. Let's say these men weren't from DEFRA.'

'What? You think Adam's right?'

'All I'm saying is it's logical to check. And if they're not who they claim to be, it needs looking into. Wouldn't you agree?'

'In the end, that's why I sent you the clip.'

Samir takes a deep breath. He knows he's standing on the edge of a precipice. He should probably discuss his suspicions about Babcock with a more senior officer, one of the DCI's perhaps? But where would that get him? Babcock has a huge reputation. She's not someone to mess with. And they're all stuffed suits. He doubts any of them would confront her. If he carries on, that could be it, brilliant career over. He hesitates, but only for a moment.

'Yeah, well, I explained about that. It's Sunday, I don't want to trek into the office. Can you access the system from here, trace the plates? Then we'll see.' He makes the request sound as casual as possible.

Jason gazes up at him. 'Seriously? I'm in enough trouble for illegally accessing the databases.'

'I'm asking you. So you're authorised to do it.' Will Jason buy this? Samir hopes curiosity will win out.

But Jason frowns. 'I could forward the clip to your team. Wouldn't that be easier?'

'They're snowed under and I don't want to wait for an answer. Okay?' The impatience in the DI's voice betrays his nerves. He's blown it. Jason will smell a rat.

However, Jason gets up, goes over to his bag and takes out his laptop. 'Fair enough' he says.

Opening the laptop, he switches it on. 'You want me to use my codes?'

'Yeah. Don't look at me like that, Jason. We both want the same thing here.'

'I doubt it. I want to protect Adam. But I've no idea what you think you're playing at.'

45

Zoe is exasperated. She's been up since six, wrangling the kids, cleaning the house. Being a domestic goddess has never formed any part of her ambition. Her cooking is functional but rarely inspired. She can follow a recipe if she has to. Adam knows all of this. But her husband seems obsessed with creating a good impression, although it appears to be down to her to do it.

The only part of his promise that he's kept was driving back from Birmingham. He's spent the morning tucked away with his laptop. When questioned, he replied vaguely that he was checking out a couple of things.

In desperation, Zoe called her mother. Ruth Rowett came over with a joint of meat—there was no time to thaw out what they had in the freezer, as Adam had suggested. Ruth prepped the lamb with garlic and rosemary, got it in the Aga and persuaded Lily to help her chop vegetables, which occupied the little girl for half an hour, until she insisted on going off to see what Daddy was doing.

Thanks to Ruth, there's a chance they will manage to put an acceptable meal on the table. But what Zoe could do without are her mother's probing questions.

'So you've never even met this woman and Adam's only met her once?'

'Mum, don't tell me it's mad. I already know that. But he's got a bee in his bonnet.'

Ruth gives her daughter a vexed look. 'As a rule, I'm not inclined to agree with your father, as you well know. But, Zoe, much as I feel for Adam—what's happened to him is terrible—things can't go on like this.'

'Like what?' Zoe is laying the table, rooting in the cupboards for serving dishes that match and giving them a brisk wipe.

'He's running you ragged. His behaviour is odd, you have to admit' says her mother. 'This is not the man you married.'

'There's nothing I can do about that.'

'There's a limit to what you can be expected to put up with.'

'Mum, it's not his fault.'

'Maybe he should see someone else. Like a psychiatrist?'

Zoe huffs. 'We can't fix him. Or pay someone to fix him. It's a process, a healing process, that's what Chang says. The truth is he's been experiencing some pretty weird things.'

'What sort of things?'

'Look, I can't go into that now.'

'Darling, we worry about you. And the children. Lily in particular is–'

'Don't! Please.' Zoe finds a tear on her cheek. She brushes it away and says, 'Oh, sod it. I haven't got time for this.'

Ruth envelopes her daughter in a hug. 'Sweetheart, I'm sorry. No one's criticising you. It's an impossible situation. But you're our daughter. Of course we're concerned.'

'I know this is affecting the kids. Ryan not so much. But Lily picks up on the tiniest thing. I know it's fear and insecurity that makes her kick off, but then I get annoyed with her. I shouldn't, but I can't seem to help myself. And now he's obsessed with this bloody woman.'

'What's it actually about? You think he's looking for an affair to boost his ego? Some men do that when they feel weak. Though I wouldn't have thought Adam was like that.'

'She was his donor's girlfriend.'

Ruth rolls her eyes. 'Oh, so it's this cell memory nonsense?'

'How do you know about that?'

'You know your father. He overheard something Jason said. He's been looking into it.'

'It's crazy, I know, but there does seem to be some truth to it.'

Ruth wipes her daughter's face with her thumb. 'Okay, well, listen to me, sweetheart. You need to calm down and see this for what it is: part of his illness.'

'You mean don't turn into a jealous harpy?'

'Exactly.'

Zoe gives her mother a kiss on the cheek. 'You're so smart.'

Ruth smiles. 'So are you, Zoe. You need to remember that.'

A squeal of excitement filters through from the hall. It's Lily. Zoe glances out of the kitchen window. A taxi is pulling up outside.

'Oh no! I don't believe it. They're here already.'

'You go and say hello. I'll sort the rest of this out,' says Ruth.

'I was going to change. Christ, I haven't even had time to brush my hair.'

'You look fine.'

'Do I?' says Zoe. 'I'm sweating like a pig.'

She cranes forward to peer out of the window as Mia Cunningham gets out of the back of the taxi. Adam and Lily are on the doorstep to meet her.

There's a young man with her, thin and dark. But Zoe hardly notices him. She can't take her eyes off Mia.

She's tall and blonde, cropped leather jacket and tight designer jeans accentuating a perfect figure. As she smiles and holds out her hand to Adam, Zoe feels her gut contract. Now Adam's determination to see her again makes sense. The toss of the head, the laugh. She's stunning. The sort of woman few men could resist.

46

DAY 32. 3.30pm

All day Adam has felt as if he's walking on air. The infection, his collapse, the difficult days back in hospital, but now he's found a new lease of life. It's like stepping out of a dank wood and finding a glorious patch of sunshine.

The lunch went well. The lamb was perfect; he managed to carve it without hacking it to pieces. Ruth joined them; it was a proper family occasion, normal and light-hearted.

It took a while, but even Nizar began to relax. Adam knew nothing about him before he arrived. Mia's suggestion that she should bring David's brother had taken him totally by surprise.

But Ruth stepped into the breach. She has the polite but unobtrusive manner of a woman who has hosted enough dinner parties to know how to ask questions without giving offence. She put the young man at his ease. They learnt that Nizar loved his new life in the UK, had been granted refugee status and was in the second year of his studies as a medical student, which had been his father's profession. He didn't mention his brother and nor did anyone else.

After lunch, Zoe served coffee in the sitting room. Nizar sat on the carpet and played with Ryan and his toy cars. Lily happily joined in. Ruth and Zoe retreated to the kitchen to clear up.

Mia watched from an armchair at the other end of the room. Legs neatly crossed, she seemed so contained. But she had a wry smile, which Adam liked. He was aware he couldn't stop staring at her. He forced himself to look away, to focus his attention on Nizar and the children. He didn't want to come over as leery or rude. They sat in silence for a while.

Then she turned to him and said. 'You've done a brilliant, generous thing, letting him come here today.'

He shrugged 'I'm glad you could both come.'

For a moment, they watched the boisterous game at the other end of the room. Ryan babbled with glee as Nizar and Lily raced the cars around him.

Mia finished her coffee and said, 'It's why I accepted your invitation.' She lowered her voice. 'Means he can feel that something good has come out of this tragedy. And David would've wanted that.'

'So he knows?'

'Oh, yes. In the circumstances, I thought you wouldn't mind.'

Adam met her gaze. She had a directness he admired. 'If it helps him.'

'He took the decision, you know.'

'The decision?'

'As David's next-of-kin he consented to his brother's heart being used. I hope that doesn't make you feel uncomfortable.'

Adam wasn't sure what it made him feel. He glanced at Nizar, this stranger who'd saved his life.

'It's... weird, I'll admit,' he said.

She tilted her head, flicked back her hair and there it was again, that teasing, wry smile.

'I disagree with all this secrecy,' she said. 'Why shouldn't the donor's family and recipient meet? Keeping people apart, pretending. It's so constipated and English.'

'I don't think we're the only ones who do that.'

'Well, I think openness is the best policy. Tell people the truth, let them make up their own mind.'

The thought seemed to energise her. She jumped up and said, 'But you promised to show us the farm.'

He smiled. 'Okay.'

Zoe provided Mia with a pair of wellingtons. She declined to come with them, leaving Adam to escort their visitors.

Adam assumed that Mia was the sort of woman who wouldn't like to get messy. Her clothes were elegant and expensive. So he was delighted when this turned out to be way off the mark. She splashed through the mud in the yard, let the slobbering young heifers in the barn lick her fingers. She knelt down in the straw to pet the dogs and ran around playing catch with Nizar and Lily with an old punctured football they found.

It was cold but, like Adam, she seemed to relish being outside. Her nose became pink and damp but she simply brushed it with the heel of her hand. And they laughed a lot.

In the fading afternoon light, as they troop wearily through the paddocks and back towards the house, Adam is aware that if he's going to speak seriously to her, he must seize the moment.

'Look,' he says, 'this is awkward. I want to talk to you about David. Maybe ask some things. Is that okay?'

She sweeps her blonde hair out of her eyes and gazes at him. 'Ask away.'

'I know you've said you didn't know that much about him, although you knew he was probably into some things that weren't exactly legal.'

Chuckling, she says 'I like bad boys, I should never have admitted that, should I?'

'Why not? I used to be a bit of a bad boy myself.'

She laughs. 'I don't believe that. David and I had an understanding. He didn't talk to me about what he did and I didn't ask. So have the police told you they were after him?'

'It's a bit more complicated. Have you ever heard of cell memory? Transplant recipients who sort of inherit traits from their donors?'

She shoots him a wary look 'You saying you've acquired some habits from David?'

'Habits. And I have certain thoughts in my head.'

'What kind of thoughts?'

'They feel more like memories, but they're not mine.'

'David's memories? Wow! That's spooky.'

'Yeah.'

'Give me an example.'

Adam hesitates. He wants to be honest. She deserves that. But telling her David was murdered doesn't feel right. Not yet.

'You were with him that evening? Before he died.'

She frowns 'How do you know that?'

'Did you try to stop him from leaving?'

Her brow darkens and she says, 'We had words. Okay,

let's be honest, a blazing row. And he stormed out. Got on his bike and rode off.'

'But you tried to warn him in some way?'

'He had an explosive temper. It made him completely reckless. He needed reminding. That's what I was trying to do.' Folding her arms, she turns away and says, 'But I didn't try hard enough, did I? I should've never let him go.'

'It's not your fault' says Adam.

'Isn't it?'

She turns back to face him. The blue eyes glisten. Adam is seized by the impulse to take her in his arms and comfort her. But his little daughter is tugging at his sleeve.

'Daddy...'

'What, sweet pea?'

And then he sees his wife watching them from the kitchen window.

47

DAY 32. 11.15pm

Adam stands in the bathroom doorway, gazing at his wife. Shoulders hunched, she's in bra and knickers. She looks girlish and fragile. The Zoe he remembers from years ago. And he finds that turns him on.

He thinks back to the night they spent in Stratford-upon-Avon. That was surprising and special, the best sex they'd had in years.

The day has been a real buzz. All he wants now is to reach out, stroke her skin, kiss the nape of her neck. But something in her manner makes him hesitate.

'It went well today, I think, don't you?' he says.

Zoe doesn't reply. She's cleaning her teeth. Since their guests left, they haven't spoken much. She's been putting the children to bed. Lily was over-excited and wouldn't settle.

She returns the electric toothbrush to its base and says, 'Did you find what you were looking for on the net? You spent most of the evening at it.'

He can tell from the snippy tone that she's not happy. She's been unusually subdued most of the day. Something's simmering. The prospect of sex evaporates. He gets the impression she's spoiling for a fight. *Why? He doesn't need this.* He's tempted to walk away.

Instead, he says, 'I do appreciate the effort you made today.'

'But not enough to help clear up or to thank Mum for coming over.'

He feels his annoyance rising. *Why does she have to spoil it? Can't she be glad for him?*

'I can see you're upset,' he says.

'Only because I've told you. So, are you going to London to see her?'

Here we go. All that desire, there a moment ago, vaporised.

'She's invited both of us. Feels to me like you're jealous and that is completely daft. You know that.'

'Daft? I'm daft? What are you doing, Adam? What's this all about?'

'You know what I'm doing. We agreed.'

'We didn't agree to this.'

'I'm trying to find a way to... I dunno if I can explain—'

'No, you don't know, do you! You didn't even pay any attention to him.'

'Him?'

'Nizar. Your donor's brother. You invite him here and then you completely ignore him.'

'I didn't ignore him. I didn't want to be heavy or anything. Didn't want to upset him.'

'I think it was pretty obvious that the only person you were interested in was her.'

'That's not true.'

'He's the one who can tell you about David, which I

thought was what this was about. And he even had questions he wanted to ask you.'

'How do you know that?'

'He told me, Adam, wondered if you'd mind if he had our email address.'

'Well, okay. Perhaps it's easier for him to put things in writing.'

She shakes her head. Her eyes are blazing. 'You're being a total and utter dick!'

That stings. Why does she need to be such a bitch? He's tempted to ask. But she pushes past him into the bedroom and picks up her pyjamas.

'I'm going to sleep in Lily's room,' she says. 'Then you can fantasise about her to your heart's content and have a good wank.'

He feels perplexed. Is this his fault? He sits down on the end of the bed and puts his face in his hands. Mia drifts through his mind. He's attracted. Of course he is. Was it that obvious? He doesn't think so.

Out of the window the fields are black, the wind is up, gales are forecast, another Atlantic low sweeping in. The moon appears briefly from behind the fast-scudding clouds. In the yard, one of the dogs barks. They're sensitive to the weather. Their kennels are snug enough, but they're always trying to sneak into the kitchen to curl up near the Aga. That's where they'd prefer to sleep, but Zoe won't allow it.

Adam lays down full length on the bed and closes his eyes. He needs rest. But she's tipped his mood. Now his head spins with querulous thoughts. Why does she have to be like this? He'd never be unfaithful. *But is that even true?* The question nags. He thinks of Mia, her teasing smile. *Is he lying to himself? Probably.*

He decides he's too wired to sleep and goes back downstairs. The laptop is on the kitchen table where he left it. Opening it, the site he was looking at earlier—True Health News—pops up. Reports on the avian flu outbreak are legion and contradictory. He's been sifting through it all, trying to get his head round what's going on. It's important. Why couldn't she understand that?

He scrolls. The sense that David was involved or knew about this niggles at the edge of his conscious mind. Then there are the white tiles. The white tiles, cold and stark, they invade his psyche repeatedly, but what do they mean? Is it that he's been trapped in a clinical environment for too long? That was Chang's view.

A sudden squall of rain slaps the kitchen window. Something crashes in the yard. A bucket being blown about? The dogs start to bark. He decides to defy his wife's rule and let them in. Going to the back door, he finds it unlocked. Zoe must've forgotten. He should've checked.

He looks for some boots, pulls them on and as he goes to open the door, a voice behind him in the dark hallway says 'I wouldn't go out there if I was you. Bloody awful.'

48

DAY 32. 11.45pm

Adam spins round to face the intruder. His fist clenches and his thoughts dart to the nearest weapons: an old iron poker beside the Aga, the knives in the block on the kitchen worktop.

But the man steps out of the shadows, smiles and says, 'You want to smash my face in, of course you do, Adam. But you've got your wife and children upstairs, so a wiser course of action might be to listen to what I have to say.'

Adam's heart is thumping. He knows this man. He's seen him in his dreams and glimpsed him in the barn talking to Zoe. But the reality of David's killer in the flesh, standing barely a metre away, is even more disturbing.

'What the fuck? How did you get in?' says Adam.

The man tilts his head. 'I've heard a story about you' he says. 'Weirdest thing I've ever come across. You can access a dead man's memories. Is that true?'

'What the fuck—'

'We don't mean any harm, either to you or your family. That I promise you.'

'Who's we?'

'All I want is a chat.'

'What if I call the police?'

The man grins. 'Middle of Devon, middle of the night. They haven't got the resources. I doubt they'd come.'

He pulls down the zip on his heavy jacket, opens it slowly and says, 'Look, I'm unarmed. And I'm here to reassure you, because I think you may have got the wrong end of the stick.'

'You mean you weren't driving the van that ran David Taylor off the road and killed him?'

The man's jaw tightens and he nods to himself. 'So you did recognise me,' he says, 'when you saw me in the barn talking to your wife. I thought so at the time.'

'The police know about you' says Adam, 'not the locals, Counter Terrorism.'

'Do they?' He doesn't seem too bothered. 'Okay, you've proved you've got the balls to front up to me. Now can we sit down in a civilised manner in your nice warm kitchen and talk about this? Cause I'm guessing you've got some questions you'd like to ask.'

Adam takes a deep breath. He's right about that. The initial shock and adrenaline punch have subsided. He nods, but his gaze remains fiercely focused on the interloper. He backs slowly into the kitchen. The man follows.

'Nice and cosy in here,' the man says, warming his hands on the rail of the Aga.

'First question then,' Adam says. 'What's your name?'

'You can call me Tony.'

Tom or Tony. Adam had begun to think he'd imagined the name. Suddenly it's there: Tony Franklin.

Tony strolls round the kitchen. Big and broad shouldered, he holds himself erect. Time in the military, thinks Adam. Hair shaved close to the scalp, the balding middle-aged man cut, but he could be anything from late forties to late fifties. His face is more than clean-shaven, it's scraped down to the pink flesh. The shoes are leather, buffed to a shine.

He turns to Adam and says 'Lovely place you've got here. This would be many people's dream, nice old farmhouse in the country but with all mod cons.'

'It's a working farm,' says Adam.

'Yes it is' Tony replies earnestly, 'and we need our farmers, now more than ever. You put food on the table.'

'I'm sure you didn't come here to discuss agricultural policy. Or are we back on the bovine TB campaign?'

Tony smiles and wags his finger. 'See, I knew I'd like you, Adam Hardy. You've seen some tough times, but you've kept a sense of humour. Spit in the eye of fortune. Bit like me, in fact.'

'I'm nothing like you.'

'Give it a few years, son.'

They face each other across the kitchen. The long pine table stands between them. Adam has the advantage of knowing the room and he's rapidly calculating. He can see from the open jacket that there's not an ounce of flab on the intruder. He probably is as tough as he looks. So Adam's weapon of choice is the poker, used to rake out the wood burner in the sitting room. It lives in a corner next to the Aga. Adam has already located it in his peripheral vision. He'll rely on surprise and a single blow to the skull.

Tony tilts his head thoughtfully again, cricks his neck and says, 'So now you're thinking how to take me out. Grab a knife from the block over there, maybe whack me over the head with a frying pan. Or maybe that nice old poker in the corner that you've been eyeing. But I wouldn't advise it, Adam. You may succeed, but then what? Jail is not a good option for a man in your state of health. They're under-funded and feral. I doubt you'd survive. Do you want to do that to your lovely family?'

Adam meets his steely gaze. 'What makes you think I care?'

'Tough talk, son. But let's get down to the facts. I'm assuming you're a patriotic Englishman and I'm going to appeal to that. How do you think that you and Zoe and Lily and little Ryan get to live here in safety and security in the beautiful Devon countryside? It's because this way of life is protected by people like me.'

Adam huffs in disbelief. 'What? You telling me you work for the government?'

'I work for the British people.'

'You murdered David Taylor in the name of national security?'

'David Taylor is a fiction. A false name on a fake pass-port belonging to a dangerous criminal called Feras Khalid. Khalid was a Syrian who got rich trafficking drugs and guns and people into this country. He's not a man you would've wanted to know.'

'What was he then? Some kind of jihadist or terrorist?'

'No, I don't think he believed in anything. He was a crim-inal and a murderer who took what he wanted and destroyed anyone who got in his way.'

'And the flu thing. How does that fit in? Why was he involved in that?'

'I don't know. Someone paid him probably. Thing is Adam, what I'm here to say is that you need to leave this alone.'

'The police came to me.'

'Yeah well, sometimes PC Plod, and I include so-called Counter Terrorism in that, goes lumbering in with his big boots when he shouldn't. Forget about all this. Forget about what you think you know or can remember. All it'll bring you is more grief.'

Adam sighs. His brain is reeling. 'I didn't think the secret service, or whoever you are, were allowed to kill people. Not in this country.'

'Not in this country?' Tony laughs. 'You're a young man, Adam. There's a lot your generation doesn't appreciate or understand. You take the life you have for granted. My dad fought in the last war, my granddad the war before that. And I'm fighting this one.'

Adam's impulse is to resist. But there's a horrible sense in what he's being told. He feels confused. 'I think the police want to talk to me.'

'Ignore them. They can't force you. Stay at home, get yourself well and healthy, look after your family, and leave this to the people who know what they're doing.'

'That's you?'

'Me? I'm a foot soldier, an ordinary bloke doing my bit.'

'Then who?'

'You've got to trust. Not easy, I'll give you that. Least that scumbag did one decent thing. He gave you a chance to get your life back. So take it. Forget him. Put the past behind you and move on. It's the best advice anyone can give you. Do that and I promise, everything will be all right.'

Twitter Feed

DAY 32.

True Health News @truehealthnews
@DHSCgovuk refuses to confirm infected escapees from immigration detention centre walked into primary school and collapsed#Governmentlies #safeandsound
15.9k Retweets 18k Likes

Department of Health and Social Care @DHSCgovuk
Replying to @truehealthnews
This is fake news. Totally untrue. No inmates of any immigration detention centre have succumbed to the H7N9 strain of the flu virus. Outbreaks remain sporadic and are being successfully contained. #Staywell
409 Retweets 513 Likes

True Health News @truehealthnews
Replying to @DHSCgovuk
Seriously! Does anyone believe a bunch of corrupt officials trying to cover up their own incompetence? PEOPLE ARE DYING! But Dame Felicity gets £210,000 a year of your money #governmentlies #holdthemtoaccount
18.7k Retweets 20k Likes

Anushka Anand @AA539
Replying to @truehealthnews
Fully qualified nurses in London, on the front line, risking their lives to save lives, get less than 25 grand a year.
#holdthemtoaccount
10.8k Retweets 12k Likes

Mark Carter @MCB666

Replying to @truehealthnews

SEE FOR YOURSELF. For actual visual proof that the Dame
went at night to Yarls Wood to manage the cover-up go to
keepsafeandsound.com #pandemic #callthemtoaccout

10.3k Retweets 11.3k Likes

49

DAY 33. 8.30am

Adam plods up a steep incline towards a small wooded copse. It leaves him breathless; he's loath to admit that his energy levels are so depleted. Whether from the transplant or the subsequent infection, his body is sore and battered. Leaving the house shortly after sunrise, he released the dogs from their kennels and set off with them across the fields into a blanket of morning mist.

Zoe was busy getting the children up. He heard her moving about upstairs as he slipped out of the back door; he'd managed to avoid any contact. As far as he knew, she was unaware of their late night visitor.

He'd laid down on the bed fully clothed, but sleep had eluded him. The invasion of his home by David's killer disturbed him deeply. The man's smug confidence repulsed him, although the tale he told sounded credible. Now he doesn't know what to think.

The encounter left Adam with a sharp anger rising in his

gullet. Though it was couched in the form of advice he'd been warned off, told to forget what he thought he knew and move on with his life. Was that even possible? And what if he didn't?

A brisk walk has always helped him clear his head. But this morning, like the stubborn mist clinging in the hollows, his mind refuses to relinquish its doubts.

The accusations that bastard made churn in his brain. What evidence did he offer? None at all, and Adam sensed more than a whiff of racism in his attitude. He spoke the name Feras Khalid as if that in itself was an indictment. Is this how the secret service in the UK operates? Is this the new normal? He doesn't want to believe it, but perhaps he's being naïve. If David was guilty of crimes, he should've been tried in a court of law, not murdered.

The more he thinks about it, the more enraged he becomes. Whatever Feras Khalid was or became, there were reasons for it. A teenage boy trapped in a war zone struggling to carry the body of his dead mother—the memory springs into his mind and brings a stab of pain. And the boy who followed him, who carried the rifle, was that Nizar? Nizar, the shy young man, who came to his house and played with his children.

Adam sits down to rest on a fallen log. Before him the grey-green vista has a chilly beauty, the steep sides of the combe rimed in frost. But his thoughts are far away, in another place that's hot and dry and dusty. And it becomes obvious to him what he must do. A murder was committed. He knows this. He is its witness. Ignoring that fact is not an option. He feels a compulsion deep down inside: he has to act. He owes it to his donor. They can't be allowed to get away with it. He wants justice. David deserves justice. *Or is it revenge? Does it matter what you call it?*

His emotions are frayed and his thoughts keep straying back to her. They've hardly left her since the previous day. She's the only one who can help him. She's already proved that by bringing him Nizar. Knowing what David was, she loved him. *She does love him, that's why she came.* It's the only thing in this whole mess that he can trust.

The two dogs, Border collies, mother and son, have settled near his feet. They gaze up at him, alert but patiently waiting, ready to follow. Their loyalty, their steadfastness, is inspiring. But he can't take them with him. He strokes their silky heads. They nuzzle his hand.

'Listen to me,' he says. 'Take care of Zoe and the kids. Keep watch. Because I have to go. It's the only way.'

50

DAY 33. 10.15am

Escorted up to Counter Terrorism's offices by an awkward young DC she's never seen before, Felicity Oldroyd feels uncomfortable bordering on tetchy. It's nearly a week since she last saw Pat Babcock and they didn't part on the best of terms. On top of this, she's not in the habit of asking for help. She helps other people, that's her job.

After her fruitless attempt to hypnotise Adam Hardy, she had given the Chief Superintendent a piece of her mind. Pat had responded in similarly robust terms and their informal alliance had ceased there and then. She'd glimpsed her former ally in a Whitehall corridor after an interminable briefing meeting, but Babcock had sailed by without giving her any eye contact.

She feels a certain trepidation as she's ushered into the Chief Superintendent's office, but Pat gets up from behind her desk, wreathed in smiles, holds out her hand and says

'Felicity, I'm so glad you've come. I owe you the most sincere apology. Several probably.'

The charm is disarming. The Professor allows her hand to be shaken and squeezed.

Accepting the invitation to sit, she says with some relief, 'Well, I think we both got a little overwrought.'

'We did,' says Babcock, 'but I put you in a ridiculous position. I should never have done it. Blame the stresses of the job.'

'I know how much pressure you're under.'

'You too. But I admit, it was a completely desperate idea.'

Felicity smiles. She feels like a schoolgirl who's upset her favourite teacher but been unexpectedly forgiven.

'What's happened to Mr. Hardy?' she says.

'He's at home in Devon. I don't think he's any the worse for the experience.'

'That's a relief.'

Pat nods and smiles. 'And, on a personal note, I'm glad to see you. You're the one government boffin in this whole farrago that talks sense. I've missed you.'

Boffin. Who uses a term like that anymore except Pat? But Felicity secretly likes that view of herself. It suggests she has opinions that should be taken seriously.

She meets the cop's unremitting gaze and says, 'You might not be so delighted when you hear why I've come.'

Babcock opens her palms. 'Tell me.'

'I think it's nonsense, but my family insisted. They think I'm being targeted.'

'In what form? Have you received a personal threat?'

'Depends what you mean by personal. There's a thing on the internet called True Health News.'

'We're aware of them.'

'According to my daughter, they've been accusing me of

all sorts and demanding my resignation. Well, obviously they're entitled to their opinion.'

'However ill-informed.'

'Phoebe—that's my daughter—she keeps an eye on them. True Health News, they're a news site. But their stories crop up and get shared in lots of other places.'

Pat shakes her head wearily 'I hate social media. We were better off without it.'

'I agree. Anyway, there's another website; they share all the True Health News stories, but they also put out these gross pictures of people being decapitated. And slogans like 'Off with the traitor's head'. They've used my picture in some of them.'

'We can certainly report this to the platform provider. Get it taken down.'

'Phoebe has been in touch with them.'

'They tend to be a bit more co-operative when they hear from us.'

'Thank you. Personally, I think it's vicious nonsense. Nasty inadequate people hiding behind their computer screens. But Phoebe thinks it's more co-ordinated than that.

'In what way?'

'She's found more than half a dozen separate sites that seem to be orchestrating the same message. They use the hashtag safe and sound. Broadly speaking they're stoking people's fears, saying there is a pandemic, insisting that loads of people are dying, but they're being buried secretly in mass graves and that officials like me are deliberately lying to the public. They have videos they show which they say prove it. And interviews with supposed health care workers.'

'Easy enough to fake. Nowadays you don't need much expertise to manufacture high quality propaganda.'

'It made me think about what you said to me when we first met. Terrorism's not about killing people, it's about creating a climate of fear.'

The Chief Superintendent steeples her fingers. 'I know this may sound like an odd question, Felicity, but you're sure this isn't a pandemic?'

'Pandemic means it's out of control. And this is simply not true. The outbreaks remain sporadic and, for the most part, they've been successfully contained. We've got highly effective systems in place for collecting data so we do know what's going on.'

'They keep cropping up. In twos and threes.'

'I'm not denying the seriousness of the outbreaks. The fact that people are dying is serious. But I think each outbreak has a common single source, which is why it hasn't turned into a pandemic. We think people have to come in contact with the source fairly directly and there doesn't seem to be much contagion between individuals that we can prove.'

'We find who's doing this, we can stop it.'

'I think so.'

'You think so?'

Felicity smiles. 'I'm a scientist. I think so until I'm proved wrong. But look, I'm not criticising the police. I can see it's not any easy task.'

'Perhaps the perpetrators hoped it would turn into a pandemic, but it hasn't. Terrorists, as a rule, aren't that competent.'

'Maybe. We keep saying it isn't a pandemic. The problem now seems to be that we're not being believed by the public. But a PR campaign is being launched to deal with that and to promote the new anti-viral drug. Ryder is convinced that's the answer.'

'Is it?'

'It's largely untested. In medical terms, it's unnecessary.'

Babcock nods. 'Hmm, but the theory is, if people believe it, who cares?'

'Well, sort of. But I assure you, Pat, I in no way support this approach.'

The cop rocks back in her chair. 'Have you asked yourself why we're being pushed down this route?'

The Professor shrugs. 'I don't know. Because all politicians worry about is what the voters think?'

Babcock smiles. 'I wonder. When you're looking for the motivation for a crime, you always need to ask who gains?'

'Who gains? I can tell you that. One Dr. Henry Shawcross. An unknown researcher who fairly soon will be a multi-millionaire.'

'Interesting' says Babcock.

51

DAY 33. 11.30am

Even though they started early, traffic out of London was sluggish and it was late morning before they hit the M5. Mehta insisted on driving. He'd collected Jason in an anonymous-looking Ford Focus with some interesting bits of extra kit on the dash. Cruising, needle on 70 precisely, Jason wished the cop would let rip, put the blues on and hit the pedal. But Mehta's whole manner exuded tension and control.

After several futile attempts to start a conversation, Jason put his earbuds in, closed his eyes, and listened to music on his phone. He'd become accustomed to the DI's lack of ease.

They'd spent most of Sunday together, him on his laptop, the cop pacing. Jason had come to the conclusion that Mehta was wired most of the time. Part of him was always on the move, even when sitting his knee jiggled relentlessly.

When it got to six in the evening and they'd eaten every

biscuit, snack and piece of fruit in the flat and drunk a gallon of coffee, hunger drove them out, at Jason's suggestion, to his local Indian.

Mehta had perused the menu with sniffy disdain. 'This is shit. You like this stuff?'

'They do a great curry,' said Jason. 'Evening Standard gave them five stars.'

Mehta continued to tut his way through the menu. 'Call this curry? You like curry. I'll take you to my dad's place in Leicester. Treat you to some food actual Indian people eat.'

'I look forward to it, mate.'

Jason smiled to himself. The thaw had been glacially slow. Mehta's awkwardness and barely suppressed aggression were hardly puzzling. Did he think Jason was going to out him? Or was it a bit more basic than that? To Jason, the sexual frisson zinging between them was obvious. He may lack his brother's breezy confidence, but he knew when another man desired him. Why else had the cop turned up on his doorstep on a Sunday morning, supposedly needing Jason's help?

But Mehta remained an enigma. Jason could sense the longing in that gaze. But he guessed the cop's private story was that he was bi-sexual. Denial. Suppression. Marriage to the right girl would sort him out.

Jason had tried that tack himself for a while. Being out nowadays was neither as straightforward or acceptable as people assumed. He was circumspect about who he told, always careful to order a cab if he left a club late at night. And then there was the residual shame he could never quite shrug off. The lingering playground taunts and the disappointment that had always tinged his parent's apparent acceptance. He wasn't about to judge Samir Mehta for his repressed attitude.

What he wanted was to reach out, touch his hand, not as a come-on, but in a brotherly way. Let Samir know that they could be allies, even friends. However, he'd already got the message loud and clear. The DI would not welcome physical contact.

But in spite of their personal tensions, or perhaps because of them, they made an effective team. Mehta was peremptory in his instructions but he was quick and thorough. Jason liked that; it led to clear analysis.

They'd established pretty quickly that the number plate on the supposed DEFRA vehicle was cloned. Jason got the impression that this wasn't news to Mehta. After that they floundered around for some time, eating crisps, drinking coffee, arguing. The question they came back to was simple: could this vehicle be connected or shed any light on David Taylor's accident in the Blackwall Tunnel?

It was Jason who remembered that the witnesses in the accident report drove a BMW X5, same make and model as the DEFRA clone.

Mehta shook his head and said, 'Yeah, but didn't your brother say it was an old Luton van that ran him off the road?'

'He did. But I'm sure the report says these blokes in the BMW stopped and told the first responder that David Taylor had been speeding, lost control and crashed into a wall. Their statements ensured it was treated as an accident.'

A glint came into the cop's eye. 'Nah, too easy. Twenty quid says the plates don't match.'

Jason pulled up the accident report on his laptop, which included the driver's name and phone number and the licence plate. It matched.

He grinned and held out his hand. 'Probably lied about the name, but they couldn't about the licence number.'

'I expect you think you're a clever bastard,' said the cop. But he smiled.

They were on a roll.

Allowing a two-hour window either side of the accident and a radius of three miles around the tunnel, they soon had the BMW pinging on half a dozen ANPR cameras. Mehta drew a rough map of its likely route. It had travelled north to south through the tunnel an hour and thirty-five minutes before the crash and then had re-entered the north-bound tunnel four and a half minutes before the 999 call was logged.

'So let's look for a Luton van,' Jason said. 'See if he was right about that, too.'

'It must've entered from the south and been slightly ahead of David. Try a fifteen minute window.'

Comparing the ANPR data with the DVLA records, in order to identify the make and model, they ran every plate of every vehicle that had entered the tunnel from the south in that time frame. Of the several hundred vehicles that passed through, they found six transits but only one Luton van. It gave them another licence plate to check.

'Shit,' said the cop. 'Now we're getting somewhere. Let's see if the BMW and the van were travelling in tandem.'

On the southbound journey, the ANPR system picked them up close together three times.

He shook his head. 'It could be a co-incidence. Happened to be going in the same direction.'

'What if we add in the plates on David Taylor's motorcy-cle?' said Jason.

Once this licence number was lifted from the accident report, it didn't take long for them to sketch out a possible route across South London.

The BMW and the van both travelled from north of the

Thames and through the tunnel. They wound their way through Greenwich and Deptford to Jamaica Road, where they both appeared to stop. Twenty minutes later, the Luton van pinged off an ANPR camera close to Southwark Park travelling back the other way. It had turned round.

Another fifteen minutes passed and Taylor's motorcycle pinged off the same camera, followed immediately by the BMW.

'It was a set up,' said the cop. 'The whole bloody thing! Somehow, they knew he was on the road. Perhaps they even knew where he was going. They travelled south together to pick him up, waited and then followed him into the tunnel.'

'Look at the van,' said Jason, 'the gap between these two cameras. It must've stopped again near the tunnel approach, waited for them to catch up, so they could get the timing right and get in position.'

'I've got to say, Jason, your crazy brother appears to be right. These scumbags targeted Taylor and followed him.'

'And killed him?'

Mehta shrugged. 'That we've yet to prove.'

'But what do you think?'

'I need to pin down the accident investigator, find out why it was never followed up.'

'That could be as simple as over-stretched, lack of time, it fell through the net.'

The cop had nodded. 'We need to find the van. And talk to your brother.'

Jason had suggested they phone him. But Mehta shook his head.

'C'mon,' said the cop. 'He's freaked out once already. I have to do this carefully, talk to him in person, on his own turf.'

'Okay' said Jason.

'I think you should come with me. Put your brother at ease. I don't need another punch in the mouth.'

Jason smiled.

'Best if we arrive unannounced,' the cop added.

Mehta had an agenda. That was clear. But he wasn't about to reveal it.

'Okay' said Jason. What choice did he have?

As the motorway snakes south across the Somerset Levels, Jason turns off the music on his phone and makes another attempt to get the DI to open up.

'What does your boss think about this?' he says.

He's had a whole night to wonder what the DI is up to. Counter Terrorism is known for its machinations. But this feels like a freelance operation.

Mehta gives him a side-eyed glance. 'Why d'you want to know?'

'So she doesn't approve?'

'I never said that.'

'Yeah you did. More or less.'

Mehta sighs. 'It's a complicated situation, Jason.'

'Does she even know you're doing this?'

Mehta doesn't answer. His fingers tighten on the steering wheel.

'You mean it's not just me, we're both about to lose our jobs?'

The DI gives him a tepid smile. 'Yeah, good chance.'

Jason shrugs. 'You're lucky. You can always join your dad in the restaurant business.'

'How's that lucky?'

'Mate, it's better than what I'll be doing, sitting in some scabby sales centre making cold calls.'

52

DAY 33. 12.25pm

As they drive up to the farm, Jason's heart sinks; Phil Rowett's new Porsche is parked outside.

'Oh, bloody hell,' he says.

Mehta gives him a quizzical glance.

'Zoe's dad,' Jason explains. 'Prepare to be pissed off.'

'Leave him to me,' says Mehta.

They get out of the car at the same time as the front door opens and Zoe comes flying out.

'Do you know where he is?' she shouts.

'What?' says Jason.

'Adam. I thought he must be with you.' She sounds desperate. 'I've been calling you, Jason. Why didn't you pick up?'

'We were driving. Crap reception. Sorry.' Following the agreement with Mehta to arrive unannounced, he'd ignored her calls.

He sighs. It's clear she doesn't believe him. She rakes her fingers through her hair.

He glances at the cop, who says nothing.

Phil Rowett appears in the doorway and scowls at Mehta.

'Who the hell's this?' he says. 'One of your buddies, Jason?'

Mehta steps forward, pulls out his warrant card. 'DI Mehta, Counter Terrorism. And you are, sir?'

Jason enjoys the moment. But Rowett doesn't even blink. He paints on a smile.

'Phil Rowett, Adam's father-in-law.' He holds out his hand to shake. 'Do come inside, Inspector.'

Mehta follows Rowett into the house.

Zoe turns to Jason. She's close to panic.

'He's disappeared, Jace. I came back from taking Lily to school and he was gone. No note, nothing.'

'I bet he's gone for a long walk. Maybe that's a good sign.'

'Without the dogs? He always takes the dogs.'

'Then he's wandered off somewhere. You sure he's not in the barn?'

'I've looked. You don't think maybe, the men that came, you don't think they've got him, do you?'

Jason's brain has gone into overdrive imagining scenarios.

'No' he says with all the conviction he can muster.

'Am I being completely paranoid? Tell me I am.'

Jason feels awkward, but he puts his arms round his sister-in-law and hugs her. 'Listen, it'll be okay. He'll turn up.'

She wriggles free. 'Why are you even here?'

'I've been helping Mehta. We've found out some things. He wants to talk to Adam.'

'What things?'

'Adam's story about the accident is probably true.'

'How do you know?'

'We've managed to trace the vehicles involved.'

Zoe stares at him. 'What are you saying? His donor really was murdered?'

'Looks like it.'

'Oh my god, then that could be it. They're after him too.'

'Why would they be? They don't know what he knows. Anyway, who would believe it?' The argument sounds weak. He can see from her face she doesn't buy it.

'Then why come here pretending to be from DEFRA?'

Jason shepherds her into the house. 'I don't know. But Mehta's smart. I think we can trust him. He'll get to the bottom of this.'

As they walk into the kitchen, Ruth Rowett is pouring Mehta a coffee.

Rowett has his hands on his hips. 'Zoe, where does Adam keep the keys to his pickup? Why aren't they on the hook with the others?'

'They should be,' she replies. 'He hasn't driven it in ages.'

'Can't find the keys to the outbuildings either,' says Rowett.

Zoe rushes out of the back door.

'Where's this vehicle kept?' asks Mehta.

'In the shed,' says Jason. 'I'll show you.'

Rowett turns to Mehta. 'We have to keep everything under lock and key. Theft of farm machinery is a big problem, as I'm sure you're aware.'

The DI nods and smiles politely. Cradling his mug, he follows Jason out into the yard.

'What's going on?' Mehta whispers once they're out of

earshot. 'Did you call them last night? Is this some kind of charade to protect Adam from further questioning?'

'No!'

'You sure?'

'Are you suspicious of everyone?'

'More or less.'

As they round the corner of the barn, Zoe is across the cobbled yard hauling open the double doors to one of the sheds. It's empty. There's a tarpaulin in a heap in the middle of the concrete floor.

'It's gone,' says Zoe. 'I'm surprised it would even start.'

An open padlock, keys dangling from it, is hooked over the metal loop of the door hasp. Jason lifts it off.

He glances at his sister-in-law. He's aware of the cop scanning them, judging.

'If he left under his own steam, that has to be a good sign,' he says.

She shakes her head and sighs. 'It's all so stupid.'

Phil Rowett comes across the yard and joins them.

'Okay,' says Mehta. 'First, let's do a thorough search of the house. See if he's taken anything with him. Secondly, the vehicle licence number. Have you got that, Zoe?'

She nods, then blurts out. 'Oh god, this is all my fault. We had a row. And I... I didn't even speak to him this morning.'

Rowett folds his daughter in his arms. 'It's not your fault, darling. This whole situation is increasingly bizarre. Is he in danger? I don't understand any of it.'

Jason and Samir exchange looks.

'Don't worry, Mr Rowett,' says Mehta. 'I'm sure he'll turn up. If not, we'll find him.'

53

DAY 33. 2.15pm

With the aid of the satnav, Adam locates an underground car park on the South Bank in one of the turnings behind the National Theatre. He has rarely driven into London and never in the beast. But, in spite of the fact it's been sitting unused for the best part of a year, his old Mitsubishi Trojan doesn't let him down.

Returning from his walk, he'd put the dogs back in their kennels, thrown a few clothes, his meds and a toothbrush in a small backpack, got the pickup out of the shed and driven away. He knew Zoe would be out taking Lily to school. He'd thought about leaving a note, but what would he say? *He didn't need another row.*

What he did leave was his phone; on the bedside table, switched off, a statement in itself. But if he was going off the grid, then he wanted to eliminate the possibility that the police, or anyone else, could track him. *Sensible precaution.*

London is not a place he knows well or likes. Born and

bred a West Country boy, he's travelled the world, but finds cities claustrophobic. He hates the press of people on pavements, the congestion of bodies forced up against one another but struggling to hang on to their own space. Every creature will fight to defend its turf. That's the natural order. We all need room to breathe or we become barbaric. Open countryside or the open sea are his favourite landscapes, but driving in on the M4 traffic is surprisingly light. The epidemic does seem to have brought some advantages.

The car park is a short walk from Waterloo Bridge, which Adam recalls is close to Mia's office. His determination to see her again is not backed by any sort of plan. On the drive to London, he thought little about what he was going to do. His mind felt loose and empty. The relief of being behind the wheel again. *In control.* For the first time in a long while, he felt free, unencumbered by other peoples' demands, *by his jealous wife,* by his responsibilities as a father.

But now, as he stands on the bridge, surveying the fog-bound river, fragments of City towers leaching through the mist on his right, the ghostly outline of the Houses of Parliament on his left, he feels at a loss. The city is cold and alien. The fog disorientates him. Perhaps he should've phoned her. Is she even at work? But it's a Monday afternoon. Where else would she be?

Fifteen minutes later, he stands in the reception area of the PR firm facing her unsmiling assistant.

'Mia is out of the office. You should've made an appointment,' she says.

'I know,' he says. 'But this is important. When will she be back?'

'I couldn't say.'

The woman is tiny, an exotic doll with a tough, unremitting stare. But to Adam she seems like a sullen pixie. He feels a sudden desire to tread on her. *She irritates him so why not stamp on her, snuff her out?*

But he smiles and says, 'I know you're doing your job. But this is urgent. So, let's start again. When will she be back?'

The steely tone seems to work. Or perhaps the woman is simply indifferent.

'She's at lunch with a client. You can wait if you want but I don't know how long she'll be' says the pixie before turning on her heel and walking away.

Adam sits down on one of the low slung sofas. The receptionist, who's more amicable, brings him a coffee and tries to chat about the awful weather. He picks up a glossy magazine filled with beautiful people draped over expensive furniture or cars, wearing watches with vast, multi-functional dials or diamond encrusted chains of jewellery.

After a while, he begins to feel weary. The drive was long, not something he's done for some time. The office is cosy after the freezing walk from the car park. He has a weird sinking feeling inside, a sense of drifting. The sofa is soft. He wishes he could lay full length and sleep. He needs to sleep.

His eyelids droop, his thoughts meander. What on earth is he doing here? The decision to come to London was impulsive, and why did he leave his phone behind? That feels stupid and melodramatic now. He tries to recall his brother's number, but he's not sure if it ends in 91 or 19. Perhaps he could go to Jason's flat?

He went out early with the dogs and got it into his head that he had to do something about David. But that feels increasingly absurd now. The man in his kitchen, the spook. Did that happen?

He has to focus, get a grip on reality. He's Adam Hardy. He had a heart transplant, he's been discharged from hospital following an infection, what the hell is he doing? He remembers Chang's advice: avoid stressful situations.

Feeling awkward, he rubs his face. If the receptionist's watching, she must think he's strange. He should go. But his body feels heavy, impossibly sluggish. It's an effort to stand up, and he's trawling his tired brain for a suitable excuse to leave when the outer doors swing open and Mia Cunningham appears. She's laughing, head turned back towards the man following, who holds the door open for her.

A combination of panic and embarrassment seizes Adam. The seconds before she notices him feel excruciating. She steps into the reception area and he comes into her line of sight. She raises her sculpted brows and says, 'My goodness, Adam.'

'I'm sorry,' he mutters.

'This is a surprise.'

He has to sit down.

Mia scans him. 'Are you all right?'

'Yeah, fine, I need to...'

He sucks down several deep breaths to stop himself from fainting.

The man with her matches Adam in height but he's rail thin, a short brush of greying hair and a sculpted beard. He wears an expensive tailored overcoat. He gives her a quizzical look.

She turns to the receptionist. 'Can you get some water?'

'I'll be okay' says Adam. 'Don't worry.' He's aware of the man's penetrating stare.

Mia turns to her companion and says 'This is Adam Hardy.'

'Oh,' he says.

She smiles and adds, 'He was an old friend of David Taylor.'

The man studies him; there's a stillness about him that's unnerving. He holds out his hand for Adam to shake. 'Duncan Ryder' he says, 'tragic what happened to David.'

His voice is soft, with the hint of a transatlantic drawl.

Adam glances at Mia, the tension in her face, the look says it all: she needs his complicity, and that helps him concentrate his mind.

'Sorry to turn up unannounced,' he says. 'I was hoping to visit David's brother. Then, stupidly, realised I didn't have the address. You know what it's like on these meds.'

'Oh dear, Adam,' says Mia, shaking her head with concern, 'are you sure you're well enough to travel?'

'Probably not,' he replies.

She turns to Ryder. 'Adam's recovering from surgery.'

Duncan Ryder nods. 'Not the flu, then.'

'Oh no.' Adam paints on a smile. 'I live in Devon. We've been fairly fortunate.'

'I love Devon, surfed in Newquay as a boy.'

'That's Cornwall.'

'Of course.' He continues to scan them both. The hawkish stare suggests he's noting every detail. 'Well,' he says briskly, 'I think I'll be off. We can discuss that other matter later. Lovely lunch, Mia. Thank you.'

She takes his hand. 'Always a pleasure, Duncan.'

He glances at Adam. 'Hope you feel better. Take care.'

As he walks out of the main doors, the receptionist brings a glass of water. Mia takes it and hands it to Adam.

'Thank you for playing along,' she says. 'That was a bit delicate.'

Adam sips the water. 'He looks familiar. Have I seen him on the telly?'

'Maybe. You're more likely to have seen his younger brother, Hugh Ryder, the politician. He's Secretary of State for Health. Duncan runs a hedge fund based in the States. He's rather rich.'

'Oh,' says Adam.

Mia is scrutinising him. She's impossible to read. It feels as if she's calculating, sifting through her options. Abruptly she smiles and says, 'Let's go somewhere a bit quieter, shall we?'

54

DAY 33. 4.05pm

The room is spacious with a large oval conference table and a panoramic view of the fog-bound Thames. Mia's assistant brings a small tray with a teapot and two glass cups. She doesn't look at Adam, places the tray in front of Mia, smiles at her and leaves.

Mia is watching Adam. He's feeling better, but shaky and more than a little foolish.

'Don't mind Nin,' Mia says. 'She hates men. Grew up in a Thai children's home that doubled as a brothel. I hope you like Earl Grey.'

'Thanks' says Adam.

Mia pours. They both watch the pale amber liquid trickle into the dainty cups. The activity covers the awkwardness of the situation. Neither of them knows what to say.

'Well,' says Mia. 'It's lovely to see you, of course. But I didn't expect it to be quite so soon.'

'Nor did I, but... I wasn't lying. I do want Nizar's address.'
Being with her helps. It makes everything clearer.

'I could've texted you that.'

'Yes' he says. 'But I'm here because, well, I need your
help. You and Nizar. You both knew David. Cared about
him. I have to decide what to do.'

'About what?'

'Some of the things I can remember.'

She gets up, folds her arms, walks over to the window
and stares out. There's not much to see; a sulphurous
blanket shrouds the river.

'I don't mean to upset you,' he says.

She doesn't reply.

Her height accentuates the narrowness of her shoulders.
Like angel wings they rise and fall. *Touch her, reassure her.*

She turns to face him abruptly, but she's not crying as he
thought. Her eyes are ablaze.

'He's dead, Adam. And let's be frank, you've benefited
from that. Nizar needs to get on with his life, his studies and
so do I. In fact, at the moment, I've got a lot on my plate.'

'I'm sorry. I didn't mean it to be like this.' What was he
hoping for? *She's slipping away.*

She flaps her hand and says, 'Anyway, whatever's in your
head, how do you know they're his memories?'

'Well, they are quite specific.'

'Specifically what? The transplant you've had, don't they
give you loads of drugs? To, I don't know, make it work?'

'Immunosuppressants to stop the new heart from being
rejected, yes.'

'Well, they're going to have an effect, aren't they? Perhaps
you're confused.'

'Yes, but—'

'This is not an easy situation.' Her hand shakes as she picks up her glass cup.

He feels callous. Should he take the damned spook's advice? Go home, get on with his own life, leave her in peace?

No way!

'I remember him being murdered.' The words pop out of his mouth before he can stop them.

She frowns and shakes her head. 'What? How? He had a motorcycle crash.'

Can't stop now.

'He was deliberately forced off the road. In the tunnel, there was this van, and it crashed into him. I saw the man's face. It was intentional. Some kind of trap.'

She stands stock still, staring straight at him.

'You sure?' she says, a crack in her voice. 'Why would anyone do that?'

'I think he knew some things.'

'What sort of things?'

'The flu outbreak. I think it's to do with that.'

She folds her arms. 'That's ridiculous.'

Adam sighs. *Can't stop now.*

He ploughs on. 'There may be things about him that you don't know.'

'Like what?'

'The police were interested in him.'

'Yeah, I know. They came to see me. But I told you, he never discussed his business with me.'

'Did the police tell you he was an informant? Before the flu outbreak, he warned them it would happen, told them there was going to be a bio-terrorist attack.'

She doesn't speak. Her palms are tightly clasped, making

the ends of her fingers red from the pressure. She stares out of the window.

'And that's only the half of it,' he says. 'The man who was driving the van came to my house. Twice.'

'I don't understand.' She turns to face him.

'I think the first time he was checking me out. Him and another guy pretended to be officials from DEFRA. They talked to Zoe about the farm.'

'But you saw him and recognised him?'

'Yes. Then he came back. In the middle of the night. Admitted he was responsible for killing David. He said he worked for the government.'

'The government?'

'I assume the security services in some form.'

'You sure? That's...'

'Unbelievable I know. Okay, we know David was no saint, but that's extra-judicial murder.'

'What are you going to do?'

'I don't know. This spook told me to forget all about it. Leave it to the people who know what they're doing.'

She paces, arms clutched around herself, staring out at the bare trees lining the Embankment. For several moments, she's silent.

Then she turns to face him. 'I hate this time of year. It gets dark so early.'

'Mia, I know this is unfair on you.'

'It is.' She sounds bitter. 'So what are you going to do?'

'I thought I knew. But I'm not sure. That's why I need to know what you and Nizar want.'

'My God, Adam, I can't answer that. How did this person who drove the van even know about you?'

'Has to be through the police somehow, doesn't it? Counter Terrorism and MI5, they're all connected, aren't they?' He ponders for a moment 'Or possibly, it's through this doctor they took me to see. She tried to hypnotise me to see what I could remember.'

'Hypnotise you? That sounds insane.'

'It felt insane. But I did remember things.'

'What sort of things?'

'About his life before. I'm assuming in Syria. The war. It was pretty frightening.'

'I literally don't know what to say.'

Adam hesitates. *Yes, you must tell her.* 'I know how he felt about you, too.'

'Do you?' Her eyes rest on him, blue and iridescent.

He stands up, takes a step towards her, places a tentative hand on her shoulder. 'I know he would want you to be all right. That's why I'm giving you a say in this.'

She leans towards him, lays her head on his shoulder. 'How can I? It's a nightmare. I can't deal with this. It's too crazy.'

'Neither of us wanted this.'

She begins to cry, softly at first. Her body shakes.

He wraps his arms around her, buries his face in her hair and murmurs, 'Sssh! It'll be okay. I promise.'

55

DAY 33. 4.15pm

Felicity Oldroyd has spent her afternoon in a slew of meetings, where, in her opinion, a large amount of hot air was discharged into the room, achieving precisely nothing.

As the day has worn on, having mentioned Shawcross's name to Counter Terrorism, she's been feeling increasingly guilty, like the class snitch, who has dripped a little poison into teacher's ear to satisfy her own questionable motives. Her exasperation with Hugh Ryder had been displaced onto the hapless scientist. This was her excuse to herself. Two hours after her meeting with the Detective Chief Superintendent conscience got the better of her and she texted Babcock:

I think I've been unfair to poor Dr. Shawcross. He's been working on H7N9 for over a year as have many small bio-tech outfits. It's an obvious thing to do. The fact that Ryder favours him is probably totally random.

Babcock had replied:

Don't fret. We'll cast our eye over him. It won't do any harm.

On receipt of this, Felicity's self-reproach had gone into overdrive. Without any real evidence, she had put Henry Shawcross in the police's sights. It was vindictive, the product of intellectual snobbery. She was ready enough to criticise this kind of bias in her colleagues.

Walking back from PHE's offices across Westminster Bridge, she continues to brood.

Do as you would be done by.

That was one of her mother's favourite sayings.

Her mother's inflexible morals and religious certainty had provided the teenage Felicity with something to rebel against. It'd turned her into a scientist, a questioner, a doubter and seeker after more verifiable versions of the truth. Gerry reckoned she ought to be grateful to the old girl for that, at least. But though she'd tried for most of her life, she'd never managed it.

The old lady had spent her last years in an expensive care home, paid for by Gerry, tight-lipped and judgemental, blaming her daughter for some unspecified betrayal.

The fog that has cloaked the city for most of the day casts a grey sheen over the encroaching darkness as Felicity hurries across the bridge. She's given up on her face mask, even though most people who pass her are wearing theirs. They direct suspicious sidelong glances at her; well-dressed, leather briefcase. She doesn't appear to belong to the ranks of the irresponsible and the feckless. Felicity returns their looks defiantly.

The truth will set you free. What a romantic illusion that is!

She reaches the north side of the bridge and the railings

of the Houses of Parliament and, as if from nowhere, banner-waving figures loom out of mist towards her. But she hears them before she sees them.

Someone has a megaphone, which seems touchingly old-fashioned. But his words are muffled by a surgical mask.

'WHADDA WE WAN!'

He's the wrangler of a slow-moving herd. They reply with a low rumble which sounds like: *No more lies.*

The masked protesters flow past Felicity as they trudge over the bridge. She has a suspicion she knows where they're going. Public Health England's offices have been besieged by demonstrations for over a week.

Most of the banners bear the heading: #safeandsound.

'Tel'us the bloody truth!' hollers a lanky youth, cowled like a monk, as he passes by her.

A small, heavily masked girl shoves a leaflet in her hand.

When the marchers have gone, she pauses to read it in the fading light under a streetlamp at the corner of Parliament Square.

Glossy and professionally produced, it is a carefully crafted facsimile of a tabloid newspaper's front page. The headline reads: WONDER-DRUG IS KEPT FOR THE RICH. Kids and OAPs are dying in droves as life-saving treatment is denied them. Secret night time burials as the plague spreads. Don't die of ignorance. Go to: truehealthnews.com.

Felicity stands in the shadow of Big Ben and a hollow despair seeps through her. She was returning to her office, but what's the point? Standing on the edge of the pavement, she sees a taxi approaching out of the murk with its orange light on. She throws up her arm and hails it. All she wants is to go home.

56

DAY 34. 9.20am

Adam opens his eyes to a paralysing whiteness. And he's cold. Refrigerator cold, mortuary cold. He's fading fast, receding from his body down to some fathomless place. He can't move. He can't breathe. Terror grips him.

But it gives him strength too, makes him gulp for air and, as it gushes down into his lungs, warm blood surges through his veins and he wakes. But the room is stark white.

The venetian blinds are shut, leaching narrow strips of ghostly light. Where is he? Not at home, but there's an odd familiarity. He realises he's desperate for a piss. He can hardly hold it in. He throws off the covers and jumps up. The bathroom is through the open door; he knows instinctively where. He just makes it, lifting the lid in the nick of time. The relief as he urinates. His brain starts to natter, and it all falls into place.

Did he make love to her? He can't quite remember. But

the scent of her is round his mouth, on his fingers, which suggests he did.

He returns to the bedroom, finds his pants on the floor and puts them on. The apartment isn't large. It only takes him a moment to confirm he's alone. He looks out of the sitting room's wide balcony window at the dome of St Paul's. A little flat but an expensive location. It fits a young woman of ambition perfectly.

At the other end of the room is a kitchenette. An empty wine bottle stands beside the sink and two washed and polished glasses on the drainer.

He remembers the wine, red and fruity. It was the first time he'd drunk any alcohol for over a year. And he remembers Mia, as they sat side by side on the sofa and she stroked his hand. How they came to be there was a blur.

'I've missed you so much', he'd said. It made no sense, but she didn't seem to care.

'I'm sorry,' she'd replied, although he didn't understand why.

She was the one who'd led him into the bedroom. Her initiative not his, he's pretty sure of that. He remembers her eyes, holding him, shepherding him. The desire he'd felt was a sharp hunger. He had no choice. His survival depended on it.

The clock on the oven timer says 9.24. He never sleeps this late.

On the round glass-topped table there's a folded sheet of paper.

He picks it up and reads:

You were so tired I didn't want to wake you. I sent Nizar a text. I think he's keen to see you. But be careful with him!

There's cereal and coffee and some wholemeal bread in the freezer. In the kitchen drawer on the left, you'll find a spare key. The code for the building is 7832. I've got a totally mad day. Not sure when I'll be back but call me xx

Nizar's no. 07915 301041

My no. 07782 459213

Adam finds a packet of granola in the cupboard, pours some into a bowl, adds milk from the fridge and wanders as he eats.

The neatness of the apartment borders on the obsessive. Nothing is extraneous. A couple of striking black and white photos are the only pictures. The books on the shelves are alphabetised by author. In the wardrobe the clothes are hung in categories: short-sleeved tops, long-sleeved tops, trousers, skirts. Dresses, jackets and coats are in plastic covers, shoes in neatly stacked boxes.

He opens the drawers. It doesn't feel intrusive. He wants to know her. Everything is folded precisely, perfume bottles lined up by size, make-up in a segmented tray, jewellery in matching leather cases.

When he thinks back to her visit to the farm—the way she splashed around in the mud—the order here puzzles him. The two things don't seem to go together. But if this is the real Mia, was the woman who came to the farm playing a part? Her behaviour that day had surprised and intrigued him, but perhaps that was the point. He was hooked.

Retreating to the bathroom, he turns on the shower. Standing under the steamy cascade of water, he finds himself niggled.

She's always playing a part. That's Mia.

The water is hot, he likes it scorching. The heat is cleans-

ing. The shower room is small and clinical. It fills rapidly
with steam. And the tiles are clinically white.

White tiles.

His thoughts drift. Relaxing under the soothing water
brings relief, respite for his body and his mind. The irritation slides away. His subconscious loosens. He closes his
eyes.

The vision comes to him abruptly and fully formed.

*Make-up trays? Plastic boxes? No, this is totally different. It's
a chrome container with a digital display. Fixed high up on the
wall near the ceiling. Fixed to the white tiles.*

Realisation ricochets through Adam. Swaying, he puts
out a hand to steady himself. He turns off the shower, steps
dripping from the cubicle, and buries his face in a towel.

He can't rely on his memory retaining this. He must
write it down.

Dripping and naked, he rushes through to the sitting
room, finds the note she left him, turns the paper over and
grabs a pen.

He draws it as quickly and accurately as he can. He has a
good idea of what it is. They're common enough. In public
toilets—the sort found in shopping centres, hospitals,
schools—these electronic air fresheners are everywhere
pumping out their fragrances.

Under the drawing he writes: *the virus? Is this how it's
being spread?*

57

DAY 34. 9.35am

DI Mehta strolls into the offices of Counter Terrorism and heads for the kitchen and the coffee machine. He drove back to London the previous evening alone. He had a lot to process. His head was a jumble and being around Jason Hardy didn't help.

The smug bastard thinks he's got him sussed. That was pretty obvious. Samir found the sidelong glances, and the arch smiles annoying and intrusive. Jason looks tough and masculine on the outside. And to Samir, that matters—a man should look like a man. Seeing him in a towel revealed he was ripped. A body like that takes work and Samir is fair-minded enough to admire such determination.

But then Jason would spoil it all by throwing out a look or gesture that was completely camp. Samir found this gross and unnecessary. Jason was a skilful analyst, but he'd served his purpose. Any notion that they're operating as a team needs to be quashed. Samir had already decided during the long drive back, the best course of action was to avoid him.

Fortunately, he has enough to occupy his mind. A search of the farmhouse had produced Adam Hardy's phone. This suggested either he'd left in a hurry and forgotten it or that he didn't want to be traced.

Whilst he was in Devon Mehta had called the Serious Collision Investigation Unit and discovered that Jason's theory was correct, like many areas of the Met it was totally overstretched. The harassed PC he spoke to was defensive, bordering on the aggressive. Getting a call from Counter Terrorism demanding to know why there'd been no follow up on Taylor's crash had freaked him out. It took him ages to even locate the file. One copper trying to do the jobs of three, a typical enough story.

But Mehta was stroppy and had insisted that they check all the CCTV for the tunnel and see if there was anything on the accident. The PC said peevishly that it had probably been wiped.

Mehta had set Pramiti the task of trying to trace the men in the BMW, although he suspected the details they'd provided were false. He'd also asked her to farm out to whoever else was available a trawl on the Luton van's plates on ANPR anywhere in the London area.

As he heads for his desk with his usual double shot, the DC comes over. She reminds him of one of his aunties, unflappable and shrewd.

'Morning, boss,' she says. 'The good news or the bad news?'

He grins at her. 'I could do with something good.'

'Your Luton van pinged out of the tunnel and travelled up the A12 a few miles. Disappeared in the vicinity of Hackney Wick.'

'That's the good news?'

'I did a bit of lateral thinking. It occurred to me if this individual had just caused an accident, as you thought, he might be anxious to get away. And sure enough, a speed camera clocked him putting his foot down half a mile out of the tunnel. I've been on to the ticketing office and here's what they sent.'

She hands him a grainy printout, an image of the front of a Luton van and the driver snapped by a speed camera.

'I've enhanced it as much as I can. I'd say white male, in his fifties, clean shaven.'

'Ace' says Mehta. 'Well done.'

'Bad news—BMW driver and his passenger gave false details. But you expected that, right?'

The DI nods. He's staring at the printout. The driver grasps the wheel with his left hand. His right finger appears to be pressing something into his ear. A hands-free earpiece? His mouth is open as if he's speaking. Talking to his accomplices, maybe?

'Crappy old van,' says Mehta. 'If you'd knocked a motor cyclist off his bike deliberately, what would you do with it?'

'Scrap it,' Pramiti replies. 'Want me to follow up?'

He looks at her. She hasn't asked why they're now pursuing a line of inquiry which Babcock had specifically told her to ignore. She's canny enough to realise he's going off piste.

Giving her a tentative smile, he says, 'That'd be great. Thanks.'

'You should probably know that the Chief Super was looking for you yesterday and again this morning. Wanted to know if you were still sick. She seemed a little... put out.'

'Thanks for the heads up.'

She smiles and returns to her own desk.

Samir glances in the direction of Babcock's office. In the last twenty-four hours, he's ignored three texts and two calls from the boss. He picks up the printout and gets up. He's not sure what he's going to say to her. She's certainly going to want to know what he's been doing. Is he going to challenge her and ask why she lied? Then there's the question of Adam Hardy's disappearance. Should they be looking for him? Has he made a promise to the family that he can't keep?

As he walks over towards the Chief Super's office, he tries to gather his thoughts.

But before he gets there, the door flies open and Babcock barrels out. She has a look of fury on her face.

Seeing him, she bellows 'Sami, with me! Some tosser with a machete has attacked the Chief Medical Officer and the head of Public Health England.'

'My god' says Mehta. 'Where?'

'Outside the Department of Health. SCO19 are at the scene.'

58

DAY 34. 9.45am

The pavement and part of the road has been cordoned off to accommodate the convoy of emergency response vehicles. Traffic is being allowed to filter down one side of Victoria Street in order to prevent total gridlock of the whole area. A white tent has been erected over the site of the incident to cover the bodies. Four armed officers stand guard.

The blanket of fog of the previous day has mostly dispersed thanks to a biting easterly wind straight out of Siberia, but the weather remains as wretched as the scene.

Felicity, wrapped in a foil blanket, stares out of the back of the ambulance at the broad backs of the two armed policemen placed there to protect her. Her professional brain tells her she's in shock, but her fuddled emotions aren't listening.

She looks down at her hands, shaking uncontrollably now, both palms sticky with blood. Dougie's blood. She had tried so desperately to save him, pressing hard on the wounds. But he was slashed in too many places. He bled to death in a matter of moments.

Witnesses to these things always say the same thing: it happened so quickly. Now she knows how true the cliché is.

The man came rushing at them out of nowhere. But Dougie threw out his arm to protect her. He put his body between them. The attack was frenzied. The man was shouting, his face contorted with hatred. He wielded a large blade, curved and serrated. He went at Dougie with a manic fury. Then two shots rang out, rapid little cracks and the attacker dropped to his knees and fell forwards.

A Mercedes pulls up behind the ambulance. Doors open, people get out, Felicity can't see them. But her guards step aside and Pat Babcock looms in front of her, a solid black-coated babushka.

At the sight of her a dam inside Felicity bursts, her mouth opens and she sobs. There seems no end to the pain that erupts from her.

Babcock sits down beside her and pulls her into a soft hug. Felicity becomes aware of her tears falling, making a mess of that beautiful cashmere coat. She pulls away, wipes the back of her hand across her nose.

'Your coat', she says. 'I'm so sorry—'

'Sssh, it's okay.'

The cop snaps her fingers and someone hands her a wodge of tissues. She gives them to Felicity.

'He... the blood... an arterial bleed, I couldn't stop it. I tried, I couldn't—'

'I know,' says the cop. 'There's nothing you could've done.'

'He was aiming at me, Pat. But Dougie—'

She clasps her hand over her mouth, forces the tears to stop. Pat Babcock rubs her back.

'Come on,' says the cop. 'Let's get you out of here.'

Twitter Feed

DAY 34.

True Health News @truehealthnews
OUR MISSION IS TO SAVE LIVES No-one wants violence
on our streets. We certainly don't. Sincere condolences to
the family of Douglas Lacey. But who's responsible?
#governmentlies
21k Retweets 24k Likes

Mark Carter @MCB666
Replying to @truehealthnews
Let's be honest here. One less corrupt official will save lives.
This is about survival. For the whole truth go to
keepsafeandsound.com
#Safeandsound #holdthemtoaccount
13.4k Retweets 15k Likes

Angela Peters @angieP313
Replying to @truehealthnews
I'm against all violence and extremism. I work with kids
with special needs. It's been so hard trying to keep them safe
from potential infection. The government and politicians
don't understand. People are very ANGRY. We want the
truth #governmentlies
463 Retweets 597 Likes

Jared Kent @jaredtheman
Replying to @MCB666
Ditto Mark. Feds shot him. But I say give that dude a
medal.#Safeandsound #holdthemtoaccount

106 Retweets 374 Likes

59

DAY 34. 10.15am

The black cab inches along Stamford Street. The driver wears a soft silicone respirator. He turns his head to glance at Adam. His voice is muffled but audible. 'Honestly mate, I think you'd do better to walk.'

'Is it usually like this?'

'Nah, something in Victoria Street. Terrorist related so they've cordoned it all off. Geezer went at some Whitehall suit with a zombie knife.'

'A zombie knife?'

'Chopped his bloody head clean off. That's what it says online.'

Adam sighs. 'What the hell?'

'I don't support violence. No way. But they bring it on themselves.'

'How d'you figure that?'

'Stuff that goes on behind the scenes, we don't know the half of it. The public should be told the truth.'

Adam stares at the back of the driver's head, grey and balding, shoulders hunched over the wheel. The image of David's killer slips into his mind. *The lies the spook told him.* He feels claustrophobic. The prospect of a cold, brisk walk is suddenly appealing.

'I don't know London that well,' he says. 'If I walk from here, can you tell me the way?'

'Ain't you got a phone?'

'Not that sort.'

The cabbie gives him a pitying look. 'Go over Waterloo Bridge.'

'I know that.'

'Left down the Strand, across Trafalgar Square and down Pall Mall. Then I'd ask someone. All the posh clubs are round there. I'd rap that scarf round your face, n'all. Safe and sound, mate.'

Adam gets out of the cab, pays the driver and starts to walk.

It feels odd to be in possession of a piece of information that could stop all this. The masks, the suspicion, the anger. After his realisation in the shower, he'd sat for some time staring at the drawing he'd made. The picture in his mind was clear, although it felt odd. How could it suddenly be there? If he had a computer or a smartphone, he'd have gone online and looked at some of these devices. Were they as common as he thought, and how exactly did they work?

He wished he could talk to Jason. He considered calling home, asking Zoe for the number. But then the last thing he needed was to have to explain himself to his wife.

There was no landline in Mia's flat but taking the key and the door code, Adam went downstairs to the concierge's desk. A bored-looking boy in some kind of generic uniform sat at the counter engrossed in his phone. He peered up at Adam from behind a grubby surgical mask.

'Hi,' said Adam. He held up the key. 'I'm staying with my sister in 24, had my phone nicked, she's gone to work.'

'Mia, saw her go out.'

'Know any phone shops round here?'

The boy considered this for a moment, then chuckled. 'In't none of my business who she screws. But take care bro, that is one foxy lady. Know what I'm saying?'

The boy directed him to a small shop on Southwark Street. Adam bought the most basic model available plus a ten pound sim for cash and keyed in Mia's number.

The relief of hearing her voice made his heart soar. He felt like a teenager. Confiding in her was obviously the right thing to do. She listened carefully to the information. There was silence on the line as he waited for her response.

'Right,' she said. 'The police are no good. But I know who you should speak to.'

'Okay, who?'

'Well, this is highly confidential, but we're running a campaign for the Department of Health to promote the new anti-viral drug. I think you should meet Hugh.'

'Ryder? The Minister?'

'I'll set it up and get back to you. On this number?'

'I bought a phone.'

'Sensible.' She'd hung up, leaving him oddly bereft. Why was he being so soppy? *Man up.* To distract himself as he waited, he called Nizar and left a friendly message.

It didn't occur to him to even wonder if she could arrange a meeting with a cabinet minister. She knew his brother. He'd seen that with his own eyes. So when the instructions came through by text, he followed them. They'd meet at the Carlton Club in St James's Street.

Adam finds it without further directions. The building is Regency faced in Portland stone and squashed between a redbrick and some fancy shops, it looks drab. But the hallway is much more impressive. As Adam gazes up at the ornate ceiling, he finds a young woman at his elbow.

'Good morning, sir,' she says. 'I'm wondering if you're aware of the dress code?'

'I'm here for a private meeting.'

'You should've been advised that we don't allow jeans.'

Adam glances down at his Levis and laughs. 'You're kidding me. And these are my best pair.'

She smiles apologetically. She has the air of a girl who might spend half her life in jeans.

'It's a rule we're obliged to enforce. I'm sorry.' She shrugs.

'Does it make a difference if I say I'm here for a meeting with Hugh Ryder, the Secretary of State?'

'No, I'm afraid not.'

'You're chucking me out?'

The young woman is joined by a stocky bloke with a weight-lifter's neck and a tailored waistcoat.

'Okay,' says Adam and heads out.

He's pulling the new phone from his jeans pocket when a Tesla draws up kerbside. The passenger door opens and Duncan Ryder gets out.

He seems mildly surprised but smiles at Adam. 'David's friend, isn't it?'

'Yeah, hi. Funnily enough, I'm supposed to be meeting your brother. Mia arranged it.'

Ryder looks him up and down and grins. 'Oh dear,' he says. 'The jeans. You're obviously not aware of how stuffy and up itself the British establishment is.'

'Apparently not.'

Duncan Ryder smiles. 'Rules are for fools. That's my philosophy. Follow me.'

He strolls into the club as if he's walking through his own front door. He eyes the beefy minder in the waistcoat and says, 'This gentleman is with me. Where's my brother?'

The man dips his head and says, 'I believe he's in the Thatcher Drawing Room, sir.'

Ryder places a comradely hand on Adam's arm and shepherds him up the sweeping staircase.

As they reach the top, Mia appears. She doesn't seem surprised that Adam and Duncan Ryder are arriving together.

Ryder smiles, leans in and kisses her lightly on both cheeks. 'I had to rescue our friend here' he says.

Mia frowns. 'Sorry, Adam. I did tell them.'

Tell them what, Adam wonders? That a member of the lower orders was about to rock up in a pair of jeans? But, in spite of his unsuitability, he should be admitted?

He smiles. *Seeing her is enough.*

The Drawing Room is palatial and stately; the furniture, huge paintings and chandeliers look like they could be on loan from the National Trust. Hugh Ryder is encamped in one corner, in shirt sleeves, lounging on a stripy sofa, sipping coffee and checking his phone. A young man sits on an adjacent chair with a heavy pile of papers in his lap.

Mia strides confidently across the room with Adam in her wake. Duncan Ryder pauses to chat to a portly old man, whose jowly features are familiar from a by-gone era.

Hugh Ryder looks up and beams. 'Mr Hardy! I'm so pleased to meet you.' He holds out a hand to shake. 'Some coffee?'

'Thanks.'

The Minister gestures for his guest to sit. He glances at

the young man and says, 'Give us five minutes, Tim.'

Tim nearly drops the heavy sheaf of papers as he gets up. Mia perches on his vacated chair.

'So,' says Ryder, pouring Adam a cup of coffee. 'I understand you have an interesting theory?'

Adam pulls the crumpled note from his jacket pocket and spreads it out. 'I think the virus is being spread in waterborne droplets dispensed from an electronic air freshener. Something like this. You see them in lots of public places.' He traces his finger across the drawing. 'Inside there's a small canister. The electronics are at the top here. I think they work on a timer, pumping out a little squirt of fragrance every ten minutes or so.'

'Interesting' says the Minister. 'He picks up Adam's drawing between thumb and forefinger as though it could be soiled in some way.

There's a blankness in his face that Adam finds disconcerting. The eyes don't blink, the mouth is upturned. But perhaps it's the mask that a life in politics demands; the necessity to be prepared at any instant for the flashbulbs of the paparazzi.

He waves his other hand. 'You have a background in this sort of thing?'

'No.' The question seems vague, but perhaps it's a deflection, giving Ryder time to think.

Adam glances at Mia for support. What has she actually told Ryder? How has she explained his revelation? But her face is composed and neutral too. She seems to be waiting.

Ryder waves the paper about and she takes it from him.

'I think,' he says, 'that we should definitely examine the viability of this... notion of yours.'

'Of course,' says Adam. 'I don't know much about how viruses infect people.'

'You should speak to Hal.'

'But I think water droplets can—'

'You should definitely speak to Hal.'

'Okay. Who's Hal?'

'That's best. We'll arrange it. But you must appreciate, Mr Hardy, the delicacy of the situation.'

The Minister's imperious tone grates on Adam. 'I'm not stupid, Mr Ryder. I know there's a lot of fear out there.'

'Exactly. So, we will look at this in stages and rely on your absolute discretion. No talking to the press or going online. Agreed?'

'Well, yes but—'

'I'm sure I don't need to stress that this is a matter of national security.' Ryder stares at him. The eyes are dark and glassy. He holds out his hand to shake. 'Don't think that we don't appreciate this.'

Mia stands up. The interview is over. Adam hasn't even touched his coffee.

He hesitates. This is not what he was hoping for. He wanted to say something about the spook, to raise the question of who can be trusted. But Ryder is already checking his phone.

Irritation rising, Adam stands up and says, 'I'm kind of surprised that you're not taking this more seriously.'

Ryder gives him a sour look. 'We've had, at the last count, Mr Hardy, fifty-two expert opinions on how this is being done, not to mention several thousand suggestions from the public. I am taking you seriously, and Dr. Henry Shawcross is a leading expert on the H7N9 virus. He is in a much better position than me to assess the feasibility of your theory.'

'Shall we, Adam?' says Mia. Her hand gently brushes his arm.

60

DAY 34. 11.30am

Zoe Hardy finds little to say to her brother-in-law on the drive to London. Searching for something to listen to on Spotify, she chooses an old pop playlist she made to cheer herself up when Adam first became ill. Jason slumps in the passenger seat, earbuds in, eyes shut. Her old hatchback grinds along at a steady sixty in the slow lane. At times like this, she wishes it was a Porsche; resistance to her father comes at a price.

Phil Rowett, in his usual fashion, had tried to take control of the situation the previous afternoon. But DI Mehta had remained polite and unmoved by the list of influential names her father insisted he could call upon to sort out *this God awful mess.*

Fortunately, the old man doesn't know the half of it and Zoe wasn't about to enlighten him. She knows his views: Adam Hardy hasn't lived up to expectations, so trade him in, upgrade to a new model. He wouldn't say it this bluntly. Ruth wouldn't let him, but it's basically what he thinks.

What does she think, though? Does she love him? Her gorgeous husband, the father of her children. That question has been rattling round her head for months. She's played the caring wife, but illness is a challenge. Being dutiful and patient in the face of misfortune does not suit Zoe Rowett. She was the girl with all the luck. Marriage was on her tick list, obviously. But she'd never considered what being a wife might actually entail. In sickness and in health? When they got to about eighty, maybe. If she's brutally honest, she feels she's been short-changed.

The cop had gone back to London with a vague promise to put out an ANPR alert for Adam's pickup. But since her husband had forgotten his phone, tracking him down would not be easy.

'You think he left it behind deliberately?' Jason asked, once her parents had been hustled out of the door and they were alone.

Zoe had sighed. There was no way she wanted to admit to Jason that her jealousy had caused the row with Adam. The problem was Mia Cunningham had turned out to be totally stunning and Zoe was well aware how silly men can get faced with beauty like that.

She'd evaded the question by saying, 'Where do you think he is?'

Jason had simply shrugged. His attitude annoyed her. When they tried to discuss anything serious, he would always adopt this blithe manner. Did he think he was somehow being cool? To Zoe's mind it was adolescent and ridiculous.

'Christ's sake, Jason,' she said. 'How are we going to sort this out if you insist on talking to me like a teenager?'

'You think this is easy for me?' he replied.

The look on his face was truly pathetic. She wanted to slap him.

'Oh, poor old Jace. Thinks his daddy didn't love him, then got buggered behind the bike sheds in Year 8 and has never recovered.'

He stared at her as if he'd been slapped, then he smirked and said, 'You are the most complete bitch, Zoe. Always were, always will be. I've never understood why my brother married you. God knows he's had plenty of better-looking girlfriends.'

At that moment, they'd both become aware of Lily hovering in the doorway. 'Where's Daddy?' she said, lip quivering. 'Is he sick again?'

'No, sweetheart,' said her mother, going over to the little girl and sweeping her up in a hug.

Jason went to the kitchen sink and poured himself a glass of water. Lily watched the two adults.

'Have I been bad' she asked nervously.

'No, not at all,' said Zoe. 'Uncle Jason's a bit upset with me.'

'Why?'

'Because I'm horrid to him.'

'Why are you horrid?'

Zoe sat down, cradling Lily in her lap. 'I'm a horrible person sometimes. I blame your granddad.'

'You should make up,' said Lily.

'We should,' her mother replied.

Jason turned to face them. 'You want me to find him?' he said.

'You think you know where to look?'

'Don't you?'

She did.

As a result, having deposited the children with her parents, they are on the road heading for London to search for Adam.

Initially, Jason resisted the idea that she should come too, but not much.

He'd given the habitual shrug—he and Adam were so alike—and said, 'Well, I know where her office is, but that's about all.'

'Couldn't you ask Mehta for her home address?'

'I'll text him. But, y'know, he's busy.'

Zoe didn't have the headspace to think about what was going on between Jason and Mehta. Her brother-in-law's relationships puzzled her at the best of times.

Nor could she fathom if he had a plan to find Adam. If he did he wasn't sharing it.

Her solution was to text Nizar Khalid. And, standing in the coffee queue at Leigh Delamere services on the M4, she gets a reply.

Though shy in person in the digital medium, the young man's tone is jaunty and peppered with emojis:

Hey Zoe. Adam called me. Left a message. Didn't say you both in London. Great if we can all hook up. I'm around anytime after 5.

Zoe considers whether to share this response with Jason. Even though he behaves like a dick, it doesn't mean she should follow suit. He does have a direct line to the police, which they may need. Also, if she's honest, dealing with Adam on her own is not a prospect she relishes. Like it or not, she and Jason will be more effective as a team.

61

DAY 34. 11.45am

The savage killing of Douglas Lacey, CEO of Public Health England, has flashed round the internet, the country and the world in the form of juddering phone footage taken by a stunned passer-by in Victoria Street. In some versions, the relentless blows raining down on the prostrate figure have been edited, but some platforms have retained the full horror.

It took forty-five seconds for the armed police officer stationed in the foyer of the Department of Health and Social Care to reach the incident, and five seconds later, the assailant was taken out. Both he and Lacey were pronounced dead at the scene.

The murder is being treated as terrorist related, speculation as to the attacker's identity is rife although his allegiance was in no doubt. He wore a high-vis vest emblazoned with #safeandsound.

Mehta sits at his desk pondering, turning a gel pen over end to end. He's witnessed enough random slaughter on the streets of London, especially with knives, to approach the matter with professional detachment.

The first question which needs answering is: was the attacker a lone wolf or part of a wider conspiracy? Resources and personnel have been rapidly redeployed to tackle this and assess the continuing threat.

Babcock has rushed off to a meeting with the Commissioner. Additional analysts are arriving from the National Crime Agency. Pramiti has been allocated the task of finding them all space to work.

As she hurries past him Mehta says, 'Hey, Pramiti. Don't suppose you ever found that van?'

'Yeah' comes the harassed reply. 'DVLA confirmed it was scrapped through a car breakers in Canning Town.'

'Couldn't send me the details, could you?'

'Of course.' She gives him a quizzical look. But it's not her place to question the DI's priorities.

The atmosphere in the office is taut but unusually quiet, with everyone working at full tilt to complete their designated tasks. The interpretation of data and the strategising takes place elsewhere. As a DI, Mehta's role is middle management. Babcock and those above her call the shots. The next briefing is scheduled for two o'clock when further instructions will be issued.

They do have a name for the attacker, though it's not being released. A conviction for assault put his DNA on the database. His last known address, his mother's house, is being dismantled by a forensics team. His on-line presence, *@sonofsamtheman*, is being tracked and dissected. Connections and influences are being traced. The picture is emerging of a disaffected white youth, nineteen years old, poorly educated, unemployed, angry; he fits the profile perfectly. Too perfectly. And this is what is niggling Mehta.

It feels to him as if they've been served the ideal distraction. Plenty of blood for the cameras, creating a sense of mayhem and melodrama. Hysteria is being fuelled on social media with tales of decapitation, which is not what happened. But there's only marginally less panic and doom-mongering from the mainstream press. Most television channels have their reporters lined up on Victoria Street wallowing in the horror. The media circus is in full swing.

After more than a month of the flu epidemic, the public are weary, drifting along with their individual lives. People have got used to wearing their masks, it's become a habit. It requires something shocking to get their attention again, to ramp up the sense of fear and dislocation. An attack on two senior government officials in broad daylight on a main thoroughfare is both audacious and considered.

Someone was pulling the killer's strings, either directly or indirectly. This seems clear to Mehta. The problem will be proving it.

A message from Pramiti pops up on his screen. Mehta scrolls through it. It confirms the van that killed David Taylor was discreetly disposed of by compressing it into untraceable scrap. There's a screenshot of the DVLA record and the address of the breakers in Canning Town.

Mehta picks up the grainy printout of the van driver captured on the speed camera. The pixels have been stretched to the limit to produce what is, at best, a shadowy likeness. But it's all he's got.

He stands up, hooks his jacket off the back of the chair and heads out. The question that no one is addressing, so far as he's aware, is: are the murders of David Taylor and Douglas Lacey connected?

Samir Mehta is no conspiracy theorist. But he has an uncanny sense that a much larger scheme is in play, which is neither simple nor random.

62

Zoe and Jason face each other across the melamine table. It's tucked in a corner of the motorway services area away from the main drag of travellers heading to the toilets and the various food franchises.

He traces a line with his fingertip bisecting the wet coffee rings on the unwiped top. She's ticking with irritation. He can feel it—it's easy to piss her off—and, he has to admit, it gives him perverse pleasure.

'Look,' she says with a sigh. 'Adam's been in touch with him.'

'So what are you proposing? We get Nizar to arrange a meeting with Adam and then we pop up and go Surprise!'

'I don't know.'

'Think about it, Zoe. He walked out. He left his phone. He doesn't want to be found.'

'We don't know that.'

'Don't we?'

She rakes her fingers through her hair and says, 'Okay, I'm the horrible cow you wish he'd never married because Adam Hardy is Mr. Perfect and the sun shines out of his arse.'

Her eyes flick away from him. Zoe the sarcastic shrew, always trying to undermine him, that he can handle, mostly. But this? She's visibly shaking. Her chin quivers as she tries to swallow it all down.

He sighs. It's never been easy acknowledging her claim on his brother. When they were younger, girls came and went. Adam always had his pick. But that was sex. The satisfying of bodily needs. It never impinged on the love between the brothers.

Marriage and children had changed all that, had changed Adam. The way that he looked at his kids. The sheer joy. He was besotted. And Jason was left feeling abandoned. It seemed as though Adam had turned his back. It was hard to admit this to himself, let alone say it out loud. What did it make him? A flakey fag? The queer brother who couldn't grow up? What was he supposed to do? Find a husband of his own, get a dog, adopt a kid? Play happy families like all the straight people did? He despised gay men who did that. Grindr was okay, but had its shortcomings. He preferred to pay for sex. It kept the transaction simple and free of emotional baggage.

He looks at his sister-in-law. He knows he's being a total prick. What's happened to Adam, from his illness and the transplant onwards, is killing both of them. He doesn't want to feel sorry for her, but he does.

'We can't run around like headless chickens' he says. 'We've got to get some perspective, a proper analysis of the situation.'

'What's that supposed to mean?' It seems like a genuine question, not a criticism.

'Let's start with the facts. Adam gets a new heart. But he starts to have weird nightmares or visions.'

'He insists they're memories' she says.

'Right. But they're not his memories. He's remembering stuff that's happened to someone else. His donor. Is that even possible? The doctors say no, it's the drugs.'

Zoe wipes her nose with the back of her hand. 'In my experience, doctors are completely dogmatic. No, it's not possible, total nonsense. Until someone proves it is possible and they all change their tune.'

'That's the scientific method, Zoe.' Jason attempts a smile. 'Okay, Adam says he remembers his donor being deliberately killed. He was run off the road by a Luton van in a tunnel. He remembers the face of the driver.'

'The bloke from DEFRA.'

'When Mehta and I looked into it, Adam's story makes sense. The donor was followed and targeted. Died in the Blackwall Tunnel.'

'Jason, we know all this. But I don't see where it gets us.'

'It gets us to the biggest question of all.'

'Which is?' She flashes him a sharp look, a whiff of the other Zoe.

'What has happened to Adam? I don't mean where has he gone. I mean, what's happened and is happening inside him. Inside his body, inside his head. Because, it seems to me, he's got more than another man's heart.'

'This cell memory idea?'

'Yeah.'

They stare at each other.

Zoe frowns and shakes her head. 'What are you saying? Adam's not Adam anymore?'

'Yeah, that's exactly what I'm saying.' Jason feels a rush of relief. Now it's out there. This is what's been keeping him awake, paralysing him, the fear twisting his gut.

'But,' she swallows hard, 'who is he? Some zombie has taken him over. Is that what you're saying?'

'No no, not a zombie. This is serious and real. Although I think there is a kind of fight going on inside him for control. But I have that each time I look at a jam donut.'

The attempt at humour falls flat.

Zoe leans back in her seat, stares out of the window and says, 'She was his girlfriend. He was in love with her. That's why he's gone to her, isn't it?'

'Probably.'

Jason reaches out, clasps her hand and says, 'Look, how do any of us know who we are? We're a bundle of thoughts and feelings and memories. We are who we think we are. Consciousness appears to keep the bundle together. But we use memories to construct the picture we have of the world. Our sense of self comes from that. Maybe the idea that we're one solid, separate person is an illusion.'

Zoe looks at him. The antagonism has drained out of her.

'Sometimes I watch the kids,' she says. 'Their moods change like the weather. Ryan's screaming his head off. A minute later he's smiling.'

'If there is such a thing as cell memory and Adam can feel what it's like to be Feras Khalid, then it's going to change him. He's become someone else. Not totally, but in part.'

'Can he feel it, do you think?'

'When Professor Oldroyd hypnotised him, I think he must've felt it because it completely freaked him out. I tried to tell myself it was a hallucination, an illusion brought on by the drugs.'

'You don't think that anymore?'

'No. And if you're asking what we should do, I have no idea. Not a clue.'

'But you want to help him?'

'Of course I do.'

'I've been thinking for ages that I'd lose him,' she says. 'But not like this. You think about the funeral and getting on for the sake of the kids.'

'Yeah, I know.'

'Jace, we can't abandon him. Part of him is Adam, your brother, my husband.'

'I know. He may not want it, but we have to do it. The question is how?'

She sighs. 'Well, let's look at it from the viewpoint of the new Adam. What does he want?'

'That supposes he even knows. The whole thing must be totally confusing.'

'Okay, what would you do if some bastard had tried to kill you? Me, I'd at least want to know why.'

'You think Adam's going after the killer?'

'I think he could be trying to. Trying to find out through Mia and also maybe Nizar why it all happened.'

'That's dangerous.'

'Yeah. Because whoever they are, they had a reason to kill this Feras Khalid. They'll do the same to Adam if they can. Why wouldn't they?'

63

DAY 34. 12.35pm

The black BMW X5 turns off the M11 at the A14 junction skirting the northern fringes of Cambridge. The sky is leaden, threatening rain or even snow. Adam watches the freezing, sunless landscape skittering by from the back seat.

The meeting with Hugh Ryder had left him dissatisfied. The Minister seemed pompous, but Mia had explained that was his manner. Adam was sure of one thing, he didn't like the man. Nor did he like the way his eye rested on Mia.

As they walked out of the Carlton Club, Mia had assured him that Henry Shawcross was a different proposition. A top-flight research scientist who'd run labs in the US and the UK, he was the man whose opinion counted. Ryder would always hedge his bets, she explained. It's what politicians did. But the scientist would give him a fair hearing. If he was correct and Shawcross was convinced, it would change everything.

By the time they'd stepped out into St James's Street, the

X5 was waiting for them. The man in the passenger seat had got out immediately. He was young, a shaved head and bushy beard.

'This is Lucas,' Mia said. 'He's in charge of security. With the terrorist attack this morning, we're taking no chances. We're on high alert.'

It was hard to tell if Lucas was a first name or last name. He gave Adam a curt nod and opened the back door for him.

Adam turned to Mia. He wanted answers but there seemed to be no time. 'Well, where am I going?' he said.

'Straight to Henry's lab,' she said as if this was obvious. 'In Cambridge. Don't look so worried. Lucas will look after you and I'll see you back at the flat tonight.' She smiled, stroked his forehead and kissed it. 'Okay?'

'Okay,' he replied.

He got into the car.

Neither Lucas nor the driver, who was older, seemed inclined to conversation. There was something military in their manner. Adam supposed that this may well be their background. What was curious was that neither of them wore any sort of face mask.

They travelled in silence until they reached the M11. The heater was blasting out hot air. It was making Adam feel sleepy.

'Can we have the heater off for a bit,' he said.

Lucas glanced round at him. 'Didn't want you to be cold.' He adjusted the switch.

'I'm fine. Thank you.' Then he added, 'Surprised you guys don't wear masks.'

Lucas smiled. He and the driver exchanged glances.

'Well,' said Lucas, 'it's a bit awkward with this beard. Anyway, we've both had jabs, so it's not necessary.'

'Do the jabs even work? Doesn't seem to be what most people think,' said Adam.

Lucas shrugged. 'Depends who you talk to.' He pulled a metal flask from the glove compartment and offered it to Adam. 'Here, have a drink.'

Adam thanked him, unscrewed the top and took a long draft. The water was cool and refreshing. He hadn't realised how thirsty he was. He took a couple more slugs and offered it back.

'Keep it' said Lucas.

The X5 cruised along at a steady seventy. The driver's gloved hands rested lightly on the wheel. Both men seemed alert but relaxed.

The silence didn't bother Adam, although he felt a growing impatience at their lack of urgency. He wished they'd speed up so they could get to Cambridge, see Shawcross and get back to London. He imagined Mia waiting for him in the flat. *The silky softness of her hair brushing his face.* But once he'd spoken to the researcher, and the authorities had acted on the information, what then?

He found he had no room to consider that. His mind was fixated on one thing. His brooding thoughts travelled on a well-worn loop. *Mia. Getting back to Mia.*

As they turn on to the A14, the traffic bunches and slows to a crawl. He stares blankly out of the window but sees nothing. Nearly two hours in the back of the car has left him enervated and drowsy. But somewhere on the edge of consciousness, the ghost of a recollection he can't quite grasp niggles. The frustration of it slides into annoyance. The more he tries to retrieve it, the more fuzzy his thoughts become. *Let go and it'll come. Forget it. Forget it all.* He feels hot.

He unzips his top, exhales loudly.

Lucas glances back at him and says, 'Not long now. This is the turn off to the Science Park coming up.'

The Cambridge Science Park is a high-tech hub spread over many acres of low-rise buildings shielded by trees. The ornamental lake is semi-frozen and glassy in the frosty air.

As they drive round the circular access road, Adam shudders. More heat. He's seized by a sudden impulse to vomit. The bile is rising, stinging his throat. He clasps a hand over his mouth.

'I need to stop! Now! Please.'

'It's okay, we're here,' says Lucas.

The X5 turns into a driveway and pulls up in front of a square, glass and steel building three stories high.

Adam throws open the door, leans out and pukes. The remains of his breakfast form a small puddle on the gritted concrete.

He feels a hand on his shoulder, steadying him. He's handed a tissue. Wiping his mouth, he looks up.

'I'm sorry,' he says. But the words die on his lips. *The black X5! It followed him. He was running from it.* That's what he needed to remember.

'Better out than in, I find' says Tony, patting his shoulder. 'I wasn't expecting to see you again, son. But you seem to be turning into more of a problem than we thought.'

Twitter Feed

DAY 34.

Hugh Ryder MP @hughryder
All right-minded people must share my horror at the brutal
murder of my dear friend Douglas Lacey. Staff at @DHSC-
govuk and @PHE_uk are working flat out. We must stand
together and remain united. #staywell
479 Retweets 730 Likes

Hospital Watch @hospitals24/7
An independent nationwide survey shows the number of flu
deaths falling confirming the success of @PHE_uk new anti-
viral treatment. Go to bit.ly/3AdkC567pl for survivors stories
#healthandhope
460 Retweets 591 Likes

True Health News @truehealthnews
Replying to @hospitals24/7
Independent? Guess where they get their stats –@DHSC-
govuk. It's just part of the government cover-up. Go to
truthhealthnews.com for the truly independently verified
facts. #pandemic #governmentlies
24.8k Retweets 31k Likes

Anushka Anand @AA539
Replying to @truehealthnews
These so-called survivors stories. They filmed it at our
hospital using actors. I saw them. TOTAL LIES! Bodies are
stacked in our mortuary. They didn't film that!#govern-
mentlies #pandemic #safeandsound

16.8k Retweets 20k Likes

64

Samir Mehta sits in his car and watches. The side street is a dead end and close to the River Lea. Either side of the road chain link fencing divides off small industrial lots. Some of them look vacant, weeds growing through the tarmac, rusty padlocks hanging on gates. But RapidKlean Cleaning Solutions appears to be a going concern. There's a sizeable warehouse with a one story sixties-built office block tacked on the side. Three new white Vauxhall Combo vans with the company logo are parked out front.

Their website is smart. Mehta scrolls through it on his phone, but it makes no mention of specific personnel.

He's been to the car breaker's yard in Canning Town and they were helpful. The boss was Romanian and anxious to emphasise that everything they did was above board. He followed all the regulations and didn't want any trouble. Consulting his records, he found the Luton van.

'Yeah' he said. 'Lee picked it up.'

'Is Lee around?' Mehta asked.

Lee Kelly looked about forty, tall and scrawny, with a rasping smoker's cough.

'I was helping a mate out,' he said defensively. 'But they done all the DVLA stuff.'

'Tell me about your mate,' said the DI with a smile.

'It was a heap. No reason to think it weren't completely kosher.'

'See that, Lee,' said Mehta, holding up his warrant card. 'It says Detective Inspector, I'm with Counter Terrorism. So think hard and tell me about your mate.'

Lee's mate had turned out to be his sister Wendy, who worked for a cleaning company in Hackney. Neither brother nor sister had a criminal record. Wendy Kelly was on the electoral register and paid her council tax.

But, as Mehta had turned to leave the small Portakabin office at the breaker's yard, Lee had retorted, 'Don't know what you lot think you're up to. Wendy done what her boss asked her. And he's connected to your lot, anyway.'

'My lot? How?'

'I dunno. But Wendy's done nothing wrong.'

The comings and goings at RapidKlean Cleaning Solutions in the half an hour Mehta watches comprise a transit van with a ladder on top returning and a young girl, possibly in her late teens, stepping out of the office block for a cigarette. She looks too young to be a candidate for Wendy, but Mehta decides to use the opportunity.

Getting out of his car, he strolls across the road and into the yard.

'Afternoon' he says.

The girl eyes him suspiciously and continues to suck on her cigarette. Her arms are folded, and she's shivering in her skimpy top. Mehta cannot fathom why anyone would want to smoke enough to stand out in the freezing cold to do it.

'Don't suppose you're Wendy,' he says.

She shakes her head. 'She's inside.'

'You worked here long?'

'I'm a temp. Come in when they need me.' She gives him a wary look. 'You a cop?'

'Well spotted,' says Mehta. 'You seen any others round here?'

'Uniforms, nah. Never around when you need 'em. Kid got stabbed on the High Road, bled to death 'fore the police turned up.'

'I mean, have any plain clothes officers like me been here lately?'

'I don't know nothing,' says the girl sullenly. 'Ask Wendy. She practically runs the place.'

'Thank you. I will.'

Opening the glass panel door, Mehta steps into the warm fug of the office. There's a small reception desk and an open-plan area behind. A oscillating fan heater is going full blast and seated at a computer screen beside it is a plump, rosy cheeked woman with a startling shock of bright ginger hair done in tight ringlets.

She glances up from her keyboard and removes her glasses, but she doesn't smile.

Mehta pulls out his warrant card and says 'Hello. I'm Detective Inspector Mehta. I'm presuming you're Wendy Kelly.'

Nodding, she gets up and approaches the desk. The tension pulses off her. He decides on a low-key approach.

He smiles and says, 'I'm hoping you can help me with a bit of background information about the firm. RapidKlean Cleaning Solutions, it's a clever name.'

Wendy shrugs. This doesn't appear to be what she's expecting. 'It's all right, I 'spose.'

'Tell me about the business.'

'Cleaning. All sorts, domestic and commercial.'

'How many staff?'

'We got ten teams, some two-man, some three, depending on the size of the job.'

'All men?'

'No, turn of phrase. Maybe eight women. Domestic cleans usually prefer women.'

'Are most of your contracts in London?'

'Used to be. Now we go all over.'

Mehta scans her face. The eyes are pale blue, beautiful but guarded. Her manner is on the polite side of surly. But her anxiety is palpable. Time to turn the screw.

'I met your brother, Lee, this morning,' he says.

She raises her chin. 'Yeah, I know.'

As expected, he's called to warn her.

'Let's put our cards on the table, shall we?' says Mehta. 'I know you had a Luton van scrapped for someone else. I know you probably had little choice in the matter. But we're not talking about scams or petty villainy here. I'm not interested in that. I'm here because the van you disposed of could be connected with a serious terrorist incident.'

Her face falls.

Mehta continues, 'Have you seen the news this morning?'

'Shit. Not the bloke that was hacked to death? My son had it up on YouTube. It was horrible.'

He can feel her panic. Now she knows she's in more trouble than she thought.

He fixes her with an unremitting stare. 'He was the CEO

of Public Health England. He was murdered in broad daylight on Victoria Street.'

'Listen, I don't know nothing about any of that. I haven't seen the boss for days. He's a bloody law unto himself and a complete shyster.' Her face reddens and the words spill from her with increasing rapidity. 'I try to do my job. He told me to get the van scrapped, and that's all I done. I swear on my kids' lives. And when she come round and told me to text him, I done what she said too. I thought she was a cop. Looked like one to me, but what do I know? Jesus Christ, I'd never have nothing to do with people getting murdered.'

'A woman came round? What did she look like?'

'Short, fat, well dressed. Came in a Merc.'

Mehta's stomach does a backflip. He swallows, reaches into his jacket pocket and draws out the neatly folded printout that Pramiti had obtained of the Luton van driver from the speed camera.

Unfolding it, he lays it on the counter in front of Wendy. 'Recognise him?'

She peers at the image. 'Can I get my glasses?'

Mehta nods. 'Take your time. Have a good look.'

Wendy retreats to her desk, picks up her the blue framed specs. Mehta studies her, her hands are shaking.

Returning to the counter, she sighs and hands him the printout. 'Yeah,' she says, 'bit blurred, but it's definitely the boss.'

Mehta gives her a reassuring smile and says, 'Okay, how about you make a nice cup of tea and we'll sit down and go through this bit by bit.'

'You ain't nicking me then?' She looks relieved.

'No, I'm going to take a written statement because I can see you want to help.'

She's sweating. She wipes her forehead with her fingers. 'I've never been in trouble with the law. You can check.'

'I already have.'

She takes a deep breath and blinks at him. 'Sometimes I dunno what's going on in this sodding country.'

'I agree with you there, Wendy.'

'Never had this sort of thing when I was a kid. Everyone carrying a knife. It's bonkers. I tell my three that 'til I'm blue in the face.'

He nods and smiles. Now she's decided to open up, she looks at him expectantly like a small child hoping for guidance from a kindly adult. Well, he can certainly provide that.

'Let's start with the boss, shall we? What's his name?'

'Tony Franklin. He's only been running the firm for a month or so. And he scares the shit out of me, I can tell you. There's something wrong about him. He took over all of a sudden because the old boss got killed.'

'What happened to him?'

She goes into the adjacent kitchen, lifts the kettle off its base and fills it.

Coming back she replies 'Crashed his motorbike. He was okay. Bit of a rogue, Dave. Well, this game most of them are. But I liked him. Killed outright, sad. It's down to him that we're doing so well. Tough but fair, knew how to treat people. As I say, sad. You take sugar?'

'Just a splash of milk, thanks,' says Mehta.

65

DAY 34. 2.30pm

During her party-filled, boozy university career, Zoe Hardy had several summer internships in London. She'd worked at a swanky advertising firm in Soho, owned by a business acquaintance of her father's; their office was full of long tables, sofas and beanbags and closely resembled the PR firm where Mia Cunningham works.

As she stands in the chic reception area, Zoe recognises the carefully manufactured vibe of the place and also the manner of Mia's sniffy assistant who says, 'Her schedule today is stacked, I'm afraid. She does apologise, but perhaps I can help you.'

Zoe and Jason exchange looks.

'I doubt that,' says Zoe, staring down at Nin from her superior height. 'Now go and tell her that we and also the police are trying to locate my husband as a matter of urgency. I'm sure she wouldn't wish to be obstructive.'

Nin blinks a couple of times and trots off with her message.

Several minutes later Mia herself appears, wreathed in smiles. 'I am so sorry. I was speaking to a colleague in New York and Nin can be a little overprotective.'

'I'm sure that's what you underpay her for,' says Zoe with a chilly smile.

Mia simply smiles back.

'You're looking for Adam?' she says 'Is there a problem?'

Zoe isn't about to explain herself.

'Have you seen him?'

'Only briefly. Yesterday. He came here. He wanted to get in touch with Nizar.'

'That's odd,' says Zoe, 'because Nizar did leave his number and email when you visited us.'

Mia shrugs. 'Perhaps he forgot or spaced it out. I must admit, he did seem a little confused.'

Jason has been hanging back, preferring to let the two women slug it out. He finds Mia impossible to read. There's a polite but steely implacability about her, which is difficult to penetrate.

'Confused in what way?' he asks.

Mia sighs, purses her lips. 'I don't think he's terribly well. He had a dizzy spell while he was here. And London is not a good place to be right now. Especially for someone like him.' She shakes her head with concern and adds, 'I think you're right to be worried.'

Zoe continues to glare at her. But she keeps her anger in check.

The private all girls' school she'd attended had its fair share of bitches like Mia. They had the same unassailable belief in their own superiority. The playground hierarchy had been brutal and Zoe knew from experience that showing any weakness was the worst thing she could do.

Her brain is nattering with questions. Has this woman seduced her husband away? Is he holed up in her flat somewhere? Have they slept together? Does she think she needs to protect him from his shrewish wife?

But if Mia reckons she can blatantly lie and shame Zoe into backing off, she needs to think again.

Zoe tilts her head and fixes the other woman with a penetrating stare. 'If you think you're helping him, trust me, you're not.'

'I don't know what you're talking about.' Her smile is almost teasing, but Zoe doesn't rise to the bait.

'Yeah you do,' she says equably. 'He may have David's heart, but he's not David. Okay, he's drawn to you and you may find some temporary relief from your grief in that. But what's next? He is confused. You're right about that. This whole situation is a monumental mindfuck. You sure you want to take that on? I assure you he needs a lot of looking after.'

Mia remains unmoved, her face a serene mask.

'Like I said' she replies, 'Adam came here yesterday. I was out at lunch with a client. Our receptionist gave him a coffee. When I returned, we spoke for around fifteen minutes. He was feeling unwell. I urged him to go home. He refused. He talked about David, said he wanted to understand more about who he was, what experiences had formed him. We agreed that I couldn't help him that much. But Nizar could. I took him downstairs and put him in a taxi. All of this can be verified with the staff here, should the police wish to do so.' The glacial stare doesn't waiver.

'Do you know where he went?' says Jason.

'He said he needed to find a hotel, rest, then arrange to see Nizar. I imagine the police can trace his credit card.'

Jason nods. 'Do you know the name of the hotel?'

'I'm afraid I don't.'

Zoe feels her gut churning with rage. She's aware of Mia's eyes upon her, watching her with an anthropological interest.

'I can see how stressed you are, Zoe,' she says, 'but if you think that something untoward has gone on between me and your husband, you are completely wrong. You and Adam have a wonderful marriage which has supported him through some terrible trials. Not to mention two lovely children. You don't know me, but I can assure you I'm not the kind of woman who'd wish to undermine all that.'

'I think Zoe knows that,' says Jason. 'And we're grateful for your time and your candour.'

'I only wish I could be more help. And I hope you find him.'

Jason puts a gentle hand on his sister-in-law's arm and starts to shepherd her out. It stops her from blowing a fuse. But only just.

He opens the door for her and she walks through it. She can feel Mia's gaze on her back. Now she wants to escape. She clatters down the stairs and out into the street.

Then she turns on Jason.

'Her time and her candour? Are you kidding me! What bollocks was that? You don't believe her, surely?'

'No,' says Jason calmly. 'I think she's lying through her teeth. But we don't want her to know that, do we?'

66

DAY 34. 2.45pm

The room is small and claustrophobic—a faux leather treatment couch, a desk, a cupboard. The roller blind over the tiny window is closed.

Lucas and the driver, grasping Adam's arms round their necks, had hauled him from the car, round the side of the building and in through the loading dock. He'd thought about struggling or crying out for assistance but a lethargy consumed him, his feet dragged and his limbs wouldn't support him. He felt hot and light-headed but also annoyed. Annoyed at himself for not realising who they were. *Same bastards. He knew it.*

They'd dumped him none too gently on the couch, left him and locked the door. He'd tried, but it was impossible to get up. He'd lain prostrate, drifting in and out of consciousness.

Each time he surfaced, he replayed the sequence of events. Tony was there when they'd arrived, he was sure of it. He'd thrown up, Tony had handed him a tissue and spoken to him. Then he'd disappeared.

Had the cheap burner phone Adam bought in Southwark Street been removed from his pocket by Lucas? He couldn't recall. But it was gone.

This half waking, half sleeping stupor had continued for some time.

But slowly, by degrees, his muzzy head begins to clear and his jagged vision settles.

He sits up and tries to fathom why he'd been so sick and then crashed out. He remembers the flask of water Lucas gave him and how thirsty he was because of the heat in the car. Now it makes sense. *Bloody obvious*. They drugged him. *Bastards*.

Attempting to stand, he finds he's a little giddy. His mouth is extremely dry. He manages the two steps to the window and opens the blind. It appears he's at the back of the building on the first floor. He tries the window; it's locked.

He continues to explore his makeshift cell. It's a first aid or medical room. In the cupboard there's a tray of dressings and a pack of anti-bacterial wipes.

He walks up and down. Taking some deep breaths helps him feel steadier on his feet. The door doesn't look that robust, hollow panelled MDF with an ordinary lock. Adam puts his ear to it and listens. Nothing. *Kick the bastard in.*

The impulse is strong, but he resists it. He needs to think things through, not simply react. He sits back down on the couch as he tries to make sense of what's happened. His head is filled with a cacophony of questions, a jumble of emotions.

Why is he here? Why have they done this to him? It doesn't make a lot of sense. They were taking him to

Cambridge to explain his theory to some research scientist. Are they in Cambridge? Yes. He remembers the drive up the M11 and turning off towards the Science Park. But when they arrived, Tony was waiting. How did he know? 'More of a problem than we thought', that's what he said. *Too right!*

Adam feels a surge of energy and rage. He tries to contain it. He must think not react, but his brain is squirming with conflicting drives. Mia told him this was the man to convince, this Shawcross. Has Tony waylaid him to stop him talking to Shawcross? That seems the most logical explanation. Lucas and Tony are somehow in league. They've drugged and kidnapped him to stop him getting to the scientist. To stop the truth from coming out.

He's breathing hard with the effort of holding it all together. It feels as if his head might explode. A surging fury rises in his chest. If he doesn't move it'll choke him.

He jumps up, lifts his right foot and boots the door hard below the handle. *One, two, three!* On the third blow the wood cracks tearing the lock away from the door jamb. *Yes!* He puts his shoulder against it and a shove finishes the job. The effort leaves him gasping. The door pivots on its hinges and falls open. Adam steps through the gap.

67

DAY 34. 2.48pm

Adam stands, swaying slightly, glancing from left to right along an empty corridor. He grasps the steel hand rail running along it. Through the window is a car park and beyond a row of dismal Leylandii filtering a few sparse rays of fading wintry sunshine.

He can feel his heart beating, thumping in his chest. Behind him, the broken door creaks and twists on its remaining hinge. As his anger subsides, a sense of desolation floods in to replace it.

Shawcross. Find Shawcross. Mia said he would understand.

Turning right, he sets off down the corridor. The building is light and airy. The glass of the vast windows gives way to slabs of exposed concrete and he comes to a broad spiral stairway of transparent glass treads, which rises through an imposing central atrium to a skylight.

He rests his palm on the balustrade. Which way? Up or down?

A woman in a lab coat comes strolling round the corner. Looking up from her clipboard she smiles at him, then frowns.

'Are you lost?' she says.

'Shawcross?' His voice sounds disembodied, hardly a croak.

The woman scans him, the smiles falters.

'You mean Dr. Shawcross?'

'Yeah. Does he work here?' There's no guarantee they've even brought him to the right place.

'Are you all right? You seem a bit—'

'Tell me. Please.' He doesn't mean to snap, but it comes out all wrong.

She hesitates. 'Yes, he's our CEO. Do you have an appointment? Perhaps if you go downstairs to reception, they'll be able to help you.'

Adam shakes his head. He can tell from her expression that he must look awful.

'He is expecting me.'

Pulling out her phone, she paints on a smile. 'I'll get someone to come and help you.'

Adam shakes his head and starts to walk away. He feels hot. He can hear the woman speaking, probably calling security. *Push the bitch down the stairs.*

He hurries round the corner and starts to run. Lumbering, he weaves from side to side across the corridor, trips over his own feet and crashes to the polished tile floor.

As he tumbles, he realises how ridiculous this is. He has to get a grip. He's done nothing wrong. But the woman's reaction confirms how suspicious his actions must look.

He struggles to his feet. Stand. Breathe. He leans a hand

against the wall to get his balance. Glancing up he notices that there are cameras in all the corners, compact, white and discreet. Well, there would be.

A young man, another lab coat, appears at the far end of the corridor. He's slight in build with heavily rimmed glasses, hardly the usual security tough. He walks towards Adam with a neutral expression. As he gets close, he smiles and says 'Mr Hardy? Dr Shawcross is expecting you. Please come this way.'

Adam nods and tries not to look surprised. 'Yes, thank you.'

He follows the young man, using the short walk to compose himself. None of it makes sense. But maybe it's him.

Ever since he became aware of the fragments of memory inherited from his donor, nothing has made sense. He slips in and out of the life he once knew and then sometimes he seems to drop through the net into another realm. It's full of feelings and impulses which he knows are not his, and yet strangely they are. His world has become surreal. Thoughts ambush him from hidden corners. Urges he can't control flood through him. And then sometimes it all goes quiet.

When he's in the quiet place, he knows he's safe. He imagines a room with soft sunlight and an aura of tranquility. The problem is how to find his way back there.

The young man leads him into a spacious corner office suite with floor to ceiling windows on two sides. An imposing black ash desk sits diagonally across the room, strewn with glossy photographic prints. The young lab assistant immediately retires.

Dr Shawcross, small and pot-bellied, is leaning over the desk and staring at the images through round John Lennon specs. He looks up as Adam enters, tugs at his beard and smiles. He wears a white T-shirt emblazoned with an image of the Spice Girls superimposed on a Union Jack.

'Adam!' he says. 'Glad you're feeling better. They said you got a bit car sick.' He comes round the desk, hand outstretched. 'Hal Shawcross. Been dying to meet you. You're quite a phenomenon, I understand.'

Adam shakes the damp palm and says, 'I don't know about that.'

'Cell memory. I've read about it, of course, but in the flesh. Wow! I want to know what it feels like. Is it spooky? Kind of Jekyll and Hyde?' His eyes are small and bright and brimming with enthusiasm.

'I wasn't car sick,' says Adam. 'I was drugged.'

'You sure? I don't see why anyone would do that.'

'They locked me in some kind of medical room.'

Shawcross blinks a couple of times and shrugs. 'I think they wanted to give you time to recover.'

'They want to stop me from talking to you because I'm here to tell you how it's being done, how the flu virus is being spread,' says Adam.

'Yeah, I gather' says the little researcher. 'So this is something you can actually remember? How does that work? Is it like a dream?'

'Not a dream. I was awake, staring at the white tiles in the shower. And then I realised. You know these electronic air fresheners they have. In public toilets. They're everywhere. They're on some kind of timer and at intervals they pump out a fragrance. I think that's how the virus is being spread, in the tiny droplets they spray out.'

Shawcross beams and shakes his head. 'That's amazing,' he says. 'And you didn't figure this out for yourself. You knew it, all of a sudden? It's a memory you've somehow got from your donor?'

'Yes. I think so. I don't know how he knew, but I think this is how it's being done.'

Shawcross takes off his glasses and polishes them on the baggy hem of his T-shirt. 'Man, that is such a precise memory. Amazing! And can you picture one of these devices?'

'Yes' says Adam. 'I can draw it if you like.'

'Wow.'

'So do you think I'm right? Could this be how it's being done?'

'Oh yeah,' says Shawcross blithely. 'It's right. You're spot on. It provides the perfect delivery system. How do I know?' He grins with pride. 'You're looking at the guy who worked out how to adapt these air fresheners to do it.'

68

DAY 34. 2.50pm

Felicity Oldroyd sits on the end of the double bed. Her hands are folded in her lap, she wears a fresh pair of cotton pyjamas, and her feet are snuggly slotted into the soft, fluffy mules she got for Christmas.

Phoebe sits behind her. 'Shall I dry your hair for you?' she asks.

The voice seems to drift in towards Felicity from afar. It drags her from a convoluted train of thought. Can she get back to it? No. It's gone. Her skittish mind rambles on and refuses to settle.

Raising a finger, she touches the back of her own head and yes, it does appear to be damp. Of course it is.

When she'd finally got home, all she wanted was a shower. But they were lined up in the hallway, like mourners at a funeral: Gerry, her husband, her son Alistair and Phoebe. They all looked at her as if she was a ghost. She felt like a ghost. Then there was the hugging and clutching. But all she'd wanted was to take a shower.

Doctors are used to blood, to other people's blood. She reminds herself of this. *Blood is a chemical mixture, not a compound, made up of haemoglobin and plasma... what are the four main components and their functions?*

'Mum,' says Phoebe, 'shall I get the hair dryer?'

'I can manage,' Felicity says brightly.

'You don't have to manage.'

She can hear the crack in her daughter's voice. She turns and sees that her child is weeping.

Wrapping her arms carefully round her daughter's shoulders, she cradles her. 'Oh, it's all right. Sssh!'

'This is my fault, my bloody fault!' wails Phoebe.

'Don't be silly,' says her mother. 'How can it be your fault?'

'Because I guessed it!' Phoebe spits the words out emphatically even through her tears. It reminds Felicity of when she was little and the vehemence with which she'd always fight her corner. *He pushed me, Mummy. Alistair did it!*

'What do you mean, you guessed it?'

'The signs were all there. The chat on social media. The way they kept using your photo. All the trolling.'

'Phoebe, if someone told this awful boy to do what he did, then the police will find out.'

'But what if it's more subtle than that? It's more like a grooming. Not of someone specific, but of anyone who might be floating around out there. It's how terrorists operate. Alistair talked to Freddie. Remember him, he works for this monitoring group and he said—'

'My lovely girl, I know you want to solve this and protect me but the police—'

'I know I know! But listen' Mum, what if their analytics are being applied on the basis of the wrong assumptions?'

'I'm not sure I even know what that means.'

'The police are looking for a culprit. So the data trails they're following are predicated on that: who's been spreading the virus. But what if that's beside the point?'

'You're saying the point is fear. Pat and I did talk about that.'

'But that fear is being fuelled. It may be happening haphazardly, people being idiots. But what if it's not?'

'How can you prove that?'

'Are they tracking political sentiment on social media?'

'Good Lord, Phoebe, I don't know. Are they even allowed to?'

Phoebe clutches her own head in frustration. 'Arghh!' she growls.

'You're not responsible' says Felicity gently.

Wiping her face on her sleeve, Phoebe says. 'We thought you were gone. Alistair saw an alert on his phone, but for oh, four, five minutes, they didn't say who was actually dead. If it was both of you. I thought Dad would... well, I don't know. I've never seen him like that before. I sort of expected him to be calm, but he wasn't.'

Felicity smiles. 'Poor old boy. I am so sorry I've put you all through this.'

'I think Dad's going to want you to retire.'

Felicity nods. Her husband has already enveloped her in a fierce protective hug and whispered: *no more, they can't have any more, you're too precious.* Now he's retreated to the study for, she suspects, a stiff drink or two.

Soon they'll have been together for forty years. She can't imagine life without him. But he's got some bad habits—

he's a secret smoker—and a dicky heart so, in the end, there will probably be no refuge for her.

As she contemplates the desert of old age, the idea comes to her in a rush as if her melancholy, self-pitying brain has been zapped. She feels immediately energised.

'Are there TV crews outside?' she says.

Phoebe nods. 'Loads. Dad was so relieved he took them all mugs of tea.'

Felicity stands up. 'I need to dry my hair and put some clothes on.'

'What? Why?'

'Look in the wardrobe. Find me something assertive.'

'Mum—'

'No, maybe casual would be better. Nice pair of jeans.'

Phoebe stares at her, slack-jawed.

But her mother smiles serenely. She knows exactly what she must do. For Dougie and to end this madness.

'Don't look so worried. Your father will get his wish,' she says. 'I am going to retire. But I've got one last job to do first.'

69

DAY 34. 2.53pm

Adam Hardy sits in a chair. Shawcross perches on the edge of his desk, arms folded, facing him.

'Sure you feel okay? Can I get you some water?'

'Yeah, thanks' says Adam.

Collapsing in a chair is the best ploy he can come up with. He's stunned. This is the person responsible for spreading the virus? Why would Ryder send him here? But maybe the Minister doesn't know, he's been duped too?

Adam needs to buy some time, that much he knows, although he has no intention of drinking anything he's given.

Shawcross goes to the door, puts his head round it and speaks to someone outside.

Returning, he sighs and says 'I know this is all pretty far out and a lot for you to take in.'

'No, I'm beginning to get it,' says Adam. 'I think I've figured it out.'

'Have you?' says the little scientist, tugging a tuft of beard. He has the manner of an over-excited gnome.

Keeping him talking seems a good strategy to Adam.

'Yeah,' he says, 'you've made this anti-viral drug that you want to sell. So you've taken the flu virus it's meant to cure and deliberately spread it round the country. Then when people get sick, you can tell the government you've got the answer. They buy the drug and you become filthy rich. Is that the basic plan?'

Shawcross beams. His sharp eyes twinkle. 'That's pretty astute' he says. 'You're clearly an educated man.'

'Not really. I dropped out of uni. My wife's the one with the business brain.'

'What you're suggesting has some plausibility. And I'll be honest, there will be some incidental financial gain on a personal level, but that's not what this is about. Not at all. Our ambitions are far larger than that.'

'What? You reckon you're going to save the planet by killing a few million off with the flu?'

Shawcross giggles. 'I like you, Adam. I like your ballsy attitude. You're the sort of man we need on our side.'

'Was David Taylor or Feras or whatever you called him on your side?'

Shawcross shakes his head sadly. 'He was a cog in the wheel, a small and troublesome one. Now his motive definitely was money.'

The door to the office opens and Tony strolls in. He's carrying a bamboo tray. Adam glares. It was him. He didn't imagine it. That thought at least brings him some relief.

'How you feeling, son,' Tony says. 'Not too worse for wear, I hope?'

He places the tray on the desk. On it are three cups, a teapot and milk jug, a bowl of sugar cubes and a can of coke.

'Cup of tea?' he says, lifting the pot.

'You drugged me,' says Adam.

Picking up the can of coke, Tony grins. 'Just a precaution. But here's a nice cold can of coke, completely sealed. No one's interfered with it, you can check.'

He holds the can out. Although he's thirsty, Adam shakes his head.

'Suit yourself. But you must've figured that if we wanted to get rid of you, it'd be done and dusted by now.'

The tone of voice is teasing; the bastard thinks he can toy with him.

Adam meets his gaze head on. He won't be intimidated. 'Why am I here then?'

Tony pours two cups and says, 'Hal was intrigued when he heard about you.'

Shawcross beams. 'Such a fantastic opportunity. I wanted to meet you in person,' he says. 'You're a genuine scientific curiosity. And I wanted you to understand why you can't go around telling people about how the virus is being disseminated.'

'I've only told Hugh Ryder, and he told me to talk to you.'

Tony hands Shawcross a china cup. 'This is a complex situation,' he says. 'You've been told to mind your own business. But you haven't listened to advice, have you?'

'What's this then? A demonstration of the security service's power to shut me up?'

Shawcross splutters into his tea. 'He thinks you work for those numbskulls? That's amusing.'

Tony grins and shakes his head. They seem to be sharing a private joke.

He turns towards Adam. 'I said I worked for the British people, son. Bloody government are mostly a bunch of self-serving chancers with their heads up their backsides. All politicians are. They couldn't organise a piss-up in a brewery. Civil service is no better.'

The little scientist is chortling. He has to wipe his eyes and polish his glasses.

Adam stares at them both and his blood runs cold. Who are these people? Not the government. Who then?

They're sitting in a prestigious high tech facility in Cambridge, which must've cost millions. Who's behind it?

And they murdered David. Now they want to put him under the microscope like some biological curiosity. Will he ever walk out of here alive, he wonders?

'Why did you let me think you were a spook?' says Adam. Talking fills time. 'Was it a joke?'

Tony sighs and shakes his head. 'No. I was trying my best to make you listen to reason.'

'Okay, I'm listening. Who the hell are you?'

'Concerned citizens. Ordinary people like you, who recognise that things have to change.'

'So this is political?'

'This is survival. The British people have to fight back before we lose our identity and our country.' The conviction in his tone is unwavering.

'I don't get it,' says Adam. 'What do you hope to gain by giving people the flu?'

Shawcross sips his tea, little finger extended. Behind the round glasses, his eyes are fierce and bright as any rodent. 'The public at large needs a fiction it can understand' he says. 'Fear helps them focus.'

'You're killing people for a fiction?'

Tony puts down his cup and says, 'Hal, I don't think we need to go into this.'

'Why not?' says the scientist. 'The actual mortality rate is not that high. Collateral damage has always been an accepted consequence of conflict and change. H7N9 is nasty if your immune system is compromised. But it's unlikely to turn into a pandemic. The fiction is people believe it already has.'

'You create panic. Then what?'

'We give them fear and we offer them a way out. They want safety and a solution and they want it now. So, a government of national unity will be formed—'

'Hal' says Tony in a warning tone. 'That's enough.'

Shawcross raises his hand. 'No, I think he should understand. You'd like that, wouldn't you, Adam?'

'Yes' says Adam. What's to lose? Get them engaged in a conversation. Perhaps work on the little scientist's vanity. He glances at the door. Can he make a run for it? He'd have to get past Tony.

'The planet faces problems that most people simply aren't equipped to understand' says Shawcross. 'Climate change leading to mass migration, disruptions on a global scale from AI, competition for finite resources, the sheer trajectory of scientific advance. But people don't get it. They want a tank full of cheap petrol, a nice juicy burger and loads of mind numbing telly to watch.'

He paces up and down, energised by his argument.

Adam notices that Tony is scowling. He rearranges the cups neatly on the tray, but there's a growing tension in his stance.

'Here it is,' Shawcross declares with a sweep of his arm. 'The central conundrum for Western democracies. We believe democracy is the best form of government. But most people don't understand the modern world, which makes them too stupid to vote.'

Adam glances at Tony. 'Thought you said this was about ordinary people.'

Tony sighs and pulls a pair of blue vinyl gloves out of his pocket. 'Hal's got a point' he says calmly. 'We can't continue to have our leaders pandering to a stupid electorate.'

Shawcross shoots him a tetchy look 'Oh no, Tony. No, no, no! And certainly not in my office.'

'I warned you, Hal. You run off at the mouth about all this. Now you give me no choice.'

The mood has flipped. Adam sees the steely glint in Tony's eye. He draws on the gloves, reaches in his pocket, and takes out a small semi-automatic pistol.

Adam stares at it in horror. Five inches long. Black and shiny.

So is this it? He's spent a good deal of time in the last year wondering how his life would end, but he could never have predicted this.

His throat is parched. Now he wishes he had drunk the coke. He thinks of Zoe, Lily and little Ryan. He wants them to be his last thought. He wonders if he should beg. *Fuck them. No!*

He stands up to face his assassin. He could try for the door, but he wouldn't get far.

'I absolutely forbid it,' says the gnome. 'He's unique, as far as we know. An important piece of biological data.'

'I can't help that' says Tony as he slots the magazine into the chamber and releases the safety catch.

Shawcross reaches for his phone 'You're acting beyond your authority.'

'Put the phone down, Hal.'

'How dare you come into my office waving a gun!'

Tony raises his arm, straightens it and points the gun at Adam. Adam blinks, but he doesn't flinch.

'I forbid it!' shouts Shawcross.

Pivoting on his toes, Tony twists abruptly, turns the gun on Shawcross and pulls the trigger. Three staccato cracks ring out and the scientist slumps forward, blood soaking his T-shirt.

Every nerve in Adam's body is jangling. He stares in disbelief.

Tony takes a step towards the body, turns it over. The torso is a gory mess, three bullets to the heart, the eyes wide and frozen. Dr Shawcross is dead.

'Well,' says Tony. 'That's that then. Two birds with one stone.'

70

DAY 34. 2.56pm

When the front door opens, the assembled media are ready. The afternoon light is fast fading and Felicity Oldroyd is greeted with an explosion of flashes on cameras, large and small. And a cacophony of shouted questions.

She simply raises her palm for quiet. Staring out at the sea of muffled, expectant faces, she wonders who else might be out there. Other assailants? The flustered young police protection officer on duty has advised her against this course of action. She can see him out of the corner of her eye, on the phone. He's probably calling Babcock.

But she can feel Gerry standing inches behind her right shoulder and Alistair beside him. Although he's been told categorically not to, she suspects her son has a Sabatier knife from the block in the kitchen in his jacket pocket. She can feel his readiness. Her family will protect her.

Taking a breath of chilly London air, she notices the

familiar taint of diesel. She will miss her beloved city, but she's ready for a simpler life.

She raises her chin to project her voice. Whatever else, she will be heard.

'This morning' she says, 'my dear friend and colleague Douglas Lacey was brutally murdered on the streets of London. He stepped forward to protect me from a violent attacker. I can hardly bring myself to express how devastated I am. There are no words. But what I can do, here and now, to pay tribute to my dear friend, is to speak up for the work he did and the values and principles he held dear. Values which he and I shared.

His job was to understand and investigate threats to public health and safety. Like me, he was a public servant. But we have been accused of lying about the nature of the current outbreak of the H7N9 avian flu virus and misleading the public as to its seriousness and the number of fatalities. This is categorically untrue.

I don't know who is accusing us of this or what their motives are. They operate from the anonymity of the internet. They bring no concrete, verifiable proof to support their accusations. But the murderer of Douglas Lacey believed and had been encouraged to believe that he was a bad man who should be punished. And this is the most pernicious lie.

So let's talk about the flu. There are various strains in circulation and they change from year to year. It's a challenge to produce a vaccine that keeps up with the virus. Some years it works better than others because it's a complicated problem. There's unlikely to be a universal jab any time soon. But the overall death rate is low and most healthy adults recover without medical intervention.

H7N9 is a form of avian flu. People in Asia contract it

through close contact with contaminated birds and poultry. The fear that it may mutate to become transmissible between humans has been around for some time.

But as yet, there is no verifiable evidence that this has happened here in the UK. The current outbreak has occurred in small pockets, which suggests a handful of individuals at random locations have been deliberately and directly exposed through some mechanism of which we are not yet aware. Illegal immigrants in detention centres are not the source of the virus.

The police and security services are working hard to find out who is doing this. The assumption is it is a terrorist act. I'm probably breaking all kinds of rules by telling you this. But my view is there's so much misinformation out there, it's time to tell the truth.

And the truth is, this is not a pandemic, and it's unlikely to become one. The public at large are not in mortal danger. The number of fatalities from all forms of flu is elevated for the time of year but only by a few hundred cases. All the data we have is available for scrutiny and I invite all legitimate news organisations to examine it. There are no secret mass graves.

We do not need some brand new anti-viral wonder drug as the Secretary of State proposes, and I have told him as much. Most patients that need it are being successfully treated. Sadly, some are not, but generally these are people with already weakened immune systems.

I'm not saying this is not a serious situation and a national emergency. But it's a problem that many highly skilled experts are working to contain and resolve. And I have no doubt that it will be resolved very soon. They have no reason to lie to the public and nor do I. And nor did Douglas Lacey.

But when a man is stabbed to death in broad daylight for doing his job, I think there are some other questions we need to ask.

Who are the liars here? Why won't they face the cameras? They make their false accusations from the cover of social media. Who is behind truth health news? Why do they want you to be frightened? What is the purpose of undermining people's belief in the healthcare system we have in place to protect ourselves? Who hopes to gain from the ensuing chaos?

If you're worried, wear a face mask. But fear and misinformation and panic are far more deadly than H7N9.

For over thirty years, I have been a doctor. I take the ethics of my profession seriously and above all, the injunction to do no harm.

What I've told you today is the truth. I am resigning from my position as Chief Medical Officer and I therefore have no reason to follow any sort of government line.

There may be people out there who want to harm me, but they will not intimidate me and they will not stop me from telling the truth. Thank you for listening.'

There's silence in the chilly street, a collective holding of breath, then an eruption of questions.

Gerry Oldroyd puts a protective arm round his wife's waist and shepherds her back into the house.

71

The door opens, Lucas and the X5 driver step briskly into the room. They too wear vinyl gloves. Adam is in shock. He finds his arms pinioned as they drag him towards the desk.

Tony gives Lucas a nod and says 'Right-handed, are you, Adam?'

Lucas grasps Adam's right hand and squeezes the bone hard to force the palm open. Removing the clip, Tony places the gun in his hand and forces his fingers to close round the handle.

He feels the indentions from the stippling on the grip digging into his palm and curled fingers. But the pistol is surprisingly light.

His hand imprisoned in Tony's iron clasp, Adam meets his captor's gaze. For a man who's just shot someone dead, Tony seems relaxed and detached.

He smiles and says, 'Bit of a fright for you there, Adam.

Sorry about that. But this is a fast moving situation. We have to improvise.'

Releasing the pressure on Adam's hand, he takes the gun and puts it on the desk.

The corpse lies on its back on the floor, blood pooling around it.

'Good' says Tony, in a matter-of-fact tone. 'Fancy that can of coke now?'

Adam simply glares at him. 'You're a complete psycho!'

Tony laughs. 'I'm afraid you're the one who'll be labelled a psycho. You're about to become one of the most hated figures in the country, Adam, because, as you've probably guessed, you've murdered a national hero. Dr. Henry Shaw-cross, who has battled selflessly to save lives, gunned down by a madman in his own office.'

'You'll never pin this on me.'

'Your prints are on the murder weapon. CCTV will provide footage of you wildly careening down the corridor and asking directions to his office. I think the over-stretched local plods'll be grateful for such an open and shut case.'

Twitter Feed

DAY 34.

True Health News @truehealthnews
Dame Felicity's speech on YouTube is so moving. Clearly the woman believes what she's saying. But does that make it true? Maybe the suits at @PHE_uk are lying to her too? #felicityfooled #governmentlies
25.9k Retweets 32k Likes

Surinder Chakrabarti @suriChak25
Replying to @truehealthnews
I worked in the CMOs office as a temp. Lovely lady. Well-meaning. Bit old-fashioned. But at @PHE_uk they do treat her as a joke. They were always pulling the wool over her eyes. #felicityfooled #governmentlies
359 Retweets 742 Likes

Anushka Anand @AA539
Replying to @truehealthnews
As a nurse on the frontline I don't buy these excuses. People are right to be angry. These high-paid bureaucrats don't give a shit. You want to see the posh house where this "lovely lady" lives go to: keepsafeandsound.com
16k Retweets 21k Likes

Mark Carter @MCB666
Replying to @AA539
Spot On! These so-called experts don't give a F...K about us. Get a mask they say.FACT: thousands have died. FACT: and been dumped in mass graves. FACT: you could be next.

Go to truehealthnews.com for the real independently verified FACTS. Reject their LIES. #dontdieofignorance #safeandsound

14.7k Retweets 23kLikes

72

DAY 34. 6.25pm

Plonking the two-ounce shot glass on the granite counter, the Right Honourable Hugh Ryder MP pours himself a Jim Beam. It goes down in one. It's been that sort of day. He refills the glass.

His brother taught him to drink in their teens, explained to him that bourbon was far cooler than the cheap blended Scotch favoured by their austere and distant father. But Duncan is teetotal, has been for years. Now he drinks wheatgrass from his shot glasses, scoffs about fifty vitamin pills a day and is planning to live to be a hundred. Such is the vanity of rich men or, as Duncan prefers, ultra-high-net-worth individuals. He regards the term 'rich' as vulgar, insists it's never been about the money. Hugh doesn't believe this for a moment.

He takes his drink over to the window. Ordinarily, he ignores the view. The flat is convenient for the House and secure, a suitable London pied-a-terre for a busy man plus an escape from the irritations of family life.

The river below looks black with mercurial flecks of light. The Palace of Westminster is shrouded in scaffolding, which could well be an appropriate comment on the state of the nation. Decaying stonework, medieval plumbing, treacherous electrics; in his view, the whole place needs to be torn down. Gazing at it dispassionately, Hugh drains his glass and belches as acid reflux burns his gullet.

The door buzzer sounds. He doesn't move. His police protection officer, stationed outside the door, is simply alerting him to the fact someone is about to enter.

He turns and a moment later Mia Cunningham walks into the room. Even with her hair awry and a red nose from the wintry cold, she's still the most gorgeously fuckable woman he's ever met.

She dumps her briefcase on the coffee table and takes off her coat.

Holding up his glass he says 'Drink?'

'I'm fine.'

Sitting down, she slides her laptop from its sleeve and opens it. He watches her. She gives the impression of being both contained and unobtainable. You may want her, but she doesn't give a damn about you. It's probably a trick she's learnt. Nevertheless, it makes him feel awkward, like a schoolboy in a lap dancing club.

She continues to ignore him. Her attention is on the screen as she logs into a secure, encrypted transatlantic line.

Returning to the counter, he pours himself another slug.

'I cannot believe it,' he says. 'What on earth does the stupid cow hope to gain?'

'I doubt she planned it. It has all the hallmarks of an emotional outburst, which is probably why it's gone viral.'

'You reckon? It's always been her agenda to fuck me over. So how bad is it?'

Mia shrugs. 'I've got Nin running some more in depth analysis but, preliminary assessment, this is having a huge impact. Even before this, Professor Oldroyd's trust ratings were high.'

'God knows why?'

'Dignity and grief is a potent mix. The way she made it about Lacey's murder gets engagement. Explains why it's gone stratospheric. Trending on all social media platforms. Record numbers of views and shares across all channels. Approval ratings to die for.'

Ryder takes another hit of bourbon. 'Y'know, the hypocrisy of the woman! Her bloody husband has made a mint from pharmaceuticals so she can afford to be squeaky clean and righteous.'

'Have you tried to speak to her?'

'No I bloody haven't!'

'Perhaps you should.'

'Why?'

'To reassure her. To tell her how moved you were and that you agree with every word. To ride on her coat-tails.'

The Minister sighs. 'Is that necessary?'

'Yes.' She fixes him with a chilly stare. 'And Duncan agrees with me.'

He glares at her, shakes his head and says, 'So you've talked to him already? Yeah, course you have.'

Mia gives him that look, disdainful and dismissive. She can be a complete shrew.

He doesn't want to sound petulant, but he can't seem to help it. 'Y'know, it's becoming inconvenient' he says, 'that you're screwing my brother.'

She tilts her head, gives him that condescending smile.

'Hugh, you probably need to stop drinking and calm down. This is a glitch.'

'Isn't it your job to sort such things out?'

'That's what I'm doing. Nin and the boys are on it. We'll contain it and turn it around.'

'He won't marry you, y'know. You may think he will, but I know my brother. Even with a watertight pre-nup, he regards it as too risky. He's a careful man. Plans to hang on to his billions.'

Getting up, she sighs and says. 'He's on another call, but he'll be with us in a couple of minutes. Can I make you some coffee?'

Ryder pours himself another shot. 'Seriously, you've picked the wrong brother. I'd marry you.'

'Imogen might have something to say about that. And what about your two lovely little girls?'

'Nah. Y'know, strikes me she might be a dyke, my lovely wife.'

'I think she's probably just bored with you.'

He laughs. 'You are a piece of work, Ms Cunningham. The cold-hearted psycho bitch to end all bitches. S'pose the clue's in the name.' He flicks his tongue suggestively over his lower lip.

'Always such a gentleman, Minister.'

'What's made you like this, eh? Crappy childhood? Bullied at school?'

'I'm lucky, I guess' she says. Her smile remains serene, unconcerned. And those eyes. Like lasers. He has the feeling she can see straight through him.

The laptop emits a singsong tone and a pixilated image of Duncan Ryder pops up.

'Ah, here's Duncan.' She swivels the computer round so they can both view it.

On screen, Duncan Ryder smiles and says, 'I've been having a pleasant lunch with a surprisingly attractive new Congresswoman.'

'Are you screwing her?' says his brother.

Duncan frowns in annoyance. 'No. Nor am I screwing up, which is what appears to be happening at your end, Hugh.'

'He's drunk', says Mia.

'Oh, for pity's sake, get a grip.'

'Bloody hell, Duncan,' says the Minister. 'You can't blame this on me. What is it now, day 34? This whole thing is stalling. Where are the people on the streets demanding change? One pathetic demo of a couple of hundred head-bangers. I have to say, your game plan doesn't appear to be working.'

'It'll happen. As Mia will explain to you, it'll take a while for online engagement and anger to turn into action. People need to be more upset. But I'm dealing with that.'

'Meanwhile, I'm the one exposed here. Oldroyd decides to tell the public it's not a pandemic and they believe her.'

Duncan Ryder sighs and steeples his fingers. 'Okay, let's think this through. She's CMO and she's technically correct, so what do we do?'

'I dunno. Discredit her? Maybe we could get Hal Shaw-cross to say her old man's bought some shares in his company and accuse him of insider dealing?'

Duncan shakes his head. 'Forget about Shawcross. He's out of the picture.'

'What do you mean?'

'Sadly, he's no longer with us.'

'He's dead?'

'He's been murdered.'

'Murdered? Christ sake, Lacey, then him. When?'

'Little brother, what have I always told you? A setback is only a setback if you regard it as such. In fact, it's an opportunity. Unfortunately, Lacey's rapidly becoming a martyr, so we had to respond.'

The Right Honourable Hugh Ryder heaves a sigh. 'Oh my god, you haven't let that nutter loose again.'

'Hugh, calm down.'

'He's a thug!'

'Now is not the time to become squeamish. The situation has been handled and by the evening news, we will have a martyr of our own. People will soon forget about Lacey. We'll regain control of the agenda. Tell him, Mia.'

She smiles 'Duncan's right.'

Hugh shakes his head and frowns. 'But how's this going to play out? What about the police?'

'I've told you, it's being handled. Let's get back to Oldroyd. She tells the public there's no pandemic. What we do is we turn it around. Prove her wrong.'

'Yeah, easy-peasy. How?'

'You were moaning about a loss of impetus. Well, I agree. I think it's time to escalate. Two hundred and fifty units of the virus targeted specifically at hospitals in the London area. All at once. Now it may not technically be a pandemic, but after that it'll certainly look like one.'

73

DAY 34. 6.30pm

The first thing Zoe notices is the neatness of the room, spartan as a monk's cell; the only articles not tidily housed or shelved are two medical text books lying open on the desk. Nizar Khalid lives on the third floor of a purpose-built, upmarket student residence on the Mile End Road.

Invited to sit by their host, Zoe perches on the end of the narrow bed and Jason takes the desk chair.

Nizar opens a cupboard to reveal a kettle and a silver tray with a small ceramic pot and three glasses.

'Do you like mint tea?' he says.

'Lovely' Zoe replies.

He smiles nervously. The tray has already been prepared and the kettle filled, although Zoe suspects he doesn't get many visitors. It feels like a ritual from his homeland that he's clinging on to, but maybe he needs that.

'Studying medicine, that's hard work,' says Jason. 'You like it?'

Nizar nods. He turns the kettle on, closes the books, places the tray on the desk, and smiles.

Zoe has to stop herself from fidgeting. Her impatience is in danger of overwhelming her. Where is Adam? That's what she wants to ask. Has Nizar seen him, spoken to him? Also, she hates mint tea.

Her tension must be obvious because Jason shoots her a cautionary glance then says, 'Your dad was a doctor? So was it sort of expected?'

The young man nods again, hesitates then says 'Feras was the eldest, obviously it would've been him but, well, y'know...' He shrugs.

There's an uncomfortable silence. Their earlier exchange of texts was easy. This is like pulling teeth. Zoe realises she was right. He's far happier with the detachment of the digital communication. But how to make him relax?

She tries a different tack. 'I didn't have a chance to say when you came to the farm, but we're grateful that you agreed to the donation of your brother's organs.' As soon as the words are out of her mouth, they sound disingenuous, even to Zoe.

Now she gets a baleful look from her brother-in-law.

But Nizar inclines his head politely and replies, 'It was the right thing. My father would've wanted it and so would Feras.'

The kettle comes to the boil. It clicks off. Nizar's lips are pursed; more silence.

Jason gets up, slots his hands in the pocket of his jeans. 'Listen, Nizar,' he says, 'we need to come clean about some things. But it's difficult to explain.'

The young Syrian turns to face him. Behind the guard-edness, there's a flash of defiance. 'What things?' he says.

'I don't know where to begin.'

The young man stares. He looks so young, a teenager, but the eyes are old with cynicism.

'Maybe begin with cell memory?' he says.

'You know about that?'

'I'm not stupid. Adam has some of Feras's memories. You want to find out if they're true. Isn't that what this is about?'

'Do you believe that's possible?' says Zoe.

Nizar shrugs. 'My father said a doctor must always remain a scientist. But the frontiers of science are way out there. Medicine is always playing catch-up. We never know what's possible until we witness it.'

Zoe takes a deep breath 'What if we told you Adam thinks he can remember the manner of Feras's death?'

'Can he?'

Jason joins in. 'This will shock you, Nizar, but Adam thinks your brother was murdered.'

'What? How?'

'The accident in the tunnel was caused deliberately. He was run off the road.' Zoe says. 'And Adam can recognise the man who did it.'

Nizar lifts the kettle off its base and carefully pours water into the little pot. His face remains impassive.

Jason and Zoe exchange looks. It's hard to tell if he's even taken in what they've said?

Then he opens the desk drawer and pulls out a postcard. 'I wanted to show this to Adam' he says.

Jason takes the postcard from Nizar's outstretched hand.

On one side is a picture, some kind of religious painting, an icon perhaps. The other side bears the student's address, in English, and then several lines of neat Arabic script.

'It came the day after the accident. It's an apology.'

'Apology for what?' says Jason.

'We argued. Surviving the war, coming here, was hard.

Feras did things, many of them criminal things. He had no choice. He protected me. Got asylum status for me. Sent me to a private school so I could pass the necessary exams. It was expensive. I had no right to criticise him.'

'Did you criticise him?' asks Zoe.

Nizar nods and swallows hard. 'I was so superior. His expensive clothes, his fast motorbike. I told him it was all wrong. He'd become as greedy and corrupt as the regime my father fought. David! Stupid English name.'

He wipes his face with the back of his hand. 'I told him Feras was my brother, not David. I said I hated David. These are the last words we spoke.'

Zoe puts a hand on his shoulder. 'I'm so sorry, Nizar.'

He shakes his head briskly, takes the postcard from Jason, stares at it and says, 'Let me translate what he wrote: "I hear you my brother. And you are right. But I will always be your brother. I will stop all this. I will honour our father and do no more harm to any man. This I swear."

'You see, I thought—' Nizar has to swallow hard again. He continues, 'I thought he'd gone out on his bike and deliberately killed himself. Because of me and what I said. I thought it was my fault.'

'Well, it wasn't,' says Jason.

Nizar smiles and says, 'Maybe not.'

Zoe's brain is buzzing. Getting closer to David, understanding who he was, feels like a portal, a way back to Adam.

'I will stop all this?' she says. 'What do you think he meant by that? What did he have to stop?'

74

DAY 34. 6.40pm

The pitch-black darkness swathes him like a fetid blanket. Adam holds up his hands. They've been bound in front of him with plastic zip ties. The room they've locked him in this time is far more secure. It's in the basement, a storeroom with a heavy metal door.

Two birds with one stone. That's what Tony said. It didn't make sense at the time. Adam was in shock. He'd assumed he was the one about to be shot. But what if it was Tony's plan all along to kill Shawcross and set him up? Is that why he was brought here?

Sitting in the dark, on the freezing concrete floor, Adam has plenty of time to brood. He has no watch or phone, no light, no accurate notion of how much time could've passed. Sensory deprivation is a form of torture. It sends people mad, destroys them. Is this what they want?

But they won't succeed. *Not this time. Bastards!*

He marshals his thoughts, going back through the day since he left Mia's flat that morning.

Mia.

It's clear that Tony must've duped her. She didn't know Lucas was working with him. She couldn't have. She was expecting him back at the flat. He must get back to London. He's told Ryder how the virus is being spread, he gave them the drawing. But Ryder didn't seem convinced.

Inside his head, thoughts collide. Who can be trusted? *He must stop this. Get to the cop.*

Suddenly, he remembers the cop, the DI that took him to meet Mia. The one he punched. Was his name Mehta?

Counter Terrorism, these are the police he needs to contact. Mehta and his fat boss with the beady eye. They're the ones who can use the information to stop this.

Footsteps in the corridor, distant at first, then getting closer. They're coming back. This is his chance. Adam readies himself. He manages to stand up. As soon as they open the door, he'll rush them.

A bolt slides back. He's expecting Tony or Lucas. But as the door opens, the figure it frames is much smaller. A woman? He hesitates. The light goes on, completely blinding him. Sharp white diamonds explode on his retinas. He puts up his palms to shield his eyes.

A hand thrusts something in front of his face. He blinks at it. Some form of ID?

The voice is reedy and female. 'I'm DC Janine Sawyer. My colleague is DC Thomas. Adam Hardy, I'm arresting you for the murder of Dr. Henry Shawcross. You do not have to say anything. But, it may harm your defence, if you do not mention when questioned something which you later rely on in court. Anything you do say may be given in evidence.'

Adam finally manages to focus on the figure in front of

him. Small, unsmiling, and those blue vinyl gloves. 'I'm going to release your wrists, Mr. Hardy.'

'I've been set up,' he says.

'You'll be formally charged and interviewed. Then you'll have a chance to give your account of what happened.'

'It wasn't me. It was Tony.'

'Who's Tony?'

'He was here, in Shawcross's office. He brought tea.'

'The office staff have all been questioned. There's no one of that name.'

He holds up his wrists. 'Then who tied me up and put me here?'

'You were detained by security.'

75

DAY 34. 7.55pm

By the time he gets back to the office there's been a shift change. Pramiti has gone home, but she's left a cryptic post-it on his desk.

Hope you managed to get the toothache sorted, boss

DI Mehta smiles to himself. She's covered for him. Even so, it's time to grasp the nettle. He glances in the direction of Babcock's office.

Taking the folded printout from his pocket, he heads for the Chief Super's door. He can glimpse her through the glass. Her swivel chair turned away, phone to her ear.

He taps. She beckons him in.

She's frowning. 'Okay, I'll get straight back to you. We'll send someone. Yes, definitely. Thanks for your call, sir.'

Hanging up, she smiles. 'Well, Sami,' she says, 'are you ready to tell me what the bloody hell you're playing at?'

'Yes, ma'am,' he replies with deliberate formality. 'Although I'd like to ask you the same question. I've been continuing to look at David Taylor or we should probably call him Feras Khalid. It seems to me that it's pertinent to the investigation that our source was murdered. And I can now identify the man who killed him.'

Babcock nods. 'I see.'

The DI unfolds the printout and lays it on her desk. 'This is the man. Tony Franklin. He runs a cleaning company in Hackney, RapidKlean Cleaning Solutions. And it transpires that he took it over from Khalid. But you already know all this, don't you, ma'am? Because, like me, you've been there.'

Pat lounges back in her chair and smiles. 'You're a smart lad. I've always thought so.'

Mehta responds with a chilly stare. 'I'm thirty-two, ma'am. Hardly a lad.'

She meets his gaze. 'You're right, Inspector. Not very PC. I do apologise.'

He stands in front of the desk, feet firmly planted, hands behind his back, like a soldier standing at ease; his height gives him confidence. The stance is deliberate. Babcock has to look up at him. She has to know that he won't be bullied.

The corners of her mouth twitch, but he can't tell if it's amusement or nerves. Babcock on the ropes should not be under-estimated. He wonders if his career is effectively over.

But her gaze travels beyond him to rest on the far wall. She sighs and says, 'So our informant ran this place before Franklin? That's interesting. I didn't know that.'

'But you admit you know Tony Franklin and you tried to contact him?'

Babcock smiles and says, 'Sit down, Sami. You're giving me a crick in the neck.'

She opens a file on her laptop. 'Yes, I do know Tony Franklin. But his real name is Peter Grazinski. These files, as

you will see, are classified. He was an undercover officer
with the Special Demonstration Squad in the early nineties.
And I was his handler.'

She turns the laptop screen to face Mehta. A younger,
handsome version of Franklin in a Fred Perry polo shirt
gazes out of the screen at him.

He stares at it. 'He's a police officer?'

'He was once.' Babcock smiles wistfully and says, 'Most
of the SDS targets were left-wing groups, that's what people
know about. That's where it all went pear-shaped. But our
unit targeted football hooligans. It was dangerous. There
were frequent crossovers with drug dealing and criminal
gangs. Pete spent five years in and out of one of the most
violent London football firms. I pretended to be his girlfriend. That was our cover. But he was brilliant at it. Possibly
the best undercover officer in the SDS.'

Mehta settles in the chair opposite the desk with a
mixture of confusion and relief.

'What happened?' he says

'Hard to say exactly. Some elements in the firm became
involved in the National Front and we were told to follow
that line, find out what they were up to. Then one day Pete
went off the grid, disappeared completely. I suppose somewhere along the line he flipped, became what he'd been
pretending to be for so long.'

'Went rogue?'

'Sadly, yes.'

'Was no attempt made to bring him in?'

'Oh, believe me, we tried. Then he got involved in some
serious criminality, dealing drugs, probably taking them too,
and that was difficult to ignore. By then, the SDS was under
fire, anyway. We offered him a debrief, tried to secure his

resignation. He refused to co-operate. So it was decided by the powers that be to write him off.'

'They were afraid of the scandal if it got out?'

'Course they were. Easier to deny he was ever connected to us. His wife divorced him, he has a child he never sees. I suppose I felt guilty. I should've given him more support. So over the years, I've tried to keep tabs on him. He's turned into a complete far-right fanatic, linked to groups in the States and eastern Europe. MI5 has got a file on him this thick.' She measures a gap of several inches with thumb and index finger.

'Why did you go looking for him now?'

'Because what we're dealing with now, we need an informant.'

'You think this is some kind of far right conspiracy?'

'Yes, that's the consensus. National Crime Agency has been drilling down through all the social media noise. There would appear to be an orchestrated campaign to disrupt, using the flu as a scare tactic. It has all the hall-marks we've come to expect from ultra-right neo-fascists. The Lacey murderer is certainly a follower of these groups.'

'Any theories who's actually behind it?'

'None that we can prove. That's why 5 wanted to see if we could get to Franklin.'

'You think you can turn him?'

'I was probably being naïve. Anyway, he hasn't responded to my message. But the fact he and Feras Khalid are connected through this cleaning firm, that's interesting, well done. Suggests we're on the right track.'

'I'm embarrassed, boss,' says Mehta. 'I should never have doubted—'

'Don't be. You sniffed a rat and you followed your nose. I wish I had more officers with the brains and balls to do that.

If in doubt, be suspicious. Isn't that what I've taught you? These are strange times.'

He feels a fool. 'What do we do now?'

Babcock rubs her face. Mehta scans her. She looks old and exhausted.

'Okay,' she says, 'what do we know about this cleaning firm? The woman who runs it, Wendy, is she involved?'

Mehta shakes his head. 'I don't think so. Could be a front. A legitimate cover.'

'To do what? To spread the virus?'

He frowns. 'Yeah, but how?'

Babcock steeples her fingers. 'I think Khalid knew, and somehow he and his cleaning company were involved. But he decided to stop it, that's why he came to us. That's why he was killed.'

'So what do we do, take the place apart and see what we find?'

Babcock sighs and says 'We spook them, they'll go to ground. Which brings us back to Adam Hardy.'

'He was certainly right about Franklin.'

'The call I was on was from the Deputy Chief Constable of Cambridgeshire. They've arrested Adam Hardy for murder.'

'Seriously? Who the hell has he murdered?'

'Dr Henry Shawcross.'

'The one involved with this new anti-viral?'

'Yep. Professor Oldroyd did point a finger at him. And he certainly would've made a fortune out of his drug if the government bought it.'

Mehta frowns 'Why would Hardy kill him?'

Babcock nods. 'Even more interesting, why would Hardy shoot him three times through the heart with a Sig Sauer 9mm pocket pistol?'

'How would a Devon farmer get hold of a gun like that? Shotgun maybe.'

'Indeed. And it gets even more curious. Guess what Mr Hardy is telling anyone who'll listen?'

'That he didn't do it?'

'He's saying he was set up. Someone called Tony Franklin did it.'

76

DAY 34. 8.40pm

Zoe drives, Nizar sits beside her, Jason is in the back. They park a couple of hundred meters down the road. The warehouse and office block are in darkness, the gate is closed and secured with a heavy padlock.

'I only came here once' says Nizar. 'About a year ago. Feras had bought the business. He was excited. Said he could make loads of money, but it would all be legal.'

'Where did he get the money to buy it?' says Zoe.

Nizar shrugs and looks away.

'We're not judging him or you' she says. 'We need to find out what he was doing? He said he was going to stop? Stop what?'

'It's a cleaning company,' says Nizar. 'He was just running a cleaning company.'

Jason opens the back door of the car and says, 'Maybe we should take a closer look?'

As he gets out, Zoe winds down her window. 'What are you going to do?'

'Walk round the perimeter. Have a snoop.'

'They might have CCTV or something.'

Jason smiles and pulls up the hood on his sweatshirt. 'How's that?'

'Be careful' says Zoe.

He raises his eyebrows and says, 'Zo, never knew you cared.'

In the seat beside her, Nizar wriggles, he's a bundle of nerves.

She watches Jason stroll across the road and skirt along the side of the fence. From behind he could be Adam, similar build, broad shoulders. She feels her gut cramp with fear. Where is her stupid husband?

Adam had contacted Nizar, said he wanted to meet him. But that was this morning. Since then, there has been no further communication. She can't see that Nizar would have any reason to lie about it. But that cow Mia certainly was lying. Zoe feels sure she knows where Adam is. This feels like a wild goose chase.

Jason disappears into the darkness. She gets out her phone, checks it for the umpteenth time. Two more unanswered texts, plus a missed call from her father. Questions, concerns, diktats. Nothing new there.

She glances at Nizar. 'Are you all right?' she says.

It seems a bit of a stupid question considering his history. There must've been times in his young life when he's been totally petrified. War is something she watches on the television news, it happens to other people in foreign places. She can't imagine what it would be like. Being bombed out of your home, running for your life. Losing everything.

'I don't see the point of this,' Nizar says wearily. 'Adam is not here.'

Zoe knows he's right. They lapse into silence.

The road is a cul-de-sac, the concrete surface cracked and uneven. It provides access to RapidKlean Cleaning Solutions, an electrical wholesaler and another vacant site full of drifts of dumped rubbish. Two more vehicles are parked on the other side of the road; one, a battered Nissan Micra, looks as though it might've been abandoned.

Zoe checks the time on her phone. Jason has only been gone a few minutes, but sitting there in the darkness with only a distant streetlamp, it feels longer. She can hear the rumble of traffic from the main road, but the industrial estate itself is deserted and eerily quiet.

At the junction with the access road, a dark transit van appears. Zoe and Nizar both stare at it, tense as rabbits.

Turning left, the arc of the headlights swings round towards them and it heads down the road in their direction.

'Shit' says Zoe. 'It's coming this way.'

There's an awkward scramble as they both slide down in their seats to conceal themselves.

The vehicle drives past them and stops at the gates to RapidKlean.

Zoe peeps over the dashboard. It's a large Ford Transit, brand new, black. Opening the video app on her phone, she points and hits record.

The passenger door of the van opens, a man gets out, a tight beanie hat pulled down over his ears. As he walks towards the gate, the security light above it comes on. He slots a key in the padlock and unlocks it, removing the chain. Pushing the gates open, he stands back for the van to drive through.

That's when Zoe sees his face. Panic surges through her. It's the man who came to the farm, pretending to be from DEFRA, the man Adam said had murdered his donor.

As he shuts the gate behind the van, he glances in their direction. She ducks down and prays he hasn't seen them.

77

DAY 34. 8.47pm

Adam has been taken into custody, stripped, photographed, finger-printed, forensic and DNA samples taken. He's been given a sweatshirt and tracksuit pants to wear. He tried to explain what had happened to the officers who arrested him —he was drugged, set up—but they weren't interested. He mentioned Counter Terrorism and the vital information he must pass on revealing the source of the flu virus. They remained cold and unsmiling.

'We'll deal with that later,' that's all they'd say. Their job was to transport him. He was taken out of the building to a waiting police van. The main entrance had been cordoned off, there were various police vehicles parked up. At the sight of him, several reporters came running from the other side of the road. They shouted questions, the name Shaw-cross. Cameras flashed. Adam's handlers bundled him swiftly into the cage in the back of the van. It was only a short drive.

Out of all the bizarre things that had happened to him, being processed as a common criminal was the most disturbing. In the custody suite, in the cells, the officers seemed to be going through a well-worn ritual. No one looked him in the eye. No one listened to his garbled explanation of events or his pleas. He was a murder suspect. They treated him as an alien creature to be handled with vinyl gloves and restrained if necessary.

It was explained to him that once the duty solicitor arrived, he'd have the opportunity to give his account. When they asked if he had any medical conditions they should be aware of, he laughed.

Being shut up in the dark had been bad enough, but being locked in a starkly lit police cell feels worse. His body aches, his wrists are cut from the zip ties although they've been removed. But he can't afford to sink into self-pity. He must hold it together and make them understand. *Play the game. Wait.*

As he takes deep breaths to calm his rattled brain, it's hard not to feel paranoid. It would be naïve to think that innocent people don't get convicted of murder. The evidence against him, engineered by Franklin, is incriminating. It had all been planned. That seems clear now.

If he could just get in touch with Mia, she would help him. *Or would she?*

His thoughts skip to his wife and he feels ashamed. He can't call Zoe. No way. Even if she asked her father, would he get a lawyer for Adam? This would simply confirm the opinion Phil Rowett has always had of him. There's only one person he can call when he gets the opportunity: Jason. That seems the most sensible course.

He's racking his brains to recall his brother's number when the cell door opens.

'You owe me a bloody apology!' says DI Mehta. 'I nearly lost a tooth.'

Adam stares at the cop. *The prick cop.* Relief floods through him and he smiles.

'I am sorry,' he says. 'I hope Jason told you that.'

'You seem to be in quite a mess.'

'I didn't kill anyone. I swear. I was kidnapped. I was drugged. Tony Franklin, the man who killed my donor, he shot Shawcross. I thought he was about to shoot me. You have to believe me.'

'The murder team here seems convinced. They've got a stack of evidence.'

'Franklin put the gun in my hand. But they're behind it. They're the ones spreading the flu virus.'

'How do you know?'

'I realised how it's being done. I told Ryder.'

'The health minister?'

'He sent me to Shawcross. But then Shawcross admitted it was him.'

'Admitted what was him? I'm confused.'

'Okay, look, for ages I kept seeing white tiles. I knew they were important, but I couldn't quite get to it. Then it all came to me in a rush. Electronic air fresheners. They have them on the walls in public toilets.'

'Those things that pump out perfume?'

'Yeah. The outer casing is plastic. It's fixed to the wall near the ceiling. You open it. Inside there's a timer, the canister with the fragrance—'

'That's where the virus is?'

Adam nods. 'Yes. It sprays out a fine mist at regular intervals. If you've got a piece of paper and a pen, I'll draw it for you.'

'Who would fit them, service them? A cleaning company?'

'Probably.'

Mehta looks tense but excited too. 'You think this is what David knew?'

'Yes. He knew, and I think he wanted to stop it. And I didn't kill anyone.'

'I believe you. Just hang on in there, Adam. I'll be back.'

'Yeah but—'

He has no chance to say more. Mehta is gone. The cell door slams behind him.

78

DAY 34. 8.48pm

The chain-link fence is secured to heavy concrete posts and topped with rolls of razor wire. Picking his way over the uneven ground, Jason follows it to the back of the site. The only light is a pervasive orange glow from the main road. There's a steep bank and rustling bushes; beyond that he can glimpse a patch of dark water. It seems to be moving, flowing, so he guesses this is the River Lea, which borders the industrial estate.

Where the fence meets the river bank, he finds the bases of several posts have subsided, creating a sag in the wire mesh and a gap. He squeezes through. The back flank of the warehouse is corrugated metal, rusty in places. Jason uses the torch on his phone to scan it.

He's spent the day wondering what they're actually doing. Looking for his brother? He has a sense that perhaps Adam doesn't want to be found. But is that accurate? What if he's in trouble?

The question he's asked himself is what would Adam do if the boot was on the other foot? And he knows the answer. His brother would find him. He'd never give up.

Earlier in the day, he tried to call Mehta and got no response. The police are under severe pressure; he understands that, and Adam is only as useful to them as the information he provides. But David was killed for a reason and the answer could be inside this building.

He discovers a side door, secured with a padlock on the outside. But the zinc plated hasp is corroded. He jerks it and it comes loose.

The phone in his hand vibrates with an incoming call. It's Zoe.

'Hey, Zoe.'

She whispers, but her voice is tense with alarm. 'Get out of there now, Jace! The bloke from DEFRA has driven up in a van with another bloke.'

'You sure it's him?'

'Yes. Where are you?'

'At the back of the warehouse. I got through a gap in the fence. There's a door. I think I can get in.'

'No! For Christ's sake. Get back here.'

'What are they actually doing?'

'They've driven into the yard. He's fiddling with some keys. I think he's going to open the shutter doors on the front of the warehouse.'

Jason can feel the adrenaline rush. He gets hold of the edge of the metal door with his free hand and gives it a sharp tug. The hasp shears off, the door opens.

'I'm going to take a look,' he says. 'See what they're up to.' The warehouse is sizeable. It'll be okay. There'll be places to hide.

'No, Jace—'

Ignoring her, he ends the call and steps through the door. In seconds his brain is buzzing, his body pumped. If he's honest, he knows he's a risk junkie.

But this is for Adam. If Tony is here, it's for a reason. He's come to David's cleaning company, but to do what? This is an opportunity to get some answers. Mehta slips briefly into his mind and he feels competitive and superior. Would the cop have the balls for this, he wonders? Walking into the unknown with no back-up? Truth is, the DI would probably regard him as a fool.

He finds himself in a small storeroom. It smells of oil and mildew. A quick scan with the phone torch reveals a rack of mouldy shelves, rubbish on the floor. The door is thin plywood. Jason depresses the handle and opens it a crack.

It leads into a narrow corridor. As he turns off the torch, he notices the screen furiously flashing with an incoming call. Zoe again. He slips the phone in his pocket.

The corridor is short and gives access to the hangar-like warehouse. Even though it's unlit, Jason can see shadowy stacks of cardboard boxes on pallets. He can also hear the clunking of the metal door shutters as they rise and glimpse the cool blue beam of the headlights on the waiting transit van.

He has only seconds to decide. If he can find a hiding place in the main body of the building, he'll be able to spy on them. He sprints down the corridor and veers left behind the boxes. Dropping onto his hands and knees, he scrabbles along the floor. There's a pungent smell of detergents, chemical solvents and bleach.

As he squats behind the pallets of cleaning supplies, the main lights come on, flooding the space in fluorescent brilliance and making him squint. He realises in an instant how exposed he is and dives for cover. Have they seen him? It's impossible to tell.

In the gap beneath the pallets, he can see the wheels of the transit driving in and stopping only feet away. His heart is pounding. He waits.

A van door slams. Then nothing. Moments pass.

A scuffling behind him, he spins round. A young bloke with a bushy beard is standing and staring straight at him.

He doesn't hesitate. He leaps to his feet and charges. The best form of defence is attack. The bloke is smaller and slighter than him. Running at him hard, he clenches his fist, pulls his arm back readying the punch. A sharp sock in the face will take him out. But as his arm flies forward, it meets something solid and metal whacking in from the side. He hears the bone in his forearm crack, followed by intense pain.

Staggering, he sees the second man, Tony, a raised crowbar in his hand. He throws up his good arm to protect himself, but the blow thwacks into the side of his skull.

An explosion of fireworks in his head, he reels, the floor flies up to meet him, then the world goes black.

79

DAY 34. 8.52pm

Tony Franklin stares down at the prostrate body, a small dribble of blood seeping from the head wound.

Lucas grunts and says, 'Recognise him?'

Franklin shakes his head. 'No. Though he does look familiar, don't you think?'

Lucas shrugs 'Fucked if I know. Think he's dead?'

Squatting down, Franklin places two fingers on the windpipe.

'Still got a pulse.'

'What you wanna do?'

Franklin stands up. 'Well, he ain't going anywhere at the moment, is he? So let's get this van unloaded.'

Lucas shrugs again. That's his default setting. Franklin watches him walk back to the van. A young man living out on the edge, pretending not to give a fuck. The movement has attracted plenty like him and it's turned their lives around because, like pack dogs, they're happiest when they know who's boss.

The back of the van contains ten carefully secured boxes of "Mountain Jade", twenty-five fragrance canisters to a box, each one laced with the H7N9 virus. The lab in Cambridge had prepared them several days ago on Duncan Ryder's instructions. But Franklin had only been given the go-ahead for phase two a few hours ago.

As Lucas starts to unstrap the first box from its secure housing, Franklin checks his phone. He does this every fifteen minutes. For security reasons, he keeps the phone switched off. But he's a man of precise habits. He finds sticking to a disciplined regime is the best way to keep things under control and get results.

The life he has chosen is a solitary one, but he doesn't mind that. He has no regrets. He trains for at least two hours each day, either at the gym, or with weights if he's out on the road. His hair may have gone, but he has the body and aerobic fitness of a man less than half his age. It all comes down to discipline and purpose.

He thinks rarely about the way he lived before. The stress and chaos of that life turned him into an addict until the movement gave him the clarity and ambition to get clean. But his ambition is not personal or greedy like most people. He doesn't need stuff. The lads tease him sometimes, call him the monk, because his lifestyle is so ascetic. His goal is to secure the future of the country; he's convinced that without strong leadership and a change of direction we're all doomed.

Only the seriously stupid believe that the threat of climate change is not real. That's going to be bad enough, but the global migration crisis that will come as a result is the true issue. It will be a tsunami. Britain is an island but it must become a fortress. It's the only way we'll survive. It's a war. Most people haven't woken up to that fact yet.

Watching Lucas carefully lifting the boxes out of the van gives Franklin a sense of satisfaction. He found the lad as a spotty youth, hanging out on a run-down estate, bullied and lost. Taking kids like him, channelling their natural aggression and putting it to proper use has shown Franklin the gateway to change.

The weakness of the liberal elite had been obvious to him for years before he worked out how to fight back. Politicians, in his view, were the worst offenders, always trying to second guess what the fickle electorate would support. But once a government of national unity was in power, they'd do away with all that. The people didn't need elections; what they needed was leadership and security.

Building a political movement takes time, but it needed the vision of a man like Duncan Ryder to see that the tipping point had come. Franklin has little patience in general for the parasitic super-rich, but Ryder is different.

Like him, the billionaire has the ruthlessness necessary to carry this project forward. The need to counter the hysterics around Lacey's death by turning Shawcross into an alternative martyr was a no-brainer. They'd agreed to it in a phone call.

Lucas is lining up all the boxes in a neat row on the floor. Tomorrow morning, they will be opened and distributed to the cleaning teams. The new targets are hospitals within the M25 perimeter, so the canisters should be in place and operating by the end of the day.

Strolling back to the unconscious intruder, Franklin takes a closer look at him. Why is he here? At this crucial juncture, they can't afford a breach in security.

Franklin has the crowbar in his hand. He's looking

around for some plastic sheeting to wrap the body in when he sees her.

Zoe Hardy emerges from behind the stacks of cleaning supplies. She's holding her phone out in front of her and filming.

He smiles to himself. So he was right. 'Well, Mrs Hardy,' he says. 'This is a surprise. But I did think our friend here looks familiar.'

'I'm live streaming this on Facebook. And my father's on the phone to the police.' Her voice is surprisingly steady. 'I suggest you put that crowbar down and step back.'

He tilts his head and sighs. Why don't people like her get it? 'You don't need to involve yourself in this,' he says. 'Go home to your children. I don't want to hurt you.'

But Zoe steps forward, placing herself between Jason and Franklin and says, 'And what are you planning to do to Jason? You need to think about the consequences of what you do next.'

Franklin gives a sour laugh. The consequences! Making history will be the consequence.

'I did that many years ago,' he says. 'And believe me, you standing there, waving a camera in my face, will not scare or deflect me one iota. Nor will it make a difference in the long run. So let's be quite clear, move away. If I have to kill you both, then I will.'

80

DAY 34. 8.58pm

Pat Babcock clutches the armrest as the Mercedes takes the tight corner at speed. In her hand she holds her phone horizontally as she anxiously watches Zoe Hardy's streamed video. He's standing there with a crowbar in his hand, older than when they last met, but it's definitely him and he still causes that fluttering in her belly. The sound quality is poor. She can't decipher what they're saying.

She glances forward at the back of the driver's head and says, 'How long, Martin?'

'Less than two minutes, guv,' he replies.

SCO19 has operational control and their armed response team should be there before that. But, as Babcock well knows, seconds could be the difference between life and death.

Usually, she watches an operation unfold from the control room. But tonight she feels the need to be there in person. Why? The clashing emotions are hard to admit, even to herself. This investigation is one of the toughest she's handled. Somehow it seems as if her whole career is being weighed up in this one moment.

Counter Terrorism is a battle to stay one step ahead, to anticipate the threat and get there before it's manifested. The many successes go largely unreported, the failures are measured in the body count. Dead children, for her that's the real heartbreak. The Manchester Arena bombing will be forever etched in her mind.

Over the years, she's developed a strong stomach and a resilient mindset. But the stress has taken its toll on her body. If Pete looked at her now, would he even recognise the girl she once was? Would he be shocked? Maybe even repelled?

The Mercedes turns off the main road onto the industrial estate.

Her gaze is fixed on the screen. Zoe Hardy is trying to protect her unconscious brother-in-law. A brave move certainly, but extremely dangerous. Will that give him pause? Pete Grazinski couldn't have bludgeoned a woman to death. But Tony Franklin? Babcock doubts he'll hesitate.

Suddenly, on screen, the young bloke with the beard appears behind Franklin and he's gesticulating. Franklin turns away from Zoe and they run towards the van.

The Mercedes veers round a corner and through the front window Babcock can see blue lights ahead. Two ARVs are disgorging a team of sixteen Counter Terrorist Specialist Firearms Officers and they're pouring through the gates into the front yard of the cleaning company.

But as Babcock's car pulls up a black van roars out of the warehouse straight at the armed police. A volley of shots ring out aimed at the tyres, which rupture, causing the van to skid and crash into a concrete fence post. The passenger door opens. Tony Franklin steps out with a pistol in his hand.

There's a cacophony of shouts from officers. 'Armed police! Drop the gun now!'

Tony holds it up and laughs. His body is speckled in red dots as the guns lock onto him. He wiggles his pistol in the air and hollers, 'Come on, lads, decide! Do their dirty work for them! They'll pay you crap wages and let you take the rap when it goes shit-shaped.'

More shouts. 'Drop the gun now!'

'Okay,' says Tony, 'I'll make it easy for you.'

He points the gun straight at the police. A short fusillade of shots follows, but it's impossible for Babcock to tell if he actually fired. He topples backwards and lands on his back.

She gets out of the car and walks across the road towards the yard. Armed officers surround Franklin, one of them kicks the gun clear of his outstretched hand.

The sergeant leading the team approaches Babcock. 'Not sure it's safe yet, ma'am.'

'Is he dead?'

'We're checking.'

'I need to talk to him.' She'll contaminate the scene, but that's the least of her worries.

The sergeant nods and escorts her to where Franklin lies. One officer is trying to apply a dressing to the wound in his chest but, with great effort, he shoves the helping hand away. Blood gurgles up and trickles from his mouth.

Pat stands over Franklin and says, 'Can you hear me, Pete? Who's behind this? Give me a name.'

He coughs and shakes his head. He's looking straight at her and she meets his gaze. But there's not even the ghost of any recognition on his face. Has she changed that much since their time together?

He splutters. 'You... won't... stop us.'

'I bloody well will,' she says. 'You know I will.'

With difficulty, he shakes his head. The eyes boring into hers are filled only with hate.

He coughs. 'Fuck...you.'

More blood bubbles up to choke him. He goes into cardiac arrest.

Pat Babcock turns on her heel and walks briskly away.

The sergeant falls into step beside her.

'Have you found the Hardys?' she says.

'Bringing them out now,' he replies. 'We've arrested the van driver.'

'Secure the perimeter, but no one goes in that warehouse until the bio-hazard team arrives. Check IOPC and SOCOs are on their way.'

'Yes, ma'am.'

He trots off. She heads for her car. There's a mountain of things to be done. A couple of the SCO19 team are standing round his body, one is trying CPR. But she doesn't give them a backward glance.

81

DAY 34. 11.15pm

Adam Hardy strides into the A&E department at the Royal London Hospital. His gaze skims over the drunks and the walking wounded until he sees his wife hunched in a corner at the back. She's tapping away on her phone and doesn't see him.

He's been released under investigation and Mehta has driven him back to London. The murder team in Cambridge had questioned him relentlessly for over an hour, and Adam concluded that Mehta wasn't coming back as he'd promised. But then there was a break in proceedings. They gave him a mug of tea and said new evidence had come to light. On the journey back to London, he'd fallen into a fitful doze. His brain was on overload. The cop had let him sleep.

They were already on the Mile End Road when he woke and the DI gave him an edited version of what had happened. Tony was dead, shot by police, Lucas had been arrested. Facing a lengthy jail term, the young man decided to co-operate with Counter Terrorism and had provided the new evidence. He corroborated Adam's account of Shawcross' murder and confirmed that Adam had been deliberately set up. CCTV evidence had also been unearthed of Tony with a tray of tea in Shawcross' outer office.

It was only when they pulled into the hospital car park that Mehta also explained Jason and Zoe had ended up in the warehouse that was being used to dispatch the H7N9-laced canisters? Jason had been injured. Adam couldn't get his head round that. But it didn't stop him from being consumed with guilt.

As he approaches Zoe, she looks up. For a moment, they simply stare at one another.

Then she says, 'He's gone to X-ray. He might have a skull fracture.'

Adam pulls her to her feet and envelopes her in a hug. She feels so fragile. They cling to each other for a long moment.

Releasing her, he says, 'What the hell were you doing there, Zo?'

'Looking for you.' She gazes at him. It's hard to tell if she's angry, in shock, or worn out. He feels awkward. His brother's in the hospital. None of it makes sense.

Samir Mehta joins them and Adam has to admit that the presence of a third person is a relief. He can see from his wife's face that she has questions he can't answer.

'Is Jason okay?' the DI says. 'Did he regain consciousness?'

'He came to in the ambulance,' Zoe says. 'Don't know how bad the head injury is yet. He was more pissed off about his broken arm.'

'I heard about what you did,' says Mehta, 'and I want to

say how brave that was. Not many people could've done that.'

Zoe shrugs and turns away. To Adam, she seems tearful and small.

He stares at his wife. 'What did you do?'

'Your brother was unconscious on the floor. She stepped between him and the assailant. Undoubtedly, she saved his life,' says the cop.

Zoe sighs. 'They turned up. I didn't know what else to do. That bastard, Tony. I'm glad the police shot him.'

'Tony?' says her husband.

'That's his name, isn't it? The bloke that pretended to be from DEFRA, that you think murdered your donor.'

'Tony Franklin is one of his names' says Mehta.

'My God, Zo! He could've killed you.'

She shrugs. 'I suppose I didn't think about that. I was so bloody angry.'

A staff nurse approaches them. 'Mrs Hardy? Jason's back from X ray. You can come and see him.'

'Has he got a skull fracture?' says Adam.

'The doctor will talk to you, but I believe the X-ray was clear.'

She leads them through a set of double doors into the treatment area.

Jason is in the third cubicle along, propped up with pillows on a trolley, his right arm in a sling across his chest, a dressing on his forehead.

He glares at Adam 'Where the bloody hell have you been?'

'Long story,' his brother replies. 'Are you all right?'

Jason huffs, 'Do I look all right?'

Adam scans him, hurt but stroppy. But when he was injured as a kid, belligerence was generally a good sign.

'Thing is,' says Jason 'all the painkillers they give you, I'm high as a kite.' He glances at his sister-in-law. 'Your chance to get rid of me once and for all, Zo. And you blew it.'

She smiles 'I know. But then I'd have to find someone else to bitch about, wouldn't I?'

Samir Mehta is hanging back. Adam draws him forward.

Mehta gives the patient a nod. 'How you doing, mate?'

Jason manages a smile. 'Up yours, Mehta. Why didn't you take my call this morning?'

'I'm sorry. I should've done. But it was a rapidly evolving situation.'

Shaking his head, Jason turns to the other two. 'That's police jargon for complete shitshow.'

'That's another way of putting it,' the DI says. He meets Jason's gaze for a moment, then looks away. It's clear to Adam the cop is awkward and embarrassed. Is there something going on between him and Jason? It's impossible to tell.

'Well, what is happening?' Adam asks.

'You were right about the electronic air fresheners' says Mehta. 'Feras Khalid ran a cleaning company. They had commercial as well as domestic contracts. So they went round the country servicing these air fresheners in public toilets. That is how the virus was spread.'

'He was part of it all, then?' says Zoe.

'He must've been to start with. Then he had a change of heart. I think that's why he came to us offering information. We don't know his motive, though.'

'He changed his mind because of Nizar,' says Jason. 'He made him a promise he'd do no more harm.'

'Well, if he changed his mind, that's probably why they murdered him,' says Adam.

The cop nods. 'Khalid's involvement is the tip of the iceberg.'

Adam's thoughts are churning. *He was a cog in the wheel.* Shawcross's rant is echoing through his brain.

How did Franklin know where he was that night? *How did he know he was on his motorcycle and headed for the Blackwall Tunnel?*

He turns to his wife 'I've got to go. Will you be all right?'

'Do you even care?' she says. She looks desolate.

'I'm sorry. I have to talk to someone. I can't explain right now.'

Zoe shrugs. 'You'll do what you want, anyway. I can't stop you.'

Adam finds it hard to meet her gaze. The guilt stabs at him. But his thoughts are skittering out of control. 'I'm sorry', he mumbles.

82

DAY 34. 11.25pm

The concierge on the desk has changed since this morning. He looks up as Adam taps in the door code:7832. That much he remembers. His appearance is ragged; a cheap grey tracksuit supplied by Cambridge police and trainers that rub his bare feet. But the man gives him a polite nod. Heading for the lifts' he wonders if she'll even be there. The spare key from her kitchen drawer was in the pocket of the blood-stained jeans that the police took from him.

He'd borrowed some money for a cab from DI Mehta. The cop had tried hard to stop him.

'You're still under investigation.'

'They didn't set any conditions. I'm not about to skip the country.'

'What are you doing? Have you remembered something else?'

'No.' Only partly a lie. What did he even think Mia could tell him? *He has to see her.*

'Keep me in the loop,' said the cop.

'I will.'

At the door to flat 24, he pauses. He feels hot and nervous. He takes a deep breath, then presses the buzzer.

Moments pass and nothing happens. He wonders where she is. She could be anywhere. If he summarises the things he actually knows about her, they amount to virtually nothing.

He presses the buzzer again, leans on it hard and abruptly the door opens.

Nin stares up at him with a scowl on her face.

'It is him,' she calls over her shoulder.

Then he hears her voice, *soft, seductive,* from another room. 'Let him in.'

Adam finds her in the bedroom packing a suitcase.

She smiles but doesn't look at him. 'This is a lovely surprise' she says. There's a blitheness to her tone.

'You said come back.'

The wardrobe is open and a selection of clothes is neatly stacked on the bed. She picks up a dress, looks at it, sighs, returns it to the cupboard.

'Did I? Yes, of course. It's been a hectic day. And now I have to go to New York.' She laughs 'I'm awful at packing. Can never decide what to take.'

'Did you know Lucas would take me to Tony Franklin?' he says.

'No, of course not.'

She's lying.

'So you do know who Tony Franklin is, then?'

She stops to stare at him. Then she sighs and says, 'Poor sweet Adam. Are you as naïve as you seem?'

She's smiling and completely gorgeous. Those blue eyes are as cold as ice. A ripple of horror runs right through him. This woman may well be a monster. *But she's his monster.*

'If trusting people is naïve,' he says evenly, 'then I suppose I am. David trusted you too, didn't he?'

She inhales and is about to answer when Nin's voice floats through from the sitting room. 'You should come and look at this.'

'Excuse me' she says and gives him a polite smile as if they were two complete strangers who'd met in a corridor and he was standing aside to let her pass.

But then they are strangers. Adam follows her into the other room.

Nin has her laptop open on the coffee table. On screen is the BBC's 24 hour news channel. The picture is of Hugh Ryder, in a barrage of flashbulbs, on the doorstep of a Georgian townhouse with a woman at his side. He waves away reporters' questions with his hand and turns to go back into the house.

'Turn it up', says Mia.

Nin adjusts the volume.

−*"Senior Cabinet colleagues expressed surprise at the Minister's sudden resignation. But a spokesperson for the Department of Health said the prolonged stress of the current crisis had taken its toll and Hugh Ryder planned to spend more time with his family."*

Snapping the laptop shut, Nin jumps up and says, 'We need to go, like now.'

'You sure everything is down and squared away?' says Mia.

Nin throws up her hands 'The sites were down and the twitter accounts deleted half an hour ago.'

'Then there's no need to panic.'

Adam watches the two women. What are they? Co-

conspirators? Partners? Nin's attitude suggests they're equals; she's not merely the assistant.

With a sigh, Nin picks up the laptop and puts it in her backpack. 'I'll wait for you downstairs in the cab,' she says. 'Hurry up.'

She disappears out of the door.

Mia looks at Adam. 'As you can see, we're in a bit of a rush.'

'You're in this up to your neck, aren't you?'

'I don't know what you mean.' There's a hardness round those lips that he hasn't noticed before.

'Franklin's dead, y'know' he says. 'The police shot him.'

Ignoring him, she returns to the bedroom. He follows.

'You must know that,' he says, 'which is why you're running. That in itself is an admission of guilt.'

'Guilty of what?' she says.

'For starters, it was you who set David up. He wanted to stop and so you called Franklin and had him murdered?'

She laughs. 'What? I ordered a hit? Like some kind of gangster. How melodramatic.'

'You told them where he was and that he needed to be stopped, so, yeah, it amounts to that.'

She takes a blouse off its hanger and folds it neatly.

'David,' she says, 'was Feras Khalid, a people-trafficker, occasional drug dealer and cold-blooded killer. He'd been contracted to do a job and he reneged on the deal. But the people who he was dealing with don't find that kind of behaviour acceptable.'

'People like Duncan Ryder, you mean?'

She laughs again, tinkling and high-pitched, scans the suitcase and the piles of clothes. 'Oh well,' she says, 'I think perhaps I'll leave all this. Probably time for a new wardrobe.'

Adam pulls open his track suit top 'Look, I'm not wearing a wire or anything. This is between us. Just tell me the truth.'

'Whose truth? You want to know my truth? Believe me, Adam Hardy, it would shock you to your oh-so-decent core. With your nice farm in Devon and your lovely safe English life. Personally, I've had enough of being English. I think being American will suit me better.'

'Didn't you care for David even a bit?'

'Yes, I enjoyed fucking him,' she smiles. 'And I quite enjoyed fucking you. But he understood the transaction. I suspect you didn't.'

'Who the hell are you?' says Adam.

'I am what you see. I'm not responsible for your assumptions or your pathetic male fantasies.'

'Then tell me, did you set him up?'

Tilting her head, she brushes back her hair with her middle fingers. The gesture is habitual and tantalising. She's trying to bewitch him again. But not this time.

'If David hadn't crashed his motorcycle,' she says 'and died in the manner he did, you wouldn't be here. You want to call it murder? Well then, the direct beneficiary of David's murder is you, Adam. His murder saved your life. That's the truth.'

She picks up her coat and puts it on. 'Now you'll have to excuse me. I have a jet waiting for me and we need to take off before midnight.'

Is that it? She walks away?

Adam grabs her arm. 'The police will arrest you.'

Shrugging him off, she replies, 'No. The police will settle for what they've got. Decisions will be taken based on finite resources and political expediency. Why? Because no one will want to admit how close we came to pulling it off.'

83

DAY 35. 12.46am

It's well after midnight in the Counter Terrorism offices when the briefing ends. But the mood in the room is celebratory, boosted by a sense of relief. After the double shifts and relentless pressure of the last five weeks, everyone is on a high, although there's still plenty to be done.

Reports are filtering in from the forensic examination of the warehouse. It will take days to go through the place properly. But the canisters have been safely removed and a sample from each batch flown by helicopter to Porton Down. A preliminary analysis suggests they do contain the H7N9 virus.

Wendy Kelly has been arrested but is co-operating fully and has provided the police with a comprehensive list of the sites where RapidKlean had installed and serviced electronic air fresheners. Numbering nearly a hundred around the country, these have all been secured and sealed off.

Pat Babcock's address to her officers is full of praise for

their efforts and dedication. But as she wanders back to her own bolt-hole Samir Mehta can see that she's still carrying a weight on her shoulders.

He taps on the glass door and she waves him in.

'Congratulations, boss,' he says with a smile. 'A good result.'

'A partial result,' she says with a sigh. 'All the websites, Twitter accounts and YouTube channels the NCA's been monitoring have disappeared in a puff of smoke.'

'Can't we lean on the tech companies?'

'They say it's all routed through the dark web and they can't trace any of it. I don't know if that's true. Personally, I don't really understand this stuff.'

'What about Shawcross's place in Cambridge?'

'Owned and financed offshore through a series of shell companies. The people who work in the laboratories there are being interviewed. But my guess is most of them know nothing. There was a "special projects" lab overseen by Shawcross himself. That had a staff of five. They've all done a runner.'

'Well, we've stopped any further spread of the virus. That's the main thing.'

Babcock opens her desk drawer and lifts out a bottle of Scotch. 'Indeed, it is. And we should be proud of that.'

'I saw on the news that Ryder's resigned.'

'Interestingly, he fell on his sword even before 5 gave him a grilling. Said he felt responsible even though he absolutely denies any knowledge of what Shawcross was up to.'

'Smart move, I suppose. Makes him look principled.'

'As a nest of vipers' says Babcock. 'His billionaire brother is, of course, an American citizen and out of the jurisdiction.'

'Won't the FBI help? Mia Cunningham was supposed to

be Hugh Ryder's PR adviser. What if she was running this whole fake news show all along?'

Pat Babcock shrugs. 'How would we ever prove that?'

Getting up, she takes two mugs off the shelf and holds them up. 'Will you have a drink with me, Sami?'

'I'd be honoured, boss,' he says with a smile. Then he adds, 'Do you think we'll ever get to any of the real perpetrators behind this?'

Sloshing hefty measures into the mugs, she heaves another sigh and says, 'Probably not this time. But it's a bit like serial killers and rapists. You can guarantee that sooner or later they'll have another go.'

84

DAY 40. 2.30pm

Adam Hardy steps out of the taxi first and holds the door open for his wife. The street of imposing Edwardian villas is bathed in early spring sunshine and the police officer, stationed on the doorstep, cradling an MP5 submachine gun, is wearing sunglasses.

Zoe glances up at Adam as she gets out of the cab. There's a wariness in her look. It feels like she doesn't trust him. All the charges against him have been dropped, but he doubts that cuts much ice with his father-in-law.

He and Zoe have spoken little since his return home. Mostly it's been practicalities to do with the farm or the kids. Adam expects that, after a respectable interval, she'll tell him she wants a divorce. The prospect of this saddens him deeply but part of him is resigned. He's lost most of the life he once took for granted. This feels, in a way, inevitable. He wants her to have a chance to be happy.

The police officer rings the doorbell for them and they

are ushered inside. Felicity Oldroyd greets them in the hall-way. She seems younger than he remembers; she wears jeans and a sweatshirt.

'Thank you for agreeing to see us' says Adam.

She smiles warmly and touches his arm. 'I'm glad you don't bear me a grudge. I've been thinking about you quite a lot. And you must be Zoe?'

Zoe holds out her hand to shake.

'Come through to the kitchen. It's the sunniest part of the house. I'll make us some tea, or coffee if you'd prefer.'

Felicity leads them to the back of the house, where the bi-fold doors are partly open. The room is airy, light shim-mering off highly polished granite and tile.

'Do make yourselves comfortable' says Felicity, indi-cating the two sofas by the window overlooking the garden.

'You have a beautiful home,' says Zoe.

Felicity grins. 'Oh, my husband and I are always arguing about what we want and don't want. He'd stuff the place with antiques if I let him. I like things much more minimalist.'

'I can see who wins the argument' says Zoe.

Once the tea is served, biscuits handed around and they're settled facing each other on the sofas, Felicity says, 'So, Adam. What can I do for you?'

He takes a breath. He's been thinking about this for days and even more during sleepless nights. The pressure to be normal and to get on has been constant. Yet he feels trapped in a strange liminal place. He can't go back, but he can't move forward.

'I need to find a way to get on with my life,' he says, 'and I suppose what I'm looking for is advice. James Chang is an excellent surgeon. But he doesn't get it or accept what's happened to me. But, well, you saw it.'

'Yes, I did,' she replies.

'I'm not faking it. It's not drugs. I do have fragments of memory from my donor.'

Felicity nods 'I think that's been proven by the information you gave the police.'

Adam hesitates. He's aware of Zoe watching him like a hawk.

Then he says, 'But I also have occasional impulses that I don't feel are my own. And the most important question now for me is, am I a danger to my children, my wife, well, to anyone?'

'Do you feel you are?'

'I'm walking around with a killer's heart.'

He's said it. It's out there.

Felicity takes a sip of her tea. 'The medical profession can be mechanistic in its view of the human body. It's like a machine, one bit breaks, you get a spare part and replace it. But many people, including myself, would say that's out of date. It's too simplistic. The question is where does that leave us.' She turns to Zoe. 'Do you feel he might hurt you or the children?'

Zoe shrugs 'I don't feel threatened. I just don't know who he is any more. I can see he's working hard to reassure us. But it's like he's putting on a front all the time.'

'Have you talked about this?' asks Felicity.

'I–' Zoe avoids his eye. 'After all he's been through, I don't want to upset him.'

'Be honest. Are you scared of me, Zo?' Adam asks.

His wife stares out of the window at the garden. 'I'm not sure. I don't think so.'

Felicity watches the two of them. She's delivered enough bad news in her time to recognise the good manners being deployed by each to cover their despair.

'Well,' she says, 'neuroscientists can tell us a lot about the human brain. How it makes a picture of the world, how it relies on memory. But they can tell us nothing about consciousness. What even is it? How does it work? And where are memories kept? Have you got little tracers in your brain or nervous system of all the things that have ever happened to you? Or is there something else going on between memory and consciousness?'

Adam sighs, 'Sounds complicated. Where does that leave me?'

Felicity smiles and says, 'What I'm saying is I can't give you facts to explain this, Adam. We don't know. But I can tell you what I've observed in all my years as a doctor. And it's simply this: your beliefs are a central and crucial factor.'

'So it's what I think that matters?'

'I'd say it's what you feel and think combined. The little voice in your head or that deep gut feeling. I've seen patients who were by all objective measures terminally ill recover. A miracle? I've seen people, who I'd expected to survive, give up the ghost. You've heard of placeboes and how they work?'

'You think something's medicine, but it's a fake. It works anyway because you believe in it.'

'That happens all the time.'

He smiles 'James Chang told me it's all in the mind.'

'And in a sense, he's right. I'm not saying any of this is easy. But you can decide what to believe. You can turn your donor into a monster who's invaded you or you can welcome him as a saviour who should be embraced and loved.'

'Someone else said something similar. But what if he is a monster?'

'Let's suppose elements of him may exist in your body at

a cellular level. It's up to your mind to interpret them. Must I follow this impulse now or can I think about it?'

'I can choose? You make it sound simple.'

'You can learn to choose. It's doable, but it takes practise.'

'So Adam's never going to be the person he was?' says Zoe.

Felicity smiles. 'I've been married for nearly forty years. The young man I married was a whirlwind of energy and confidence. But each experience we have changes us incrementally. If it happens slowly, we don't notice it as much. He's different now, my husband, much slower. He had a hip replacement last year. I'm different too, I'm sure. But I wouldn't be without him.'

Zoe turns to Adam. She holds out her hand to him and says, 'I suppose I'm angry for everything you've put us through.'

'I'd call it more suppressed fury' he says. 'But then that's you, Zo. You like things to go your way and when they don't, you get mad. You're exactly like your old man.'

'Wow!' she says. 'That's harsh.'

'Is it? Makes you strong and resilient. It's one of things I've always loved about you. You know what you want and you get it. You're not a silly, giggly girl. It's your strength that's got me through this last year. And it saved Jason's life.'

'And what about Mia?'

'She's a mirage. A pretty malevolent one, too. And I think Feras knew that.'

'But you want her, don't you?'

'No. I don't. I felt desire. But that was his, not mine.' *Is that true?* Will he ever confess that he acted on it? *She doesn't need to know that.*

He smiles. 'When I go to my quiet place, all I think about is you.'

Zoe gets up, folds her arms and walks over to the window. He can see the tremor in her shoulders. Walking away is what she always does to conceal her hurt.

'Tell us about your quiet place' says Felicity.

'All the chatter stops and I can see things clearly. When I'm there, I know I'm all right.' His eyes are resting on his wife's back.

'Do you have some kind of dialogue with him?' says Felicity.

'Less now than before.' *Fibber.*

He stands up abruptly and says, 'Listen Zoe, if you want a divorce, say so. They'll be no hard feelings. This isn't the life you planned, I know that.'

She turns to face him. 'Is that what you want?'

'Absolutely not. But I'm asking what you want.'

'Okay,' she says. 'If I can't have the old Adam back, I'll settle for the new one.'

He grins. 'Adam Hardy 2.0. He may be a better version.' *He's definitely a better version.*

'He may be,' says Zoe. 'Let's hope so.'

EPILOGUE

Adam Hardy lounges on the garden recliner in the warm summer sunshine. Through half-closed lids he can see a cerulean blue sky and the odd fluffy cloud. Today he's okay.

He watches his wife scurry across the lawn. Ryan is tottering towards the roses. He makes a grab for a perfect flower head but his mother scoops him up before he can grasp the petals.

'Come on, monkey,' she says. 'Your grandma spent a long time on those roses. She doesn't want you wrecking them.'

Phil Rowett stands at the gas barbecue—an anniversary present to his daughter and son-in-law—flipping burgers. Ruth Rowett and Lily are ferrying various salads and side dishes from the kitchen.

Zoe carries her son over to Adam. She sits down on a deckchair next to him. Ryan wriggles free and heads off in the direction of the rose bed. Adam watches the little boy and feels a surge of love.

Zoe's attention is on her father. She giggles and says, 'Have you ever in your entire life seen a bigger barbecue?'

'I don't think so,' says Adam. 'I didn't even know they made them that big.'

'Nor did I.'

They share an intimate smile. Is she happy, he wonders? It's impossible to tell.

She gives him a searching look. 'You okay? Not nervous?'

She's a bit of a nagger.

He kisses the back of her hand and smiles. 'I'm not nervous. Stop worrying.'

She laughs 'I know, I'm a control freak but I'm working on it.'

Jumping up, she sprints off in pursuit of Ryan.

There's a crunching of gravel on the drive as a car pulls up.

At last!

Doors slam. A moment later the back gate opens and Jason appears.

Adam gets up. 'Ahh, here they are!'

Jason walks across the grass towards his brother. Nizar follows him through the gate.

Opening his arms for a hug, Jason says, 'Sorry we're late folks, we've been crawling for miles. Big holiday traffic tail-back on the A30 and Niz insisted on playing some crappy underground Belgian band full blast with the windows open. I think we frightened the tourists.'

'You said you liked them,' says Nizar.

Adam puts an arm round each of their shoulders. 'How old are you, Jace? Niz, you're bringing out the worst in him.'

'You've turned into an old fart,' Jason replies.

Zoe comes forward and gives Nizar a kiss on the cheek. 'How were the exams?' she asks.

'Hard,' he replies. 'But they're over. That's all I care about at the moment.'

'Right,' says Phil Rowett 'these burgers are more than ready, so get your plates.'

'Didn't anyone tell you, Phil?' says Jason 'We've become vegan.'

Rowett's face falls 'Oh,' he says.

Zoe grins. 'Dad, they're winding you up.'

'Oh,' he laughs. 'Ruthie, get some plates over here!'

Adam pulls Nizar into a tight hug. 'Glad you could come, buddy.' Gripping the young man's shoulder, he feels a lump in his throat. *Safe now, brother.*

Nizar gives him a shy look. 'I love it here. You are so lucky.'

'I know that,' Adam replies. *Yes, we love it here.*

'You always make me feel welcome.'

'That's because you are welcome,' says Adam. 'This is your second home. But, hey, since you're going to be here the whole summer, we'll be putting you to work. It's a busy time on the farm.'

'No problem,' says Nizar. 'I'm looking forward to it.'

A MESSAGE FROM SUSAN

Thank you for choosing to read *A Killer's Heart*. If you enjoyed it and would like to keep up to date with my latest book releases and news, please go to

susanwilkins.co.uk/sign-up

*Your email address will never be shared, and you can unsubscribe at any time.

Do get in touch and let me know what you thought of *A Killer's Heart*. I love hearing from readers. You can message me via my website and find me on Facebook, Instagram, Goodreads and Twitter.

Also if you feel like writing a review, I'd be most grateful. The choice of books out there is vast. Reviews do help readers discover one of my books for the first time.

Scan QR code to review A Killer's Heart.

BOOKS BY SUSAN

The Informant

The Mourner

The Killer

It Should Have Been Me

Buried Deep

Close To The Bone

The Shout + The Right Side Of The Line (Free when you sign up to Susan's newsletter)

A Killer's Heart

She's Gone

Her Perfect Husband

BOOKS CONT.

PLUS SUSAN'S SOCIAL MEDIA

You can find me on Facebook, Instagram, and Twitter.

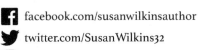

facebook.com/susanwilkinsauthor

twitter.com/SusanWilkins32

instagram.com/susan_wilkins32

ACKNOWLEDGMENTS

Huge thanks to Colin James and Graham Bartlett, who are always so generous with their time and professional expertise.

Thanks to the usual suspects, my back-up crew of fellow crime writers, who provide help, advice and encouragement. You know who you are.

And last but never least, my love and thanks to my support team: Jenny Kenyon and Sue Kenyon. Without you this book would still be sitting in a file on my computer.

Published by Herkimer Limited in 2022
Summit House
170 Finchley Road
London NW3 6BP

Scan QR code to go to susanwilkins.co.uk

ISBN 978-1-9169012-5-4

Printed in Great Britain
by Amazon